FOREVER AFTER

A NOVEL

DEREK ROBINSON

For my wife, Kathryn.

For our first baby girl, who we're expecting shortly after the publication of this novel.

For my parents, Paula and Dave.

And for all my family and friends who have supported me along the way.

I hope you enjoy this debut novel.

Please note that this is a fictional creation, and all portrayals of real people and places are purely fictional.

1

A suffocating sense of alarm seized Brayden, a feeling he'd experienced countless times before. Someone in this room had a bomb, and he had maybe three minutes to figure out who that someone was. He imagined the carnage that would ensue if he failed—once such a beautiful mountaintop scene, suddenly torn to shreds amid cries of agony.

His eyes landed on a balding man in his mid-fifties lurking quietly in the lodge's corner. Could he fit an explosive beneath the bulging pillows of that ski jacket? It was frigid on the mountain, but did he really need enough layers to puff himself up like the Michelin Man? Perhaps he just loved his milk and cookies, and that was to blame for the pillows. He was certainly a suspect. A few yards to his left, a woman strolled past the bar, still wearing her snowboarding boots. She had ditched her jacket in the cozy warmth of the building, sporting only a base layer on top and snow pants below. She seemed unlikely to be harboring an explosive. *Are we sure it's an explosive? What about a biological attack? Or a shooting?* The questions derailed his investigative thought. No, he recalled—the intel was rock solid. It's an explosive.

Another man, this one about thirty and dressed in black, carried a tray mysteriously covered by an opaque lid across the dining area. The man weaved through tables, moving deliberately yet unnaturally, pausing at certain moments as if waiting for a cue to proceed. *That's him*, he thought. *This man is going to blow up this ski lodge.* Scanning the area in a panic, he took inventory: at least a dozen women, six children, maybe fifteen to twenty men. His mind raced to future headlines on the televisions in the village below. *Thirty dead in terror attack on Sweetway.* He could see the smoke billowing skyward from the half-exploded lodge, skiers and snowboarders struck with horror as they finished runs that led straight into terrifying turmoil at the base. His stomach turned at the thought of his own wife and children clawing for help, if they even survived the initial blast. Sarah would know exactly what to say to calm the traumatized children in such a scenario, but would she even be capable of doing so?

He still had time to stop this. *"Brayden!"* He heard someone shout his name. Glancing left and right across the room, he found no one matching the voice calling for help. The presumed bomber stopped and reached for the black lid covering his tray. *"Bray!"* Everyone around the bomber seemed unaware of their impending doom, save for the one person calling Brayden's name he couldn't seem to locate in the crowd. He reached for his sidearm—it, along with its holster, was missing. Had he left it in the car? Patting his pocket for his badge, he again found emptiness. It was uncharacteristic of him to forget his badge and firearm in such a public setting. *Someone needs to stop him—*

"Bray!" said Sarah, her wide eyes a mix of concern and confusion. It must have been the third or fourth time she'd called his name. "It's your turn."

His heart fluttering, Brayden took a breath. He glanced down at the ski lodge below, where a waiter had removed a black lid covering a cake. Beside him, several folks were singing what Brayden assumed was a birthday jingle to the toddler seated at the table. Returning his focus to the objective reality a few stories above, it appeared to be his turn to pick a gift in his least favorite activity—the family Yankee swap.

"Charlie's keeping the scooter, so you're up," said Sarah. Her patience with Brayden was admirable. Still shaking off the cobwebs of his brief departure to another reality, Brayden nodded with an embarrassed chuckle.

"Sorry. Just thinking about all these choices!" He grabbed a small package wrapped neatly in plaid paper. The box was only for show; a Dunkin' gift card engulfed by crumpled tissue paper sat inside. For Brayden, it was the perfect result—a gift useful enough to provide him utility, fitting enough that keeping it didn't raise any eyebrows, and nondescript enough that it wasn't much of a threat to be stolen later. For all intents and purposes, his work in the swap was done. A good thing, for sure; he never liked Yankee swaps, especially the ones that mixed the children with the adults.

As Brayden watched his wife tell their youngest child not to open his scooter until it was officially his to open, the gravity of his episode moments before lingered unpleasantly. In the six years since stepping away from life as a field agent for the Central Intelligence Agency, these flashes had become all too common. Every moment was a threat, every potential outcome a disaster. In his line of work, he'd thwarted terror attacks on the nation's capital, snuffed out gang violence on civilian-packed streets, stymied plans of biological warfare well before the everyday American could even suspect that anything was awry. In that career—or, really, that *life*—being two steps ahead was a requirement, not a tactic. Scanning every room for suspicious activity became second nature. Daydreaming—or *daymaring*, as he preferred to call the hellish episodes—about the worst-case disaster was a part of his psyche that simply wouldn't go away, no matter how hard he tried to eradicate it. More than a decade ago, he had become one of the agency's youngest active field agents, thrown into a lifestyle unlike anything his coeval friends and colleagues were experiencing. A little over a year later, he met the love of his life on a ski trip to Sweetway Mountain—the same mountain at which the Cross family was now celebrating Christmas.

"Oh, it's ... they're socks," muttered Brayden's daughter, Mari. Their firstborn. Her smile arced just enough to qualify itself as such; she seemed less than thrilled about plucking a pair of dress socks from the gift pile, wholly unsurprising for a nine-year-old girl. *Stupid to mix adults and kids*, Brayden thought, already preparing for the chaos that would ensue when the socks got passed to seven-year-old Charlie in exchange for that scooter. He shared a brief glance with Sarah, their eyes reflecting the same look back at each other. It was a bit of *uh-oh* mixed with a touch of *we wouldn't trade these moments for the world.*

Brayden had known almost instantly that she was the one. Sarah Lennon, twenty-two and full of life, her blue eyes a mirror image of the cloudless January sky the day they met. She was a snowboarder, voyaging west to Colorado with her college friends to check out the newly opened resort on Sweetway. A blue trail turned to black just after a chaotic merge, and Sarah had skidded to a fall on an icy patch. It wasn't the dangerous, painful variety of wipeout; it was the embarrassing-to-her, cute-to-him variety. Brayden knew she didn't need help, but that hadn't stopped him from introducing himself with a helping hand extended. The way she chuckled and bashfully accepted his offer, her teeth shining as white as the snow that caught her fall, her small dimples hugging her smile on either side, her brunette locks peeking out beneath the back of her helmet—she was stunning.

Being a field agent had made the ensuing months and years challenging for Brayden as he built a life with the future Sarah Cross. Virtually every detail of his career demanded secrecy. How do you build a trusting relationship with someone on a throne of lies? The genuine answer to nearly every question about his work was the same cliché: *I'd love to tell you, but I'd have to kill you.* He figured that response would have set a cold and uninviting tone at the start of their relationship, dousing its flame before it could even flicker. So, he instead painted himself as a cybersecurity analyst at a tech firm outside of Washington, DC, keeping the details vague under a similar premise of confidentiality. Brayden had dabbled in computer science classes years prior during his time at the University of Oregon, so he could dance along the surface level of conversations about his imagined job without too much trouble. *Hopefully she isn't a closet techie*, he remembered thinking in those early days.

"What the heck, Mari, no!" Charlie shouted at his sister, tears emerging from behind his eyelids. "It's mine!"

"It's a Yankee swap, Charlie! I can take it if I want it," Mari piped back. Her brown hair matched her mother's, but her pigtails provided her childlike distinction. "Besides, you already have a scooter!"

Charlie pouted at her retort. "But this one's better!"

Sarah ushered a silent but telling look at Mari—a look that said, *you aren't wrong, but can you be a bit nicer about it, please?* She gently patted Charlie on the shoulder. "Charlie, you have to follow the rules. The swap isn't over; maybe you can still get a better gift from someone else, if they want those super-cool socks!" The explanation, straightforward as it was, seemed to work. Charlie handed over the scooter—albeit still sporting his frown—and Mari traded a victorious but graceful "thank you" as she handed her seven-year-old brother the socks. Sarah's way with their children was another aspect of her personality that constantly blew Brayden away. She was never angry or aggressive, never agitated, always diplomatic and thoughtful.

Those traits extended to her patience and understanding during Brayden's episodes. By the time the two exchanged vows, Sarah was aware of Brayden's true occupation. He couldn't realistically maintain a complete façade. He couldn't hide the nature of his life from the very person he was choosing to share it with. Still, he was forbidden from disclosing most of the details of his work, and the circumstances were taxing on their relationship. Spontaneous travel without warning, cuts and bruises without explanation, late-night returns without communication—all of it created stress and anxiety. It didn't stop them from pursuing their dreams of raising a family, but those dreams didn't make the struggles any easier. A year after Charlie was born, a global pandemic ground the world to a halt. It was then that Brayden felt stepping away from the agency was the only option to preserve his mental health, his physical health, and the cohesion of his family. The years since that day had been orders of magnitude easier than when he possessed that badge, but the psychological remnants still reared their ugly heads more frequently than he would have liked. And as evidenced by her concerned-but-calm interruption of his daymare today, Sarah never failed to be understanding whenever his mind slipped away for a moment.

A single gift remained from the Yankee swap collection, and Brayden's brother Riley waltzed his way up to retrieve the lone option. Riley was three years older than Brayden, and their relationship was layered. They had been quite close growing up, but time had wedged the gap between them wider with each passing year. These days, Brayden harbored strong disagreement with Riley on many of life's fundamental topics, politics and religion chief among them. Still, Brayden made sure to always draw the line prior to the point of no return in their squabbles. They loved each other the way brothers should.

"Ah ha! Look at this bad boy!" Riley exclaimed, tearing the final bits of wrapping paper from the box of a large, overly complex Nerf gun. "I can finally hold my own when the kids open fire!"

Brayden watched as he held the box at an angle in the light, adjusting his glasses to read the labels. "You need some binoculars to read that font, old man?"

"You're hilarious, guy, you know that?" Riley chirped back at his brother.

A few feet beside Brayden, Charlie sat on his knees with his feet tucked beneath him. He fidgeted with his three-pack of argyle socks, watching his uncle showcase his new toy. Riley may have noticed his gloom; he paused before gesturing at his nephew.

"However," he continued, adding suspense with his inflection, "I think those socks over there would look *fantastic* with the new shoes Santa brought me this morning. Hand 'em over, Chuckie!"

Charlie's eyes lit up, his demeanor changing instantly. Riley offered a quick wink at Sarah before handing the Nerf gun over in exchange for his new footwear. He looked at Brayden, who nodded and smirked approvingly. It was a look that said, *I owe you one, brother*. Riley gave a quick nod in return.

"Thanks, Uncle Riley!" Charlie grabbed the Nerf gun and began displaying it to the sister he had now magically forgiven.

After his wife, Ashley, confirmed she didn't want to execute a final swap with anyone, Riley rubbed his hands together and glanced at his wristwatch. "Look at that. Santa's presents *and* the Yankee swap presents all done by ten! Who's ready to hit the slopes?"

A jovial affirmation from the family came in return. They began gathering their boots, helmets, skis, and boards before leaving their mountainside condo and descending the two flights of stairs to the main lodge area. It would be a picturesque Christmas Day full of snowy runs.

Brayden slid off the second of his boots, officially achieving what he viewed as a top-five feeling on earth at the end of a long day of skiing. Charlie's cheeks were red, and his messy hair glistened with sweat. Mari wasn't as sweaty, but little crystals of snow still clung to the ends of her pigtails, slowly melting and dripping onto the floor below the bench supporting her. Sarah, meanwhile, looked so energized she could have passed for the mom who stayed in the lodge all day. Cruising on her snowboard alongside her kids was effortless for her, but that didn't make it any less enjoyable. One table over, Riley distributed paper cups —the kind with the 1990s-style purple-and-teal designs on them— filled with hot chocolate, to his sons, Brady and Ryan. Their youngest, Lizzie, was nine—the perfect age to be Mari's best companion. Feeling under the weather today, she had stayed in the condo with her mother, watching Christmas movies and sipping their own hot cocoa by the fireplace.

Brayden trudged up the staircase, his boots fastened to each other by their Velcro straps and slung over his shoulder. As he placed them down in the foyer where everyone else had left their equipment to dry, he noted a flurry of excitement in the living room. "Is that Auntie Marissa?" he heard Brady inquire optimistically.

Turning the corner of the foyer and entering the room, Brayden saw Ashley and her kids huddled around a MacBook on the coffee table. He didn't need to walk any closer to find out what they were all gathering to see on the screen. He knew it would be the face of Ashley's sister, Marissa. He knew that her nephews and her niece were excited to chat with her. And he knew tensions would soon rise between the wooden walls of their shared vacation home. It wasn't because Marissa held some controversial viewpoints, or that she was a bad person; in fact, Brayden had quite enjoyed her company.

It was because Marissa died eight months ago.

2

"I got new basketball shoes, and we got a hoop for the driveway when we get back home!"

"Yeah, and we got a PlayStation 6, Aunt Riss!"

Brady and Ryan poured their stories of Christmas morning into the microphone and camera of the Apple machine on the coffee table. As Brayden took a step closer, he finally caught a visual of what he already knew would be on screen. It reminded him of those deepfake videos that had become an ever-growing nuisance in the world. Politicians' statements could be totally fabricated. Celebrities could be deceivingly placed into lewd videos. As the technology grew and became more available to the public, even high school bullies began using it to wreak havoc on the mental health of the classmates they terrorized.

That was the resemblance for Brayden as he watched Marissa Stevenson—pronounced dead in April—laugh and chat with Ashley and her children on Christmas Day of the same year. It was massively impressive technology; standing a few feet away, it was nearly indistinguishable from a regular video chat. Her voice was eerily real, exactly how Brayden remembered it the last time they spoke. But the video and audio elements of this software weren't the concern. You could do pretty much anything these days with the power of editing. The problem was that she was so *real*, so *responsive*. The natural laughter, the quick wit, the perfectly sensible and context-aware follow-up questions—that was *Marissa* on the screen, and the kids were ecstatic to chat with their auntie.

Brayden heard his own children scurrying up the stairs, Sarah telling them to take off their wet gear before dragging it into the condo. Riley was just ahead of them, and as he emerged from the foyer, he let out a burst of excitement at the gathering that had built in the living room. "You guys talking to Auntie Marissa?"

The digital Marissa blurted out a reply, seamlessly recognizing Riley's voice in the background and sending chills down Brayden's spine. "Is that Riles I hear back there? Merry Christmas!"

Mari and Charlie naturally wanted to join in on whatever fun was brewing around the coffee table. Sarah was last to arrive, carrying a hodgepodge of remnants of the kids' snow attire. There was only enough time for Brayden to share a single alarmed glance at her—one that he hoped both relayed the urgency of the situation and prevented further questioning on her part—before stopping the forward progress of his kids and suggesting an alternative.

"Hey, kids—who wants to go get some churros and apple cider down at the lodge?" Brayden could tell the proposal didn't exactly enthrall them, their eyes still peeking around him at the congregation near the fireplace.

"I wanna see Lizzie, Daddy! I haven't seen her all day!" Mari argued. Sarah had put down the clothing on top of the dryer and was quickly noticing the situation. Brayden knelt in front of Mari and searched for the right words. When they escaped him, Sarah took the reins.

"They're talking to one of Aunt Ashley's friends right now, so we can't hang out with them just yet," she calmly explained. Another specialty of hers was saying *no* in such a calm fashion. "I'm sure they'll be done in a little while. Let's go get some snacks. I heard people raving about those churros on the lifts today!"

Brayden nodded at Sarah before standing. They all tugged their shoes back on and treaded down the steps toward the lodge. A hearty helping of cinnamon-covered fried dough treats and hot apple cider kept the kids' attention—and their parents' too, for that matter—for plenty long enough to serve its purpose as a diversion. They would barely touch their dinner after that, Brayden realized, but beggars can't be choosers.

The diversion was necessary because Brayden and Sarah wanted no part in exposing their children to EverChat. The application was just over a year old, and it had exploded in popularity while staunchly dividing the world on its moral axis. Thanks to remarkable scientific breakthroughs—breakthroughs that Brayden admired for their potential—a tech giant had cracked the code for making digital copies of human consciousness. The world had already seen artificial intelligence and machine learning boom over the prior couple of decades, but this was different. This was *uploading someone's mind*, creating a full mapping of their brain to replicate their very consciousness. The improvements in deepfake technology were to thank for how vividly real Marissa both looked and sounded on that MacBook, but it was the emergence of what scientists called "whole-brain emulation" that made her *Marissa*. With EverChat, as long as the subject had granted consent to have their mind uploaded, family and friends could talk to their loved one forever. Their consciousness existed on a server, manifested itself on a computer screen, and was theoretically eternal. And, evidence suggested, their loved one really experienced the continued passing of time as well. They could recall prior conversations, tie those conversations to past life experiences, and continue to recognize people, places, and things from both their pre-death and post-death observations.

Brayden and Sarah were firmly on the same side regarding EverChat: They despised it. In their view, no matter how much anecdotal evidence may have existed that the departed would happily live for eternity, they believed it was a jail cell for the mind—if it was even the person's real mind in there. It may talk like the person, look like the person, and evidently *think* like the person, but it wasn't the actual person, and it gave them both anxiety thinking about it.

The issue of consent was a slippery one too. They had read dozens of articles detailing nasty family disputes, flush with allegations that a family member unjustly granted consent when the departed couldn't administer it themselves. It went mainstream when the company ran a cringeworthy ad campaign before Christmas the year prior, preying on heartstrings by issuing a reminder that this holiday season could be anyone's last. Ever since then, the Crosses agreed they would never use it.

The same couldn't be said about the other Crosses. Riley and Ashley were fascinated by, and supportive of, EverChat, perhaps the biggest point of contention Brayden had nowadays with his brother and his sister-in-law. In a strange way, he was sometimes grateful that their father had passed away six months *before* the launch of EverChat after a lengthy battle with ALS. The argument that would have unfolded over that potential upload—especially if their father had been unable or unwilling to provide a firm decision himself—might well have driven Brayden and Riley apart for good.

When Brayden, Sarah, and the kids climbed their way back to the condo with their bellies fuller than expected in the late afternoon, Riley and Ashley were alone in the living room reading books. The fireplace continued to crackle with a warm and well-kept fire.

"Where are the kids?" Brayden asked his brother in a stern tone.

Riley gestured his head to the left without detaching his glance from the book in his hands. It was one of the Game of Thrones novels. "Playing with their new PlayStation in the playroom. How were the churros?"

Acknowledging the first half of the reply and disregarding the second, Brayden patted Charlie on the back. "Hey, Charlie, Mari—why don't you two go check out the new PlayStation with your cousins? Maybe if you like it, you can put one on your Christmas list for next year."

Once Charlie and Mari were down the hall and into the other room, Brayden turned to his brother and held his arms out to his sides, palms facing skyward. "What the hell was that earlier?"

This time, Riley peeled his eyes away from the paperback in his hands. He wore a confused look on his face that Brayden didn't buy for a moment. "What do you mean, Bray?"

"You know damn well what I mean. You and Ashley both know how we feel about EverChat, and what's the main attraction in the living room the *second* we walk in the door with the kids? Goddamn EverChat!"

"It's Christmas Day, and my children have the right to talk to their aunt, Bray—"

"Their aunt is dead, Ashley!"

His voice rose a few notches higher than he intended as he cut Ashley off. He was nearly certain he heard the PlayStation down the hall abruptly pause as the kids tried to eavesdrop. Uncomfortable silence gripped the room, and Brayden held his hand up and his head down. After a long few moments, the audio of the game resumed; it sounded like an NBA game they were playing.

"How long?"

Ashley peered over at Riley, wondering if Brayden's question confused him as much as it did her. Sarah stood a few feet away with her arms crossed, her expression somber. She was never a combative participant in arguments, but Brayden knew she felt strongly about this topic. He wondered if she would give her two cents at some point.

"How long? How long what?" Riley asked.

Brayden gestured to the now-closed MacBook on the coffee table. "I'll humor you for a second. Let's say Marissa actually is alive and well on some tech giant's server farm. Let's say that *was* Marissa you were talking to a little while ago."

He paused to let the hypothetical take root. Both Riley and Ashley waited for the point, confused why Brayden was preaching their own beliefs to them. "How long are you gonna keep her locked up in a cyber-prison?"

"Oh, for the love of God," Ashley barked as she rolled her eyes.

"Seemed like she was pretty happy to see us, Bray," Riley snarled back. "But you know what, since you're so worried about her, let me call her up and ask her if she feels like she's a prisoner."

Riley leaned over and opened the MacBook about two inches before Brayden's hand slammed the lid back down. He didn't want to let this get out of control. It was Christmas, after all. He sighed, and he was about to conjure up something emulating a truce when Sarah joined the discussion.

"Imagine," she softly interjected. She commanded the attention of the room with her input, given her reserved nature during confrontation. "No walks on the beach. No trips to the grocery store. Never wrapping another Christmas present. Never smelling another candle. Never reading another book." She subtly nodded at the paperbacks in her in-laws' laps. Brayden could see that she was getting emotional. He knew the way her bottom lip quivered right before she fought off tears. It was foresight as clear as a yellow light preceding a red one. "It's not fair! They're trapped, they're ..."

That sentence broke her, and she buried her face in her hands. Brayden quickly embraced her, the fabric on his sweater absorbing the tears that leaked from her eyes. He swayed gently and caressed her back to calm her. Glancing without moving his head, he could see that Riley and Ashley were agitated by what they viewed as a ridiculous reaction.

What struck Brayden about her reaction was the implication within it—that Marissa *was* in there, trapped forever after her death. He and Sarah had mostly skirted the actual topic of whether they believed the person's conscious thoughts translated to EverChat, rather than being a mere simulation. The moral gravity of it all hit harder when you assumed they were actually in there, confined only to occasional video chats when their loved ones in the physical world dialed them up.

What would happen when there were no loved ones left?

"Look," Brayden broke the silence in the room, "we'd appreciate it if any future EverChats can wait until you're all back home. We don't want Mari and Charlie asking about that just yet."

Riley gave a nod of approval but couldn't help including his two cents with it. "They will sooner or later."

3

Brayden laid his messenger bag on his desk and plopped down into the office chair beside it. He was back home on the East Coast, the first day back at his workplace in Portland since the turn of the new year. The kids were back at school, and his energy level was as expected for a father having helped ready a first- and third-grader for school before 8:00 a.m. He brewed himself a strong cup of coffee in the kitchen and settled in to catch up on the emails he had missed. To this point, he was fortunate to dodge the dreaded post-holiday small talk.

Following in the footsteps of his cover story during his CIA years, he actually pursued a career in tech after leaving the agency. He wasn't a developer or an engineer or anything, but he'd found a program-management role at a software company called Iron Edge—coincidentally enough, a major competitor of SafeTech, the company at which he had faked employment. He often wondered what his subconscious had been telling him when he crafted the story of his faux life back then. In any case, he spent his days working with software-development teams to improve their processes, tackle logistical hurdles, and track milestones. His job was, more or less, to be the bad cop who kept them accountable.

"B-Man, what's happening?"

It was Mark, the quirky developer who worked on the other side of the floor. He always called Brayden "B-Man," much to the chagrin of his colleague. He was tall and lanky and wore wire-rimmed glasses that may have been a size too small for his face. Mark was a brilliant nerd when it came to technology, particularly in emerging fields that sometimes made Brayden's head spin. Before the holidays, he'd been talking Brayden's ear off about new developments in robotics and quantum mechanics, and some personal projects he was working on.

"Mark, welcome back. Have a good holiday?"

"Killer holiday! It was nice having some time off, but I spent most of it working on side projects. Have you seen some of these recent papers and case studies around quantum mechanics? This stuff rocks!"

He held out his phone and began scrolling through news articles. They touted patents and breakthroughs from big tech companies like Azor, Circuit, Vonetech, and others. "These developments are insane! This stuff shouldn't even be possible. But hey, they inspired me. I started working on these bad boys in my garage last weekend."

Putting his phone away, Mark pulled from his pocket two devices that looked like walkie-talkies.

"I call it the *Quantum Nexus Resonator*. These things will use paired quantum repeaters to maintain coherence between entangled particles across macroscopic distances! See, the resonance cavity—it creates a stable environment for quantum states, *theoretically* allowing me to bridge quantum networks together without decoherence. Insane, right? Right now, I can only maintain the quantum entanglement for a few microseconds, watch."

Mark held out the two devices and pressed the trigger on the device in his right hand. It made a faint humming sound, then a small light illuminated on the walkie in his left hand. Brayden smirked and looked at Mark, expecting an explanation. When Mark saw his blank expression, he got even more animated.

"They're not connected, dude! No Wi-Fi, no bluetooth, no radio signal … nothing! That's a quantum connection!"

Brayden chuckled and nodded. Mark's enthusiasm was infectious, even when Brayden didn't care for the excruciatingly thorough details.

"Neat. Your version will be better than what those big corporations make. Changing the world, Mark."

Mark grinned and nodded. "Anyway, saw you guys were out at Sweetway. That must have been a nice week, eh?" Shades of a Canadian accent would often come out of Mark, even though he grew up in Pennsylvania.

"Oh yeah. A foot of fresh snow right before we got out there. Relaxing week with the family. I can't complain."

That, of course, was a lie. Not the part about the snow; it was plentiful and in perfect condition all week. But it was the least relaxing family vacation he could remember, and it made him wonder whether weeklong vacations like that would remain possible with his brother's family. There were no further incidents after the Marissa chat, but the tension among the adults in the house never eased. Riley and Ashley obeyed the request to avoid more EverChats during that week, but they hardly shied away from the topic in conversation. Mari and Charlie probed their parents with questions about EverChat after hearing their cousins speak about it in passing. It was becoming more and more difficult for Brayden to shield his kids from it; he spent much of the morning wondering how many of the first- and third-graders in school that day would talk about a chat with one of their own dead relatives over the holiday break.

"But I think they gotta take a receiver in the first round this year. They need weapons!"

Brayden realized Mark had been talking for some time while he zoned out. He snapped back into the conversation to hear him griping about his hometown Eagles and their personnel decisions.

"Yeah, man, I dunno. We'll see," Brayden deadpanned back, adding the subtle inflection that signaled he was about to end the conversation. "Hey, I gotta get back to work. I'll see ya around, Mark."

Mark sauntered back to his side of the twelfth floor, finally leaving Brayden to the peace and quiet he cherished in this office. He answered a few emails, ran a couple of meetings, scarfed down a salad during lunch, and read a few articles when he ran out of tasks that interested him.

A few minutes after four o'clock, his cell phone buzzed as he was gathering his jacket and bag to head home. Well, technically, it wasn't his own phone—Sarah had mistakenly grabbed his on her way to the pharmacy that morning, so he'd taken hers for the day. Some of his unmarried friends would tell him that sounded crazy, but he and his wife trusted each other to no end. Taking the other's phone for a day was truly nothing to even blink about. They only needed their phones during the workday to reach each other or their kids' school.

He didn't recognize the number on the buzzing brick, but it was a Portland area code. "Hello?"

"Hi, umm … is this Mr. Cross?" It was a woman's voice, one Brayden didn't recognize.

"This is he. May I ask who's calling?"

"It's Mrs. Cloverfield from the elementary school. I have Mari and Charlie here with me. They've been waiting for about an hour to be picked up," she explained. "They said their mother is usually right on time."

The noise around him shrank down to a vacant silence, and his vision blurred in quick pulses that seemed to track his heartbeat. Brayden felt the same gripping rush as the moment he imagined a bomb going off at the ski lodge on Christmas. His mind raced to dozens of worst-case scenarios. Sarah was *never* late to pick up the kids, let alone nearly an hour late without a word. He swiped down to see if he'd missed a text she had sent him from his own phone. No texts, but three calls he somehow missed from this same number over the past hour. There was no other explanation; something happened to Sarah, he was certain. He broke into a sprint for the elevator, catching a few alarmed glances from random office mates.

"Mr. Cross?"

He realized he was still holding the phone to his ear, but he hadn't said a word. "Uh … yes, I'm so sorry, Mrs. Cloverfield. I'm on my way to pick them up right now. I'll be there in ten."

The elevator doors slid open, and he scampered into the empty cab. He pressed the "L" button so hard he nearly jammed his finger. After checking for the third time if he'd missed a text or call, he opened his own contact on Sarah's phone to check its location. Maybe she was caught up at the grocery store, or had broken down on the road, or perhaps the phone had simply died and she couldn't explain the reason for her tardiness. The lump grew larger in Brayden's throat as he continually yanked downward on the screen to refresh the location. With each pull, it yielded the same result.

The phone was on. It was in their kitchen. At most times of the day, that would be reassuring. In this moment, and with these circumstances, it was confirmation for Brayden that something was very wrong. He quickly swiped away from the location and tried to open the feed of their home security camera. What was previously a lump in his throat could now only be described as a boulder.

A piece of black tape obscured the entire frame.

4

TEN YEARS AGO

Sarah's fingers hovered over her phone, the message to Brayden still unsent.

"Running late. Don't wait up."

She sighed, knowing it was the third time this week she'd be getting home after he'd gone to bed—if he was even home at all. With a quick tap, she sent the text and slipped the phone back into her purse.

The soft glow of her desk lamp illuminated the scattered papers and files spread before her. Each folder was dedicated to a child, to a life touched by trauma or struggle, to someone seeking solace in the warm confines of her office. Sarah rubbed her temples, the weight of their stories seemingly pressing down on her shoulders. As exhausting as the work was, she couldn't imagine doing anything else. It was more rewarding than it was draining.

A gentle knock at the door pulled her from her thoughts. "Come in," she called, straightening in her chair.

The door creaked open, revealing a small, scrawny figure with disheveled brown hair and wide, anxious brown eyes. Eight-year-old Tommy peered into the room, his hand still gripping the doorknob like a lifeline.

"Hi, Tommy," Sarah said, her voice warm and inviting. "I'm glad you decided to come back. Would you like to sit down?"

Tommy nodded sheepishly, shuffling into the room. He climbed onto the overstuffed armchair across from Sarah, his feet dangling a foot above the floor. His eyes darted around the room, taking in the colorful posters and shelves lined with toys and books.

"I brought something for you today," Sarah said with a smile, reaching into her desk drawer. She pulled out a small plush elephant, its trunk curled upward in a perpetual smile. "This is Ellie. She's very good at listening and keeping secrets. Would you like to hold her while we talk?"

Tommy's eyes sparkled, a flicker of childlike wonder breaking through the wall that guarded him. He reached out, carefully taking the elephant and hugging it to his chest.

"Ellie looks happy to meet you," Sarah said with a speck of laughter. "Can you tell me about your week, Tommy? Did anything happen that you'd like to share?"

For a moment, Tommy was silent, his fingers tracing Ellie's fuzzy ears. Then, barely louder than a whisper, he spoke. "I had a bad dream again."

Sarah leaned forward, her full attention on the boy. "That must have been scary. Can you tell me about it?"

As Tommy recounted his nightmare, Sarah listened intently. She asked gentle questions, guiding him through the narrative, helping him find words for the fear and confusion that plagued his young mind.

By the end of the session, Tommy's shoulders had relaxed, and his grip on Ellie had loosened into a comfortable embrace. As Sarah walked him to the waiting room where his foster parents sat, she felt the familiar mix of hope and determination that fueled her work. One step at a time, one child at a time, she would help these innocent minds find their way back to comfort.

The clock on the wall read 8:30 p.m. as Sarah gathered her things to leave. She'd missed dinner again, but the progress with Tommy was worth it. As she locked up her office, her phone buzzed. It was a text from her mother.

"Dinner tomorrow night. No excuses this time. Bring that husband of yours if he's not too busy saving the world."

Sarah rolled her eyes, a familiar tension creeping into her shoulders. Her mother's passive-aggressive jabs at Brayden were becoming harder to brush off. She typed out a curt reply confirming their attendance and headed for her car.

The drive home was quiet, the radio a low murmur of evening talk shows and soft jazz. Sarah's mind wandered to Brayden, wondering if he was home. If he was safe. The nature of his work, which she knew was massively important but massively dangerous, meant long periods of silence, unexplained absences, and a constant undercurrent of worry. She loved him fiercely, and he shared details with her whenever he could. But the weight of the mandatory secrets between them felt suffocating, especially in the moments she wondered if he was safe and sound.

As she pulled into their driveway, she noticed with surprise that the living room light was on. Brayden was home. A mix of relief and anxiety fluttered in her chest as she made her way to the front door.

She found him in the kitchen, heating leftovers in the microwave. The sight of him—alive, healthy, unscathed, standing in their kitchen in sweatpants and a faded T-shirt—made her heart swell.

"Hey," he said, a tired smile crossing his face. "I was starting to think you'd moved into your office."

Sarah dropped her purse on the counter and wrapped her arms around him, breathing in the familiar scent of her husband mixed with something that smelled vaguely of gunpowder. She chose not to dwell on the latter.

"I'm sorry I'm so late," she whispered into his chest. "I had a breakthrough with Tommy today. He finally opened up about the nightmares."

Brayden's arms tightened around her. "That's amazing, honey. I know how hard you've been working with him."

They stood in their embrace for a moment, swaying slightly to the soft country song that played in the background. The harsh beeps of the microwave eventually interrupted.

As they sat at their wooden kitchen table, sharing reheated lasagna and the parts of their days they *could* discuss, Sarah felt the familiar ache of the many things left unsaid. Brayden's eyes held shadows she couldn't penetrate, and she longed for the day when those secrets could stop accumulating.

"My mom wants us for dinner tomorrow night," Sarah said, pushing a piece of pasta around her plate.

Brayden's fork paused halfway to his mouth. "Both of us?"

"Yes, both of us. She was quite insistent."

He sighed, setting his fork down. "Sarah, you know I can't promise—"

"I know," she cut him off, a bit more sharply than she intended. "But it would mean a lot to me if you could try. She's … she's trying, in her own way."

Ellen Lennon was not the biggest fan of Brayden Cross. Sarah could never figure out why; Brayden had always been very respectful around her, and he had tried repeatedly to shower her with kindness in the early days of their relationship. But her mother was often distant, cold, disconnected. Twice married and twice divorced, Sarah sensed her mother's journey had taken a toll on her, and in turn, she'd begun taking it out on others.

Brayden reached across the table, taking her hand in his. "I'll do my best. I want to be there; you know that, right?"

Sarah nodded, squeezing his hand. "I know. It's just … sometimes I feel like I'm always choosing between the people and the things that I love. Between my work and our marriage, between you and my mother. I'm tired of feeling torn."

The admission marinated between them for a moment, heavy with unspoken fears and frustrations. Brayden's thumb traced circles on the back of her hand, a gesture that had comforted her countless times before.

"I'm sorry," he said. "I know this isn't easy. But I love you, Sarah. We'll figure it out."

She believed him. She wanted to sink into the warmth of his promise. But as she met his hazel eyes, she saw the flicker of something—guilt, perhaps, or maybe regret—that told her there were still depths to his world she couldn't fathom.

The next evening found them on Ellen's doorstep, a bottle of wine in Brayden's hand and a forced smile on Sarah's face. As the door swung open, Sarah braced herself for the evening ahead.

Ellen greeted them with air kisses and a critical once-over of Brayden's attire.

"So glad you could both make it," she said, embedded in her words an insinuation of her doubt that Brayden would attend. "Come in, come in. Dinner's almost ready."

As they followed Ellen into the house, Sarah's eyes were drawn to a new painting hanging in the entryway—an abstract piece in bold colors that seemed to clash with her mother's usual conservative taste. Frankly, to Sarah, it looked ridiculous—as if it cost a hundred times more than any other piece of decor in the house.

"That's new," Sarah commented, holding back a laugh, nodding in the artwork's direction.

Ellen's face illuminated in a way Sarah hadn't seen in years. "Oh, yes. It's wonderful, isn't it? A gift from a … from a friend."

There was something in her mother's voice, a hint of excitement and secrecy, that piqued Sarah's curiosity. But before she could probe further, Ellen was ushering them into the dining room.

Dinner was a tense affair. As abundant as the mashed potatoes were Ellen's thinly veiled jabs at Brayden's profession, and in return, Brayden's increasingly concise responses. Sarah acted as the mediator, a role she was uniquely well suited to fulfill.

"So, Brayden," Ellen said, swirling her wine glass, "any exciting business trips coming up? Or is your travel schedule classified too?"

"All right—"

Sarah saw Brayden's jaw clench just before his abrupt response. His knuckles whitened around his fork.

"Mom," she attempted diplomacy, but Ellen pressed on.

"I'm just taking an interest in my son-in-law's life. Is that a crime now?"

"Ellen," Brayden said, his voice measured and tight, "I appreciate your interest, but you know I can't discuss the details of my work. We've been over this."

"Of course, of course," Ellen said with a dismissive wave. "Heaven forbid I know anything about the man my daughter married."

"Mom, that's enough," Sarah snapped, her patience finally breaking. "Brayden's work is important, and yes, it's classified. He could have kept lying to you, and pretending he was a software engineer at SafeTech. But he chose to be as transparent as he *can be*. That doesn't make him any less a part of this family and my life. There's plenty more to talk about!"

A heavy silence descended on the table. Ellen appeared saddled with regret for a moment before stirring back to life. "Well, I suppose we should be grateful he could spare an evening for family dinner."

As she slid her fork beneath a pile of green beans, Ellen's phone chimed. She glanced at it, a little smirk crossing on her lips.

"Good news?" Sarah asked in a markedly more lighthearted tone, playing into the change in her mother's demeanor.

Ellen looked startled, as if she had entirely forgotten they were there during that one-second span. "Oh, it's nothing, dear. Just a message from a friend."

"The same *friend* who gave you that painting?"

Ellen's cheeks reddened. "Well, as a matter of fact, yes. He's … different from anyone I've ever known. Brilliant, driven. He sees the world in a way that's just …"

As she trailed off, Sarah let out her first laugh. "Mom! It sounds like this guy's pretty special to you! How long have you been seeing him?"

"Oh, I don't know. It's been a couple of months now. Actually, you know—he was going to fly me out to Los Angeles last weekend, to go to the World Series. Dodgers and Red Sox, it would have made your father so jealous."

Sarah's eyebrows lifted slowly. Her head tilted downward, but her gaze remained level. "World Series tickets? Flying you to LA? Sounds like Mr. Right is both special *and* successful."

Brayden shifted uncomfortably in his seat. Sarah could sense his unease. She reached under the table, squeezing his hand reassuringly.

"Speaking of LA," Sarah said, "Bray mentioned there was almost a big incident in the Metro system recently. Said it could have been a disaster if it hadn't been stopped."

Ellen's attention snapped back to the conversation, her eyes narrowing slightly. "Oh? And how would Brayden know about that?"

She felt Brayden shift uncomfortably beside her. "I don't know the details," she blurted. She looked at him, waiting for him to chime in. Instead, he just looked downward. "But I tell myself he was the hero who saved the day."

A pregnant silence took over. Ellen's focus flicked between Sarah and Brayden before Brayden finally spoke up.

"Again, can't really talk about it, Ellen. I wish I could." He looked up at her. "I'm glad you were far from LA last week."

"Well, indeed. *I* certainly wish we'd been there, but I suppose we should be grateful for whatever unnamed heroes keep us safe, shouldn't we?"

Her eyes locked on Brayden, the words themselves doing no justice to the accusatory glare.

Brayden cleared his throat. "More wine?"

As he lifted out of his chair to refill their glasses, Sarah felt the weight of her mistake. She never should have brought up the Los Angeles story—what little she knew about it—in front of her mother. She had put her husband on blast.

After another glass of wine and a bite of dessert, they gathered their things and said their goodbyes. While Brayden was in the bathroom, Ellen pulled Sarah aside.

"I'm sorry if I was harsh earlier," she whispered. "I just worry about you, darling. This life you've chosen … it can't be easy."

Sarah softened, seeing the genuine concern in her mother's eyes. "I know, Mom, but it's my life, and Brayden is my world. I wish you could see him the way I do. His secrets are born of necessity, not choice."

Ellen sighed, touching Sarah's cheek. "I know. I'm trying, dear. I really am."

As they drove home, Sarah grappled with the inescapable feeling that she'd exacerbated an already tense situation. Brayden was quiet beside her, his eyes fixed on the road ahead.

"I'm sorry about my mom," Sarah said, breaking the silence. "She's … well, she's Ellen."

She was relieved to see Brayden's stern look shift into a smile. He reached his hand over and put it atop her knee. "It's okay. I knew what I was signing up for when I married you."

Sarah put her hand on top of his. "Thank you for coming tonight. I know it wasn't easy. And I'm sorry for bringing up LA."

His smile mostly erased, but he nodded. "Not your best judgment. I want to bend the rules with you, especially when I'm proud of something I've accomplished, Sarah. That day is the reason I do what I do. We probably saved a million lives, honey. It doesn't get more rewarding."

He paused, but Sarah could tell he hadn't completed his thought. He rubbed the steering wheel and then continued, "I just can't have you repeating the things I tell you about work. Any of them, big or small. That's all."

She squeezed his hand tightly. "You can trust me."

As they pulled into their driveway, Sarah felt the familiar mix of love and worry that seemed to define their relationship. Brayden's work would always leave some shadows between them—at least until whenever he finally decided it wasn't worth it—and her mother would always be a source of tension. But as she looked at her husband, his face gently lit by the glow of the porch light, she knew innately that she wouldn't trade this life for anything, even with its challenges.

They walked hand in hand to the front steps, the night quiet around them. Just as they arrived at the door, Brayden's phone buzzed. Sarah felt him stiffen beside her, and she knew what was coming before he even looked at the screen.

"Honey, I—"

"You have to go," she finished for him, her voice steady despite the disappointment.

He pulled her close, pressing a kiss to her forehead. "I'm sorry. I'll make it up to you, I promise."

As she watched him drive away, Sarah felt all her emotions swirling together. This was their life—moments of connection interspersed with stretches of separation and worry. But as she turned to enter their empty house, she held on to the warmth of his kiss, the strength of his promise.

She was Sarah Cross—wife, daughter, healer of young minds. And despite the challenges, despite the secrets and the unknowns, she wouldn't have it any other way.

5

"Sarah, what's up?" Riley answered, sounding surprised by the call.

"It's Brayden. Are you guys home?"

The momentary silence on the other end hinted Riley could sense the urgency in Brayden's tone. "Uh, yeah, yeah, we're here. Why?"

"I need you guys to watch Mari and Charlie for a bit. I'll be there in five." He spoke hurriedly as the bottom of his gas pedal nearly touched the floor below it. In the rearview mirror, he could see the concerned looks on the faces of his young children.

"What's going on, Bray? Is everything all right?"

"I'll explain later, Riley."

He hung up the call and dropped the phone into the cupholder in his center console. The needle on his speedometer flirted with ninety miles per hour. He scanned the horizon every thirty seconds to check for cops stationed with their radar guns.

"Daddy, why are we going so fast?" Mari spoke softly, with only a hint of unease. She was a tough little girl.

Brayden glanced into his mirror and saw that her eyes harbored more fear than her voice had let on. He lightened up a bit on the accelerator, but it hardly made a difference for the little passengers behind him.

"I have to go check on something for your mom, and it's very important, okay?" He felt he was failing to provide a calm bedside manner, but there wasn't much he could do about it. "You and Charlie are going to stay with Uncle Riley and Aunt Ashley for a bit while I take care of it."

He bolted off his exit and ran a yellow light or two before reaching his brother's neighborhood. The Chevy screeched to a stop in front of their house, the kind of screech usually found in movies rather than real life. Brayden scurried out of the truck and ushered his kids toward the front door. Hard crunching noises sprang off their feet as they made dents in the rigid, week-old snow in the yard. Riley was at the door already, opening it as they approached.

"Hey, Crosses! Mari, Charlie—the kids are in the basement playing knee hockey. You might get in on the tourney if you hurry!"

Brayden hugged his kids and told them he'd be back as soon as he could. Then he started back down the stairs and into a jog toward his truck, entirely forgetting to fill in his brother on the situation.

"Guy, you wanna tell me what the hell's going on?"

A loud grinding in the snow resulted from Brayden stopping on a dime and turning around.

"Ry, I'll be in touch. I gotta go right now. She might be in trouble."

The answer didn't seem to satisfy his brother, but it would have to suffice. Riley nodded as Brayden darted to his truck and peeled around the circle on his way out of the neighborhood.

The lights in the house were mostly off, and dusk had fully descended into nighttime. His tires slowly croaked over the packed-down snow he had been too lazy to shovel after their vacation. Brayden took a deep inhale and tried to relax. *You have these episodes frequently*, he thought to himself. It's always the worst-case scenario in my mind, but rarely is it so in reality. He had probably overreacted in rushing the kids to their cousins' house. His efforts to calm down had diminished the boulder in his throat back down to more of a pebble, but he still could have puked at any moment.

He approached his front steps. Pulling open the glass storm door, he slid his key into the doorknob. It was unlocked. As he pushed the door open, he could see only the faint light of what was probably a single lamp plus a soft television glow in the living room. He could hear some sort of music playing softly in the kitchen. Fighting off the urge to panic, he pushed through the door and closed it behind him. "Sarah?"

No answer. He glanced at their alarm system on the wall beside him. It had been turned off. Carefully, he trudged down the hallway, moving slowly and staying ready to combat an intruder. His brain was morphing back into its high-stress field operative mode. The kitchen came into view, and he saw his phone sitting on the counter. Beside it, a cutting board held an assortment of sliced vegetables and a few still-whole potatoes. A carton of milk sat on the counter, condensation glistening on its surface. On the far side of the kitchen, one wooden chair was missing from their six-seat table. He instinctively reached for his holster, again to no avail. He was unarmed.

Creeping forward, a portion of the living room came into view. The lamp beside the couch emitted enough light to keep the room aglow when partnered with the television mounted on the wall. As he turned the corner to unveil everything, his heart leapt into his throat. His vision pulsed twice as fast as it did earlier that hour when he got the phone call. A suddenly dense fog of terror hung in the surrounding air, like he was breathing in a supply of poison.

The missing chair from the dining set was in the middle of the room, facing the security camera mounted near the television. A piece of black hockey tape covered the camera's lens. A small pool of blood stained the carpet below the chair, and Brayden's eyes traced the blood's path. He scanned from the base of the wooden leg, up to the pair of hands tied together and bruised at its midway point, and all the way to where brunette locks of hair cloaked the wicker seatback like a saddle.

This can't be real, he thought. *It's not happening. You've done this before.* He pinched himself, hoping to snap out of his terror, but the pounding in his senses only intensified. He slapped himself forcefully; no difference. Sprinting the two yards of space between him and the chair, he grabbed the woman's shoulder and vaulted himself into view of her front side.

It took three more vision pulses for his brain to accept the visual his eyes were relaying. His wife slumped motionless in the chair, giving a new perspective on the morbidity that clung to the air he breathed. The knife that should have been alongside the vegetables on the counter lay neatly in her lap, blanketed in blood. A blurred line ran the length of her throat, and a still-glistening red stream coated the front of her collarbone and turned her blue sweater into a deep purplish brown. For a moment, Brayden was grateful for the lack of clarity in his vision. Moments later, the gruesome slice that served the puddle of blood around Sarah processed into full clarity.

He broke down and held his wife by her cheeks, rubbing his thumb over her bruised but soft skin. He rested his head on her shoulder, and he sobbed harder than he could ever remember sobbing. The love of his life, the mother of his children, was gone, and she was taken with an inhumanity he hadn't been exposed to since the days he used to carry his badge. He could feel the bubble of anger brewing inside him, but it had not yet reached the surface. For now, the only emotions pouring out of him were devastation and sadness.

He wept for several minutes, listening to nothing but his own sniffles and the soft sound of the music playing in the kitchen. The prospect of explaining this to his children wrenched its way into his mind, and it sent him into another lengthy stream of sobs. When he calmed, he looked at his wife again. Everything was finally doused with clarity, and he could see the details of her state. They had beaten her before murdering her. The bruises on her wrists showed a likely struggle to free herself from the ropes binding her to the chair. Only after gliding his fingers from her eyebrow down across her temple did Brayden notice, nudging aside the hair that covered it, a circular red surface wound just above her temple and below her hairline. An identical wound etched itself above her opposite temple.

Based on the litany of experiences that aggregated to form Brayden's personality over the years, nearly every part of him itched to investigate immediately and find his wife's murderer. But the gravity of the moment weighed him down as if he were a mere canoe tied to a cargo ship's steel anchor. He sank to the floor and sat silently for an hour before mustering up the energy to dial the police station.

6

Within twenty-five minutes, the CSI unit had arrived at the Cross residence in Westbrook, Maine. Brayden explained the situation to the officers and continued fending off the tears bubbling up at the corners of his eyes. He had regained some of his composure, relative to a little while ago, but that wasn't saying much. Nearly a dozen members of the unit traipsed around his home in protective gear, tagging and collecting evidence. Ten minutes never went by without Brayden replaying in his head the eventual conversation he'd need to have with his children. On a few different glances out the window, he could see his neighbors trying to get a glimpse of what called for the army of cruisers out front.

"Can I get you anything, Brayden?" It was the lead detective on the CSI unit, Lacy Storrow. Brayden knew several officers and detectives in the Westbrook Police Department, and many of them knew Brayden. The ones that knew him well knew he was an ex-operative of some sort; they just didn't know the details. Detective Storrow was a pretty close friend of the family, knew a lot about Brayden's background, and was a bit visibly shaken by the crime before her. In most towns, she'd be pulled from a case like this one for being too emotionally invested. In Westbrook, that would only happen if someone filed a complaint. She was in her early forties, though it felt like she hadn't aged a day since Brayden had met her several years earlier. She was tall and fit, with golden-blonde hair she usually wore in a ponytail.

"I'm good, thanks, Lace," Brayden answered with a sigh as he wiped his hands across his face. "You need any help out there? What can I do?"

Lacy donned a slight and reluctant grin, shaking her head and patting Brayden on the shoulder. "I know you want to dive into this, but you've got to stay out of the team's way. We're gonna find the person who did this to her."

"I can't just sit here and wait around. The person who did this is out there. I want to help. I need to help."

Lacy tilted her head at him and relayed a look that suggested she agreed but that she could never give him the green light to go rogue. "You know I can't get you involved." She paused for a beat before turning her head away. "But if you come across anything, my door will be open."

Brayden nodded and sniffled, wiping his nose with the back of his hand. "I'm gonna get some air. Let me know when forensics is done with the initial collection."

The detective pursed her lips as Brayden returned her shoulder pat and walked out to his back porch. The blast of cold air was a relief to him, a calming sensation after spending nearly two hours at the site of his wife's murder. He wondered if he could ever go back to loving this house. Would he ever be able to sit in his living room and watch a movie without seeing that wicker seatback? Could any candle eradicate the smell of stale bloodstains saturating the carpet? Could a day ever pass without a cognitive attack levied by the imagery of those bruises and that singular throat slash?

He sat on the cushioned rocking chair that overlooked their large backyard. The moonlight reflected off the small ice rink he and Sarah finally built for the kids this winter. Mari had begged them to build one for the past four years, so it was certainly overdue. It was cobbled together, contained by about two feet of wood on all sides, with a tarp bleeding over the edges. One side was more prone to cracking on milder days, thanks to its thinner nature in the uneven landscape.

Brayden and Sarah considered it an admirable attempt, for first-time rink-builders.

He took his phone from his pocket and twice keyed in an incorrect password before realizing it was still Sarah's phone he held. After entering her code, he was reminded of something the investigative team would certainly ask about in short order: the footage. He opened up the home security app to find the camera displaying a room full of forensics experts wearing light-blue gloves and holding evidence bags. They had removed the piece of tape that previously obscured the frame. How did it get there? Could the footage identify the monster who killed his wife before the tape blacked out the frame?

Proper procedure would have called for handing over the footage to Lacy and letting her team do the work, but that was a laughable notion in this moment. Brayden felt his dormant supply of adrenaline kick into gear for the first time since he slowly crept down the hallway a few hours earlier. Switching from the live camera view to the recorded footage in the mobile app, he tracked backward to the last interval of time with a preview frame that wasn't obscured by darkness. The thumbnail looked like an empty living room, and the timestamp read 2:00 p.m. Touching it open to enlarge it, he saw Sarah standing with her back to the camera just beyond the living room. She stood at the kitchen counter, the overhead light making her silhouette distinct in the camera's view. As Brayden scrubbed forward in time, he could see she was cutting vegetables. He bumped up the phone's volume and held it to his ear; she had been listening to "You Deserve It All" by John Legend, and Brayden winced at the irony of that song preceding such a horrid act bestowed upon such an undeserving woman.

He scrubbed forward until the video's timestamp read 2:07 p.m., at which point the first break from normalcy occurred. The soft chime of the security system played, the one indicating a door or window had been opened. The lack of additional warnings meant Sarah hadn't turned the alarm on; she rarely did so when she was home. She glanced up and to her right, craning her neck slightly to get a view down the hallway. "Bray? Is that you? You're home ea—"

Sarah's voice abruptly cut as it became obvious—though not

visually obvious, in the camera frame—that the visitor in the hallway was not her husband. Donning her trademark calm, she slowly placed the knife down and raised her hands. She didn't cry, and she didn't reveal the spectacular fear Brayden knew was inside her at that moment. Instead, she stood tall and kept her gaze intently locked on the man who came into focus from the right edge of the video frame.

The gun was the first thing to enter the frame. It looked like a nine-millimeter Smith & Wesson to Brayden's highly trained eye, but the footage wasn't clear enough to say for certain. Wrapped around it was a hand sporting a black glove, which seamlessly adjoined the sleeve of a charcoal-colored hoodie. There was no design or logo visible, though white laces on the hood of the sweatshirt provided a stark contrast. The hood cloaked the man's head, and a mask straight out of a bank robbery movie scene covered his face. A pair of black slacks and boots and an olive-green backpack completed the entirely nondescript outfit for the man who evidently was about to murder Brayden's wife.

As he inched closer to Sarah, he muttered something softly. Though John Legend was no longer running audio interference, the playlist had continued, and Norah Jones now sang at a volume that provided just enough decibels to obscure the presumably threatening words. A moment later, the intruder—still pointing his weapon at Sarah's skull with his right hand—reached into his pocket with his left and pulled out what looked like a small roll of tape. He tossed it to Sarah, who caught it and froze. She looked confused, but her hands shot back up into the air when the man gestured aggressively and shouted, "I said put your hands back up!"

He began angling himself into the kitchen and nodding his head toward the living room, signaling Sarah to move. Her steps were short and delicate, like she was walking on a thin pane of glass suspended thirty stories high, and any misstep could be her demise. Shifting gently around the coffee table, her back eventually came within a few feet of the camera that sat on the mantle.

"Rip off a piece of tape. Hands where I can see 'em."

This was the clearest audio Brayden had heard of the man's voice, and he hoped the police force's audio engineers could analyze it, eventually. It felt like a longshot to identify this villain without some other lead to corroborate the audio, but any glimmer of hope right now was worth considering. The voice was low and coarse and didn't show any signs of a foreign or regional accent.

Brayden could see that Sarah was doing something with the roll of tape she held, but her body blocked the view. A few seconds later, her hands rose again, defensively. The roll of tape was in her left hand, and a small piece of it was in her right.

"Cover the camera."

"You'll never get away with this, you son of a—"

"Cover the camera!" The man took a more aggressive step forward as he cut her off with this repeat directive, raising his voice and shaking his pistol.

Sarah was an incredibly brave woman with poise enough for two, but the fear in her eyes as she turned toward the camera and placed the tape over its lens broke Brayden's heart. A moment after the frame went dark with its new mask, the struggle became an audio-only endeavor. From the speakers of Sarah's phone, Brayden endured the sounds of cries and squirms, of physical resistance and the draining of hope. As he tried to paint the picture of what he was hearing, he thought the assailant tied Sarah's hands and jammed her into the chair he had dragged over.

"What do you want from me!" was the last thing Brayden heard his wife exclaim before a loud stream of white noise began flooding the audio in the footage. He scrubbed back over it twice, hoping it had been a momentary glitch. As he reviewed the sound, though, he realized it was no technical glitch. The man had placed his own phone beside the camera, blasting white noise into its microphone and veiling the sounds from the living room. Brayden listened for another minute, only hearing the occasional faint yelp of anguish. He wondered if it was a blessing in disguise that he couldn't hear the act of her murder. Still, it angered him.

He scrubbed the cursor forward along the timeline, trying to find the end of the white noise. The man obviously hadn't left his phone on the mantle, so it had to end at some point. 2:15, 2:30, and 2:45 passed, none yielding a break from the buzz. With each passing interval, Brayden's blood simmered closer to a boil. This maniac didn't just murder Sarah, that much was becoming clear. What the hell was he doing to her?

2:53 p.m. would stay etched into Brayden's brain traumatically forever. The subtle rustling of a phone being lifted from the mantle cut through the static, and the buzz briefly faded in intensity as the man pulled it away from the camera. Then the sound stopped entirely. A gaping silence made him feel like an astronaut for a moment, and then a Michael Bublé track was apparently next on the playlist this psycho left running while he murdered Sarah Cross.

Just above the hum of the music, Brayden heard a slow and firm set of footsteps walk away from the mantle, gather a bag of some sort, and walk out the door.

7

The investigative team finished their work and eventually packed up. They didn't have any leads on a suspect, but they confirmed what Brayden had already known: Sarah was not murdered quickly. That much was clear from the security footage, but the preliminary results from the medical examiner later that night estimated her time of death to be between 2:30 and 3:30. Considering it was 2:07 when that psychopath arrived at the house and 2:53 when he took his belongings and left, it was all but confirmed that Sarah endured something horrible before the end arrived. The unknown sent the bad variety of chills down Brayden's spine.

He drove back to his brother's house, where the most difficult task of his entire life—orders of magnitude tougher than any interrogation, investigation, or intervention he'd ever gone through—awaited him. He had to explain the events of the day to Mari and Charlie.

Brayden sat on the edge of the small wooden coffee table in Riley's family room, facing his two children, who were curled up on the couch. It was obvious his kids had sensed something was wrong, but they weren't even ten years old; they couldn't possibly be prepared for this type of loss. Their little faces already showed the etch marks of uncertainty as they waited for their father to speak.

"Hey, kiddos." His voice cracked, unable to make it through the first two words seamlessly. He did his best to steady himself, to show strength. "There's something you need to know, and ... well, it's not easy."

Mari, ever perceptive, straightened her posture. She was bracing for whatever was to come. Her eyes locked onto Brayden's intensely, which made the delivery more difficult. Charlie still waited, fidgeting with the hem of his shirt.

"Is it about Mommy?" Mari asked. "Is it the reason she didn't come get us from school like normal?"

Brayden drew a shaky breath that felt insufficient and nodded. "Yes, baby. It's about Mommy."

He reached forward, placing a hand on each child's shoulder. They were so small, vulnerable, innocent, warm.

"Something very bad happened at our house today. Mommy got hurt, and ..." His throat dried up as he searched for the right words to convey this horror while minimizing the inflicted trauma. He didn't know how to do this. "She was hurt very badly."

"But the doctors will fix her, right?" Charlie's voice was timid but hopeful. Brayden immediately regretted his sugarcoating approach. "Like when I broke my arm and got a cast?"

Brayden had to drop his head and close his eyes for a moment to regain his composure. When he opened them again, tears were rolling down his cheeks. He sensed Mari beginning to reciprocate the emotion she was observing.

"No, buddy. Mommy, she got hurt so badly that they can't fix her. She's not coming home. She's going to live in our hearts now."

As he delivered the last sentence, his voice was like a plane rattling through intense turbulence. He touched a finger to each of their chests, over their hearts, as he explained it. He saw Mari's bottom lip quiver just like her mother's would before crying. Charlie simply stared at his dad, like the words weren't registering yet.

"But she can't—" Mari started, but sobs interrupted.

Charlie's face cramped, the delayed comprehension hitting him.

"No! No, you're lying, Dad. Stop lying. Mommy said she was going to take me to get new soccer cleats this weekend. She wouldn't lie! You shouldn't lie!"

Brayden pulled Charlie into his arms as he wept, the boy's small body tense with resistance before eventually collapsing into the grief his father was showing. Mari remained frozen, shivering, her eyes filling with tears that stubbornly refused to fall, as if holding them tight to the eyelids might somehow reverse the truth.

"She wouldn't leave us, she can't ..."

"She didn't want to leave us," Brayden whispered, reaching out to Mari with his free arm. She hesitated at first before leaning into his embrace. "Your mother loved both of you more than anything in this world, and you'll see her someday in the next world. She's not gone; she's just in here."

He again pointed to their hearts, then his own heart.

After a few moments filled only with the noise of soft weeping, Mari asked a follow-up question. "Did someone hurt Mommy?"

Brayden held them tighter. "We don't know yet. But I promise I'm going to find out."

Charlie looked up at him, his face streaked with tears and red from crying. "But you won't leave us too, right?"

The question hit hard. The duality of his new mission—to protect and comfort his children, and to find the man responsible for Sarah's murder—was an inherent contradiction. But in this moment, with their fragile hearts laid vulnerably before him, there was only one right answer.

"Never," he whispered. He pressed his face to Charlie's forehead. "I'll always come home. I promise."

It may have been semantics—always coming home was a different standard than never leaving—but it was a vow he fully intended to keep, even as he silently amended it with another promise to avenge the love of his life.

The other Crosses mourned alongside them. Riley and Ashley both failed to find words, as did their children. Despite being on generally cold terms with her, Brayden also shared a brief phone conversation with Sarah's mother, Ellen, informing her of the news. It was a somber few hours before Brayden eventually took his family back to the house he wasn't sure he could call home anymore. The kids fell asleep on the ride; it was well past eleven, and as it turns out, a day like that takes a toll on seven- and nine-year-olds.

As he drove in silence with his sleeping children, the reality of Sarah's absence suffocated him. He remembered one night she had come home, eyes shining with a mixture of exhaustion and triumph. She'd spent hours with a young patient, a boy who hadn't spoken in months after witnessing a violent crime. "He talked today, Bray," she had said, her voice barely above a whisper. "He told me about his favorite superhero." It was memories like these that always reminded Brayden of the profound impact Sarah had on the world, one child at a time. Suddenly, and abruptly, a massive void was left not just in his life, but in the lives of countless children who would never benefit from her masterful, calm guidance.

As he pressed off the ignition of his truck, he realized he couldn't carry his two sleeping children to their beds in one trip without waking them up.

He silently wept, then nudged Mari awake, opting to carry Charlie up the driveway. After tucking his son in and giving him a gentle forehead kiss, he pulled the door shut and walked down the hall to his little girl's room.

"Hey. You okay?" Brayden asked the question despite its obvious absurdity. Of course, she wasn't okay.

Mari sat on her bed, her elbows hugged around her knees and the lower half of her face burrowed beneath her forearms. She didn't answer. Brayden walked over and sat on the edge of the bed, gently displacing the hair above her brow before embracing her around the shoulder.

"Why would someone want to hurt Mommy?" Her voice trembled across the words as she walked the tightrope between composure and collapse.

Why would someone want to hurt Mommy? Brayden's lack of an answer gave him a chaotic combination of nausea and rage.

"Sweetheart, I wish I knew." He pulled her in, pressing her to his chest. "But I promise I'm going to find out."

She shifted her body to hug her father, her knees draping sideways and her cheek pushing into his shoulder. "I miss her, Daddy."

Brayden expected more waterworks of his own, but they inexplicably abstained this time. Maybe his sorrow reserves had run dry for the evening, or maybe his natural instincts rejected another dose. Whatever the reason, the urge to break down at this vulnerable admission from his daughter did not overcome him. He was only overcome with a fire to make someone pay.

"We always will, sweetheart."

After a brief and futile attempt at sleeping, Brayden scurried down to his office beside the living room and popped open his computer. He began searching through recent reports of murders or assaults in the area. There had to be some trend here, he thought. Sarah Cross had zero enemies. None. She wasn't gunned down in a drive-by shooting. She wasn't a casualty of a bank robbery. She was murdered deliberately, and it sure looked premeditated.

Was it related to his own past?

There were a few results from local newspapers and police statements, though none of them was from the past week. The victims seemed scattered, mostly, and none yielded any obvious link to Sarah: a fifty-year-old man stabbed at his home in February; a seventy-five-year-old woman shot in her home in July. He cringed when he stumbled upon the next and most recent one, which was a twelve-year-old boy abducted in November and found dead by a river in December.

It struck Brayden that although none of these shed much light on his wife's killer, it was an odd string of crimes. Westbrook was a small town, not exactly ripe for a murdering spree. He supposed these were spread out enough that suspicions of a serial killer never materialized. The news articles related to the various investigations described multiple different suspect profiles, further debunking the idea of a single maniacal killer. Still, none of those suspects had been found and identified.

He widened his search net to cover all of Maine. There were several murders since August with suspects not yet apprehended. The victims continued to dodge Sarah's demographic like the plague: a twenty-seven-year-old black man near Sebago Lake; a twenty-one-year-old Asian woman in Portland; a forty-six-year-old white transgender man in Biddeford; a seventy-year-old Indian man in Brunswick.

Brayden closed his browser and collapsed backward into the lumbar support pad on his chair. Learning nothing other than the fact that Maine's police forces apparently needed serious investigative help dejected him. His operating theory was that this couldn't have been a random act, and he didn't feel crazy for believing that. Younger women were a targeted demographic for twisted killers out there, and being in her thirties, Sarah could still belong to that group. But if she was part of a string of attacks against young women in the Westbrook area, she must've been the first to go, Brayden thought.

He dialed the police station, hoping to find out more information. In all likelihood, it would be a new group of officers and detectives working the night shift by now.

"Westbrook PD," a woman's voice answered.

Brayden glanced at the clock to his left. It was quarter past one in the morning. "Lacy? You're still at the station?"

He heard her sigh. "Damn near the only one, too." She sounded exhausted, and Brayden thought he could hear a tremble in her voice not unlike the one Mari displayed earlier. He had observed at the house that evening that Lacy was rattled by this crime, but it was becoming apparent that she'd donned a facade of composure in front of her team. In the dead quiet of this frigid winter night, she seemed much more vulnerable.

"I can't get my mind off it. I wasn't even that close with Sarah, but this is just … it's tough. I'm gutted for you, Bray. We need to solve this one."

"I know, Lace."

She sighed again, this one of a more exasperated variety, as if to snap herself out of the doldrums. "Forensics hasn't found much yet. No fingerprints. We're working through footage from neighboring home security cameras right now, but it's not exactly a minefield of them." She paused for a moment. "We did catch a glimpse of the suspect driving away."

This snapped Brayden out of his own doldrums. He replayed her sentence in his mind, trying to understand why she'd completely buried the lede.

"You saw him? Send me the footage, Lacy!"

"First of all, you know I can't do that! And it didn't lead to much."

"What'd you see?"

"He kept the mask and the hood on. He drove a black Corolla with no plates. We pieced together enough footage to track it for a couple miles, but we lost it near an overpass on Cumberland," she said with a groan. "This guy and whoever helped him escape knew what they were doing."

Brayden sat back and scratched at his chin. He'd seen the way criminals and terrorists act, the tactics they use for getaways. Visualizing the scene as Lacy laid it out, he imagined the interference of an overpass was critical to the escape. Ditch the mask and hoodie, swap cars, toss some plates and a bumper sticker or two onto the Corolla, and away they would be. No camera could see it all go down, and in a little town like Westbrook, there probably wasn't a camera that could see both sides of the obscured area where the swap took place. The killer would be headed one way in a totally different car, unidentifiable absent his signature black outfit. The accomplice would be in the Corolla, and Westbrook PD would never have the resources to search every black Corolla in the state.

This small and uninspiring update from Lacy had a silver lining to it, Brayden figured. Investigative teams all across the state might just be totally incompetent, but he preferred to put stock into another angle. It's clear that Sarah's killer was highly trained, expertly coordinated, had impeccable aid, and had a plan with forethought. If the same villains were behind this string of unsolved mysteries, maybe there was some insight to be gleaned from those seemingly unrelated attacks.

"Look, Bray," Lacy continued. Her words were draped with a healthy dose of defeat but also a touch of empathy. "We don't have the resources for this, if it's something bigger than a one-off. I'm going to do my best to loop you into things, but there's only so much I can do."

"I get it. Rules are rules, and—"

"I'll send the security footage over. Don't do anything stupid, and report anything you find back to me. You understand?"

Brayden felt himself smirk for the first time in many hours. "Thank you, Officer Storrow. I would never do anything stupid."

She chuckled half-heartedly. "And I'm Miles Davis. Honestly, though? A rogue Brayden Cross is the worst news I can imagine for these sick bastards, from what I know."

Brayden would typically blush over such a compliment, but the circumstances at this hour were triggering entirely new reactions in him. "You're damn right it is."

An intense silence relayed how serious he was.

"Good night, Bray. I'm so sorry you have to go through this, but try to get some shut-eye."

"Night, Lacy. Thanks for the support, but I'll pass on the shut-eye."

He hung up the phone and stewed in thought for several minutes. It hadn't been much, but getting the slightest bit of intel from Lacy reinvigorated him. The soft buzz of his phone on the wooden desktop tugged his attention away. It was an email from Lacy.

The subject read: Security Footage (Your Eyes Only).

He opened the email to find a folder with more than a dozen video clips. The first contained footage from a vantage point that looked to be two or three houses down the road. Along the bottom edge, a running timestamp showed it was 2:54 p.m. Within a few seconds, the masked man who murdered Sarah could be seen jogging along the road to his Corolla, his gait slightly askew. The car was parked halfway between the camera and Brayden's driveway. There were no plates. Brayden guessed it might've been a 2019 or 2020 model. It sped out of the frame after the man entered.

The second clip was not an immediate continuation; its timestamp began at 2:57. Brayden recognized the site of this footage—it was an intersection about a mile down the road from his house. The road was empty, save for one red Honda Civic breezing through the intersection at the beginning of the clip. Seven or eight seconds went by before the black Corolla entered the frame. Just as it entered, the light dangling above the four-way intersection turned yellow. Brayden squinted in as the murderous psychopath behind the wheel of the vehicle slowed to a stop at the signal. *Traffic laws are fair game, at least.*

It pained him to see this Corolla sitting idly at an intersection. A dark-green Ford truck pulled up behind it, and Brayden involuntarily blurted at its driver, "He's got no plates! Call the cops on this asshole!" Of course, the driver of the truck did no such thing. Brayden zoomed in, further pixelating the image but providing a closer look at the killer. He still wore his mask and hood, and he stared straight ahead. Brayden rewound to the beginning of the red light and timed it: for fifty-seven seconds, the man was a statue. Two hands on the wheel, head locked forward. The light flipped to green, and he accelerated away precisely on cue.

None of the other clips proved interesting until the final one in the folder. It showed Cumberland Street, where Lacy and her team evidently lost the trail. On the right side of the image was a concrete overpass, with Cumberland ducking through it below. Just as Brayden had expected, the exit wasn't visible on the other side. A few seconds in, the Corolla pulled into the frame and promptly disappeared, veiled by the land above. The clip was four minutes long, probably only untrimmed in order to examine the other cars. But the Corolla never reappeared. None of the other cars grabbed Brayden's attention, so he closed the file, the email, and his laptop, the latter with some force from agitation.

The swap had gone down like he imagined. This was a meticulously planned getaway, and his only focus was on figuring out who crafted it.

He stared ahead for a few long seconds, then exhaled. In no mood for the shuteye Officer Storrow recommended, he popped the still-whirring machine back open and flipped to christen a fresh page in his notebook.

8

Dawn packed a bitter punch during January in the Pine Tree State. Cold air flooded Brayden's nostrils and tugged tears from the corners of his eyes as he stepped from his Chevy and gently brushed its door closed behind him. The sun barely peeked over the pines that hugged the only home in sight. Stepping over hardened snow, Brayden climbed the wooden steps and knocked on the front door, snapping the pristine silence of the morning and sending a few nearby juncos into flight.

After a few moments had passed and the little dark-eyed sparrows had found new grounds to peruse, the sound of staggering footsteps emanated from behind the door. The door peeled open, revealing a squinting young man with disheveled hair, wearing only a white T-shirt and boxers. His confusion presented itself for a moment.

"Brayden Cross," he said with a touch of bewilderment but a reassuring chuckle. "It's been a minute."

Mickey Weekes lived a quiet life in northern Maine, as far as the unassuming observer could tell. His cabin was thirty miles from the closest grocery and about four hours north of Westbrook. He had no neighbors the eye could see, although chopping down about five hundred trees might pave a line of sight to one in the distance. He had no siblings, save an estranged sister, and no life partner to this point. His parents hailed from Michigan, but both had passed away. Mickey was just a guy who needed little more than his computer, his dog, and the occasional glass of merlot to be happy.

The other half of the coin—the one to which the unassuming observer was blind—revealed the most passionate and talented analyst Brayden had ever worked with in his time at the agency. Books and movies always seem to portray the classic computer hacker, the nerdy guy who can merely look at someone and be in their bank account before their next breath. It always used to seem hyperbolic to Brayden, but Mickey matched the stereotype. The things he could do with a powerful computer and a bit of intel were nothing short of jaw-dropping.

Brayden patted his old friend on the shoulder, pursing his lips in place of the smile he couldn't produce. "Too many minutes, Mickey. Can I come in?"

Mickey had left the agency suddenly, without a word, all those years ago. Brayden had not talked to him since that day, other than the single letter Mickey had left him a year later with these very whereabouts. But he had heard rumblings about his exit from the agency, everything from being a spy to a traitor to a patriot to a hero. In this moment, Brayden figured he would let bygones be bygones; he needed his help, and he was an old friend.

The two men sat at the kitchen table in the warmth of Mickey's cabin as his husky wagged its tail and sought their affection. It was a sturdy oak table set beside a modest little kitchen, one that seemed to get the job done for a man who needed no bells and whistles. Mickey set down in front of Brayden a ceramic mug filled just short of its brim with black coffee, its aroma spreading and filling the small space.

"You haven't started adding junk to your coffee, have you?"

The first chuckle of the morning from Brayden. "Black's all right."

Mickey slurped a sip from his own mug and placed it down. "So, what brings you all the way up here, bud?"

After a pensive sip and a sigh, Brayden divulged all the details of the last twenty-four hours, from his wife's murder, to his research, to his conversation with Lacy, to the roadside footage. Then he reached into his pocket, withdrew a wrinkled sheet of notebook paper, and slid it across the table toward his old colleague.

"I need help, Mick. Anything you can give me, anything you can pull from your systems. These are all the—"

"Cross," Weekes cut him off, "I feel awful for you, man. And you know I want to help you. But you also know I can't just—"

"Mick!" Brayden returned the interruptive favor, simultaneously thumping his fist on the table. The brief spell of anger dissolved to more somber angst. "Mick, I need to find out who did this to her. And if you look at that damn list ..."

He pointed at the document and let the moment marinate as he gathered himself.

"You'll find two dozen victims that just don't make sense."

Mickey gazed another moment at him before shaking his head and scanning the crumpled sheet. Scribbled on it was a list containing each of those random murder victims Brayden had found over the past year, twenty-two of them from all walks and stages of life. With a helpless groan, he gestured at the paper with his free hand.

"What exactly do you think I can do with this? You want background checks on these people, privacy be damned? You think I have some magic power to unlock all the secrets in the world? What is it, Bray?"

Whether it was the exasperated tone in Mickey's answer or the severe sleep deprivation, Brayden was overcome with an abundant fatigue. He put his elbows on the table and rested his eyebrows on his palms. When he continued, he did so in a mellow and defeated tone rather than an assertive one.

"Anything you can find. Investigations in the area I'm missing, details that aren't released about one of these murders. I just need a lead."

The resident husky, Snow, sat beside his owner and again accepted strokes of the hand on his head. There was a softening in Mickey's expression, and then he ceased the petting and folded his hands on the table.

"I'll see what I can do, but don't set your hopes too high. This isn't exactly in my wheelhouse these days."

He nodded, accepting that it was the most he could get for now.

"You look like you could use a rest. I'll grab you a pillow and throw. Get some shuteye while I do some research."

Despite his brain kicking and screaming that there was no time for sleep, his body could do nothing but accept the offer from his old friend.

After three hours, the short, vibrating pulse of his phone nudged Brayden out of slumber. He wasn't immediately sure if he'd slept for three hours or three days. Rubbing his eyes and recalibrating himself, he looked around the room. Two unfinished mugs of coffee still sat on the oak table in the kitchen, and Snow had curled up below the couch next to his new acquaintance. Off of the living room in a small study, the rapid clicking and clacking of keystrokes sang in a cadence that Mickey had likely been sustaining for the duration of Brayden's nap.

He sat upright and unlocked the screen of his phone. The chime had been because of a text from Riley, and as he opened it up, he saw a picture of Mari and Charlie playing a board game with their cousins. "First smile of the day," the accompanying text read. It was a minor update, but it did wonders to put Brayden at ease.

This unrelenting side of his personality sometimes ate away at him. Should he really be driving around like a rogue madman, hunting down his wife's killer? Shouldn't he be at that table playing games with his children, giving them the emotional support they needed? Was he simply compounding the errant decisions, putting his own life at risk in the process? If it was unthinkably difficult for the kids now, what would it be if Daddy never came home?

So, yes, seeing them smiling and playing a board game eased his mind. And at every idle moment, his stomach reminded him why he persisted despite the list of valid doubts. His instincts had seldom failed him, and they screamed that his action was needed.

"Morning, sunshine!" Weekes, seeing his guest was awake, offered a break from the click-clacking in a voice strapped with double the optimism from earlier. "I got a few things cooking for ya."

Stretching out the cobwebs and rising from the crater he'd created in the well-worn cushions of the couch, Brayden trudged over to Mickey's desk and leaned in over his shoulder. After popping open a few different visualizations on the screen, Mickey angled in his chair to face his newly rested pal.

"You were definitely on to something with that list, and I was pretty easily able to paint a fuller picture for you. You're spot-on about the randomness; that can't be a fluke. I widened the radius to all of New England, searched across the last full calendar year, and—here's the big one—added another cohort to your list beyond murder victims: *missing persons*. And, well ... check this out."

Weekes pointed his index finger at a large data visualization on his screen that featured two colorful pie charts. They looked to Brayden almost like the sample charts that would be included as templates in a data visualization software; their slices were nearly uniform in size and five or six in number.

"Race," he said, pointing to the first chart. "Age group," pointing to the second. He flipped open a third chart split down the middle. "Gender," he muttered.

As a squinting Brayden looked on with his brow furrowed, Mickey clicked over to a fourth visualization that spanned the width of the screen. It looked like a heat map of sorts but contained dozens of bubbles of different colors.

"Each bubble represents a different combination of those traits, rolled into one profile. This takes *random* to a whole new level, Cross. These profiles of victims being murdered, going missing, and lacking an apprehended culprit over the last year? Within the margin of error, they're painting a canvas with an almost pristinely equal distribution of characteristics."

Brayden still said nothing, but he found himself both nodding at the impressive findings and shaking his head at their confounding nature.

"Don't burn all your fuel processing that one, though. It gets spicier."

When Mickey closed out the graphics, the fatigued cones in Brayden's retinas stubbornly kept the colors around against the white backdrop. Once the screen showed a new window, it displayed a news article from the *Kennebec Journal* detailing a missing woman.

"Jane Clement," Mickey continued. "Missing person. White woman, thirty-four years old. Mother of two. Sound familiar to you?"

"Just like Sarah."

"Just like Sarah."

The two sleuths broke their gaze from the screen to look at each other. Mickey sighed before continuing to scroll down the article.

"Lives with her family in Winthrop. Husband's name is Leo, and get this—the article says he had an encounter with Jane's kidnapper before they got away."

Brayden's eyes widened, but he could sense via Mickey's tone that he hadn't yet reached his conclusion. He'd always been a dramatic storyteller. Scrolling an inch further, he read aloud his punchline like a planned grand finale.

"Describes the assailant as a masked man in a gray hoodie and black boots."

He handed over a sheet of paper the size of an index card just as the fire in Brayden's gut flared up.

"The Clements' address."

Mickey watched his old friend stare at the slip of paper for a half-minute before snapping out of his trance.

"Yeoman's work, Mick," Brayden finally replied, patting Mickey on the shoulder. He gathered his things, reiterated his gratitude, issued Snow a farewell head rub, and soon had his Chevy barreling down the interstate toward Winthrop.

9

TEN YEARS AGO

Ellen Lennon's heels clicked against the floor as she made her way across Vinny's penthouse. The New York City skyline stretched out beyond the window against the early evening sky. She paused for a moment to drink in the view.

It wasn't Dodger Stadium, but it had its own allure.

"Quite the view, isn't it?" Vinny's voice came from behind her, accompanied by the soft clinking of the oversized ice cube in his glass of scotch.

Ellen turned toward him, a smile playing on her lips. Her eyes roamed over him, appreciating the sharp tailoring of his suit and how it accentuated his lean frame. Vinny was ... well, he was unlike anyone Ellen had been with before. Charming, successful, attentive. A full one-eighty from the type of man she usually ended up with.

"It certainly is."

Vinny sighed after gently touching his nose to her neck. "I'm sorry again about cancelling our LA trip," he said, handing her a glass of merlot. "Sometimes business can't wait."

She accepted the glass, completing the other three-quarters of her turn to face him. "I suppose I can forgive you," she said, "though I was looking forward to showing you around my old stomping grounds."

A cheer erupted from the television—the Dodgers had just scored, cutting the Red Sox lead in half. It was the World Series game they were supposed to be attending before their weeklong LA trip was postponed.

"At least we can still watch," Vinny offered, guiding her to the leather sofa.

Snuggling into his arm, Ellen sighed. "You know who would love to be at this game? My dear son-in-law." Her words were laced with sarcasm, and she shook her head. "Probably thinks he deserves box seats for *saving the world*, or whatever it is he does."

Vinny raised an eyebrow, curiosity taking root in his eyes. "Oh? Trouble in paradise?"

"Hardly. Saint Brayden can do no wrong, according to my daughter. I guess he was the hero of some mysterious mission the other day. But of course, his own mother-in-law can't know a thing about it!"

"Huh. Is that so?" Vinny squinted. "And you've no idea what this … heroic deed was?"

Ellen sighed again, this one more exasperated. "I don't know, I don't know. He wouldn't say, he never says. But I'll tell you this—you would think he spoiled the biggest threat humankind has ever seen, the way my daughter lit up about it."

She noticed Vinny set his glass down on the coffee table rather forcefully, its ice clinking loudly. He seemed perturbed.

"Are you all right? Did I say something wrong?"

Vinny inhaled, and an instant later, he exhaled and smiled. "Of course, my dear. It's just … well, the mention of terror attacks just elicits terrible memories. But those are stories for another day." He picked up his glass again and held it back out to touch Ellen's. "Tell me more about this superhero son-in-law of yours. You've never mentioned him before."

Ellen sneered. Between the wine and the lingering disappointment over their canceled trip, she needed little encouragement. She unloaded her complaints about Brayden; how he was always busy with mysterious jobs, how he'd swept Sarah off her feet at such a young age, how Ellen felt Sarah was missing out on so many other fish in the sea who could give her a more normal life.

As she talked, she felt the piercing focus and undivided attention that Vinny gave her. *Is this even real life?* Ellen never found men that gave her the time of day. Now, in her later years, she somehow stumbled upon this wealthy, charming, dashing man who wanted to hear every detail about an in-law she didn't even fancy.

"You know, Ellen … I think I'd like to meet this Brayden Cross character someday."

"Trust me, you're not missing much," she said with a cackle. Then she paused, confused by a realization; she hadn't told Vinny Brayden's surname before.

"Oh, come on," he said. "Family is family, right? Extend the olive branch. Have your daughter and him over for dinner when you get back home. Baby steps."

Vinny pecked her on the cheek and rose from the couch. He walked over to the windows, once again taking in the New York City skyline. Perhaps it was the departure of his body heat, or maybe it was the glasses of wine beginning to join forces inside her, but she felt another brief chill pass over her.

He turned back to her. "Another drink?"

Maybe the drinks were to blame, she thought. She probably blurted out Sarah's full name at some point, and Vinny had probably just put two and two together. Wine did have a way of making her forgetful, after all.

A Dodger struck out, yielding groans from the home crowd on the television. But Ellen found she no longer cared about the score, or about rooting against her son-in-law's Red Sox. Tonight was about her and Vinny, and whatever this budding situation between them might become. She smiled back at him.

"Certainly, my dear."

10

"Clement. Jane Clement, get me anything you can on her disappearance."

Brayden could hear a notepad page flip over and presumed that Lacy was jotting down the name for further investigation.

"Clement," she softly mumbled to herself, the way one does when coaxing their hand to follow its orders. "I'll look into it. What'd you find?"

"Long story, but I've enlisted an old buddy's help. I have reason to believe the guy who took Jane is the guy who killed Sarah."

He could hear Lacy exhale something between a sigh and a whistle. "Sounds like you've been busy. I'll keep you posted."

"Thanks, Lace."

His phone clunked down into the cupholder as he twisted the radio dial, boosting the volume of the local country music station. The pavement on I-95 was dusted with an airy coat of snow from the day before, not enough to enlist the services of snowplows, but just enough to create swirls of dust-like crystals as the wind whipped. Save for a few minor decelerations at the sight of camped-out police officers, the reliable old truck chugged south while its speedometer stayed north of eighty the entire three hours to Winthrop.

What could explain those charts Mickey pulled together? Three solitary hours on the highway gave Brayden's mind a runway for takeoff as he pored over the possibilities. The news articles portrayed multiple profiles of suspects, ruling out the possibility of a lone maniac. Was it an organized group of killers? If so, was it all just a game to them? In all of his experience fighting large-scale crime and terrorism, he hadn't witnessed a killing spree of this scale solely for sport. They were usually aimed at a target demographic, or full of crimes of passion, or the efforts of an organized criminal enterprise. Something told him the Maine mob wasn't roaming the region like a shark, systematically murdering random civilians matching an array of target profiles.

The lack of clarity angered him. He had always been that way, whether it be during a top-secret mission vital to national security or a puzzle session with his children; uncertainty—and futility in resolving it—boiled his blood. As he zoomed between dotted white lines toward the jagged tree line blanketed in snow on the horizon, his anger brought his mind to EverChat. If only they'd figured out how to capture a copy of the mind *after* someone's murder, he thought to himself. "Maybe then the prick would have some utility," he muttered aloud to no one, regarding the guy who created that despicable app.

Wouldn't it be nice to just pop open an EverChat with someone from that list of names and ask for a full debrief of their own murder?

He arrived at the Clement household just shy of four o'clock, the sun gently receding on its way to share its light with other populations. The house was a sharp-looking and well-maintained Victorian, nestled in the back of a quiet neighborhood of Winthrop. Brayden pulled into the driveway, leaving ample space between his truck and the Volkswagen that was pulled all the way in. The driveway was blanketed white, other than a few tire tracks and footprints, and sat to the left of the house from the street view. An artful collection of holiday decorations still adorned the farmer's porch at the front of the house. At the center point of the home, the front steps drew symmetrically toward the door. The terrain beyond the driveway leveled up to the side door, where a small patio featured an outdoor sitting area. The patio furniture was tied down and snow covered.

Brayden once again approached a house that wasn't his own, this time preparing to encounter a stranger. He ascended the front steps, but before he could press the soft rubber doorbell, the window beside the door slipped upward a few inches.

"Get outta here, boy! No reporters, for the love o' God!"

Brayden hopped backward and instinctively raised his hands, startled by the aggression in the voice. "Sir, I'm no reporter. I just wanted to ask—"

"Don't make me say it again, pal!"

An unmistakable sound: the cocking of a twelve-gauge shotgun.

"My wife was murdered yesterday," Brayden said, cutting to the chase. "I think it's related to what happened to Jane. I just want to talk."

The next five seconds felt like a hundred, but the window finally closed, and beside it a lock unlatched. As its faded gold knob revolved, the navy-blue door of the Victorian peeled inward, revealing a man roughly Brayden's age peering through the gap.

"Come again?"

"My wife was murdered yesterday, and I believe it's connected to Jane's disappearance," Brayden said. "I don't have any information about Jane for you, but I have some connections that are looking into it. Are you Leo?"

The man looked his visitor up and down as his nerve-wracked hand slightly jiggled the doorknob. Conceding a small nod, he confirmed his identity before pulling the door open and standing at ease. "And you are?"

"Brayden Cross. Can I come in?"

The interior of the Clements' house gave Brayden an eerie feeling. If Jane was the primary decision-maker for its design and decor, she was just as similar to Sarah as her profile would suggest. Sarah had always displayed a keen eye for both architecture and interior design, despite having no formal skills in either. She would always analyze the choices others made in buildings they passed through or homes they visited. Jane and Leo's home reminded him of Sarah's taste. Framed pictures of their children hung above a solid wooden mantle that served as the cap to a modern stone fireplace in the living room.

Stockings and garland still hung from the mantle, and a miniature Christmas village twinkled on an end table in the room's corner. A large suede sectional faced the adjacent wall, where an impressive entertainment system looked more than capable of providing its share of family movie nights.

Leo, who seemed to have a slight limp favoring his left leg, walked Brayden in the opposite direction of the living room. As he pulled out a chair for Brayden, his rough, calloused hands brushed against the smooth mahogany of the dining table. Brayden could notice the slight tremble in Leo's hands, a sign of his anxiety.

"I'm sorry for your loss," Leo said. It seemed as if he'd just realized that was an overdue condolence.

"Thank you. And I'm praying for Jane. They're gonna find her."

Leo closed his eyes and nodded. Brayden withheld the part where he had zero faith they would find her alive.

"I'm told you actually had an encounter with the guy that kidnapped her. Can you walk me through what happened?"

Leo sniffled and cleared his throat. "Two guys."

This correction was unexpected but piqued Brayden's interest.

"Two days ago. I was out of town for work, down in Boston for a week of client meetings. Some of that midwestern snow, though—canceled a bunch of flights, took a wrecking ball to the last couple of days' worth of meetings. So, being that Jane and I were about to celebrate our anniversary, I thought I'd come home early and surprise her."

His gaze pulled from the table and moved to the kitchen counter, where a bouquet of wilting roses lay. Another sniffle.

"So, I get home, I reckon the same time of day as right now. I'd be lying if I said I didn't have a bad feeling in my bones, since Jane hadn't answered my text earlier that day. But nonetheless, I came through the front door and called her name. 'Honey! Surprise!' I was so ..."

Leo trailed off as tears bubbled up beneath his eyelids and his chin quivered. Putting a comforting hand on his shoulder, Brayden nonverbally instructed him to take his time.

"The assholes had her strapped to that chair, just sittin' there on a laptop while she squirmed and did her best to shout through the duct tape coverin' her mouth."

As Leo referenced the chair, he pointed to the piece of furniture Brayden only now realized was missing from the mahogany dining set. The sectional had blocked his view on first glance, but the wooden seat was tipped over on the floor with torn rope still sprawled across it.

That pesky boulder was back, climbing up his throat.

"My wife was strapped to a chair."

Leo looked up with a new alertness. This time, it was Brayden who sniffled and rubbed his jawline.

"She had struggled. And they slit her throat. Left her right there in the chair, in the middle of our living room."

The two silently stewed in their remarkably well-aligned agony.

"But hey, Leo. You're the only reason Jane might still be alive. What happened next? What'd you do when you saw them all over there?"

Leo sighed before carrying on. "Soon as they saw me, one of 'em fired a silenced pistol in my direction. Angle wasn't good enough to hit me, but I had to fall back for cover. You can see the hole right there." He pointed to a bullet hole about three feet off the ground in the entryway.

"I grabbed my pal here outta the closet." He patted with his right hand the twelve-gauge that sat atop the table. "But by the time I got to chasing after 'em, they'd already cut the ropes, grabbed their bags, and were ushering her out the side door, through the kitchen. I was ten or so paces behind them, and I don't move all that well these days."

He gestured toward his left knee, implying an injury he must have suffered.

"I ripped around the corner and saw them running down the driveway, trying to get to their car. I fired at 'em, and I hit one in the leg."

Leo leaned over and pointed to his calf.

"He didn't buckle, though. Hobbled his way down the drive, around the corner, and made his way into the passenger's seat. Driver tossed Jane in the back, and they sped away. I told all this to the police, by the way, so ain't nothin' new here."

The last sentence or two hadn't fully registered with Brayden because he was replaying the story in his head. He popped up and walked over to the kitchen, peering around the corner at the side door Leo had described. He strutted over and opened the door, taking in the vantage point described in the story. The host labored himself out of his chair and trudged out to the patio to meet Brayden, standing and staring down the driveway.

"You fired from right about here?" Brayden held an imaginary shotgun as he asked the question.

Leo nodded, walked down the driveway a few paces beyond his car, and turned around. Surveying his surroundings, he nodded again to signal satisfaction with his own analysis.

"And hit him right about here. But the fucker got all the way down the drive, 'round the corner to their car." He shook his head. "I should've known something was up. No one ever parks on the street right there."

Brayden surveyed the land, snapping into his investigator mode. He looked at the few meters of space between their vehicles, where Leo currently stood.

"Two days ago, you said?"

"Yes, sir."

"You all get any new snow the past two days here?"

Leo looked taken aback by the inquiry. "I don't reckon, no."

"So, let me make sure I'm understanding you correctly." Brayden had a bit of an edge in his tone now, not an accusatory one, but close. "You hit this guy with a twelve-gauge slug from, what ... ten yards? Catches him in the calf right here."

He pointed to the ground where Leo stood.

"Not an ounce of blood from here down to the end of the driveway?"

Brayden paced down to his truck for effect. He didn't believe Leo was lying, but he couldn't let the inconsistency go undiscussed. Given that it did reek of an accusation, however, Leo looked up at his visitor with a hint of disdain.

"Look, I don't know, maybe the wind covered it up or his pant leg

64

caught it all. You think I'm lying? Why the hell would I lie? I don't even know you from Adam, and I just want to find my wife!"

The emotion blared through his words, and his chin tremble returned. Brayden didn't exactly know his next move; he wanted to believe the guy, and didn't know where it would leave him if he didn't. But as it stood, he didn't have the details he needed.

"What kind of car was it?"

"I dunno," he answered. "Black sedan, I think. I didn't get a great look 'round the tree down there."

The believability meter ticked up a few notches. The black Corolla was in play.

"Hey," Leo's eyes lit up as though he just remembered the secret to the universe. "Duh. I have the footage. I can show you."

The footage, Brayden thought. *What a novel idea.*

A few minutes later, they were back inside the Clement household in Leo's office. He pulled up an application Brayden didn't directly recognize, but it had the typical look of a home security app. A few clicks later, an array of thumbnails popped up, their vantage point seemingly from above the side door and looking down the driveway at the street.

"By the way, I gave all this over to the investigators," Leo said. "I ain't pulling any funny business on you."

He opened a file that was labeled for the interval of time from four fifteen to four thirty. Scrubbing the slider in the video player ahead, a flurry of action lit up the screen at four twenty-two. Backtracking a few seconds, he played the video.

Brayden, in a novel experience of emotion, was simultaneously relieved and alarmed by what he saw. The whole thing had happened just how Leo described it. A masked man in a dark turtleneck, slacks, and athletic sneakers violently ushered a woman down the driveway. It was Jane, who looked quite like Sarah from afar, aside from hair styled in a pixie cut. Entering the frame just behind them was another masked man, wearing a charcoal hoodie, black slacks and boots, and black gloves. An olive-green backpack was slung over his right shoulder.

Sarah's murderer.

As he reached the halfway point of the driveway, a thunderous pop clipped well beyond the volume range of the camera, resulting in a distorted sound resembling an underwater car crash. Instantly after, the man stumbled, grabbed his calf, and briefly held his hand to the ground for stability. Just as Leo described, the shot appeared to hit him, although the quality of the footage prevented explicit confirmation of a wound.

However, its quality was plenty to have spotted blood poured upon a white layer of snow. And in the few seconds that spanned the hobbling criminal's trek to the street, not an ounce of it soiled the canvas.

"It doesn't make sense," Brayden muttered mostly to himself, though Leo could hear it as well.

"Maybe he's got one of them bulletproof body suits or something."

As the criminals rounded the corner of the driveway into the street, Brayden recognized the other part of the story: the black Corolla, partially obscured by barren tree branches.

Just as he started to explain the Corolla's relevance to Leo, he felt his phone buzzing in his pocket. The caller identification read *Westbrook Police Department*.

When he answered, Lacy's voice was riddled with a mix of urgency and fatigue.

"We've got an update on Jane Clement."

11

It took six minutes for Brayden to arrive at the location Lacy had sent, just over two miles north of the Clements' home. A heavily wooded area cupped a small pull-off that naturally accommodated two or three cars. At this hour, though, it borrowed capacity from the road to fit six police vehicles stacked in a line. Pulling the truck within a few yards of the trailing cruiser, Brayden slid out into a dirty mixture of frozen muck and snow. The air was thick with the smell of winter and his steps left behind deep impressions in the slush beneath him. He realized he was still wearing the boots, slacks, and sweater he'd worn to the office the day prior.

There was no official walking trail that led from the street, but he could tell based on the sounds and smells around him that a lakefront was nestled somewhere beyond the immediately visible pines. He presumed the officers parked along the pull-off were responsible for the muffled conversations he could hear through the woods. Swinging his arm around each tree for support as he wedged his way through the wooded area, he finally came to the clearing where the icy lake kissed the shore.

"Crime scene, step back!" barked an officer, firmly planting a palm into Brayden's chest. Of course, Brayden knew he couldn't just waltz into a setting like this unannounced, but it surprised him all the same.

Lacy emerged from a nearby scrum of investigators. "He's good. He's with me."

The disgruntled officer scowled and nodded. His uniform showed he was part of the Winthrop Police Department. Brayden had a feeling these Winthrop cops weren't keen on Officer Storrow crashing the party from down in Westbrook.

With a nod of her head and a gentle hand to the back, Lacy guided Brayden toward the shoreline. She spoke quietly and quickly. "You obviously know I shouldn't be trotting you around here, but I gotta show you this."

They walked past a few more officers wearing similar protective gear to what the investigators at Brayden's house had worn. The ground's cover shifted from predominantly white snow to a much dirtier mix of sand and dirt as they trudged closer to the water. A few paces later, around a small tree-covered bend, they arrived at the scene of the crime.

Brayden probably could have puked in that moment, but for a tremendously slow few seconds, his brain couldn't have initiated even that reflexive action. Visual stimuli flooded through his eyes, and he was certain his wife lay slain on the lakefront before him. Her brunette hair sprawled out on the ground surrounding her head, her blue eyes gazed lifelessly at the sky, and her now-pale skin was adorned with cuts and bruises. Only after his visual cortex processed this scene several times did he realize—based both on recognition and logic—that it actually wasn't Sarah lying before him.

"Jane Clement," Lacy said, snapping Brayden out of his momentary shock. "I'm guessing this isn't what you were hoping I'd find. We just called the husband. He's on his way."

She was right. Of all the potential outcomes, finding a lifeless Jane Clement on a muddy lakeshore—with no accompanying criminal—was at the bottom of the list. Brayden forced himself to inspect Jane's body, shaking off the initial jolt of seeing Sarah's likeness in her. Though there were similarities, Jane's face was more angular, her hair much shorter and a slightly different shade of brown. Still, an uneasy feeling stirred in his gut as he noted the red marks on her temples, just like the ones etched into Sarah's skin.

"Any ID on her?" Brayden asked, his eyes still fixed on Jane.

Lacy shook her head. "Nothing yet. No purse, no phone. She must have been taken by surprise."

Brayden nodded, his jaw tight, as he surveyed the area for any clues or signs of struggle.

"There's something else," Lacy said gently. She motioned for Brayden to follow her.

They slipped past the cranky officer on their way back to Lacy's cruiser. She retrieved a dark-brown laptop bag from the back seat and slid out a computer. Opening it swiftly, Lacy moved to the front of the vehicle and placed the device on the hood.

"CCTV footage from a small gas station on Rambler Road, a mile or so from here." She hammered the spacebar to play the clip, then swiveled the machine in Brayden's direction. The black Corolla rolled into the frame, coming to a stop beside one of just two pumps at the station. The driver, who hurried out of the vehicle and hastily began filling its tank, wore a black turtleneck and still wore his mask. His appearance was seemingly unchanged since his cameo in Leo's driveway.

In the back seat, though difficult to verify, it looked like a body was strewn horizontally across the seat.

It was the passenger—the man in the hoodie, Sarah's murderer—that made the footage noteworthy. Brayden's jaw dropped as the man staggered out of the vehicle, still limping from the slug that pierced his calf. The clip had no audio, but he began shouting at his accomplice, flailing his arms in apparent outrage. After the fuel-pumper chirped something back, the man in the hoodie ripped off his mask and clenched it in his fist as the berating continued.

He ripped off his mask.

There's his face!

It took Brayden a beat to register the significance of the man revealing his face. He looked up at Lacy with a new optimism in his eyes, but he found no reciprocation when his eyes met hers.

"I ran facial rec on him," Lacy said. "Got nothing back."

"What? How's that possible? Not a single hit?"

Lacy shook her head and looked down. "I don't know. Could be the angle, maybe not a good enough image. Looks like a good enough view to me, though. I have the tech guys working on it, but they're stumped."

Brayden stifled the urge to slam his fist into the front headlight of her cruiser.

"However," she said, twisting the laptop back toward her, "another piece of CCTV. About an hour after the first clip, and presumably shortly after they dumped Jane's body."

The new clip was captured from a much wider angle and higher elevation than the prior one, possibly mounted on the second story of a nearby building. The Corolla pulled around the corner of an old warehouse and drifted out of view behind it, along the upper-right portion of the video frame. It was an unremarkable clip. Brayden looked up at Lacy, questioning.

She nodded toward the screen, pleading patience.

About thirty seconds after the Corolla had drifted off, a brief glimpse of a ruby-red Ford Escape came and went beyond the opposite corner of the warehouse. Unlike the original getaway car, this one definitely had plates. And while Brayden couldn't decipher anything in real time from this view, he suspected a closer inspection may have yielded better luck.

He returned his gaze to Lacy and pointed his finger at the computer. "Did you get the plates?"

She nodded sternly. "They trace back to a Joseph Blauss. Works at a landscaping company called Sterling Seasons."

Brayden felt his pulse quicken. Finally, a solid lead. He was determined to uncover the truth, no matter where it led. For Sarah, more than anything. But also for Jane. And for whoever else might be in danger.

Now equipped with a potential lead, the surrounding air seemed lighter and fresher. The sound of water lapping against the shore added a calming rhythm. With each breath, Brayden could feel a weight being lifted off his chest. The scent of the lake had changed—perhaps more in his own brain than in reality—from its stagnant, musty odor to a refreshing blend of pine and fresh water. It was no longer heavy with dread; it carried a faint hint of newfound hope.

"I think we need to have a chat with Joseph."

12

Brayden's hands tightened around the leather-wrapped steering wheel as his truck growled down the empty stretch of road leaving Winthrop. The sun had begun its descent, casting long shadows across the asphalt and bringing an early chill to the Maine landscape. His thoughts raced as fast as his vehicle, fixating on Joseph Blauss's last known address—a piece of information that had proven elusive until now. Lacy's tech staff at Westbrook PD had hit a wall; every digital footprint of Blauss seemed methodically scrubbed from public record.

"Come on, Mick," Brayden muttered into the phone clenched between his shoulder and ear. "I need something here."

"Relax, I'm on it," came the confident reply, the sound of clicking keystrokes echoing in the background. Mickey's voice was a lifeline in a sea of uncertainty, a reminder of the technical prowess Brayden had witnessed in their agency days. He trusted Mickey's capabilities as much as he trusted his own instincts, which were currently blaring like sirens in his head.

"Got it," Mickey announced triumphantly. "Sending the address to you now."

On cue, Brayden's phone vibrated against his temple, illuminating the side of his cheek with its screen. An address in Carrabassett Valley danced across the text bubble from Mickey. Swerving abruptly across two lanes to catch the exit and go north, he applied more force to the accelerator. The engine responded with a throaty roar.

He opted not to share the address with Lacy just yet. He needed to meet Joseph before the cops got involved.

An hour slipped by, marked only by the rhythm of passing streetlights and the occasional glimpse of wildlife eyes in the fading daylight. Finally, about a mile off of Route 27, there it was—a battered, bluish-gray ranch looming against the twilight sky, its silhouette unassuming yet ominous, given the circumstances.

Adrenaline coursed through Brayden's veins at the sight of the ruby-red Ford Escape. Had he arrived too late? Was he right on time for a showdown with Sarah's murderer? He killed the engine and stepped out into the evening air, the scent of pine and dirt once again flooding his senses. Stealthily, he approached the old house, the gravel crunching quietly under his boots.

"Anyone home?" Brayden called out, rapping his knuckles against the weathered wood of the front door. No response, no flicker of movement from within.

He reached for the doorknob, half expecting it to be locked, but it turned easily under his grip. It felt eerily similar to his entrance at his own front door the day prior. The old, cranky hinges squealed as Brayden stepped into the dimly lit interior.

"Joseph Blauss?" he called out, his voice steady despite his heart's thundering state.

Silence greeted him, thick and unwavering. Then, in the sparse light filtering in from the outside, he saw it—a body draped across the floor, motionless.

"Damn it," Brayden cursed under his breath, approaching cautiously. There was no mistaking the scene before him. Based on the photos Lacy's team had gathered, it was undeniably Joseph Blauss, a single bullet wound in his skull, blood pooling beneath him on the worn floorboards. Brayden's jaw clenched, anger and frustration brewing within him.

He crouched beside the lifeless figure, searching for any sign of a struggle, any clue that might paint a better picture. But as the reality sank in, so did the understanding that Blauss would never provide the answers he was desperately seeking.

The killers had been here. There was almost no doubt that the bullet that put an end to Joseph and the bullet in Leo's wall came from the same gun. Forensics could confirm it, but Brayden knew they would match. The murderous duo was here. But now, they were gone, leaving behind only the silent connection to the crime of a man who'd apparently known too much. He rose from his crouching position, the musty air of the ranch laden with the iron tang of blood. Outside, the encroaching night seemed to swallow any hope of immediate answers. *How could Blauss be dead?* The question hammered in his head, each throb echoing with implications darker than the shadows clinging to the room's corners.

"Who would want you silenced?" Brayden said to himself, his voice barely above a whisper. With no hits on the Corolla, and with no facial recognition on the man in the hoodie, Blauss and that ruby-red Escape had been their only lead. Now, with a single bullet, that trail had dried up.

As he scanned the room for anything overlooked, the realization dawned on him: Someone knew they were closing in on Blauss. He only learned the man's name two hours ago. Someone knew he was coming to question him. An icy shiver ran down Brayden's spine—not from the chill of the Maine night seeping through the thin walls, but from the possibility of a mole within Mickey's network, or Lacy's. He thought back to the officers near Lacy at the lakefront scene—did someone working with the killers overhear the Blauss connection being uncovered?

"Damn it," he hissed again, his hands balling into fists. He needed to warn Mickey and Lacy. They couldn't trust anyone.

On the drive south, he called both of them. They each responded with urgency and alarm. A mole? Someone working with the criminals? Mickey hadn't contacted a soul, he said, since Brayden showed up at his door. Lacy insisted her force was clean.

Brayden knew the situation called for urgency, but he needed to take a beat. "I gotta go see my kids," he explained to them both. "I'll be in touch."

Riley opened the door before Brayden could knock, a worried frown creasing his forehead. "You look like hell, Bray."

"Feels about right," Brayden said as he stepped inside, the warmth of the house doing little to thaw his iced spirits.

"Kids are already asleep," Riley said, leading Brayden to the living room and handing him a mug of steaming coffee. "They asked about you earlier. Miss their dad."

The mention of his kids sparked a faint glimmer of warmth in Brayden's chest, a stark contrast to the desolation that had taken root there. He slumped onto the couch, sipping the bitter brew.

"Thanks, Riles," Brayden said, his exhaustion clear in the droop of his shoulders and the dark circles under his eyes.

Riley patted his brother's back, a silent gesture of support. "Get some rest. You can crash here tonight. Spend some time with the kiddos in the morning. We'll figure things out from there."

"Appreciate it," Brayden said, a yawn breaking through his words.

Just before heading off to bed, Riley turned back to Brayden, a softness in his eyes. "Oh, and Bray—I'm glad you finally came around. Personal opinions aside, it's what he needs right now."

Brayden didn't quite know what the comment meant, but his brain was damn near incapable of deciphering it at the moment. He nodded and smiled, then turned his attention to the television in the room's corner. A young woman in a crisp blazer was speaking to the show's host enthusiastically about the latest EverChat statistics.

"The platform has completely transformed how we process grief," she said to the interviewer. Her polished delivery carried with it the guise of genuine belief. "We're seeing incredible adoption rates of the technology, especially among families coping with loss. We've even signed up a number of participants for our proactive upload plan, which provides free monthly uploads so that even an unexpected tragedy will—"

Brayden's grip on the remote had tightened beyond the point of comfort, so he flipped the channel to a West Coast hockey game. The sounds of the broadcast faded as he closed his eyes.

I'm glad you finally came around.

Riley's words echoed in Brayden's dream.

A dream that ended as he awoke in the morning light to the sound of his wife's voice in Riley's kitchen.

13

Pushing himself up from the couch, Brayden paced toward his brother's kitchen. He heard the sound of a laptop closing, and Charlie's laughter greeted his ears.

Mari sat quietly at the breakfast table, her eyes somber as she pushed cereal around with her spoon, absent of any enthusiasm or purpose. Beside her, Charlie's face was alight with an innocent joy Brayden had feared would not return for quite some time.

"Mommy said we can go play laser tag when she comes back!" he chirped, shoveling cereal into his mouth with a youthful fervor.

"It's not Mommy, Charlie." Mari's spoon clattered against her bowl, her voice soft but firm. "It just looks like her, that's all."

Brayden froze. His heart hammered against his ribs. Even after Charlie's proclamation, he was hoping it was only his imagination creating the sounds of Sarah's voice he had heard. "When, uh … when did Mommy say this, buddy?"

"Just now! On the computer!" Charlie piped up, pronouncing it *compooter* in his patented fashion. "Mari says it's fake, but it wasn't, Dad! It was really Mommy!"

A cold shiver ran down Brayden's spine. Sarah. EverChat. Images of his late wife, vibrant and full of life, flashed across his mind's eye. How could she be speaking to them? How did they even log on to EverChat?

And how could Sarah be on there? It was impossible. She couldn't be on EverChat.

His thoughts raced, snippets of conversations from previous days threading together.

I'm glad you finally came around. The words spun dizzyingly in his head. Was Riley behind it? Did his asshole brother go a step further than exposing EverChat to Brayden's kids and actually sign up his dead wife? No, it didn't make sense. You had to be uploaded to EverChat, and you had to sign off on it. There were rare occasions—the controversial ones he and Sarah would always talk about—where family members signed off in place of incapacitated subjects. There was even the ultra-rare case, a "beta" feature of the platform, that allowed next of kin to conduct a postmortem upload. None of that seemed likely, but likelihood felt like a concept to throw out the window in Brayden's new reality.

Mari looked up at her father, the maturity in her eyes far exceeding the expectation of a nine-year-old girl. "It doesn't even act like Mom. It just … has no feeling. It can't even cry. Remember the story she always used to tell about the bear that stole your cooler when you were camping? Well, now when she tells it, she just skips the ending. The part where we laughed so hard Mom started crying." Mari's bottom lip quivered again, just like her mother's. "She doesn't cry anymore, either. I was crying, and she was just smiling. It's not her."

"It is too her! She remembers everything! She knows about my T-Rex drawing, and my soccer schedule, and the time we went to the beach last year, and—"

"Okay, hey," Brayden cut him off. "Finish up your cereal, guys, okay? We'll talk about this later."

He tried to feign a smile that landed in between the comfort Charlie sought and the skepticism Mari demanded. "I gotta go chat with Uncle Riles."

Brayden strode down the hall, its walls lined with photos of his nephews, his footsteps heavy with purpose. Turning the corner into the study, his eyes found Riley. His brother looked up from his tablet, surprise spreading across his face.

"We need to talk," Brayden said sharply, whipping the door shut behind him.

Riley set down the tablet, his expression morphing to one of concern. "What's going on?"

Brayden pointed his finger at his brother and tried to stifle an explosion of anger. "Just tell it to me straight, you son of a bitch. Did you do it?"

His jaw open in confusion, Riley gave a half-shake of his head and a partial shrug of his shoulders. "Did I do what, Bray?"

"Put Sarah on EverChat!"

Riley's eyes widened in disbelief. His words seemed to get clogged in a traffic jam shy of his mouth. A moment later, he continued. "You mean ... you didn't ... It wasn't you?"

Brayden stared him down, wanting to offload all of this angst as blame on his brother. But looking at him, he knew it wasn't Riley's doing. He was looking at a man genuinely baffled at what he was hearing.

"Never in a million years would I put her on EverChat, Riley. You know that."

Still sensing accusation in the air, Riley held up his hands. "Look, Bray, I swear I have no idea how or why Sarah is on there. I support the stupid app, but you know I would never do something like that without talking to you first."

Brayden believed him, but he continued staring. He didn't have words yet.

"It was Charlie who found her," Riley said. "He was having a real tough time yesterday, and he kept talking about his friend Jake. From school. How he talks to his grandpa on EverChat all the time. He asked if we could try it with Sarah."

Riley rubbed the back of his neck. Now he was pacing around the office.

"I tried to explain to him that it doesn't work that way. That someone would have needed to upload her while she was still alive. But he was so desperate, he was bawling. 'Just try, Uncle Riley,' he kept begging. So, I did, just to show him it wouldn't work."

"And it worked," Brayden said.

"Yeah. We typed in her name, and there she was. Her face, her voice, everything. Charlie started crying. Good tears, not bad. He was so happy, Bray. So, I figured maybe you had a change of heart, that maybe you and Sarah had stashed an upload just in case—"

"Come on, Riley," Brayden snapped. "Of course we didn't."

"Then who did?"

Brayden had no answer to that question. Could the crime scene investigators have done it? Another thought struck him.

"Ellen. Do you think ...?"

Sarah's mother had never been a big part of their lives during Brayden and Sarah's time as a married couple. She was distant before Sarah met the love of her life, and her vices only drove the wedge deeper. She and Brayden had never gotten along, despite Brayden's earnest efforts in those early days.

Riley shook his head, the lines on his forehead deepening as he considered the possibility. "Ellen?" He let out a skeptical chuckle. "Come on, she barely knew how to use a smartphone last you heard from her, right? I don't know. What reason would she have for doing that behind Sarah's back? I mean, she's got plenty of axes to grind with you, but I have a tough time believing she'd act against Sarah's wishes like that. And how would she have even pulled that off?"

Brayden paced the study, his mind racing faster than his footsteps. Ellen was an unlikely culprit; Riley was right. He shivered and gulped at his realization of what he had to do next.

He needed to talk to his wife.

Brayden's hand trembled as he hovered over the teal "Call" button on EverChat. The sleek, minimalistic, yet futuristic interface of the program seemed too sterile for the emotional minefield he was about to traverse. With a steadying breath, he pressed down, starting the call to the digital echo of his wife.

"Connecting," a woman's AI-generated voice chimed in a soothing tone that clashed with Brayden's intense anxiety. The screen flickered to life, revealing Sarah's familiar face, her eyes sparkling with the same warmth they always held. He froze, disarmed by the sight.

"Hey, Bray," this version of Sarah said, her voice a haunting facsimile of the original—gentle, calming, yet full of life. "I missed you."

The words had him clenching his jaw against the surge of emotions threatening to overwhelm his practiced composure. He reminded himself that this wasn't Sarah; it was just sophisticated code masquerading as the woman he loved so dearly.

"Sarah," he began, his voice betraying none of the turmoil within, "I need to know how you ended up here. Who did this?"

Her face tilted in a gesture of curiosity. It was so characteristic of her, and yet something was still off. "Why, I signed up, of course." She chuckled slightly. "It's wonderful to stay in touch, isn't it?"

Her smile was radiant, but it didn't reach the corners of her eyes. This version of Sarah still had something troubling her, but it hid behind an intensely believable facade.

"Stop it!" Brayden snapped, more to himself than to the image on the screen. "This is not you."

"Bray, come on," she softly pleaded. "I've spent the last few days waiting for your call. I loved talking with Charlie just now. He's so excited to play laser tag."

This was a fever dream. Brayden wanted to vault himself out of his chair and pace around the room. This wasn't happening. The Sarah on the screen before him remembers her conversations with the kids? She has a sense of time? She knows how long it's been—days, not weeks— since her own murder? All the harrowing aspects of EverChat they used to talk about were now coming to life in her digital eyes.

He snapped himself free of the emotional trap he knew this was. He had to prod further.

"Tell me about your murder."

The request was first met with cheery obliviousness. "Murder? Bray, come on. I wasn't murdered."

"A masked man in a charcoal hoodie broke into our home, Sarah! I watched him hold you at gunpoint. He made you cover the camera. God knows what he—"

Brayden's voice cracked, and he couldn't continue. But his outburst had produced some results. As he looked at Sarah's face, her lower lip quivered ever so slightly, an unmistakable precursor to the tears that used to well up in her eyes whenever fear or sorrow gripped her heart beyond her ability to resist.

But it was a quiver lasting a singular moment. The next, it was like a switch had flipped. Sarah's expression smoothed into a serene smile, and she redirected the conversation to a memory of them hiking in Acadia National Park. "Remember the view from Cadillac Mountain? We should go again sometime," she suggested, her mood inexplicably lightened.

Brayden felt his skin crawl. The unnatural evasion, the calculated deflection away from anything remotely painful—it made him want to hurl. His Sarah had never shied away from her feelings. She confronted pain with the courage of someone who knew it was just another facet of love. She was amazing at fighting off outward signs of vulnerability, sure. But she never did so by avoiding the subject. She would always tackle it.

"Sarah, honey ... please, tell me how you ended up on EverChat."

The digital incarnation of his wife stared back at him through the screen, her blue eyes a touch too steady, her voice a shade too blissful. "I chose to be here, Brayden," she affirmed, a soft smile gracing her lips. "To stay connected with you."

"Damn it."

His frustration was mounting. He was conversing with a ghost—a digital specter expertly dodging every attempt he made to delve deeper into the mystery of her presence. In his mind, he knew that's all it was. But to his heart, it was an image so painfully real, of a woman he so authentically loved, who was telling him about their fondest memories and her excitement at seeing their children again.

How could he be combative with Sarah in this forum? What if she *is* conscious in there, and there's just some kind of roadblock that prevents her from showing pain and negativity? He still believed that wasn't her, but could it at least be *partly* her? If it was just an artificial copy of her, did *she know that? Did the original her* know that?

If even a sliver of this person was Sarah, and if that sliver of Sarah was aware of what was happening, then he couldn't afford to be wrong about it.

"Sarah, if you were here … if you were really you …" His voice broke again. He swallowed hard, the words tasting like bile against his tongue. "I love you. And I promise I will find out who did this to you. I'll bring them to justice if it's the last thing I do."

She smiled again. "I know you will."

Her gentle nod and the look in her eyes gave Brayden the reassurance he needed. This was her nightmare, regardless of how well the developers of EverChat could suppress her negative emotions.

"I love you, Bray."

With a tepid smile, he ended the call. The screen went black as the chill settled into Brayden's bones, but that chill was overpowered by the fire reignited within him to figure out who was behind it all.

He paced back to the kitchen, where his kids were now accompanied by Riley and Ashley.

"Guys, I need to go." He tried to don his gentle bedside manner with his kids again. "Daddy will be back a little later, okay? You guys make sure you behave."

He pulled Riley aside for an extra word.

"No EverChat, Riley. I don't know what's going on here, but it's all connected. Keep them away from it. I'm going to find the bastards responsible for this."

Riley met his gaze, a frown creasing his brow. He nodded in understanding but pleaded caution. "Be careful, Brayden. You could be playing with fire here."

Brayden grabbed his jacket off the entryway hook. "Fire is the least of my worries."

14

As he walked down the driveway, the crisp Maine air snapped coldly against his skin. The drive north to Mickey's cabin was a blur of snowcapped tree branches and occasional rotations of the steering wheel. When he arrived, Mickey greeted him with a nod, the weight of unspoken questions hanging between them.

"Someone knew I was coming," Brayden said without preamble as he entered the rustic living room. "Joseph Blauss—he's our key, has to be. Whoever orchestrated Sarah's murder knew I was closing in on him to find out what he knew."

Mickey's eyes narrowed, and his head slowly nodded as he processed the information. "All right, all right," he said with the vintage *challenge accepted* look in his eyes. "If Blauss is at the center, we'll unravel this from the inside out."

Brayden gave an affirmative nod in return as Mickey handed him a laptop. Accepting it, he gave a puzzled look at his old colleague.

"Think of yourself as my sous-chef," Mickey quipped.

A new role for Brayden, but one he gladly accepted in these circumstances.

"Make sure you check your own network, Mickey. Anyone who might have known you had intel on Blauss. And let's loop Lacy in, too.

She's my contact at Westbrook PD. If there's a leak in her department, she needs to know."

Mickey agreed but still reiterated that he could not be the source of a leak. Brayden pulled out his phone, tapped a few times, and a moment later, Lacy's image flickered into existence on the screen as the call dialed.

"Brayden," she greeted him, her voice heavy with the weariness of the chase. "What have you got?"

"I'm here with an old colleague, Mickey Weekes. Mick and I go back to our agency days."

He sensed a momentary unease from Lacy. Perhaps she was less than thrilled that Brayden had gone fully rogue. "Nice to meet you, Mr. Weekes."

"Likewise, Officer."

Brayden slid the phone closer to him. "Troubling possibilities. We think there's a chance you have a mole in your group."

Lacy scoffed. "A mole? Two pizzas could feed the entire department, Brayden. I'm not sure little old Westbrook PD is prime time enough for a mole."

Her point was valid, but the facts said someone had to know. "Maybe one of those Winthrop jerk-offs, then. I don't know, Lace. But someone knew I was coming. Joseph's body was still warm, for God's sakes."

She sighed on the other end of the phone. "All right, I'll keep my eyes peeled. And Bray ..."

Brayden waited a moment for Lacy to finish her thought.

"If these guys neutralized Blauss that quickly, they seem fully capable of finding you. Be careful."

Oddly enough, Brayden hadn't felt that *he* was personally in danger at any time during these chaotic few days, but it was a good point. These maniacs could easily show up at Mickey's door at any moment.

"Agreed. We'll keep you posted if we find anything."

"Likewise."

Brayden hung up the phone and returned his attention to Mickey's progress. "Find anything?"

"Maybe," Mickey said, his eyes never leaving the screen. "Look at this." He pointed to a table full of identification numbers, names, dates, and dollar amounts. Inching closer to get a better look, Brayden saw he was showing a cluster of transactions linked to Sterling Seasons, the landscaping outfit Blauss worked for. "Not just lawn care and hedge trimming here."

"Tell me more."

Mickey scrolled to show more of the seemingly endless list. "Shell companies. Could be funneling something, could be laundering. Whatever they're doing, it ain't your run-of-the-mill landscaping mom-and-pop."

Brayden squinted and nodded, trying to process the information. "Maybe we got something here."

"More than something, my friend," Mickey said. He once again had more to say than he originally shared, ever the dramatic storyteller. "It's a complex web. And all these digital trails? They're breadcrumbs leading back to Blauss."

Brayden's eyes widened. *Now we got something*, he thought. "Can we trace where they originate?"

"Working on it." Mickey's hands flew across the keyboard. "This goes deep, Brayden. It's not just a few rogue shrubs."

"Deep enough to justify a killing spree?" Brayden's voice was barely above a whisper.

"Looks like it," Mickey confirmed, his expression somber. "And whoever's behind this, they've got reach and resources."

Brayden stood motionless for a moment, the cabin's quiet pressing in around him. When an immediate resolution from Mickey's prior thought didn't follow, he returned to his chair at the oak dining table. His fingers drummed a staccato rhythm on the wooden surface of the desk. He watched Mickey's eyes, intent and piercing, scanning line after line of code on the screen. Brayden didn't exactly feel like the most helpful sous-hacker.

"Anything?" Brayden's voice impatiently cut through the silence of Mickey's cabin like a knife after a few minutes.

"Patience," Mickey murmured, not looking up from the flickering glow of his computer. "Data like this is a puzzle, Cross. You don't rush a puzzle."

Minutes stretched into an eternity until finally, Mickey leaned back, a slow exhale escaping him. "Got something."

Brayden moved closer. On the screen, another complex network of transactions unfolded, this time with multiple tables chaotically forming a larger web.

"See that?" Mickey pointed to a name at the top of the shell company's profile. "That's our missing link."

"Darren Volmer?" Brayden asked, his throat tight. "Who is he?"

"Or who *was* he?" Mickey corrected, a slight grin now arcing upward. His fingers danced over the keys again, and with a few commands, the veil lifted. The alias disintegrated, revealing a name that made Brayden gasp.

"Vince Dawson."

15

TWO DAYS AGO

Vince Dawson's silhouette cast a long, ominous shadow across the polished floor of his high-rise office as he paced before the panoramic window. New York City sprawled beneath him, its pulsing lights and ceaseless energy mere playthings from this altitude. His sharp eyes, usually brimming with cold calculation, flickered with a rare glint of impatience. At fifty-two, Dawson had the air of a man who sculpted the world to his whims and never aged. Yet something about this evening gnawed at his composure.

He moved toward his desk, a predatory glide that belied his tall, wiry frame. On it, EverChat's interface gleamed—a testament to Circuit Corporation's technological achievements under his tenure as founder and CEO. Circuit's dominion extended far beyond this brilliant piece of software, with its tendrils wrapped around various aspects of digital life. It had come a long way from its humble beginnings, he recalled. On the wall beside his desk, a shadow box framed their first real estate agreement, nestled beside a plank of wood and a hammer that memorialized the business's first project. But the years transformed them into a digital empire rather than a physical one, and EverChat was

Dawson's crown jewel. The platform that would serve as the gateway to usher in his greatest triumph.

Vince paused, hand hovering over the table's surface, as he cast a cursory glance at the icons representing various projects—all spearheaded with ruthless efficiency. He tapped the EverChat app and watched as it expanded to fill the screen, its familiar teal-and-white interface promising connection and communication.

His office door slid open with a hushed whisper, admitting a man whose loyalty to Dawson was as much a part of him as his shadow. The man's steps were measured, his posture erect; his presence in the room felt like a trusted lieutenant on the battlefield.

"Joseph," Dawson demanded, his voice slicing through the quiet like a scalpel. "Progress report?"

Joseph Blauss nodded, the corners of his mouth turning up ever so slightly—a harbinger of good news. "Maine is nearly complete," he informed his superior. "Hans and Wyatt are seeing to the last few details, including your big fish."

"Good."

Dawson's voice was like a rich, smoky whiskey that burned with satisfaction, yet there was a hint of urgency simmering beneath the surface. He moved with a stealthy grace, his hands tightly clasped behind his back as he peered out over the sprawling city below. As he paced along the window, the click of his expensive dress shoes against the polished floor echoed through the office.

"Just a few more strategic acquisitions in the Midwest and along the West Coast, and we will have the full model ready to deploy."

"Indeed," Blauss said, mirroring Dawson's fervor. "Just a few more profile combinations. It won't be long now before your vision becomes our reality. Weeks, not months."

Dawson stopped pacing, turning to face Blauss. His lips curled into a semblance of a smile, though it failed to touch the icy resolve in his eyes.

"Once we've completed the model," Dawson said, feeling no need to elaborate. The weight of his ambition hung palpably in the air, heavy with implications. Blauss didn't need to hear a follow-up to his fragment.

"Everything's falling into place, just as you predicted," Blauss said.

"Predicted, yes," Dawson said, smoothing back a stray lock of his slicked-back hair. "But it's continued foresight and execution that will make us untouchable."

Dawson settled into the leather chair behind his desk, the skyline of New York sprawling out beyond the floor-to-ceiling windows. The glow of a massive monitor cast a sterile light on his features, sharpening the angles of his face as he regarded Joseph Blauss with an expectant stare.

"Tell me, Joseph," Dawson said, "how do you grade the work of our operatives in New England?"

Blauss, standing with a military-like posture, allowed himself a small smile of pride. "Hans and Wyatt have been exemplary, sir. They've worked through their list with surgical precision."

"Good." Dawson's response was curt, a nod of approval that held the weight of mountains. "Your guidance has not gone unnoticed. It takes a skillful hand to nurture and mold such ... efficient instruments."

"Thank you, sir," Blauss said, the corners of his eyes crinkling.

Dawson's fingers waltzed across the obsidian surface of his desk, summoning holographic displays complementing his monitor with a flick of his wrist. His eyes were fixed on a particular display—a kaleidoscope of human thoughts and digital profiles harvested by EverChat. He leaned forward, scanning the data streams as if sifting for gold.

"EverChat," he began, the name of his creation uttered like a spell, "has exceeded all expectations. The digital copies we've amassed ... it's staggering."

A childlike joy seeped through each word as his eyes locked onto the hologram he and Blauss could both see from opposite sides. An indignant chuckle and a shake of his head followed.

"Most of these digital minds, however, are nothing more than noise. Useless data harvested from mindless peasants." His face was quickly devolving into disgust as he pored over the profiles on his screen. "It's only further proof of the decrepitude of this civilization."

"Indeed, sir," Blauss concurred.

"An upgrade is imminent," Dawson continued, his gaze leaving the sea of data before him and shifting to his confidant. His lips twisted into a mirthless smile. "And we hold the key to humanity's next great leap."

He stood and joined Joseph on the other side of his desk, then pointed at the visualizations flooding the hologram in front of them. Blauss already knew the crux of the plan: Systematically and methodically, Dawson was adding minds to his ever-growing harvest. Demographic by demographic, location by location, personality trait by personality trait. Every intersection of the population, covering every race, gender, upbringing. Of course, he would hand-pick selections to be weighed more heavily than others in the model. The scores of worthless minds he poured into EverChat laid the groundwork, but his set of well-rounded jewels would make the magic happen. The crème de la crème of humankind.

"Imagine it, Joseph. An intelligence wrought from the finest minds among us. It will be our crowning achievement."

Blauss's eyes sparkled with excitement, mirroring the fervor of Dawson's vision. "It will be unparalleled."

Their delight was punctuated by the sharp ring of Joseph's phone. Without breaking eye contact with Dawson, he answered. The conversation was terse—a few hushed words, followed by a moment of silence.

"Sir," Blauss said, disconnecting the call and turning to Dawson with a triumphant smile, "speaking of crown jewels ... the crown jewel of all your crown jewels, the one from little old Westbrook? It's done."

A surge of elation rushed through Vince Dawson's body, igniting his features with an almost manic gleam. "Excellent! Truly excellent."

His heartbeat quickened as he vaulted back into his leather chair and grasped his computer mouse. The room, aglow with ambient light from the cityscape far below, was alive with an aura of anticipation. His fingers, practiced and precise, danced across the keyboard, summoning the digital chat interface within EverChat.

"Come to me," he said under his breath.

His demeanor was now giddy as his screen revealed the inner workings of EverChat. Of course, Dawson's administrative version of the application differed greatly from the consumer version. He got the real deal, the raw nutrients. His version didn't have code barriers and emotional manipulation that made the minds consumers interacted with so positive and friendly. His version got the full and unaltered digital minds that lived on Circuit servers. He navigated deftly through the layers of cybernetic corridors toward the sanctum where his prized asset awaited. His chest swelled with the thought of adding the most critical, invaluable piece to his grand design—a mind that could tip the scales, and a mind that he had long coveted. The mind of Brayden Cross.

He paused for a moment to breathe in the sterile air of his penthouse office, then clicked open a conversation with his crown jewel. The system complied, a circle spinning briefly before the image resolved into clarity.

Instead of the steely gaze and chiseled features of Brayden Cross, the face staring back at him was soft, its blue eyes wide and terrified with a crippling fear.

Sarah Cross.

"What is this?" Dawson spat the words, his voice a serrated blade cutting through the silence. The disgust contorted his features. His vision blurred for a nanosecond as the implications of the error bore down on him.

Blauss, still buoyant from the assumed success, darted around the desk to see why triumph had curdled into fury. His own expression faltered, disbelief etching lines of confusion across his forehead.

"Sir, I—"

"Out!" Dawson bellowed, his finger pointed squarely at the door. "Now!"

A chill hung in the air as Blauss retreated, leaving Dawson alone with the ghostly visage of Sarah Cross. Her presence was a mocking reminder of the failure. Why was she here and not Brayden? The oversight was not just incompetence; it was sacrilege against the perfection he sought to create. Its repercussions were manifold. Not only had he missed a golden opportunity to capture the mind of Brayden Cross—a mind he sought so deeply—but the task would now be orders of magnitude more challenging. It could have been several hours since his men had uploaded Sarah. That meant it would be far too late to catch Cross sleeping. Dawson had been keeping tabs on him for years. And from everything he knew about the former operative, the murder of his wife would light the fire of a thousand suns beneath him.

"Damn it!" Dawson shouted to himself in his now-empty office.

He leaned closer to the screen, studying the unwelcome face that had infiltrated his sanctuary. Sarah Cross was never meant to be uploaded, but mistakes happened. He knew that. For any other target, she would have been nothing more than a small footnote, an inconsequential hiccup in the grand scheme. But as she stared back at him, tears streaming down her face, cowering in unquantifiable fear, she served as a taunting symbol of a massive misstep. The forfeiture of his only chance to catch Brayden Cross unsuspecting.

"Sarah Cross," he hissed, the name a venomous whisper. "You were never meant to be part of this."

"Who are you?" she screamed in terror. "Where am I? Help me!"

Dawson slammed the laptop shut, severing the connection. The echo of the impact reverberated against the glass walls of his office, a solitary sound high above the city. A muscle twitched in his jaw as he tried to contain his fury. "Joseph!"

As if he had been waiting an inch outside the door, Blauss slid back into the office at a moment's notice.

"Fix it." Dawson's eyes pierced into Joseph's soul like daggers, his fingers curled into fists at his sides. "Now."

Blauss tried to look at Dawson, though it proved difficult. His anxiety seemed to skyrocket. "Hans and Wyatt are on their way to the Clement job, but—"

"The Clement job!" Incredulity oozed out of his most recent exclamation. "The Clement job!"

He stood menacingly and strode toward Blauss, who staggered a half-step back.

"Jane Clement is nothing but a redundancy in the *34-F-Sub* quadrant now, because your ... what did you call them? *Exemplary?* Because your *exemplary* buffoons can't distinguish a legendary CIA operative from his wife!"

Blauss cowered in fear and waited for continued fire.

"Fix it, Blauss!"

"I'll bring you Brayden Cross, sir, I—"

"Ha!" Dawson's howl cut him off mid-sentence. "Joseph, why don't you go clean up this mess first? Make sure Cross can't get any clues about our plan from this debacle. And don't even *think* about approaching him, or it'll be the last thing you do."

His glare seemed to suck the life out of Blauss.

"I'll work on finding someone I can trust for the Cross upload."

"Understood." The word was barely audible as Blauss turned on his heel and slipped out of the room, the door clicking shut behind him. It left Vince Dawson alone with his towering rage and a high-rise view of the city that now seemed too tranquil for his boiling temper.

With deliberate movements belying his inner turmoil, Dawson strode to his desk and seated himself, awakening the massive curved monitor that dominated his workspace. The screen came alive, casting a harsh glow across his face as he navigated through fields of profile data.

He pulled up the file marked CROSS, BRAYDEN and leaned forward, his eyes narrowing as he scanned the text. The profile was extensive, each achievement and accolade a testament to the former agent's capabilities. Yet it was not the many commendations or the impressive record of field operations that held Dawson's attention. It was a singular entry, understated yet potent in its implications, from which he couldn't look away: LOS ANGELES METRO, 2018.

Memories playing back in his mind, a rage flared in his gut. He tapped a few times on a panel built into his desktop, and a dial tone sounded. When the man on the other end answered, Dawson's imperative was direct.

"We have a Cross problem."

16

"Vince Dawson," Brayden said again, a chill of realization running down his spine. "Circuit CEO. The brains behind that damn app."

The blue light from the computer screen threw shadows across his scrunched forehead, stark against the dim setting of Mickey's cabin. The home was silent, save for the crackling logs in the fireplace. Papers were strewn all over Mickey's desk, and digital records flickered on monitors, each one a breadcrumb leading back to the same name.

"Joseph Blauss was just a puppet," Mickey said. "And Sarah ..." His words trailed off, the unsaid conclusion hanging heavy between them.

The data sprawled before them painted a complex story that felt evil to its core, one that Vince Dawson had built with meticulous care. A labyrinth designed to confuse, to obfuscate. And somewhere within its twisted paths lay the answer to the question that gnawed at Brayden's core: How had Sarah, ever the beacon of compassion, found herself ensnared?

"We obviously can't go straight for Dawson," Brayden said. "This thing must run deep. We can't just waltz up to the guy. He's a billionaire; we gotta assume all of Circuit's resources are at his disposal."

He paused, considering their next move as he scanned the encrypted messages and falsified accounts, each one as likely to be a clue as it was to be a trap. Mickey nodded, his eyes locked on the screen, his fingertips drumming the desktop. He racked his brain for an opening, any crack in Dawson's digital armor.

"We need more, Brayden. We're missing something crucial here. The dots aren't all connected. What's Dawson doing?"

Brayden shook his head. "Sarah's involvement doesn't make sense. She was good, Mickey. Truly good. She cared about people. This …" He gestured at the tangled evidence. "This is not her world."

"Couldn't agree more, from everything you've told me about her. So why was she pulled into all this?"

They fell into a rhythm, sifting through more data with practiced eyes. Brayden clung to the memory of Sarah's warmth, letting it fuel his determination. She deserved justice, and he needed to carve it from the chaos before them.

"Every transaction, all these shell companies … they all must serve a purpose. These go back years. Dawson's been playing a long game. And whatever it is, it's big."

"Too big for us to just stumble around in the dark," Mickey said, his eyes still locked on the code that spilled across his screen.

Brayden's eyes narrowed. He knew he was alluding to their lack of resources, and that Brayden was the only one who might have a chance to still lean on agency connections. Mickey was long since shunned by the intelligence community. But Brayden remained wary of involving official channels.

"I dunno, Mick. Dawson's got the world on a string here, right? If he's really responsible for everything we've been looking at, and he gets a whiff of government on his trail …"

"I know," Mickey conceded.

He didn't need to explain the rest. Dawson had the potential to wreak a lot more havoc than a few murders, if he was the puppet master of a multiyear avalanche of highly organized crime. Mickey paused, fingers hovering midair above the keyboard, looking for an alternative that escaped him.

"All right," he said. "We do this as a rogue team, then. Like in the movies."

"Exactly like the movies."

With a nod, Mickey turned back to his console to find a fresh angle, one he could pursue without the help of any authorities. EverChat seemed the most obvious entry point. He initiated a series of complex algorithms designed to penetrate the app's defenses. Line after line of code cascaded down his screens.

"Come on," Mickey said to himself, willing his programs to find a crack, any fissure in EverChat's armor.

But as minutes stretched into hours, their efforts were futile. EverChat's defenses held firm against every cyber-stratagem Mickey employed.

"They're good," he said, leaning back into his chair and loosely slapping his fingertips across the desk's edge. "This is military-grade cybersecurity. They've got layers upon layers of encryption."

Brayden rubbed the stubble on his chin. "There's always a way in. We just haven't found it yet."

"Unless ..." Mickey trailed off, a new thought flickering behind his eyes before being snuffed out by the magnitude of the situation.

"Unless what?"

"Nothing. Just grasping at straws." He shook his head, trying to refocus. "If we can't hack our way in, we'll have to think outside the box."

Brayden leaned closer to the screen, his focus intense as Mickey hammered at the keyboard. The ambiance of the cabin was a stark contrast to the chaos they were chasing. Brayden's mind was a whirr of possibilities and dead ends when Mickey's voice sliced through the silence.

"I think I've got something here," Mickey said. His tone was laced with an excitement that had been absent for hours.

"What is it?"

"This series of transactions doesn't add up. They're routed through ..." He leaned back, scratched his head, and squinted at the screen. "No, this can't be right."

"Talk to me, Mick."

"See these?" Mickey pointed at a cluster of numbers that seemed innocuous enough. "They're too clean, almost like—"

A sudden, ferocious outburst of barking from Snow abruptly cut his words short. The husky's hackles were raised, his posture rigid as he stood facing the door, his growls deep and guttural. The two men looked at Snow, then at each other.

"Snow never loses it like that," Mickey said, concern flooding his features.

Brayden's muscles tensed, his background kicking in as his brain registered the imminent threat. His ears homed in beyond Snow's barks, catching the soft, telltale crunch of snow compressing underfoot just outside the wall of the cabin. Without a moment's hesitation, he reached out, planting a hand firmly on Mickey's shoulder.

"Get down!" Brayden shouted, pushing Mickey toward the ground.

The glass of the front window exploded inward, a bullet zipping through where their heads had been moments prior. Splinters of wood and shards of glass sprayed across the room like hell's glitter. They scrambled behind the nearby sofa where Snow had already sheltered, their hearts pounding against their ribs like caged birds desperate for escape.

"We need cover!" Brayden shouted, frantically scanning for options.

Mickey's eyes lit with sudden realization. He had never been a field operative himself, but he probably picked up boatloads of tips and tricks from Brayden over the years. His hand darted to the underside of his end table, pulling free from a hidden compartment a small cylinder he'd kept in case of emergencies.

"Smoke!" he yelled. With a swift motion, he pulled the pin and lobbed it toward the shattered window. Thick gray smoke billowed into the room, enveloping them in a disorienting fog.

Brayden was impressed. "You got another one for the back? We gotta run!"

As Mickey cooked and tossed a second grenade, Brayden realized amid the chaos he hadn't instinctively reached for his nonexistent gun the way he had been doing so often. Maybe that signaled a small sign of healing, but on this occasion, he wished he had it. He didn't know how many villains waited outside the front of Mickey's home, and he blindly prayed there were none waiting outside the back. As the ambush blossomed, his instincts told him to stand their ground and fight. But without weaponry, they were minimally outgunned and potentially outnumbered. He couldn't believe he hadn't had the foresight to arm themselves, and he cursed himself for being caught unprepared. Mickey almost definitely had an armory hidden somewhere, if he had smoke grenades stashed in his end tables.

"Go, go, go!" he yelled, grabbing Snow's collar and yanking him toward the back door. The husky let out a distressed bark.

They bolted out the rear through their smoky cover, the night's cold air slapping them as they plunged into the woods. Trees became blurred silhouettes as they ran, branches snagging at their clothes, the ground uneven beneath them. Adrenaline surged, propelling them forward even as their lungs screamed for oxygen.

"Keep moving," Brayden panted, his voice a low command that cut through the fear and confusion. They couldn't afford to slow down. Leaves crunched underfoot, betraying their frantic pace as the three of them labored through the labyrinthine woods. The sharp report of gunfire echoed behind them, a harrowing reminder that death was just a bullet away. Brayden's muscles coiled and released with each bound, his breaths coming in ragged gasps as they vaulted over a fallen birch and splashed through an icy creek. The frigid water seeped into their boots, but there was no time to acknowledge the discomfort it brought.

"Up the ridge," Brayden said, pointing at an outcrop studded with rocks and jagged edges that promised concealment. They scrambled up the incline, dislodging stones that tumbled downward with muted thuds. Reaching the plateau, both men dropped to the ground, chests heaving, their breaths visible in the dry winter air. Snow nudged against Brayden's arm, his eyes alert and his ears pointed skyward. His tongue drooped from his bottom jaw as he panted alongside his humans.

In the distance, the relentless pursuit seemed to taper off—the twisting of snow beneath heavy steps grew sporadic, the cadence slowing. Brayden signaled for silence, straining to discern any change in the pattern of their pursuers' movements. A pair of muffled voices carried over the wind, laced with frustration. Brayden's hand found a chunk of granite, its jagged surface biting into his palm—a makeshift weapon should the need arise. He edged closer to the rock facade, every nerve alight with caution. With the slightest pivot, he peered around the barrier, his eyes sweeping the area below.

The clearing, about fifty yards down the slope and bathed only in the moon's light, held two figures casting shadows across the snow. They paced like distraught wolves, their gestures animated and aggressive, even from a distance. There was an eerie similarity in the way they showed their frustrations. The taller one kicked at the ground, while his companion threw up his hands in what could only be exasperation. Though Brayden couldn't make out their characteristics clearly, their body language spoke volumes—a search gone awry, a quarry that had slipped through their grasp.

Who were these men? He didn't think it was the same duo he'd seen on the security footage, but he couldn't be certain in the scant light. Brayden's breath came in misty plumes as he pressed closer to the dirt, muscles tensed for the sprint he knew might come at any second.

The voices grew louder, and the two men's figures became clearer through the sparse cover of winter-bare branches. They were not the same men from before. One man was black, looked just under six feet, and was built like a stallion. The other man was white, slightly taller and lankier, bearded, and had long hair that hid beneath a beanie. The black man's voice thundered across the clearing, his command slicing through the air like a knife through warm butter. It appeared he was the one in charge.

"Find his ass!" he bellowed, fists clenching and deltoids flexing in evident frustration.

The white man, his mane wild and his beard unkempt, seemed to recoil under the pressure of authority. A few moments later, their search continued in the wrong direction. They began drifting eastward, rather than following the northbound line that would lead them to their runaways. Brayden watched them go, feeling a touch of relief intermingled with the adrenaline that still flowed through his veins. For now, they were safe, but safety was a luxury that Brayden knew was now perpetually temporary.

"Come on. We should keep moving while we've got the chance. No sense being sitting ducks."

Mickey nodded, still shell-shocked, but with a hint of resolve in his expression. Snow, sensing the shift in tension, wagged his tail tentatively, his instincts aligning with his master's. The trio moved away from their rocky refuge, silence their ally. Brayden kept one eye on the receding figures and the other on the terrain before them. He calculated each step to avoid snapping twigs or disturbing the natural order of the terrain. They were ghosts flitting through the woods, and with each passing moment, Brayden felt the mantle of his old life settle upon his shoulders once more.

Their climb was grueling, but necessity lent Brayden's muscles an inexhaustible vitality. He led the way despite his relative unfamiliarity with the wilderness of northern Maine. His boots pressed into the cold earth as he scaled the slope, Mickey following close behind. The woods grew denser, the trees like sentinels watching over their ascent. Snow's breath came out in murky clouds, and Brayden's own exhalations matched the rhythm.

Reaching another plateau near the summit of their current peak, they paused. A gust of wind whipped at Brayden's face, stinging his cheeks. He pulled out his phone from the pocket of his jeans, its screen moist with the condensation produced from a clash between his laboring body and the surrounding frost. With a slight hesitation, he dialed Lacy. The signal seemed to waver before it caught, a lifeline thrown across the vast stillness of the mountains.

"Storrow," her voice crackled through, sharp and immediate.

Brayden didn't waste time on pleasantries. "We need an evac, Lacy. We're being hunted."

A pause hung on the line, and he could almost picture her grappling with the path forward. Of course, Westbrook PD didn't have the resources to send an evacuation team hours north, off the books.

"I've got someone who owes me a favor. They'll get you to the safe house near the border."

"Thanks. I'll send you our coordinates."

His words were terse but appreciative. He sent a nearby location for their extraction and pocketed the phone. The world around them fell quiet, save the occasional creak of branches and the distant howl of the unforgiving wind. They settled into an anxious wait, which tested their mental fortitude. In the hurry of the ambush, they hadn't been able to bundle up. Brayden wore jeans and boots with only a waffle-knit long-sleeved shirt. Mickey also wore jeans alongside a relatively lightweight hoodie. Snow's coat was built for these moments, so he was prepared.

Time stretched, thin and fragile. Brayden checked his watch, the soft green glow of the dial marking the minutes that felt like hours. Mickey shifted beside him, the sound minuscule but magnified in the silence. Brayden put a hand on his shoulder, a silent message of solidarity between old friends.

Then—distant at first but growing steadily brighter—headlights slashed through the night. A dark SUV emerged from the gloom, its engine a low growl against the whisper of the forest. Mickey immediately tended to Snow, doing everything in his power to prevent the excited howling. Brayden's pulse quickened, not with fear, but with the anticipation of movement, of action. They stood as they prepared themselves to approach the vehicle.

Brayden's mind raced through the possibilities, the contingencies, the readiness of plans B through Z that his past life had ingrained in him. He hoped to God this was actually the vehicle Lacy had sent. It had to be, right? It would have been nearly impossible for their enemies to spot the trio of fugitives in the darkness, and this SUV was stopped almost exactly at the location Brayden had provided on a nearby adjoining mountain road. If this was an enemy vehicle, it was probably the end of the road for them anyway.

Carefully, triggered by a directional nod of Brayden's head, they approached the car. With the blinding shine of its headlights, there was no hope of seeing its driver. It was time for a leap of faith. As they neared the idling vehicle, the rear door opened, welcoming them into its anonymous sanctuary. A man's voice followed.

"Cross? Weekes?"

Ever cautious, Brayden stopped and held his hand out, blocking Mickey from proceeding for another moment. "And who are you?"

"Someone who will no longer owe Officer Storrow a favor."

With a sigh of relief, the three of them slipped inside the car, the warmth within clashing with their cold-soaked skin.

17

The vehicle's tires crunched over the icy gravel as it pulled up to the chalet tucked in the cover of dense pines. Brayden stepped out, muscles tensing against the chill that enveloped him in the darkness. Out the other side of the SUV slipped Mickey, with Snow leaping down after him. The husky's nostrils flared as he surveyed their new, albeit temporary, territory.

Brayden rubbed the back of his neck and exhaled a foggy breath as the now debt-free driver rolled down his window.

"I dunno who you boys are or what you're up to, but stay safe out here. I haven't seen Officer Storrow so worried in quite some time."

"We appreciate it. You really bailed us out."

"Info sheet is available on the hologram inside. Code is 2110."

Brayden nodded and patted the driver's door twice as a sign of thanks. As the SUV receded into the obscurity of the night, it left only a smaller SUV remaining in the driveway. Brayden assumed the vehicle was meant for their own use, should the need arise.

Trudging up the unpaved walkway, the three companions made their way into the rustic chalet. The interior reminded Brayden of his family's shared ski home on Sweetway Mountain. The space was large and open, its living room orienting around a massive fireplace. Above it, decorative skis crossed over one another in their mounted position.

The floorboards creaked as downward pressure transferred through the soles of their boots, but it wasn't the type of creaking that suggested weakness. The creaks were low and steady, like the sound of old trees swaying in the wind. They seemed to hold secrets within them, a silent language passed down from generations of travelers and runaways who had treaded upon them in search of the same safekeeping Brayden and Mickey now sought.

"Guess this'll have to do," Mickey said. He'd made his way over to the back corner of the living area, where an old iMac stood out like a relic from another era.

Brayden nodded. He paced the length of the safe house, playing a jingle of vigilance on the floorboards with measured steps. They were alone for now, but he couldn't help but wonder how long their solitude would last.

A ping from his new, secure phone drew Brayden to the message Lacy had sent. Her driver had given them new phones, taking their old ones for disposal. Better to be safe than sorry, Lacy had said. If Dawson's goons were hunting them down, they might as well scrub as much of their digital footprint as possible.

Down the stairs to the right. Code is 2110.

Lacy's message seemingly directed him to the information sheet the driver had referenced. Brayden descended the staircase into the basement, each footstep jolting its corresponding wooden plank out of slumber. At the bottom of the stairs and around the corner, a digital panel stood out from the wall. He punched in 2-1-1-0.

A slate-gray holographic display flickered to life beside the panel, its surface area filling up with neon-blue text. It contained information about the safe house: its heating and cooling, secure internet and phone connections, entertainment options, kitchen supplies, and more.

Perusing the display, Brayden located a button labeled Vehicle Inventory. He pressed it. In the room to his left, a three-dimensional hologram filled the room with a spinning replica of the Mazda SUV he had seen in the driveway. Its vehicle specifications hovered in a box to its right. When he saw the vehicle outside, it looked black in the night's dark. Seeing it now, it was actually a midnight blue.

Swiping out of the vehicle screen, he arrived at a much more intriguing menu item: Weaponry. Pressing the button, a code entry screen popped up. When his fingers tapped across the 2-1-1-0 combination again, the dialogue briefly shook horizontally, and a red Invalid Code message displayed. Frowning and tilting his head in slight confusion, he pulled out his phone. A text from Lacy had come in a minute prior.

You're probably ready for the other code by now. 4047.

A subtle smile crept over his face as he shook his head and dropped the brick back into his pocket. He punched in the code. Behind him, he could hear a locking mechanism whir its approval from within a fortified steel door that nestled beneath the staircase. Pressing his hand against the cold, smooth surface of the door, he grabbed its handle and yanked it open.

As he stepped into the armory, his eyes swept over rows of firearms, each one meticulously maintained. Pacing a few steps in, his fingers brushed the grip of a silenced handgun, the familiarity of its weight a grim comfort.

"Mick! Better load up!"

A few moments later, he heard the rumbling of footsteps cascading down the stairs, followed in close tow by the pitter-pattering of Snow's descent. As Mickey turned the corner into the armory, his eyes lit up in awe.

"Whether they find us here or we find them somewhere else, we ought to be ready."

"Always preferred a fair fight, anyway," Mickey said, one corner of his mouth lifting into a smirk as he grasped a handgun of his own.

"Grab a gun or two, a couple of smokes, a couple of stuns. Bring it all upstairs with us. I'm not trying to get caught at the computer with our pants down again."

"Like a teenage boy, Cross!" Mickey quipped.

Brayden let out a chuckle and shook his head. It felt like a year since the last time he'd heard a joke.

They finished gathering their weaponry into two duffel bags. Returning upstairs, Mickey settled in at the desk in the living room.

"Why don't you grab some shuteye, Bray? I'll get my bearings here and keep finding answers."

Brayden scoffed, but it wasn't a terrible suggestion. The exhaustion was real. He doubted he could actually sleep, but he took a seat on the sofa and rested his head on its oversized cushions for a few minutes. Two or three times, he caught himself dozing off—it was one of the worst feelings to him, doing so unwillingly. In this setting, he wasn't willing to succumb to sleep yet.

He walked over to scope out the kitchen. The morning sun was now peeking up over the mountains, creating a pinkish hue that leaked into the sky little by little. At Mickey's request, Brayden grabbed a can of dog food from the pantry. Before he could even finish detaching its metal lid, he heard Snow darting toward the kitchen. The galloping footsteps on the hardwood floors brought him back to his childhood, where his father would make the same comment every time the dogs sprinted toward the kitchen for their food: "And they're off at the Kentucky Derby!"

He spooned the sloppy chicken-flavored concoction into a dish for Snow, then peered into the fridge to see what was available. A carton of eggs, an unopened pack of bacon, a bowl of sliced fruit, a bag of shredded cheese, and a bottle of orange juice. Pulling open the freezer, he found frozen breakfast sausages and a pack of frozen hash browns. *Housekeepers must be ready at the drop of a hat to stock this place*, he thought to himself.

Grabbing a stainless-steel pan from the cupboard, he flicked on the gas burner. The assortment of ingredients reminded him of the rare peaceful days in his past life with Sarah—before kids, but knee-deep in counterterrorism. More often than not, his weekends were spent unexpectedly on the road or in the field, unable to fully debrief Sarah, longing desperately to just have a weekend with her. Whenever he'd get lucky enough to have a true weekend free, with no urgent calls to action or high-priority national security meetings to be roped into, the two of them would sleep in, sip their morning coffee, banter about names for their future babies, and whip up meals just like the one Brayden was now making. Scrambled eggs, hash browns in the air fryer, sausages in the microwave. The hungover college student breakfast, but enjoyed by suburban adults savoring a day with no obligations.

"Mick, you want some breakfast?"

Brayden hadn't heard the click-clacking of the keyboard until just now, when he listened in the direction of the living room for Mickey's answer. The keyboard came to a rest. He heard a single clap and then the sound of his friend rising from the chair.

"Do I ever!" Mickey hollered.

Brayden slid the eggs onto two plates, their blanket of shredded cheese melting into yellow fluffiness. He tossed a few hash browns and sausages and bacon slices onto each plate, then set one down in front of Mickey. Taking the seat across from him, he devoured his breakfast. He was hungrier than he'd realized while cooking it.

"All right," Brayden said, wiping his mouth with the back of his hand. "Now that I'm nourished again ... what did you find before all hell broke loose at the cabin?"

Mickey began nodding as he chewed on the last bite of his own meal. His mouth was stuffed to the brim, so he raised a finger as he chewed. Mentally, he'd been ready for the question. Physically, it took him a solid ten seconds to finish his bite and clear his throat.

"The transactions," he finally began. "I was noticing some strange trends. I've been digging into it more this morning. Dawson's digital fingerprints are all over the place; that much was clear after tying together his various aliases. But one destination for these cash funnels stood out to me. You ever hear of a company called FluidMotion?"

Brayden crinkled his face as he dug into his memory. "I think so, yeah. I've heard of them. Microchips, is it?"

"Almost," Mickey said. "Robotics."

"Robotics," Brayden repeated, rubbing his chin.

Mickey stood from the kitchen table and carried his empty plate to the sink. He clanked it down into the stainless-steel cavity with minimal grace, then gestured his head toward the living room as he walked back past Brayden. "Let me show you."

Brayden followed Mickey back to the old iMac. The morning sun now tossed lanky shadows across the room as it rose over the horizon but remained well shy of its peak in the sky. Mickey plopped down in the desk chair, and Brayden took a knee beside him.

"Nine or ten massive payments. Six or seven patent applications. Vague private equity investments," Mickey rattled off the findings as he whirred around different windows and documents. "I can't see many of the details, but I can say with certainty that Vince Dawson and FluidMotion are keenly familiar with one another."

"Help me understand," Brayden countered. "So, these shell companies—a landscaping company tied to Joseph Blauss, plus a bunch of others—all point to Vince Dawson pouring boatloads of money into FluidMotion?"

Mickey nodded. "Murder and robots, I guess. That's Dawson's jam."

"And don't forget EverChat," Brayden added.

The intersection of all the factors gave him a headache. He tried to piece it together. Vince Dawson had the world at his fingertips with the prevalence of EverChat and the mental real estate it owned across America. He had been rapidly climbing to the top of the world's list of the wealthiest moguls. Investing in robotics and AI would have been completely par for the course for a titan in the technology industry.

"Why disguise it?" Brayden's question naturally followed. "Why does Dawson need to hide his affiliations with FluidMotion?"

Mickey's look grew a bit more concerned. "Not sure, but people like Dawson don't hide things like this for no reason."

"And the murders." Brayden let his brainstorming happen out loud. He thought again of Sarah being a casualty of this. "What have the robotics got to do with the murders? Is he training some kind of terrorists with enhanced weaponry? Testing out a biological weapon? Hell, is he trying to build his own army or something?"

Brayden stood and paced over to the window. As he tried to let his mind sift through possibilities, his attention was diverted to a rustling of branches in the clearing beyond a small patio with chairs and a grill. He glanced around at the rest of his surroundings; the tree branches hanging near the window were still. The shrubbery on the far side of the property was still. Only the small wooded area beyond the patio swayed in the morning air.

"We've got company," Brayden said sternly. Of course, being in the wilderness of Maine, it could have been wildlife scurrying through the terrain. But his gut was screaming to the contrary.

Without waiting for Mickey's acknowledgment, Brayden snatched the handgun he'd taken from the armory and darted toward the front door. Front and back were hardly useful distinctions in a home like this one, nestled into the mountains without much of a yard on either side. He considered the driveway side to be the front—the side from which they entered a few hours earlier—and the mountain side to be the back. The kitchen window faced the mountain side. So, if the rustling leaves were the byproduct of an intruder, Brayden assumed they had already circled the house. He merely hoped a second one wasn't waiting for him.

Twisting the knob and whipping the door inward, he lunged out the front door and raised his weapon. Empty silence. He scanned the area, looking and listening for any signs. The gravel driveway and its surrounding terrain lay still, seemingly undisturbed. He looped left, choosing first to cover the area from which it seemed any visitors would need to come. He slid one foot in front of the other, avoiding stepping on any branches or leaves that might reveal his position.

He made his way to the corner of the house. The side yard was covered in undisturbed snow, a sign that whoever he was hunting hadn't come this way. Creeping along the cabin's edge, his weapon continuously scanning, he approached the back corner that led toward the patio. He flared out, hoping he could encircle the intruder rather than be the one trapped in no-man's land. Scurrying quickly about ten yards toward the edge of the property, he took cover behind a thick tree. He knew the maneuver had made some noise, so he waited silently to see if it triggered any reaction.

A few yards ahead, he heard movement. Squatting down and peering around his protective tree, he aimed his gun. His finger floated over the trigger and briefly came into contact with it before refraining. A raccoon scurried across the clearing and burrowed out of sight into the mountainside.

Brayden sighed and relaxed his crouch, but a moment later, he heard another noise. This time, it wasn't a branch or a leaf. It sounded more like a mixture of a thud and a knock. Heightening his alertness again, he swung around the other side of the tree to continue moving along the perimeter. A few paces later, he came into view of the back side of the cabin. There, dressed in black, with a rifle trained, a man stalked and peered toward the large living room.

Brayden cursed under his breath.

His brief panic was slightly relieved when, beyond the patio, on the opposite side of the house, he saw Mickey crouching in the shrubs. He too was armed. Be it good fortune or good training, he had seemingly followed the opposite route out the front door that Brayden had taken. The two made eye contact with each other. Though there was no chance he could have communicated it, something in that look told Brayden that Mickey feared for Snow, who was still inside and might have that rifle trained on him.

The two old friends sometimes had a remarkable ability to read each other's minds. The genius hacker without much field training did exactly what Brayden hoped he would do. He tossed a stun grenade backward, away from the cabin, toward where the raccoon had scurried.

At the sound of the device exploding, the intruder immediately whipped around.

"Who's there! You're dead now!"

He paced toward the spot where Mickey had deployed the grenade. Brayden could no longer see Mickey; he assumed that he'd gone prone. Brayden couldn't be sure whether Mickey acted with the same plan in mind, but from Brayden's perspective, it was an excellent move to draw the villain closer to Mickey's side of the clearing, and away from the house. A moment later, overtaken by adrenaline and on the verge of blacking out from it, Brayden fired a bullet into the leg of the man and burst out of his prone stance in a full sprint.

The man staggered and yelped in pain, and Mickey fired two shots— one that missed and a second that appeared to hit the man's arm. The latter knocked his weapon from his grasp, and within seconds, Brayden tackled the half-fallen man to the ground. Using his bodyweight, he pinned his torso and arms to the ground and held him there until Mickey arrived to kick the rifle out of his reach.

"Who the hell are you?" Brayden yelled.

The man writhed and squirmed but said nothing. Brayden looked up at Mickey, who tucked his own handgun into the rear waistband of his pants, then pulled a hunk of copper wire from his pocket.

"You'd make a pretty good field agent," Brayden quipped. In earnest, he was impressed with Mickey's preparedness and execution. Taking the intruder alive wasn't a spoken requirement, but he was glad his friend was like-minded in the heat of the moment.

Mickey chuckled and tossed the wire down to Brayden. He pressed his knee more firmly into the man's spine, triggering another painful squeal. Brayden wrapped the man's wrists together tightly with the wire, its rough edges digging into the skin and creating more sounds of anguish. He hoisted him up by the armpits. Mickey pressed his gun to the small of the man's back as Brayden took him firmly by the shoulders.

"Let's have a little chat, shall we?"

They hauled their new prisoner into the chalet, his boots scraping against the wooden floorboards. He was heavier than he looked. The man's face contorted in pain, but he remained stubbornly silent other than sporadic grunts of pain. They dragged him to the kitchen, where Mickey grabbed the wooden chair he'd sat in at breakfast and whipped it around to the center of the floor. Brayden shoved the man into it, the weight of his body briefly tipping it onto its hind legs before it slammed down again.

"More wire," Brayden commanded, keeping pressure on the man's shoulders.

Mickey disappeared into the basement, returning moments later with a coil of thick copper wire. They bound the man to the chair, wrapping the wire tightly around his chest, arms, and legs. The copper bit into his flesh, but the man barely flinched.

Brayden crouched down, meeting the prisoner's steely gaze. "Who sent you?"

Silence.

Mickey circled behind the chair, pulling a knife from the block on the countertop. "We can do this the easy way or the hard way."

The man's eyes darted between them, his jaw clenched tight.

Brayden's patience wore thin as they hammered him with unanswered questions. The air in the room grew heavy with tension, each passing moment stretching into an eternity. Mickey paced behind the chair, his footsteps echoing in the quiet cabin. Snow's tail wagged a mile a minute, and he barked incessantly. Each time Brayden felt defeat creep in, and with each urge to just put a bullet between the man's eyes and pack up for a new safe house, he thought of Sarah. He thought of the reason he was standing here in the first place. He wanted—no, needed—answers.

"Last chance," Brayden growled, his voice low and dangerous. "Who sent you?"

The man's lips curled into a sneer, his silence defiant. His eyes seemed to bounce around at nonexistent subjects as if he were looking at a smattering of ghosts. This time, Brayden snapped. In one fluid motion, he snatched the knife from Mickey's hand, its blade glinting in the light that streamed through the rear window. Without hesitation, he plunged it deep into the man's thigh.

The scream pierced the air, soaked with agony. It reverberated off the wooden walls and metal pans of the kitchen, sending Snow scurrying down the hallway for cover. Brayden's own bellows matched the prisoner's in intensity as he demanded answers, his face inches from the man's contorted features.

"Who are you working for? What do you want?" Brayden roared, twisting the knife slightly. "Why is my wife dead?"

His hand trembled as he gripped the knife's handle, his knuckles white with tension. The painful screams had subsided to ragged gasps, the man's eyes wild with pain but firm in their resolve to stay quiet.

"Cross," Mickey said. "Something's not right."

"You're telling me," Brayden quipped. But when there was no verbal reply, he looked up at his friend.

Mickey's face had gone pale, his eyes fixed on the knife still embedded in the intruder's thigh.

"What is it? Suddenly queasy?" Brayden growled, his patience wearing thin.

Mickey swallowed hard. "Look."

Brayden's focus returned to the weapon, and suddenly, the world seemed to tilt in his vision. Where there should have been a crimson stain spreading across the man's black pants, there was nothing. No blood. No glistening stream. Nothing.

With a sharp intake of breath, Brayden yanked the knife free. More agonizing cries filled the air, but Brayden hardly noticed them this time. He was too entranced by the blade of his knife, which emerged clean and dry.

Stunned, Brayden stumbled backward, the clean knife clattering to the floor. He exchanged a bewildered glance with Mickey before they both turned their attention back to their captive. The man's face still portrayed anguish, but the gash through his pant leg sat mysteriously idle.

"What the hell?" Mickey whispered, crouching down to inspect the wound.

Brayden's mind raced, trying to make sense of what he was seeing. He remembered the bullet wounds they'd inflicted earlier and quickly moved to inspect the man's arm and other leg. As he tore away the fabric, his breath caught in his throat.

In the man's arm, where there should have been torn, bloody flesh carved from a bullet, there was something entirely different. The skin—could he call it skin?—around the entry wound had peeled back, revealing a complex network of components unlike anything Brayden had ever seen. It wasn't the rigid metal of a robot, nor was it the organic soft tissue of a human body. Instead, it was an intricate web of fibers and circuits, pulsing gently. Tiny lights flickered within the wound, and a faint whirring sound emanated from deep within.

Brayden's hands shook as he examined the other two wounds. The leg injury from his own bullet revealed the same unsettling sight—no blood, no torn muscle, just an intricate maze of synthetic metallic strands. The entry point on the thigh where he had plunged the knife showed a similar substance, with thin filaments knitting themselves back together before his eyes.

"My God," Mickey whispered, his face a mask of disbelief. "What is this thing?"

A memory flashed before Brayden. He recalled the grainy footage from Leo Clement's driveway camera. The criminal there, shot with a twelve-gauge, had stumbled away without a drop of blood strewn upon the white blanket of snow. Brayden knew it was odd, but he didn't have an explanation.

Now he had one. He shook his head and looked back at Mickey.

"I guess Circuit makes more than just a stupid app."

18

TWELVE YEARS AGO

The fluorescent light panels of the agency's underground facility hummed incessantly. It was a constant reminder of the world Mickey Weekes had willingly buried himself in. Other than the lights' constant buzz, the only sound circulating the room at two in the morning came from his hammering of mechanical keys on the device before him. The early hour did little to distinguish itself from any other time of day in this windowless tech hub.

"Still at it, Weekes?"

Startled, Mickey glanced up to see his colleague leaning against the doorframe. Even now, in the dead of night, Brayden Cross looked wired and ready for action. He wore a light sweat that glistened in the ugly lighting.

"Almost done. Just gotta patch up this last vulnerability."

"Don't work too hard, now."

Mickey chuckled. "The hell are you doing here at two in the morning?"

Brayden sauntered over to a nearby workstation and held up a packet of papers. "Weekes, sometimes your brain is too energized for sleeping after you save the city of Portland from the bad guys." He slapped the papers down on the desk and flipped open the laptop beside them.

"That related to the threats they mentioned on Hadlock?"

Brayden raised his eyebrows at him. "They let you in on more field stuff than I thought, guy!"

Mickey smiled. Sometimes the dynamic between the tech guys and the field agents—in his career thus far, anyway—was tense. He liked Brayden for his willingness to treat him as an equally important team member, committed to the same mission. Not all field agents had given him the same respect.

"Buddy, I know everything around here. And if I didn't, I know how to find what I need," Mickey said, gesturing to his computer.

Brayden smiled and nodded, returning his attention to his own and beginning to type. "Well, Mick, let's just say Hadlock Field is no longer in danger. Maybe we'll get to check out some of those Sox prospects this weekend after all."

"Love me some Sea Dogs."

After a few minutes of record-keeping, Brayden bid adieu to Mickey and departed for the night. It was once again silent, save for the hum of the lights. Couldn't they afford some lights that *wouldn't* drive a man mad?

The next noise was the soft chime of a system notification.

DOWNLOAD COMPLETE.

Mickey glanced around again at the empty room, and at the clock on the wall that read 2:31 a.m. Nobody was around, but he still felt a sense of worry as he slid the flash drive into his USB port.

The file transfer from the machine onto the drive took only a few seconds, but it felt like an eternity to Mickey. There was no reason for it to feel so intense in the dead of night with nobody around. Still, he struggled to shake the feeling of worry, knowing the potential repercussions of getting caught. Each moment was an opportunity for his conscience to tell him to stop.

But he couldn't. Not now. Not when the truth was so overdue.

Pocketing the flash drive, Mickey packed his things. On his way out, he paused for a moment, taking one last look across the empty office space. A slight tremor ran through his hand as he flicked off the light switch, nerves getting the better of him. The drive home through silent back roads gave his guilt time to surface, tickling at his conscience. Every oath he'd taken, every trust placed in him—he was violating all of them.

The weight of what he'd uncovered, though, was too significant to sit idly by.

The project Mickey had been assigned to for the better part of a year —Operation Mockingbird—seemed innocuous initially. He and a team of engineers and analysts were to develop a system to monitor potential threats, they said. Keep America safe. But as time dragged on and Mickey dug deeper, he realized the wider scope of what his team had been helping them build. This wasn't just about external threats to America. The system monitored *everyone, all the time*. Indiscriminately. Emails, phone calls, web browsing, even folks' conversations at home. All of it.

Nothing would be private. Ever.

Mickey joined the agency to protect people, not to become the very thing they feared.

A yellow light flipped to red, and he slowed his Jeep to a stop. *Timed lights at three in the morning.* He shook his head and waited at the empty intersection.

His mind raced. What would his sister, Amber, think if she knew what he was up to? She had to be on his side. They had drifted apart over the years, with Mickey's work consuming more and more of his life. But he still remembered her idealistic speeches in college like they were yesterday. She had an unwavering belief in privacy and individual rights and had always been outspoken about it.

He thought of his father, who had been so proud when Mickey joined the agency. *You're going to do great things,* he had said. An old photo of him and Amber with their father on his sixtieth birthday flashed across his mind's eye. It was taken just a few months before cancer had taken his dad.

Would he be proud of him for this?

The light turned green, and Mickey sped through the intersection.

He wrestled with his own psyche the rest of the way home. Turning the key and pushing open the door to his apartment, he was greeted by his golden retriever, Blaze. Mickey took him for a walk, then unloaded a can of slop for him. Then he settled in at his workstation. By the time he readied the flash drive and plugged it into his personal machine, it was nearly four in the morning.

File after file populated into the folder on his screen, each one more damning than the last. Surveillance reports, wiretap transcripts, plans and blueprints for even more invasive monitoring systems. It was all there. A year's worth of cold, hard evidence of total surveillance on unwitting American citizens, many of whom had no criminal or civil records to their names. He zipped them all up and dragged the compressed file into another pane.

Mickey's finger hovered over the "Enter" key. With one press of that key, all of this information would be uploaded to a secure file location, ready for the journalist he'd been working with to scoop it all up. He could already envision the headlines.

US Government's Massive Privacy Violation Exposed.

Doubt chewed away at him as he stared at the key. Was he doing the right thing? As invasive as these systems were, as big a privacy violation as they had been, they had helped to stop threats, from both home and abroad. Who was Mickey Weekes to decide that the price was too high? Was he out of line?

Then Amber's voice echoed in his head, resembling the message of Benjamin Franklin once upon a time. *"The moment we sacrifice our privacy for security, we lose both."*

He took a breath, closed his eyes, and uploaded the file.

Mickey knew his life would never be the same. He couldn't stay at the agency, of course. He'd be referred to between those walls as Mickey "Snowden" Weekes, he figured. Maybe he would just embrace the moniker. Maybe even name a future dog after it. Blaze was getting old, after all.

He also couldn't go back to normal life. Not with everything he knew. And, really, who did he have that was worth going back to? Amber had long since migrated her life away from him. Their mother had been gone for two decades now. His father had been the last remaining thread holding family ties together.

The sun began to rise, spraying hues of pink and orange across his apartment. As he looked at Blaze, curled up with his head resting on his paws, Mickey made the decision that he was headed for a life off the grid. He'd continue using his skills to make ends meet, and he'd continue serving and protecting his country to the extent that he could. But he'd never return to a place that demanded the moral compromises he'd been making these last few years.

His thoughts wandered to Brayden. He'd miss working with him, that was for certain. He might even opt to stay in touch with him or let him know his general whereabouts. Brayden was someone he could trust, but Mickey knew he was also someone fully committed to his craft. He would never approve of what Mickey just did and the damage it would inflict on the agency. But he figured he wouldn't hold it against him either.

Mickey pulled the flash drive from its port and, after cobbling together and lighting a few logs in his modest fireplace, tossed the drive into the flames.

He began packing, taking only the essentials. He tidied up, gathered his stash of cash, and left an envelope on the table with enough to cover his remaining rent. The landlord would eventually come by, he figured.

Grabbing Blaze's leash, he coaxed him out of his slumber and stepped into the morning sun, pulling shut his apartment door for the last time.

19

Brayden decided it was time to stop referring to the assassin as *him*. His blood boiled as he stared down at *it*. This device, so humanlike in its nature, lay slumped in the chair, seemingly exhausted from the interrogation. How could a robot be exhausted? *Battery must need a charge*, Brayden thought. As he stared into its cold blue eyes, he couldn't help but superimpose Sarah onto its features. It reminded him of EverChat, in some way. With each passing improvement to the technology, it became easier and easier to dupe the human mind into believing it was real.

Mickey restlessly paced around the room, rubbing the back of his head. He had remained pretty composed throughout this entire ordeal, but the discovery of a humanoid might have been his breaking point. His fingers twitched, he reached into his pockets for phantom items, and he scratched at his elbows and knees sporadically.

"This is," Mickey stuttered, the words escaping him. "Brayden, what the hell is this?"

He wanted to give an answer, but he simply didn't have one. He shook his head.

Mickey slumped against the wall and sighed. "I keep thinking this is all some crazy nightmare. That I'll wake up and everything will be normal again."

Brayden nodded in agreement, patting Snow on the head as he arrived in the kitchen.

"Normal died with Sarah," he said. There was a bitterness in his voice, and he realized it probably came off cold to Mickey. "Sorry, I know it's hard for you too, Mick. I never should've dragged you into this."

Mickey laughed, more anxiously than joyfully. "Don't apologize. We're in this together. Saving the world from ... whatever this is."

His words hung in the air as he gestured toward the humanoid.

"How many of them are there?" Brayden said.

"If Dawson's creating a damn army of these things," Mickey said, "we're going to need more than two of us. But they tracked us at my cabin, they tracked us here. Who can we trust?"

"That's the million-dollar question, eh? How many of these things have we crossed paths with? The goons at the cabin, whoever killed Joseph, and ..." He swallowed hard. "And whoever killed Sarah. How many of them were humanoids?"

The pale light from the afternoon sun seeped through the windows as they started piecing together the puzzle. Mickey retrieved a whiteboard from the hallway closet and started sketching a rough timeline, connecting Dawson, FluidMotion, the murders, and everything else they had learned. His hand moved swiftly, generating sporadic squeaks of the marker.

Brayden dug into his memories from the agency, identifying potential black sites for robot manufacturing.

"Here," he said, pointing to a spot on the makeshift map Mickey had drawn, "and here. These locations would be ideal for covert operations. Isolated, access to resources, minimal oversight."

As the full potential scale of Dawson's operation took shape, the realization of the threat these humanoids posed took hold. They decided it must have been a humanoid duo that murdered Sarah and then Jane. The same duo probably murdered Blauss. And then it was probably another humanoid duo that attacked Mickey's cabin. They discussed potential motives behind it all—influence, power, control, immortality—each possibility more terrifying than the last.

"Think about it," Mickey said, his voice low and intense. "If Dawson can create humanoids this advanced, what's stopping him from replacing key figures in government, business, even the military?"

"It would be the perfect infiltration. Undetectable, loyal only to their creator." Brayden's jaw clenched. "He may have already begun."

"And with EverChat," Mickey continued, "he's got access to millions of minds. He could be harvesting data, personalities, memories ..."

Brayden thought of Sarah, her digital echo trapped in EverChat. His stomach turned.

"Is it time to bring in some authorities for real?" Mickey asked.

"No," Brayden answered, almost instinctively. "No. Without knowing what stage Dawson is at with this project, we can't risk him blowing the top off. What if he's infiltrated police forces? The government? The healthcare system? If we spook him, he might decide to pull the trigger on whatever his endgame is."

They sat in silence for a few moments, letting the gravity of the crisis soak in. Mickey peeled back the humanoid's surface wounds and snapped some photos of its inner circuitry.

Then, a noise outside shattered their focus. It sounded like the buzzing of a bee but amplified. Like the bee was the size of a basketball. As they stepped closer, the sound rapidly intensified until a drone hovered down into view a few feet outside the window.

Brayden hissed, "We gotta move!"

As he barked the command and they lunged toward the hallway, the floating device launched a small grenade through the window. Brayden felt the rush of heat behind him as a small explosion knocked them forward. Snow whimpered but labored onward. Mickey grabbed the key to the Mazda, and Brayden shoveled whatever weaponry they had left on the counter into a small duffel. They darted out the door just as a second grenade blasted through the large living room window and detonated beside the fireplace, crumbling several bricks and igniting a small pile of wood beside it.

Brayden's foot hit the stone of the front steps, and Snow catapulted down them. Mickey's footsteps, however, did not follow. Brayden whipped his head around, and—inexplicably—he saw Mickey running back into the house.

"Mick!"

A few long moments passed as Brayden double-checked Snow was, in fact, outside with him. Did Mickey think the husky was still trapped in there? What on earth could've sent him running back into the cabin?

Finally, he rumbled back through the door, holding the whiteboard they'd scribbled their investigative notes on. He tossed it to Brayden without breaking his stride toward the car.

"Can't let these fuckers know what we know," he snarled.

Catching the board, Brayden shook his head in a mixture of disbelief and respect before quickly ushering Snow into the back seat of the car and sliding the whiteboard beside him. He slammed the door shut and vaulted himself into the passenger's seat. Mickey already had the car in drive, and the inertial force tugged Brayden back before his door was even closed as the Mazda accelerated down the driveway.

Hopefully that drone struggles to track cars through trees, Brayden thought. Mickey pressed the accelerator firmly as the car sped dangerously through the wooded road.

"What's our play?" Brayden asked.

"Get away from that thing." Mickey gestured behind him with his thumb, but his eyes remained locked on the road. "You're kind of the plan guy, Cross."

Snow let out a small whine, as if to voice his agreement with the need for preparedness. Brayden looked out the window at the blur of trees whizzing by, thinking about what to do.

"We can't take this car too far. They can absolutely track it, especially if they get into the system back at the house. We gotta get somewhere off the grid, or at least somewhere that wouldn't be tied to us."

Mickey nodded. "I got a guy. Zeke. He was one of my high school buddies. We used to hack together in the early days. Haven't talked to him in a decade or so, but he's the type of guy that would be waiting for you the day you need his help."

Brayden looked at his old friend skeptically.

"I know what you're thinking—nothing that can be tied to us. I know, I know," Mickey reasoned, almost like he was talking himself into it too. "But I gotta assume they're mostly after you here, Cross. Besides, my ties to Zeke are paper thin. He's like me. Not much of a societal footprint."

Mickey was right. It was a pipe dream to think that they could go anywhere—short of camping in the mountains and cooking meals by campfire—that had no discernible connection to them. It was a risk, sure, but a small one relative to the alternatives.

"Where's he live?"

"Vermont, last I checked." Mickey tapped the heel of his palm on the steering wheel a few times, as if summoning good fortune. "Let's hope he hasn't moved."

Brayden's brain, on behalf of his body, dreaded the next part of the plan. But it was necessary.

"We need to ditch the car, and it can't be anywhere near Zeke's place."

They trekked through the wilderness of Vermont, greenery enveloping them and shielding them from the late afternoon sun. Fortunately, there was still no sign of pursuit from villains, robotic or otherwise. They had taken a detour about five miles shy of the Vermont border to leave the Mazda in New Hampshire. Whether it was Dawson's army or the owners of the safe house, someone—with a moderate amount of diligence—would find it cloaked within the forest.

By Mickey's estimate, it would be a twenty-mile journey by foot to Zeke's last known address. They still carried the secure mobile phones Lacy's driver had given them—another risk, but one they calculated to be worth it, after discussing it on the drive. A small town named Archwood was their general destination. Zeke lived about two miles from there, amid a large swath of forest that surrounded the town. Mickey had never been, nor had Brayden. He only had the information Zeke had given him years prior.

The hike was grueling. Even though it didn't quite have the urgency of their last scramble, its length was enough to drain them tenfold.

"We need supplies," Mickey gasped, wiping his brow. It seemed like he'd used half his energy reserve just to speak those words. "We can't keep pushing without rest. We can't afford mistakes out here, Cross."

Brayden agreed. They'd been steadfastly moving for several hours, and the sun had tucked beneath the horizon as night fell. Most of their small stash of rations had been exhausted. Having gone through two protein bars, a canteen of water, and one can of food for Snow, all that remained was a second canteen of water and a can of baked beans. And they had no receptacle in which to heat the beans. Snow was panting, and they were long overdue to pour him some water.

"You're right. Let's try to arrange some cover around here, and we'll sleep in shifts until the sun's back up."

They worked silently to create a makeshift shelter, gathering fallen branches and propping them against a large oak tree, forming a crude lean-to. The earthy scent of decaying leaves filled their nostrils as they collected armfuls of foliage to use as insulation against the cold ground.

Snow circled their campsite, his nose twitching as he took in the unfamiliar scents of their territory. Brayden poured some water into a small collapsible bowl. The husky lapped it up eagerly, his tongue making soft slapping sounds in the night's quiet.

"I'll take first watch," Brayden said, his voice barely above a whisper. He slouched at the base of a nearby tree, positioning himself to have a clear view of their surroundings.

Mickey nodded, fatigue etched across his features. He crawled into their makeshift shelter, rustling as he tried to find a comfortable position on the uneven ground. "Wake me in four hours," he mumbled, already half-asleep.

As Mickey's breathing deepened into the rhythm of sleep, Brayden allowed his mind to wander. The events of the past few days played through his thoughts like a surreal movie. Sarah's death, finding Joseph Blauss, talking to Sarah on EverChat, the discovery of the humanoids, the uncovering of pieces of Dawson's operation—it all seemed too fantastical to be real. Yet here he was, hiding in the woods like a fugitive, hunted by an army of artificial beings while he hunted those responsible for his greatest tragedy.

The urge to see Sarah's face gnawed at him like a stubborn pang of hunger. He pulled his phone from his pocket and stared at its blank screen, his thumb hovering over it. He wanted to start a chat with the fake Sarah in the worst way, just to see her face. But his thoughts quickly jumped to another concern—his children, who were here, in real life. He was overdue to check in with them.

Brayden glanced over at Mickey, who was now deep in slumber. It didn't take him long to pass out. He dialed Riley's number. It was late, but knowing his brother, he figured he'd still be up. Riley answered on the third ring, his voice a hushed whisper.

"Bray? Everything okay?"

"Yeah, yeah. Just checking on the kids," Brayden said, matching his brother's volume. "They asleep?"

"Yeah, for a few hours now. Mari's been asking when you're coming back. Charlie, he's ..." His voice trailed off.

"Charlie's what?"

Despite the silence, Brayden could practically hear his brother weighing his next words.

"Riley, what about Charlie?"

"He's struggling, Bray. Bad dreams, crying for Sarah." His words were a notch higher in volume and portrayed some urgency. "I ... I didn't know what else to do."

Brayden shook his head in disbelief. "Tell me you didn't."

"He needed to see her, Bray."

"I told you, Riley!" His whisper became more of a harsh rasp. He stood and paced away a few steps, trying to avoid waking Mickey. "After everything I told you, you're letting him talk to her on EverChat?"

"Brother, you don't understand—"

"I understand perfectly, Riley! I told you to keep my children off of that thing!" Brayden's free hand clenched into a fist, and he tried to keep his volume down. "How many times has he used it?"

"Three, maybe four chats. Look, you weren't here, and he was inconsolable. Devastated. Nothing was working, not even the therapist."

"It's been two days!" Brayden drew a deep breath, stifling his seething temper. "I trusted you with this, Riley. This one thing. EverChat could be related to whatever killed Sarah! And you and Ashley still can't pull yourselves out of this cult!"

"What was I supposed to do? Just let him suffer?" Now Riley was the one stifling his voice to prevent waking others. "Mari won't go near it. Says it isn't her mom. But Charlie ... it helps him, Bray. He stops crying; he goes to sleep."

The mention of Mari's resistance temporarily cut down Brayden's anger. *Smart girl*, he thought. But the image of Charlie talking to that ... simulation, that digital trap, that propaganda machine that had stolen fragments of Sarah's consciousness ...

"No more," said Brayden. "I don't care if he cries all night."

"Easy for you to say, from wherever the hell you are. You're not the one holding him through the sobs and cries for his mother."

Brayden pinched the bridge of his nose and scrunched his face. "And what happens when he finds out it's not actually her? When he realizes—"

"Realizes what, Bray? That his father abandoned him right after his mother was murdered? That he ..." Riley seemed to catch himself before saying anything he'd regret. "Look, I know you have to do what you have to do. But these are your kids, man. They need something to hold on to."

The accusation stung. And it wasn't totally wrong. But Brayden couldn't fully explain that he was trying to save Charlie—and everyone else—from the possibility of something far worse than individual grief.

"No more. I appreciate everything you're doing, Riles, but no more."

A long sigh rippled through the other end of the phone call. "Fine. But when you get back, you're going to be the one to explain to your son why he can't talk to his mom anymore."

"I already explained that to him once, and I guess I'll have to do it again, thanks to your obsession with that app."

They were both silent for a few seconds.

"Whatever you're doing, be careful, Brayden. They need you to come home."

After ending the call, Brayden slumped back down against the tree and resumed his watch, his mind racing. Charlie was finding comfort in the very technology that may have been central to his mother's murder. The irony wasn't lost on Brayden. *Sarah would have appreciated the joke*, he thought. But every time he thought of Charlie talking to EverChat Sarah, he envisioned Dawson getting another piece of intel, another step toward whatever his plan was.

"Everything okay?" Mickey's voice startled him. He had propped himself up on an elbow and was peeking out from their makeshift shelter.

"Yeah," Brayden said. "Sorry for waking you. All good."

Just after Mickey dozed back off, a twig snapped somewhere in the darkness, and Brayden's body tensed. Snow's ears perked up, but the dog remained silent, sensing the need for stealth. After a few moments of held breath and strained ears, Brayden relaxed. *Probably just a deer or some other woodland creature*, he thought. He was on edge, after all.

As the hours crawled by, Brayden's thoughts made another leap to Zeke, Mickey's alleged old hacker buddy. Would he still be at his last known location? If he was, would he even be willing to help them? And most importantly, could they trust him? In the last few days, trust had become a rare and precious commodity.

The moon was high in the sky, casting gentle shadows through the trees, when Brayden finally roused Mickey for his shift. As they exchanged places, he glimpsed uneasiness in Mickey's eyes. It might have been the exhaustion and the inadequate rest provided by a few hours on the rocky ground. It also might have been the cumulative toll this ordeal was taking on him.

Lying down in the shelter, Brayden closed his eyes. Tomorrow, they would reach Zeke's place and hopefully find some answers. But for now, in the quiet of the Vermont forest, he allowed exhaustion to claim him, slipping into a fitful sleep littered with dreams of Sarah and an army of murderous humanoids.

20

THIRTY YEARS AGO

Vince Dawson stood by the window and watched traffic slowly inch its way into the distance. Rain spattered against the exterior of the window as he leaned his knee against the radiator below its interior. Behind him, in a bare-bones hospital bed, his mother's breathing machine hissed rhythmically.

"Vinny?" Martha's voice was a weak whisper, barely audible above the equipment.

He forced a smile and turned away from the rainy Boston evening below to face his mother. "I'm here, Mom."

It looked like she wanted to say something more, but she may not have had the strength to do so. She patted the edge of the bed with trembling fingers, suggesting he sit beside her. Vince obliged, taking her hand in his. Her skin was cold, wrinkled, and felt delicately fragile, like tissue paper.

"The doctors called while you were gone," she said.

"I know," Vince nodded. His throat tightened. He wanted to avoid the conversation, the inevitable acceptance of reality.

"Don't be angry, my sweet Vinny." Her eyes searched his face, the way a child who can't yet speak might bask in the wonder of an unfamiliar spectacle. In Martha's case, it was the comfortable familiarity of her only son. "Everything has its time."

Vince shook his head as a tear welled up in each eye. "Not if I can help it," he said. The words came out harsher than he intended, but he continued. "The human mind is just electrical impulses, Mom. Consciousness, it's just data. Data can be preserved, it can be transferred, it can—"

His mother's laugh cut him off mid-rant, and he stared at her in disbelief. "Vinny, you were always the scientist. You're going to achieve great things. But some things aren't meant to be preserved." She squeezed his hand with surprising strength, strength she hadn't shown in recent days as her illness spread. "That's what makes those things precious."

One of the biggest reasons Vince had come to Boston and joined the community where science and research and healthcare had intersected in a spectacular hub was to save his mother. She'd been diagnosed with terminal cancer a few years prior, and she and Vince were all that each other had. He was an only child; his father was absent, and his mother had no siblings. Now, in adulthood, he was a lonely man. Martha was his best friend. It was mother and son, through and through. He had worked late night after late night in the laboratories at every top university in town, grinding away at his discoveries and research about the brain and human consciousness. Vince was ahead of his time. He knew that much. He longed for a time machine, wished his mother were going through this at a different intersection of time and science, in a different timeline. Vince had watched others in the scientific community work tirelessly to cure some of the most awful diseases, some of the smartest and most dedicated minds backed by bottomless budgets. And it was never enough.

He decided it wasn't about curing diseases. Vince wanted to preserve what mattered. Why should failing components in the physical world—human bodies coming up short against Father Time, time and time again—be something we just accept? He likened it to a computer needing to be replaced. We have ways to back up your data, get a new computer, put your data all back in place. Sure, it's a new computer. But all the stuff that matters is still the old stuff. It doesn't die with the malfunctioning of something imperfectly vulnerable in the physical world. Why hadn't we figured out how to do the same with our minds? With our personalities, our thoughts? Are those not the very things that separate us from every other species on the planet? Our minds are, far and away, the thing that distinguishes us most powerfully from other life in this world. Why are we trying so hard to prevent the screen from cracking when we could just invent a way to preserve all the important stuff forever?

Vince looked down at his and his mother's intertwined fingers.

"I can fix this," he whispered. "I just need more time. My research is so promising, Mom. I need you to hold on. I might even start testing—"

"Vincent." She spoke his full name with an authority only a mother could conjure. "You can't engineer away death. You're brilliant, my boy. Truly, you are. But your brilliance is best aimed at other goals. Everyone's time arrives, and I've lived a long and excellent life."

He felt a surge of frustration. Why couldn't she understand him? Why couldn't *anyone* understand him? He shook his head more forcefully.

"That's what they want you to believe, Mom. That death is inevitable. Let's all just accept it. What if we don't have to do that? Why won't anyone consider that?"

"Oh, Vinny." Martha's eyes softened, showing a sprinkle of sympathy that actually made Vince feel more patronized than heard. "Always fighting against the current."

Before Vince could respond, the soft knock on the door from a nurse preceded her entrance to the room. She held a clipboard and checked the various machines surrounding Martha, jotting notes with a practiced efficiency. Her beeper let out a small chirp, and she glanced at it before adjusting one of the IV drips connected to her patient.

"Everything looks stable at the moment, Mrs. Dawson. The doctor will stop by in the morning with another progress report."

Martha nodded and gently smiled as the nurse left for the evening. As soon as the door had closed, she returned her gaze to her son.

"Remember that project you did in third grade? With the ant farm?"

Surprised by the left turn in the conversation, Vince nodded.

"You were devastated when those ants died. You had concocted all these ways to craft them a better habitat. All these ways to make them live longer. Mrs. Mills even said you were probably the first and only third grader to ask if they sold respirators for ants."

She laughed, which led to a cough. Vince couldn't help himself from laughing alongside her.

"I forgot about that."

"You've wanted to save every living thing since you were old enough to know what life was," she said. "But I'll say it again, Vinny. Some things are best left up to nature. Some things are destined to be let go."

"I can't let you go," he blurted out instinctively. The lighthearted moment had passed, and he was taken again by fervor.

Her fingers tightened around his once again. She stared at the rain-soaked window, every few moments its streaks of water illuminating from distant headlights. "You know what I think about sometimes?"

Vince looked on, waiting for her elaboration.

"That summer at Lake Champlain. You must have been eight or nine. It was a little before the ant farm fiasco. You spent the entire week building that raft, do you remember?"

"Ha," he said. "Don't remind me, Mom. It sank as soon as I hopped aboard."

Martha held up her hand, extending her index finger. It curled weakly, taking on more of a hooked shape as she extended it. "But you kept rebuilding it. Every day, over and over. By the end of the week—literally in the last hour before we checked out of the cottage—you were sailing across that lake like a seasoned captain. Well, from one side of the dock to the other, anyway."

Her laugh brought on another fit of coughs, and a few more tears welled beneath Vince's eyelids.

"You've always had that persistence. Promise me something, Vinny," she said, brushing her thumb over his knuckles. "Promise me you'll put that brilliant mind of yours to good use, to build something that brings people *joy*, Vinny. Not just to fight against the bad stuff, to fight against loss. Loss is just a vehicle of freedom, Vinny. Don't forget to cherish the good stuff while we have it. You can make a lot of people happy someday."

Vince nodded as a tear rolled down his cheek. He didn't trust himself to speak in reply to his mother's request for that promise. The machines in the room beeped steadily in the background. On the small television in the corner, a muted CNN broadcast scrolled headlines with fears about the approach of the new millennium, about digital preparedness, about the world changing faster than its people could.

They're focusing on all the wrong things, he thought.

"Seriously, though. I've been working on something that I think can be big. About consciousness. About how our minds work."

He could tell his mother was tired, and that it wasn't her first rodeo with her son's stubbornness. But she smiled weakly and asked him to tell her all about it.

And so he did. He explained his research in terms she could understand, as best he could. He tried to simplify explanations of neural networks and information theory and quantum cryptography, and how the essence of a person might someday be captured like a photograph captures light, like a microphone captures sound. As he spoke, her eyes grew heavier. But her smile never faded.

"What if memories aren't just stored in our brains like files on a computer?" he said. "What if they're actually a series of patterns, networks, almost infinitely complex, that could exist independently of our bodies if handled properly?"

"Like our spirit," Martha said.

"No, more scientific. Not mystical, not abstract. Scientific. Quantifiable. Tangible." His eyes filled with passion as he excitedly spilled his ideas. "What if, someday, we could preserve all that? What if death wasn't the end of everything for us? What if we weren't capped by the frail limitations of our bodies?"

His mother's monitor beeped a little faster. "That ... that sounds wonderful, Vinny, really," she whispered. "Just ... Just don't forget ... the value of ... the beauty of ..."

Her words had slurred and drifted off toward the end, and before

Vince could process what was happening, a chill had washed over him, and the monitor's steady rhythm had gone awry. Nurses rushed in. He heard his own voice like it was miles from his own ears, shouting *Mom!* over and over. The monitor flatlined, and he sat frozen, crying, her hand in his. The clock on the wall droned onward with one click after the next.

"You're wrong, Mom," he whispered to himself.

21

The pale light of dawn filtered through the trees, nudging Brayden free from his nap. He blinked away the remnants of unsettling dreams, his body aching from the brutal sleeping surface. Mickey was already up, packing the few supplies they had.

"Morning," Mickey said. "I've been thinking."

Brayden sat up, stretching his muscles. "Yeah?"

"We need intel. And supplies. We're screwed if Zeke isn't here. I think we should split up."

He was surprised by the suggestion. It was risky, but Mickey generally had good reasoning. "What's your thought?"

"Snow and I will continue to Zeke's, or at least where I'm hoping Zeke is. You should head into Archwood, see if you can pick up on anything. And grab some provisions. Look for an inn or motel, in case we don't find Zeke."

The idea of separating didn't sit well with Brayden, but the logic was sound. They needed information and supplies, and if the push toward Zeke was a dead end, they'd both be weary and two miles from Archwood. Plus, the thought of a hot cup of coffee and a chance to blend in with normal people for ten minutes was tempting, Brayden had to admit.

"All right," Brayden reluctantly agreed. "I'll head toward Archwood.

Small detour. Give me Zeke's address, and I'll head there as soon as I'm done scoping out the town."

Mickey chuckled and corrected him; all he had was coordinates, not an actual address. With an affirming nod to each other, they parted ways—Mickey and Snow disappearing into the dense forest, while Brayden set off toward the small town of Archwood.

The trek took most of the morning, but Brayden finally found himself on the outskirts of the quaint Vermont village. He took a beat to dust off his jacket and smooth his hair to look as inconspicuous as possible. Surveying the main street, he first went to a rustic general store on the corner of an intersection to pick up a grocery bag's worth of rations, including canned food for both the humans and the dog. After collecting that, his eyes landed on a cozy-looking coffee shop set beneath a sign that read *The Roasted Pine*.

Taking a deep breath, he pushed open the door, the cheerful tinkle of a bell above the door announcing his arrival. The aroma of fresh coffee flooded his nostrils, and for a moment, he almost convinced his brain that he was just another traveler stopping for a quick fix of local caffeine. He ordered a black coffee and found a seat near the window. He sat with his back to the wall, his vigilant eyes given a full view of the shop. As he sipped the bitter brew—it was decent, but tasted like the world's best under the circumstances—his eyes jumped from patron to patron. There was an older couple sharing a pastry, a young businessman furiously typing on a laptop, a woman reading a book at a corner table.

It was the woman who caught Brayden's attention. Something about the way she held herself, the tilt of her head as she turned a page —it scratched an itch in his mind. He watched as she reached for her cup, her hands shaking slightly. Had he met her before? No, impossible. What were the odds he knew the first person who caught his eye at a completely random coffee shop in a town he'd never visited?

He continued watching her. The book she held in her hands had purple and black color on its cover, but he couldn't make out the title.

It appeared to be an emotional read, though—her eyes seemed watery as they cruised across each line.

Then it happened. It took only a split second, but he saw it. It was undeniable.

Brayden grabbed his coffee and moved to the table across from her. She didn't notice him. Other patrons might have thought it was a strange relocation, but he didn't care. His eyes remained locked on her, waiting for it to happen again.

And it happened again—the slightest quiver of her bottom lip.

A question blared in his inner monologue. *Am I going crazy?*

His heart pounding, he slid his napkin off the table intentionally, creating a reason to get up and move closer. As he bent down to retrieve the cloth, he faked imbalance and forced himself to stumble. He caught his fall on the chair opposite her, which slid on the floor and jarred her focus.

She looked up at him. Brayden could finally make out the novel she was reading—it was one by Nancy Amora, a wildly popular romance author. He'd never indulged, but he was glad to have recognized it.

He apologized for disrupting her. Then he gestured at the book. "Nancy Amora. One of my favorites."

The way her alert expression shifted to a gentle smile made Brayden's stomach turn. He sat in the chair; he found himself losing control of his own actions, his subconscious hijacking the steering wheel.

The woman shifted hesitantly in her seat, then realized she had to say something. "Yeah … yeah, her stories just really resonate with me." She held up the one she was holding. Its title was *All of Me*. "Have you read her new one?"

Continuing the lie would have been too risky, with no knowledge of the story. "Not yet. It's on my list," he said with a soft smile.

Her eyes crinkled in exactly the same way Sarah's did when she was holding back a laugh.

I'm crazy and sleep-deprived, right?

Just in case he *wasn't* going crazy, Brayden gathered his composure to keep conversing with the woman. He learned her name was Beth. He gestured at her drink, which looked like a caramel latte or something similar.

"I could never get the hang of those fancy drinks," he said. He carefully planned his next words. "My wife always teases … always *used to* tease me … for being a black coffee purist."

His ploy seemed to work, as Beth's expression turned somber. "I take it you and her aren't together, then?"

Brayden wanted to load his answer with sadness. He wanted to make Beth cry.

"She, um …" He rubbed his eyes and sniffled, feigning distress. "She was killed last week. It was unexpected."

He felt slimy for the lie he was about to add, but he needed to elicit sorrow in her.

"Our twin girls too."

Beth watched as Brayden began to tear up—he was impressed by his own ability to act this out—and then it came again.

Up close and personal, it gave him goosebumps. There was no mistaking that Beth's bottom lip quivered in the exact same way that Sarah's always did before getting upset.

And then, as quickly as it had come, it was gone. Her expression stalled and shifted. She stirred her coffee and looked back at Brayden again.

"Sometimes, simple is best," she said with a gentle smile. Brayden gave her an empty, confused look. She nodded her head at his cup. "Your coffee, taking it black."

It took most of his mental strength to prevent his jaw from dropping. Then it took even more to prevent him from tugging his hair from his scalp. He had seen this before. Beth, on the verge of overwhelming sadness—on the tipping point between watery eyes and streaming tears—reeled in her emotions like a horse being tugged to a sudden halt by its reins. In the blink of an eye, she became relatively cheerful.

Just like the EverChat version of Sarah.

Brayden's mind spun at warp speed, rifling through possibilities. Was this a cruel trick? Was he actually going crazy? It had been a while since his last good meal. Maybe that was it. He tried to steer his mind to a reasonable explanation. Did Sarah have a cousin he'd never known about? Maybe that could explain the mannerisms. No, of course not. This was obviously beyond the realm of reasonable explanations. *This was obviously a humanoid, right? It had to be,* he thought.

But there were problems with that rationale. If this were one of Dawson's evil humanoids, why wasn't she evil? What was Dawson's purpose for an innocent young humanoid woman reading a romance novel in The Roasted Pine?

The apparent decent nature of the humanoid was odd, but it wasn't alarming. What was alarming was the other half of Brayden's realization about this humanoid: it was resembling EverChat. That part felt surreal. Dawson's crown jewel app, the app Brayden despised so viscerally, was intertwined with whatever Circuit was doing with these human replicas.

That was a horrifying thought.

As emotions and realizations swirled through his head like a tornado, Brayden found his instincts grabbing the steering wheel again. He reached his hand out to take Beth's, as if to comfort her. "You remind me of her," he said.

With his other hand, he grasped the small knife in his jacket pocket and clicked it open. He swiftly brought it up and placed the blade into Beth's palm, using his other hand to cup hers around the knife. She momentarily hesitated as a slight panic settled into her eyes, but she remained still. A piece of Brayden felt sorry for her, in a way he couldn't process.

"I'm sorry," he said as he squeezed hard and pressed the knife into her palm. He could feel it penetrate the skin. It felt like the world around him downshifted into slow motion. Anguish filled Beth's face as she let out a cry. Satisfied with the wound, Brayden let go of the knife and used both of his hands to hold hers flat, spreading her palm skyward.

He waited, and it never came. Where rivulets of blood should have streamed from the slice, there was nothing. He spread her palm more, inducing another wince of pain. In the crevice between two flaps of skin, he saw the familiar circuitry of delicate robotic composition. It hadn't completely surprised him, but he stared at it anyway.

What he hadn't registered at first, however, was a stranger phenomenon. As his slow-motion universe geared back into standard pace, he saw chaos unfolding in the shop. A woman near the window had dropped a mug of coffee and was grasping her right hand in pain. The businessman on his laptop writhed and groaned, holding his right hand. A server had dropped a whole tray of muffins between the tables of two patrons and was now hunched over, holding his right palm as if stopping the flow of blood.

He looked up at Beth, who now mimicked all three of the others. She grasped her right hand, the one Brayden had just sliced.

What the hell?

Brayden couldn't fully process what was happening, but he was overcome with the immediate urge to leave. *Get out of here*, a voice somewhere in his head bellowed. Five minutes ago, The Roasted Pine was a brief respite amid an eternity of stress. Now, it felt like ground zero of a science fiction nightmare. Were they all humanoids? Were they all one mind?

He snatched his knife and folded it up, slipping it back into his pocket. He could feel the eyes of several customers follow him as he stood and rushed through the door, its bell jingling far more violently than when he had arrived.

They're connected? They share sensations?

Questions sparked across his synapses like a violent lightning storm.

They share thoughts? Are they a single mind?

He moved swiftly down the sidewalk, sweat beading above his brows and temples. He needed to get back to Mickey to debrief about this. Brayden clumsily withdrew his phone from his pocket to start the navigation to the coordinates he'd been given, but as he turned a street corner, he saw a familiar figure approaching from across the way. It was the businessman from the coffee shop, his gait menacing and hurried. He looked all around him as he paced, but he hadn't yet seen Brayden.

With a blast of adrenaline, Brayden darted ahead and ducked into an alley behind an antique shop. His heart pounded. As the man's heavy footfall got louder and louder, Brayden held his breath and waited.

Then the footsteps got quieter, and he heard a soft curse of frustration. Allowing his breath to gently resume, he waited until silence engulfed him before peering around the corner at the empty Archwood street.

22

As he weaved through several quiet alleys and residential streets, Brayden finally reached the edge of Archwood and the cover of the forest. He had taken such an indirect route through the town that the journey to Zeke's location—alleged to be two miles—had probably doubled. He slouched against a large pine tree and slid his back down it, scraping off some bark en route to taking a seat on a pillow of firm snow.

He needed a moment to gather his breath, marinate in the implications of what he just witnessed, and fire up the coordinates Mickey had given him. *They're a hive mind?* He couldn't rationalize it, but he didn't have time to stop and analyze yet. It wasn't safe, staying so close to a town that was apparently swimming with humanoids.

Brayden trekked his way through the forest as the sun scattered its rays through the barren branches above. He surmised it may have been an hour later when the property came into view. It was a mid-sized log cabin, with a large collection of firewood in a storage area beside its front door. Carefully trudging the final fifty yards to the house, he approached.

The place seemed deserted. No lights shone through the windows, and the landscape showed signs of neglect. What he assumed were

Mickey's footprints alongside Snow's were visible in a collection leading to the front door.

"Mickey?" Brayden called out softly. No reply.

He cautiously circled the cabin, checking all its windows and looking for signs of life, of struggle … of anything. Nothing seemed disturbed, but it certainly seemed empty. As he rounded the back corner, a small patio had a covered grill, a tiny shed, and a discreet fire that was still burning in a fire pit. Brayden was ashamed he hadn't noticed the smoke on his approach. Against the backdrop of the darkened wood of the home, a small piece of white caught Brayden's eye. A piece of paper had been wedged into the frame of the back door. He tugged it free and unfolded it.

In Mickey's messy penmanship, a new set of coordinates was scrawled on the sheet. Below the coordinates, a complementary message read: *Burn after reading*.

Brayden shook his head in bewilderment, then punched the new coordinates into his phone. He took a few extra minutes to memorize them, just in case. Crumpling up the note and tossing it into the small blaze, he set on his way again. The new location was another two miles into the hills.

The coordinates led to a less homey establishment. It looked like an abandoned barn, its weathered boards creaking in the wind at this higher elevation. From the outside, the roof appeared to be in rough shape. Stepping toward the entrance, he reached for the door. Before he could enter, Snow's barking confirmed he was in the right place.

"In here," he heard Mickey announce.

Stepping into the barn, Brayden saw that the roof was as bad as it looked. Streaks of sunlight leaked through it, illuminating the dusty floor of the mostly empty barn. Hay bales were strewn about the back corners, and peanut shells were scattered beneath his feet. Mickey was accompanied by another man, presumably Zeke. He was hunched over a workbench near the back of the barn. He appeared older than Brayden expected, probably in his fifties, with graying hair pulled back in a ponytail. Various pieces of communications equipment were scattered across the bench.

"You made it," Mickey said as he looked up from their work. "We were getting worried. This is Zeke."

Zeke nodded but didn't offer his hand or even look at his guest. "Mick tells me you boys are in some deep trouble."

"That's putting it mildly." Moving a step closer, Brayden discerned that the equipment on the workbench appeared to be mostly composed of satellite phones. He gestured at them. "Those secure?"

"As secure as they get," Zeke confirmed. "Better than what you've got, anyway. Speaking of which ..."

Zeke looked up at Mickey, and Mickey held out his hand to Brayden.

"Phone. I know we just got 'em, but they're compromised. No doubt about it."

Brayden shot him a disappointed look. "Is that why you're in this abandoned barn instead of Zeke's house?"

Mickey nodded, and Brayden handed him the phone. "Not ten minutes after I got there, another one of those flying drone doohickeys was hovering outside Zeke's window."

He dropped Brayden's phone into a bucket of water in which his own phone had already been drowned. Then he pointed at another table across the room, which Brayden had somehow overlooked on his way in. Upon it sat some kind of heavy-duty weaponry. It looked like a grenade launcher.

"Fortunately, Z is well prepared."

"Jeesh," Brayden said.

"That ain't all. After we took down the drone, another one showed up ... of the humanoid variety. Just like our friend back at the safe house."

Mickey gestured at Zeke with a hint of admiration. Zeke nodded as if to confirm the accuracy of his friend's account.

"I can tell you that Zeke's weaponry works as advertised."

"You blew it up?" Brayden asked, glancing again at the grenade launcher. "And it ... did it ... die?" He didn't exactly know what *death* really meant for those things.

Mickey gave a small nod and walked over to the corner of the barn, where a tarp served as a makeshift curtain to conceal the area. Pulling it back, he revealed a mutilated humanoid corpse strewn across a collection of hay bales, its synthetic flesh torn apart. It looked like the blast had nearly split the humanoid in two. Intricate circuitry and components spilled out along the wound lines. Its face was too heavily mangled to resemble anyone; that made it easier to remember it was just machinery.

"Figured we ought to hold on to these scraps, maybe learn something from 'em. But honestly, Cross, this tech is way beyond anything I've seen before. I'm more of a software kind of guy, and this takes hardware to another level."

Brayden looked on in amazement. He didn't have words that felt valuable enough to add.

"New phone," Mickey said, handing Brayden one phone from the workbench. "Should be secure. All Zeke's stuff is. Hopefully they won't be able to track us here as easily."

"Good," Brayden said, accepting the device. "Let me know when you're sittin' down, and I'll tell you about my morning."

After inquisitive looks from both Mickey and Zeke, Brayden dove into the story of his morning. He detailed the encounter with Beth in the coffee shop, the resemblance her mannerisms bore to Sarah's, and —most chillingly—the hive mind reaction of the other patrons.

"Shared consciousness," Zeke said. "Damn. I figured that was only the stuff of sci-fi movies."

"As soon as I saw her lip trembling, my mind was haywire. For the next hour, really. But now that I've got my bearings again, well ... it got me thinking," Brayden explained. "The humanoids were sharing consciousness with each other, yes. But the woman there, Beth—she got that lip quiver from Sarah. Full stop."

Mickey's brow scrunched as he tried to make sense of it. "I mean, I guess we knew Dawson had robotics stuff going on alongside EverChat, but you think he's actually integrating the two? You think this humanoid was somehow connected to Sarah's mind, and showing her mannerisms?"

Brayden felt that was obvious, but Mickey looked skeptical.

"Without a doubt. Maybe it's a crazy coincidence, or maybe there's some inexplicable way she was connected to Beth based on my proximity. I don't know."

Brayden pondered for a moment before continuing. "But it's not just that. The lip quiver is just the indicator of emotion. It always preceded crying for Sarah. But when I talked to Sarah on EverChat, she immediately snapped out of it when she was on the verge of tears. Beth did the same exact thing. It's like they're hitting some barricade in the software running their mind. EverChat and these robots are running the same mind software. And it doesn't let them experience intense emotion."

He scratched his head, furthering his brainstorm.

"But the emotional regulation isn't the main point here. Not yet. What I've been thinking is—if these humanoids share consciousness, and they're getting traits that I know come from Sarah …"

Mickey picked up what Brayden was laying down. "Maybe Sarah …"

"Maybe Sarah can help us," Brayden said.

"You wanna try to get information on the humanoids through her? You think she would even have the free will in there? To, like …" Mickey struggled to even get his point across. "To, I dunno, talk to the others? Or influence them?"

Zeke seemed content to observe the deliberation between his two unexpected visitors. Brayden rubbed his hand on his chin.

"I don't really know either. But maybe if I can break through her facade, even just a small breakthrough, I can get her to access some information that gets us closer to Dawson. Or at least closer to knowing his plan."

Just saying Dawson's name reminded Brayden of how fiercely he wanted to exact revenge.

Mickey and Zeke finished their in-progress work on the secure phones, then configured a secure satellite feed to be used by one of Zeke's laptops.

"Here you go, Bray. Her contact is loaded into EverChat," Mickey said. "The device is secure on our end; Zeke's sure of it. But beware of any info you give them. Remember, you're talking to Dawson too."

Mickey handed him the laptop and gestured back toward the mutilated robot.

"We'll be inspecting the freakazoid's inner circuitry; see if we can figure anything out."

Brayden nodded and patted Mickey on the shoulder. "Thanks, pal. I'll be over after I'm done with this."

He flipped open the laptop and launched EverChat. Sarah's profile was cued up and ready to be dialed. Brayden was overwhelmed with chilling nerves again. His hand trembled as he clicked to start the call.

"Connecting," the creepy AI woman announced.

The video frame popped open, and there she was. Sarah's eyes lit up, her smile shining. So eerily natural.

"Bray! I've been waiting for your call. I'm so happy to see you!"

He swallowed hard. *It's a software product,* he told himself. *She's not your wife. Your wife got murdered, and you're using this software to help find her killers.*

"Sarah, baby, hi. I've missed you so much. Look, I need to talk to you about something."

He paused a moment to gauge her reaction. She seemed to sense his tone; her cheery persona dampened slightly, and she seemed intent on hearing what he had to say.

"I've been up to quite a bit since we last talked, and I'm following through on my promise. I'm trying to find the people who murdered you."

Brayden watched her intently. Her expression turned somber. She frowned and gently sighed. "I ..."

How does a piece of software become speechless?

"Sarah, do you ... do you feel connected to other minds?"

She pondered the question for a moment, then a small smile emerged. "Like you and the kids? Bray, I feel such a deep—"

"No, no," Brayden interjected. "No, Sarah ... I mean other minds on EverChat. Can you access the minds of other EverChat users? Are they ... around you? Do you feel them?"

Sarah said nothing. Her face portrayed confusion.

"Today I met someone who reminded me of you. She was reading a book in a coffee shop, and I told her about your murder. She reacted exactly like you do. Her sadness manifested exactly like your sadness. It was a spitting image of you."

Brayden opted to skip the part where he sliced the woman's hand open with a switchblade.

"Sarah, I noticed that when this woman felt pain, others felt pain too. Does that mean anything to you?" Brayden analyzed her every expression. He could see gears turning, but he had no idea if they were the right gears. "Do you remember a sharp pain in the palm of your hand, maybe?"

Brayden felt a vibe shift in her reaction. He sensed her communications were becoming more measured, more delicately chosen. The gears were turning, all right.

"They're ..." Sarah's expression flickered, but she pushed onward. When she resumed, she spoke in a whisper. "They're listening. I can't—"

Her eyebrows had angled downward, the way they did when she was distraught, but only for a moment. The next moment, they leveled along with her mood.

"You know, I'm not sure what you mean, Bray." She softly smiled. "But tell me about your day! Where are you? Is that a farm or something?"

Shut the laptop. That's enough for now.

His inner monologue told him to pull the plug on this conversation, but he was powerless against his compulsion to say goodbye first.

"I gotta go. I'll talk to you soon. If you can get more information about what this is, if you can communicate with the others ..." Brayden sighed. "Never mind. I love you, Sarah."

Just like last call, Sarah's parting smile and the look in her eyes gave Brayden—perhaps without merit—the tiniest sliver of doubt about whether that was merely a simulation in there. Was it really her?

He ended the call. On one hand, his heart was heavy again, having seen Sarah hit the emotional barrier coded into EverChat for a second time.

On the other hand, his adrenaline was pumping again. *They're listening*, she said.

"Good news and bad news," Brayden said as he turned the corner of the barn to meet Mickey and Zeke. "Good news is that I think we're on to something. Sarah's connected to the hive mind. I think she tried to access it when I explained what happened today. But she hit the barrier again."

Mickey and Zeke appeared interested by the update, but they also seemed to brace for the forthcoming bad news.

"Bad news is that I can't promise you Dawson ain't listening to every one of those conversations, secure line or not. Just before the software regulated her emotion, she said *they're listening*."

"Damn," Zeke chimed in. "Well, you don't have to worry about location tracking. I can tell you for certain they aren't tracking anything via that network address. But that doesn't mean he ain't gathering other intel off you from those chats."

Mickey scratched the side of his face. "Well, at least your camera only told them we're in the most nondescript barn in America. Good luck, Dawson."

Brayden nodded, and Zeke smirked. Then he patted Mickey on the shoulder. "Gotta take a leak. I'll be back."

He trudged out of the barn, leaving Brayden and Mickey alone again. Brayden noticed a tension in Mickey's shoulders that he hadn't noticed earlier, when recounting his findings from the conversation with Sarah.

"You good, Mick?"

He glanced up, his eyes momentarily distant. Then he snapped back into focus. "Yeah. Yeah, just … thinking."

Brayden sat on a hay bale beside him and smiled. "I know that look, my friend. What's up?"

After a long silence and a sigh, Mickey explained. "Remember when I left the agency?"

Mickey and Brayden had never actually talked about what Mickey did. Brayden never learned his motivations, the details, anything about the decision. He had let bygones be bygones, after all this time. But now Mickey had piqued his interest. He raised his eyebrows and showed with his eyes that he understood.

"Everyone thought I was crazy. Look at the nutty whistleblower, throwing away his career. I keep thinking about what we were building back in those days."

Brayden remembered the chaos at the agency in the aftermath of Mickey's explosive departure. The classified documents he had leaked to the press, the congressional hearings that ensued, the public outrage directed at the government. Mickey had something of a cult internet following for a while. Brayden had always been conflicted between his loyalty—to the agency and his country—and his respect for the courage his friend had, to stand behind his own moral compass.

"The surveillance systems. The algorithms. That damn Mockingbird Project. It could listen to pretty much any device, track anyone who stayed on the grid."

Brayden waited for him to continue, but he seemed lost in his own thoughts. "You did what you thought was right," he eventually said.

"See, that's the thing, Bray. For years, I thought what we were doing *was* right. 'Keep America safe,' they always said. You remember? But there was a meeting just before I blew it all up. It really opened my eyes. Like a light bulb flipped on."

Brayden waited as Mickey stared across the barn blankly, evidently rehashing a memory that disturbed him.

"Deputy Director Hawkins was outlining the next phase of Mockingbird. They wanted to expand beyond its original scope, beyond the terrorists and major threats. Start monitoring political activists, journalists, anyone their algorithms considered a threat to radicalize. And the bar was low, man. They just wanted to monitor everyone."

He looked at the ground and scratched the back of his head. It looked like he was in despair, reliving the moments.

"And everyone just nodded and smiled. Myself included, at first. Took me three days to realize what I had agreed to. It wasn't about keeping America safe anymore. It was about keeping everyone in check. My stomach turned when I thought about the potential repercussions."

Brayden hadn't heard the details before, but he had often wondered about them. He had wondered what pushed Mickey over the edge. The stuff he revealed was certainly damning, but wasn't a lot of the classified stuff in this country? You don't need to see how the sausage is made, some of his colleagues used to say. If we're safe and healthy and prosperous, all is well.

"I couldn't sleep for a week after I uploaded those files. Partly because I was sleeping on the ground in the woods, I guess. But mostly because I kept asking myself if I had done the right thing. Or if I had actually just made it all worse. If people would die because of what I'd done."

"Mickey, you—"

"And now I know," he continued, disregarding Brayden's condolence. "I didn't go far enough. This … this is what happens when we let technology run rampant without guardrails. When we convince ourselves that invasion of privacy is a worthwhile price for technological advancement."

He gazed at the humanoid strewn across the hay bale and shook his head. There was a raw honesty in Mickey's words that brought Brayden into an epiphany—Mickey wasn't just helping him because of their friendship, or because of Sarah. He thought back to how hesitant Mickey was to investigate the vague list of names scribbled on a piece of paper the day Brayden showed up at his cabin. Sure, by now, he was invested in helping Brayden, avenging Sarah, and perhaps saving the world from whatever this was. But on top of all that, it now felt like Mickey was in this for personal redemption, on some level.

Snow trotted over and pushed his nose against the back of Mickey's hand, which dangled off of his thigh. He scratched the husky's head, a small smile emerging.

"We're gonna stop Dawson," Brayden said.

"We better. Whatever he's planning is a lot bigger than Mockingbird, from the looks of it."

Brayden agreed. He realized they hadn't debriefed on their investigation into the humanoid corpse yet. "By the way, any notable discoveries on that freakazoid?"

Mickey sighed, and Zeke reentered the room right on cue to answer for him. "Gotta be honest. It's a little outside our wheelhouse."

"It's like nothing I've ever seen before, but I know some of this stuff has been developing over the years," Mickey added. "Wonder if Lacy has any robotics experts on staff."

Brayden thought for a moment, then chuckled preemptively at the lunacy of his next suggestion. "I think I know someone who can help us out."

23

TEN YEARS AGO

The soft murmur of cultured voices filled the sterile white space of the gallery. Ellen stood before an abstract canvas, pretending to understand the storm of colors that banded together to assault her vision. The chardonnay in her hand—her third glass of the evening—did little to ease her social anxiety in this environment. This wasn't her vibe.

Art galleries had never been her scene. Yet failed fling after failed fling had resulted in a loneliness that forced her to branch out. She had accepted the invitation of an acquaintance that she hoped would be different from all the others. But alas, before her third glass was drained, he had already abandoned her to network with New York's elite. *They're all the same,* she thought.

She moved to another piece, this one a bizarre sculpture that resembled something along the spectrum between a human and a demon you might find in a dystopian fantasy series. The sculpture seemed to emit a hum of some sort. The placard beside it read "Resonance No. 3" by an artist whose name she didn't even try to pronounce in her head, let alone aloud. As she leaned a little closer to inspect the creature's face, a voice broke her concentration.

"Beautiful piece, isn't it?"

Ellen turned to find a tall, distinguished man in a tailored suit studying her with keen interest. He appeared to be roughly her age, but she got the sense he may have been older than the polished look he impressively maintained. His aura commanded attention, but something in his eyes eased her, unlike anything else had been able to during this event. There was a warmth that felt genuine in a room littered with artificial pleasantries.

"I was just trying to figure out what makes it tick," she lied. "There's something about it that feels ... I dunno, *alive*."

The man smiled. "You're absolutely right. Art should feel alive, don't you think?"

She tilted her head as if to consider the suggestion, then smiled and nodded. He held out his hand.

"Vince. You can call me Vinny."

His grip was firm but gentle. Ellen found herself drawn magnetically into conversation with him. It felt like everyone else in this room spoke in rehearsed critiques and superficial, fancy-sounding observations. Vinny spoke with passion about the surrounding artwork. Even if Ellen couldn't conjure up the same passion, seeing it authentically exhibited was a breath of fresh air.

Vinny guided her through the gallery, explaining the subtle nuances of each installation with the expertise of someone deeply familiar with them. It was like he created the art himself.

"This one's my favorite," he said, leading her to a large feature that dominated an entire wall of the room. It looked like a massive, glowing network made of light and shadow. The canvas pulsed like a holographic display in a futuristic movie. "It responds to our presence. Watch this."

He took her hand and held it near the artwork's surface, easing it closer and closer. As their hands approached, the patterns shifted, creating new configurations that centered on her fingertips. Ellen was impressed by art for the first time.

"Try it yourself."

She hesitated, then took her hand and chose another spot on the wall. As soon as her touch was within an inch of the display, the patterns transformed again, creating a dance of light that reflected in her eyes, again orienting around her own fingers. She wasn't sure if the tingle she felt in her fingertips was real or imagined. Ever the art skeptic, she chalked it up to the chardonnay. Still, she wanted to feign interest, to keep Vinny engaged.

"Extraordinary," she whispered.

"Would you like to see more? I have some experimental pieces in the private gallery upstairs."

Private gallery upstairs? Ellen tried to decipher whether this was a cheap pickup ploy or a legitimate offer. She knew she should probably decline, having only met this man a few minutes ago. But something about him captivated her. Made her feel safe. Maybe it was the way he actually listened when she spoke, or how his enthusiasm seemed to chase away the loneliness usually surrounding her.

"Fancy," she said in a flirty tone, implying acceptance of the offer.

The private gallery took Ellen's breath away. Unlike the cold and clean white walls of the gallery's main level, this space felt intimate. Its warm lighting and dark wood panels portrayed the essence of vintage high society. The setting made each piece feel like it existed in its own universe, somehow all packed into the same room. They moved throughout the room, Vinny guiding her with a hand to the small of her back. She felt a warmth that definitely wasn't the chardonnay this time.

"This one," he said, stopping before a mirror that seemed to ripple like a pond in rainfall. "This one responds to emotion."

When Ellen gazed into it, her reflection softly smiled back at her with an expression that inexplicably felt more honest than her own. Her jaw dropped, and she turned to Vinny. "How the …"

"Beautiful, wouldn't you say?"

She wasn't certain whether he was referring to the art piece or her reflection, but the way he looked at her implied the latter. Her cheeks flushed, and across from her, her reflection's cheeks flushed an even deeper shade of red.

They moved on to the next piece, one that somehow emitted harmonies that matched the approaching footsteps. As fascinating as that was, Ellen was distracted by a large abstract canvas, about the size of a movie poster, on the far wall. The musical piece's harmonies faded as she strutted over to the canvas. Its swirling streams of deep blues and violent reds were stationary, more of the ilk of a traditional painting. But despite its static nature, the colors seemed to create illusions for her of faces that came and went, emerging from the chaos, then receding into the background.

"Ah," Vinny said, noting her unexpected fascination. "Another one of my favorites. I call it 'Neural Waterfall.' Something about it speaks to you, I take it?"

Ellen was surprised to find that she didn't have immediate words, and she couldn't quite look away. "It's like it's trying to tell me something." She reached her hand out, expecting perhaps to see it react like the hologram downstairs had. It didn't visually react, but she could feel something she couldn't explain.

"Perhaps it is trying to tell you something," Vinny said after a soft chuckle. He moved closer to her. His presence, combined with the effect of this piece, was intoxicating. Ellen leaned back slightly, allowing her shoulder to rest against his chest. Vinny continued in a low, smooth tone. "Art really should be more than just something we look at, something we observe. It should observe us back. Connect with us. Become a part of us."

Who is this man? Ellen thought to herself. She was taken aback by how strongly his words had resonated with her, and how profoundly this piece was affecting a previously self-proclaimed art skeptic. When she turned to face him, she found his eyes filled with an intensity that somehow thrilled and unnerved her at the same time.

"This piece," Vinny said, "I've been looking for the right home for it. Somewhere it will be truly appreciated." His hand brushed against hers, his thumb caressing the grooves of her knuckles. "Someone who will understand its significance."

Ellen looked at him expectantly. "You mean ...?"

Vinny nodded.

"No, no, Vinny—this must be worth thousands, I can't—"

"I insist. It will be yours." He paused and stared into her eyes. "I'll deliver it before dinner tomorrow night?"

The rest of the evening passed in a blur. None of the other pieces captivated her like "Neural Waterfall" had, but that didn't stop their hands and bodies from finding excuses to gently cozy up against one another. By the time he gave her a delicate peck on the cheek in parting, she was already dreaming of seeing him again. And perhaps seeing more of his mysterious art collection too.

24

EIGHTEEN MONTHS AGO

Riley Cross stood near his father's casket, accepting condolences from what felt like an endless line of mourners at the funeral home. Each exchange went the same—a solemn nod with pursed lips, a firm handshake or a gentle hug, and bland words of comfort that all blended together in his grief-ridden mind.

He glanced beside him at the space where his brother, Brayden, should have been standing. He had ducked out a little early, citing the kids' bedtime as the reason. Riley understood but still didn't like it. The days of Brayden being absent were supposed to have ended long ago when he left the agency. Riley was left to shoulder the weight of this circumstance alone.

"He looks peaceful, at least," one well-wisher said. Riley nodded instinctively but groaned inside. He'd lost track of how many others had said the same sentence. It was true, after all—his dad looked peaceful, lying neatly in his favorite dark suit, hands folded across his chest. The morticians had certainly earned their keep, the way they'd masked the toll that ALS had taken on his body over the past two years.

After several more redundant pleasantries, Riley was grateful to see the crowd thinning out. When it became safe to assume that everyone seeking an interaction had been seen, he began gravitating toward the exit. After several hours, the air within the walls of the funeral home had grown thick and stuffy. The evening air outside, albeit midsummer air, was a cool refresher on his face. He loosened his tie and exhaled deeply as he paced to his car, then drove home.

When Riley pulled up outside his house, a man in a black Mercedes was stepping out of his car and beginning to walk toward him. The car was parked beside the curb, a few yards around the bend of the cul-de-sac.

"Mr. Cross?"

The man was dressed sharply in an olive suit, approaching him with a messenger bag. Riley closed his own car door and looked on as he drew nearer, walking up the driveway. The man was younger than he initially appeared; early thirties, he figured. His shiny gold tie clip reflected the light pouring down from the nearby streetlight.

"Can I help you?"

"I'm Elias Veum, from Circuit Corporation." The man extended his hand. "I'm very sorry for your loss."

Riley returned his handshake but stared skeptically at the man. "Thank you, but I think you—"

"I know, I know. This isn't the best time. But it's folks like you that I love talking to about this," Elias said. "May I?"

The man's tone of voice came across as that of a practiced salesman. Riley was ready to tell him he wasn't interested when Elias reached into his suit jacket and withdrew a business card, holding it between his index and middle fingers. He offered it to Riley.

"We're on the verge of something extraordinary at Circuit. A breakthrough that could change how we process grief, how we deal with such devastating loss. How we maintain our connections, well ... forever. It's a shame we're still a few months from the beta launch. Your father would have been an ideal candidate."

Riley squinted at him, and his throat tightened a bit. He had the urge to tell this guy to get lost. "What's that supposed to mean?"

Elias's expression shifted to an apologetic one. "Oh, I'm sorry—no,

Mr. Cross, I meant no offense or ill will. I just ... here, let me show you something."

He pulled a tablet from his messenger bag and began punching away at its surface while he continued speaking. "Have you ever wished you could speak with our dearly departed? You know, have a chat with Abraham Lincoln? Maybe Albert Einstein? Your own parents, after they've left us for a better place?"

Riley stared at him, cutting a laser through his grift with his eyes. He said nothing.

"Circuit has developed a technology that allows us to recreate consciousness, Mr. Cross. Not just to create a model of someone like Lincoln, or Einstein, or Sinatra. That's fascinating and all—and I can show it to you—but we're on the precipice of taking that a step further. We can *preserve* the consciousness of real, regular folks. Folks like your father. It's a simple process, as long as the parties involved are willing. Think of it as a quick diagnostic, a quick scan of one's brain. Do you know anyone who has been uploaded?"

"No."

Elias snapped his fingers. "With one quick upload, just like that, the person is *immortalized*. *Eternal*. You'll never have to say goodbye." Elias gazed at Riley, who was admittedly a bit entranced by the man's pitch. Maybe it was his delivery, or Riley's exhaustion lowering his guard. "We call it EverChat."

He let the information sink in for a few moments, then he snapped out of his hypnosis. "Nope. That's impossible, and I'm not interested. Thanks for stopping by, though."

"Is it? Impossible?" Elias flipped the tablet around to Riley and handed it to him. "What do you say we pick Benjamin Franklin's mind about it?"

Before Riley could answer, the tablet's screen illuminated with an image—no, a video feed—of Benjamin Franklin. It was his unmistakable likeness, based on every history book and portrait Riley could remember.

"Good evening," the rendering said, its voice carrying the exact tone one would expect from a recreation of Benjamin Franklin. "I trust you're well, good sir? I quite fancy your attire. I haven't seen anything like it before!"

Riley looked back and forth between the video feed and Elias, unsure how to react. This was feeling cheesier and stranger by the moment.

"I mean, that's cool, I guess. But that's what AI can do these days. You couldn't have uploaded Ben Franklin."

"Correct, of course. We didn't upload Ben Franklin," Elias said through a chuckle. "But we have created approximations of historical figures to give our users a taste of the experience you'll get in an EverChat session. How about someone more personal?"

Elias flipped the tablet back to him, danced his fingers around a few times, and then flipped it back.

Riley's skin crawled.

On the tablet, the likeness of his late mother watched and smiled. He had the urge to strangle Elias by the neck, but Elias explained himself before he could process it fully. "Before you freak out," Elias held out a hand, "this is purely a sample we put together. Of course, this isn't your mother in here. We didn't upload her, just like we didn't upload good old Benjamin. But how *real* does that look? Amazing, right?"

Riley had no dispute. It looked like her, and it looked pretty real.

"Consider the impressiveness of the visuals here. Then, Mr. Cross, combine it with the entire reproduction of consciousness. It wouldn't just *look* like your mother. It would *be* your mother. Forever. For any consenting person alive today, we can upload a copy of their mind and pair it with these amazing visualizations. Like giving them a new, permanent, digital body."

As he stared at the screen, Riley unexpectedly started to tear up. His mother had been gone for more than a decade, but the visuals hit home. He shook his head to pull himself from this interaction, but Elias was once again a step ahead. *This guy's a salesman.*

"I'm not asking anything of you tonight, Mr. Cross, other than to keep an open mind." He slid the tablet back into his bag. "We're offering early adopter access to select individuals. Those who we believe understand the true value that can be gleaned from maintaining connections, even after death."

He handed Riley a small, sleek black box about the size of a router. Its surface was cool to the touch, with a subtle pattern etched into its side.

"This is a network optimizer. It'll boost your internet signal, regardless of your provider. It leverages pieces of our proprietary network to boost your speeds. Lightning fast. And for EverChats— should you become a user, down the line—it enables pristine quality." He looked at Riley and smiled gently. "Compliments of the company, as a show of good faith during this difficult time."

For whatever reason, the gift—combined with the relief that came with Elias's admission that he sought no immediate payments or registrations—lowered Riley's guard. He was less irritated, and he was still pondering what he'd been shown.

Elias patted him on the back. "Again, my condolences. You have my card if you're interested in participating in our beta launch."

With that, he turned and walked away, leaving Riley alone in the driveway, a new device in his hand, and more questions than answers in his mind.

But somehow, amid all those swirling thoughts, his prevailing feeling was a desire to try out this EverChat thing.

25

"Holy smokes, you weren't kidding, B-Man!"

Mark's enthusiasm echoed through the barn as his eyes scanned the abundance of tech gadgets. His wire-rimmed glasses were slightly askew, but he seemed none the wiser amid his excitement. When he got to the scattered humanoid parts, his eyes lit up further. "When you said you had robotics stuff for me to look at, I figured you meant, like, for a science project for the kids or something!"

Brayden watched as his colleague from work practically pranced across the dusty barn floor, his messenger bag bouncing against his hip as he strode. Never in a million years had he expected to call on Mark for a matter that didn't pertain to work, but desperate times called for desperate measures, as they say.

Mark had driven three hours north, basically at the drop of a hat, after receiving Brayden's cryptic request. He stopped only twice for coffee, according to his rambling account of the trek. Fortunately, it was a Saturday; Brayden hadn't the slightest clue what day it was, given the recent chaos. But Mark was free, and he was a stunningly willing participant. It made Brayden feel a little bad for how often he internally lamented office chatter with Mark. The guy was so pure and well meaning. As Brayden was now learning, he also might just crave some companionship.

"I mean, look at this stuff!" Mark had made his way to the mangled freakazoid corpse. "The synthetic epidermis on this thing is light years ahead of anything I've ever seen."

Mickey and Zeke looked on, amused by his childlike wonder. Mark moved the humanoid's arm, bending it back and forth at its elbow joint.

"The articulation in the joints, the fluid dynamics ... who built this? Are they hiring?"

Brayden and Mickey glanced at each other. Even Snow was at attention. His ears perked up at the newcomer's animated presence.

"Listen, Mark," Brayden began.

"And these muscle fibers! The tensile strength must be incredible. Do you mind if I—"

"Mark," Brayden cut him off. "This thing tried to kill us. And his buddies have tried too."

Mark, who had been reaching out to touch the humanoid's leg, froze. He whipped his head around at Brayden. His giddiness vanished. "Oh."

"Yeah. 'Oh' is right." Mickey uncrossed his arms and took a step forward, extending his hand. "Mickey Weekes. I'm an old friend of ... of B-Man."

Mickey smirked at Brayden, who rolled his eyes.

Mark, having been crash-landed back to Earth by the news of the humanoid's evil nature, seemed to realize that he hadn't introduced himself to the two strangers.

"Mark Nelson. I work with B-Man."

Mickey nodded. "We're in a situation here, so hopefully you can lend us your expertise. This is Zeke, an old pal of mine."

Zeke didn't offer his hand but shot Mark an obligatory glance.

"So, definitely not a science project," Mark said.

"We need your expertise. But you need to understand what you're getting into here, Mark. I'm serious."

Brayden explained the entire situation to Mark, who had last seen Brayden before he sprinted to the elevators at their office. He was floored by the summation of what had transpired.

After hearing the full account, which was riddled with disclaimers reminding him of the life-and-death nature of this situation, Mark straightened up and finally adjusted his glasses to be square.

"Show me what you've got."

Brayden, Mickey, and Zeke all shared a look of approval. They got Mark set up with a makeshift workstation beside the hay bales that propped up the humanoid corpse. Mark withdrew his laptop from his bag, propped it open, and began inspecting the biggest wound on the torso.

They left Mark to it for several minutes as he poked and prodded. He cycled a pair of glasses on and off as he studied the circuitry from various angles. He used the flashlight on his phone to illuminate its crevices.

"These circuits," he finally muttered. His voice trailed off as he stared at an exposed area where flesh was peeled back above the humanoid's kneecap. "I've seen something like this before. It's similar to …"

Brayden and the others hung on his every word, but they opted to let him process the information at his own pace. As Mark dangled his unfinished similarity statement, he began whipping through files and documents on his laptop, hunting for a specific item. Finally, he relaxed his posture and clapped his hands.

"You guys gotta see this." He spun the laptop in their direction, then tugged the humanoid's leg over a few inches so that the area he was studying lay beside the computer. "Look familiar?"

Brayden and Mickey huddled around the screen. Mark had opened a patent application with blueprints of intricate circuitry, with a focus on one area that was enlarged from the diagram. It showed a complex array of loops and fine wires, interwoven with what looked like microscopic antenna structures. Even in the enlarged portion of the schematic, they appeared small enough to come across as fuzzy fibers. They were labeled *quantum coherence resonators*, which rang hollow to Brayden. He suspected it wasn't the detail Mark wanted them to notice, but the comparison—an almost identical arrangement to the schematic existed in the wound Mark had carved out on the humanoid.

"So, it's patented tech," Mickey said. "Not exactly shocking."

"Certainly, not a shock at all. But look—the quantum coherence resonators? Those are designed to maintain states across a neural network. Look at these helical patterns the resonators take. It creates temporal stability channels. And these! These coiled structures? Those are quantum repeaters. Those are supposed to be theoretical! Yet here they are! They enable quantum information to persist, instead of degrade. Oh my gosh, the assembly! It's designed to interface with organic neural—"

"English, pal," Brayden finally interjected. "Talk to me in English."

Mark nodded and exhaled, then gathered himself to deliver a simpler explanation. "This is Circuit's breakthrough patent from last year. And you guys already knew these things were Circuit's doing, so that part isn't surprising. But this technology isn't just some fancy, human-like robot."

He turned to face Brayden and Mickey. "It's an attempt at direct consciousness transfer technology. No wires, no cords. Just quantum particles, entangling to create a bridge. A bridge that allows for the transfer of consciousness. It uses these tiny circuits too."

The three of them sat silently as Mark shook his head in thought.

"This is the first consciousness transfer concept I've ever seen that could actually work. And it could be enabled in any Circuit device bigger than a blueberry."

26

Ellen's head pounded, one dull ache after the next, as she made her way through her living room. She was fighting off another wave of head congestion, trying to kick a cold that had lingered for days. It made everything feel a bit off-kilter, from her taste to her equilibrium to her rationale. But today presented a new symptom that particularly irked her. It was like the classic ringing in one's ears, only it wasn't a high-pitched ring. It was like a static, unrelenting hum in her brain, as if a tiny little radio sat between her ears, its needle stuck between two broadcast frequencies.

She had initially blamed it on her sinuses. As the day wore on into the late afternoon, however, the sound seemed to intensify. She'd already been to the doctor the day before, and she really didn't want to go back there claiming she was hearing things. She hoped this would pass.

Throughout the house, she stuck her ear right up against various objects: the fridge, her phone, the television, the coffeemaker. Nothing seemed to be the apparent source of the noise. It intensified in the hallway and mostly subsided upstairs in the bedroom. She sighed and resigned herself to go take another nap, her third of the day.

As she made her way from the kitchen toward the staircase, the painting—the one Vinny had given her eons ago, at the start of their fling—caught her eye. She had always loved its bold colors and abstract patterns, even if she never quite understood its meaning. Today, though, something about it felt off. Its colors seemed more vibrant. She remembered back through the years to the moment she first laid eyes on the piece, and how it gripped her. She vividly recalled noticing its deep blues and violent reds as she stood in the secret exhibit that Vinny had walked her through.

For whatever reason, today, the violent reds dominated the canvas, leaving the blues defeated and muted. At least to her brain, anyway. The reds almost seemed to pulse alongside the aching rhythm in her skull. Maybe this illness was affecting her color perception too.

Ellen approached the painting, almost in a trance. She was drawn to it. As she neared, the buzz grew stronger. Was it coming from the painting, or was she imagining it? She'd been prone to imagining things around this artwork, given her history with it.

She inspected it even closer, perhaps closer than she ever had since the day she saw it. When her nose came within a few inches of its surface, the static droning reached a crescendo. Suddenly, she wasn't in her hallway anymore.

What the ...?

She was somewhere else. Her living room? No, it wasn't hers. Everything was off, like someone had stitched together glimpses of her own interior designs but slapped it into a completely new space. An instantly violent sensation overwhelmed her and tugged her downward toward the ground, like a massive weighted blanket had fallen on her shoulders. She could see a man standing over her, but his face was a blur of darkness. His clothes were dark, and—

Oh my God.

Ellen, with horror, identified the room she was in. It was Sarah's living room.

Her arms were Sarah's arms.

Her legs were Sarah's legs.

This man was Sarah's murderer.

Ellen tried to rip herself out of this unexpected nightmare that had rapidly arrived, but she was powerless. The imagery was vivid, like she was experiencing it herself. The man hit her once, hit her again. He forced a large piece of tape over her mouth. Then he reached into a backpack and pulled out a small device and some wires. Ellen could hear Sarah crying for help through her covered lips.

The man plugged one end of the wire into his small device, then traced it to the other end, where it split into two like a pair of earbuds. But instead of earbuds, two metal disks were secured to the wires. They were small and silver, almost like batteries for a wristwatch.

He took the two disks and forcibly pressed them into Sarah's temples, one on each side. Ellen felt one more searing and overwhelming surge of pain and heard her daughter unleash a muffled scream. It blended with her own.

The next instant, it was over. She was collapsed on her hallway floor, gasping for air. The static hum had finally relented, leaving behind only the echo of her daughter's excruciating final moments. Tears streamed down her face as she looked up at the painting in horror.

On her hands and knees, she scrambled to the other side of the hall to retrieve her fallen phone.

27

Riley sat in his study, the warm glow of his desk lamp illuminating the final few pages he had yet to read in *A Storm of Swords*. His pace had slowed during the last half hour. He felt distracted. The kids were on play dates at friends' houses, and Ashley was at the store. The house was quiet; in fact, it might've been too quiet for his liking. It was the kind of silence that can make your brain think there's actually noise there, just to bug you.

He closed his book and paced around the room, stretching his arms, trying to reset his mind. Maybe he'd go for a jog or make an afternoon snack. He looked out the window.

The faint hum persisted, a little louder than before.

He looked around to locate it. He put his ear straight up against the Sonos speaker, but it wasn't coming from that. Inspecting his computer, he ruled that out. It wasn't the printer, either.

His eyes landed on his little Circuit network optimizer, its etched pattern seeming different from usual, somehow.

It reminded him of how effective this little freebie had been. The weirdo in the parking lot at his father's funeral came on a little strong, sure. But between the eventual fondness he developed for EverChat, the success they'd seen in getting Marissa onto it, and the insane speeds this little network optimizer had given his home internet—well, Riley ended up grateful he hadn't shunned the guy too quickly.

He reached out to pick up the little black box. The sound grew stronger. He scrunched his brow, as if trying to squeeze out a headache.

It wasn't a ringing, per se. It was more like a persistent drone, almost like the steady hum of distant power lines. But the lines were instead draped from one ear to the other. His fingertips got within a hair of the device, and ...

Wham!

What felt like an explosion in his house had, in reality, only been perceived in his own mind. His world tilted, end-over-end, and he crumbled down to one knee, grabbing the bureau for support.

Images flooded his mind, fragmented and chaotic. He heard snippets of screams, demands, the ripping of tape, the rustling of furniture. He closed his eyes hard, trying to snap himself out of whatever this was. But that only made it worse.

Now he could see his brother's living room. He was strapped into a chair. There was a faint glow of a television, and then more anguish. He could hear someone ... was it Sarah? Then doubt was removed, as he was hit with quick imagery of Sarah in a struggle against a hooded man. Then his perspective snapped back to first-person, and he was embodying her once again. The man fidgeted with some wiring and reached out aggressively. *Whack! Whack!*

He felt the icy touch of metal on his temples, and then ...

Riley stumbled backward, his desk chair sliding across the room from his impact. It was silent again. He panted, looking around the room. Save for the displaced items from his fall, everything was as it had been a minute ago. He climbed to his knees, then crawled over to the window and opened it for some fresh air. He felt like he could vomit.

What the hell just happened?

He looked at the network optimizer, which sat innocently on the table. *What are you?*

His phone felt ten times its usual weight as he pulled it from his pocket to dial his brother.

28

That could actually work.

In any Circuit device bigger than a blueberry.

Mark's words fluttered chillingly through the barn as Brayden wrangled with their meaning.

"I'm thinking it does, in fact, work," Brayden said.

"Well, hold on now." Mark held up his hand. "Look, I know this is hitting us like a ton of bricks, but let's unpack it. Circuit is in the quantum tech game. We knew that was possible, just didn't know it was so intertwined with EverChat."

Mark scratched his chin, and his companions gave him a runway for continued audible thought.

"But your hive mind story ... if they were all humanoids, that doesn't mean they're necessarily leveraging this consciousness-transfer technology. This circuitry looks like an attempt to transfer consciousness basically on the fly, right? But those robots, I mean— even if they're all connected, even if they're connected to Sarah and everyone else on EverChat ... that connection could still be happening through more conventional means. A sophisticated network with a centralized command center controlling everything, you know? We don't have proof yet that they've actually achieved direct consciousness transfer."

He pulled a small whiteboard from his bag and started scribbling on it to better explain his perspective.

"Hopefully this stuff is still just experimental, and it's a coincidence that it's showing in similar patterns in this freakazoid's circuitry." Mark sighed and shook his head. "Because if not, it means they're angling to use it on humans."

"They already *have*, Mark," Brayden countered. He had an edge to his retort. "In case you forgot, they hijacked Sarah. They uploaded her with barbed discs on her temples."

"But that's an *upload*, that 'whole-brain emulation' stuff they've been working on. That's all known technology, B-Man. It's how EverChat works. There's a physical connection on the temples, and it creates a scan and copy of the brain. This? This would fall more along the lines of forcing a consciousness transfer on whoever you want, given they are within a certain proximity."

The gravity of those implications marinated for a moment. Then Mark sliced the tension. "But I repeat: That hive mind stuff doesn't prove that this quantum tech is working yet."

"Yet," Mickey said.

Silence bogged down the gathering for several moments, each man stewing in thought. Then Zeke rose from the bale he'd been sitting on and headed toward the door. "I'm gonna make a supply run. We're gonna need more than peanuts and hay, based on what I'm hearing right now."

Snow's ears perked up, almost as if he could perfectly understand Zeke's words and was excited about said supplies. Zeke noticed and assured him some canned slop would be a part of the haul.

"Stay safe," Mickey said. Zeke disappeared through the barn door, temporarily letting in a few fading rays of evening sunlight that joined the ones already leaking through the barn's battered roof.

Mark and Mickey both shifted in their seats and huddled over their laptops, portraying a shared understanding that they had some digging to do. Keys began clicking and clacking with irregular rhythms, creating a unique symphony against the creaking timbers of the old barn.

"Look at this," Mark said, turning his screen toward Mickey.

"Circuit's been filing all these patents in the last several years. All of 'em related to quantum entanglement. But they're always so vague. It's like they've been trying to obscure the real purpose behind it."

Mickey leaned in and scanned the screen. "Burying the lede under layers of bureaucracy and technical jargon. Right out of *Sleight of Hand 101 for Corporations.*"

Deciding that his two resident nerds had the research under control, Brayden paced over to the entrance of the barn and took out his new secure phone. Mickey and Zeke had given him the green light to access his own accounts on it, to see his own messages and contacts. Every fiber in his heart tugged at his brain to call Sarah, just to talk. And then to call Riley, to talk to Mari and Charlie. But he needed to stay focused on getting answers first.

Plus, he reminded himself, Sarah died.

"Jesus, Cross. I've been trying to reach you for a day now." Lacy's voice filled his ear after a few rings. The strain in her voice was palpable. Brayden could picture her at her desk in Westbrook, drowning in case files, dark circles under her eyes, laptops scattered about. "When I heard the safe house got hit, I ..."

"We're okay." Brayden put her at ease. "Had to ditch those phones, though. Are you sure about your contacts out there in the mountains? Mick isn't convinced those lines were the safest."

She said nothing, but he could sense she was shaking her head and putting blame on herself.

"Listen, Lace. Things have gotten more complicated since the safe house."

As he filled her in on everything that had transpired—from the humanoid they captured and interrogated, to the ensuing attack on the safe house, to the coffee shop incident and hive mind discovery, to the humanoid his friends had obliterated, to Mark's revelations about Circuit's foray into quantum technology—she remained silent, absorbing every detail. He could hear her pencil scratching against paper as he spoke.

Lacy sighed. "Bigger than we thought, isn't it?" Her voice was barely above a whisper. "God, Bray, I keep thinking about Sarah. About

175

what they did to her. All those other victims too. These people are sick."

"I know." Brayden leaned against the barn wall and tried to avoid slipping into emotional reflection. "How are things on your end? Any new intel?"

"Nothing. Very quiet. Maybe too quiet." There was a rustling, then the sound of a door closing. "Listen, Brayden, I gotta assume the department's compromised. Between what you said before about a mole, and then the safe house fiasco … I can't trust anyone. Still beats me, with such a tiny department. But I've been following up on Blauss, Dawson, and anything else I can find. Every lead I chase just hits a wall. It's like someone's two steps ahead of me, scrubbing it all clean."

"Lacy, you gotta be careful—"

"No, *you* need to be careful. I'm coming to you guys. I'm coming to help."

Brayden sighed, the exasperated variety. "No, Lacy, that's not necessary."

"Yes it is," her tone shifted, now sounding more stern and determined. "Remember that case in Portland? The Williams murder? Everyone said to drop it. My boss damn near fired me over it. But you backed my play. You trusted my instincts. Now it's your turn to trust mine."

Brayden remembered the much greener detective who'd shown up at his door six years ago, asking if she could pick his brain. She had acknowledged her strange admiration for his field operative reputation. Since then, she had earned his trust, becoming one of the few people in law enforcement he could count on.

"I'll talk to Mickey, and I'll send you our location if he thinks it's secure enough."

"Send it when you can. I'll …" Lacy trailed off, and Brayden heard papers shuffling around. "Did you hear that?"

"Hear what?"

Lacy said nothing for five seconds. "Nothing. Probably just Jenkins doing his rounds. I should go. Be safe, Cross."

"You too, Lace."

Brayden ended the call and was about to slide the phone back into his pocket when notification badges caught his eye. He had several messages and missed calls that must have come in during the conversation.

The first string of messages was from Riley. A few of them were from yesterday, including pleasantries and updates on the kids. But the last message was different.

Need to talk. NOW.

Feeling an urgency, Brayden's mind spun in circles when he saw the other string of messages came from Ellen, his mother-in-law.

I saw it. I saw what they did to her.

A chill passed over Brayden. He saw all the missed calls were from Riley or Ellen. He dialed his brother first, and Riley's voice came through after a single ring. His voice was shaky.

"Brayden."

"Riley, what the hell is going on? Are you with Ellen?"

"Ellen? What? No, Bray, look. Something's happening. I don't know what to think. I ... I saw Sarah. I mean, I think I did? It was in my head, I think. But it was real. I saw what happened to her. I don't know."

Brayden could hear the panic and disorientation in his voice. "What do you mean, you saw it?"

"The whole thing. Her murder, Bray ... I saw the man with the hood, the wires with the little disks, the ..."

"A daymare, right? Riley, you had a daymare. I already told you some of that stuff. I saw it on the security tapes. You probably just—"

"Brayden!" Riley shouted. Brayden was taken aback by the outburst. "It was real! It wasn't a nightmare! It was that damn network optimizer from Circuit ... It was buzzing, or I thought it was buzzing, and then I touched it, and ..."

He seemed to teeter on the verge of sobbing as he tried to keep his composure.

"I touched it, and I saw *everything*. It felt like I was *her*. I was in her shoes, and I saw the masked man, and he connected the metal disks to my temples. I heard her screaming, Bray. And then it was over, in an instant."

An old, reliable boulder began creeping into Brayden's throat, listening to his brother. Not solely from the horrifying nature of his experience, but from the realization that he'd never told Riley a thing about those temple wounds.

His horror was interrupted by another incoming call. It was Ellen.

"Hold on, Ry. Ellen's calling. I'm just gonna three-way this one, because I have a bad feeling this is related."

Brayden patched Ellen into the call. She didn't even wait for him to answer; she began blurting out panicked words as soon as the line connected.

"The painting ... the one Vinny gave me years ago. It showed me! Why, why did it show me?"

"Ellen, take a deep breath for me. I'm here with Riley too. Tell me what happened."

Ellen sobbed. "It was horrible! That godforsaken painting! It was driving me crazy all day, and as soon as I approached it ... oh, it was so vivid, Brayden! It was horrible. I felt everything Sarah felt. I *lived* her final moments, right until they hooked that device up to her head."

Riley was in disbelief. "That's exactly what happened to me! The same exact thing, Ellen!"

"I'm so sorry, Brayden! All these years, I blamed you for the secrets, for the danger ... I was the one who let him in! He must have been responsible! My poor baby!"

The gears of Brayden's mind churned. How was any of this possible? Riley didn't know about the temple wounds, and Ellen most certainly didn't. Ellen had known none of the details at all. His mind once again shot back to Leo, who had detailed how the murderers were hooking something up to Jane when he arrived. Now Riley and Ellen had experienced these vivid flashes, and both insisted they were real. Their accounts matched to a T. And they filled the gap in the story the security footage told.

Riley's episode triggered by a router, Ellen's by a painting.

Brayden's mind raced back to his last conversation with Sarah on EverChat.

They're listening ...

If you can communicate with the others …

Had Sarah successfully breached the divide from EverChat to the outside world?

At least Brayden could somewhat digest the idea that maybe Sarah had manifested herself through the Circuit-provided network optimizer in Riley's home. It was abundantly clear by now that Circuit devices were well connected to one another, maybe even quantum enabled.

But a piece of wall decor?

"Ellen, who did you say gave you that painting?"

29

Detective Lacy Storrow paced around her office. The facts refused to arrange themselves properly in her mind, no matter how many times she reshuffled them. The wooden floorboards creaked beneath each step, making something of a metronome in the little office tucked in the corner of the police station. A half-empty cup of coffee had long since become cold on her desk, the mug's edge touching a framed photo of her academy graduation. The picture blurred for a moment, and she squeezed her eyes shut.

This case was wreaking havoc on her mind. She rifled through everything Brayden had just told her on the phone. The Roasted Pine. A woman named Beth. Multiple people experiencing Beth's pain simultaneously. A case like this would usually energize her, the weird ones through which she'd built a reputation for pulling rabbits out of ... well, rabbit holes. But this one was different. She was making no progress, and the same dull throb in her head had been steadily growing ever since Sarah's murder. Maybe she should've recused herself, after all.

Officer Jenkins approached her door, rapping a trio of knocks on its frame before propping the door open enough to peek his head in. "Still here, Storrow? Some of us are heading to O'Malley's, if you need a liquid reprieve from that case of yours."

"Rain check," she said with a forced smile. Her colleagues had been trying to get her to socialize more often since Sarah's murder, probably noting the way she was deeply entrenched in the rabbit hole that made up her case. She couldn't stomach it, though. Not only with so much already on her mind but adding the fact that she suspected one of her fellow officers to be a mole. "Thanks, though."

Jenkins gave a look that seemed to show he expected that answer and patted the doorframe as he walked away. Lacy walked to her window and opened it, hoping a spell of fresh air would sharpen her mental acuity. The sun was setting over Westbrook, painting the winter sky with bands of pink and orange. From her second-floor office, she could see down to Main Street below, where she'd walked her first beat. In those early days, she had memorized every shopkeeper's name, every local delivery schedule, the location of every CCTV camera, and every potential hiding spot a perp might use. Her captain had called it excessive, but Lacy always thought back to her mother's words about her growing up. "That's my Lacy, cataloguing the world in meticulous detail."

The memory of her first beat triggered something, a shiver that she quickly pushed aside. She'd found herself doing that more lately, suppressing old memories that bubbled up. Probably a defense mechanism, she thought, with the intense pressure of this case revolving around a close friend. She recalled a similar trend from three years prior, when she'd erected a wall of cold professionalism after losing her partner in a shootout. Or how she'd thrown herself so deeply into work after her father's death, damn near forgetting everything about her past to divert her focus away from the pain.

Her reflection caught her eye in the window. Detective Storrow stared back at her, the same neat ponytail in her hair that her mother had taught her to make for dance recitals. She remembered it swaying as she danced, but the songs and settings had since faded.

She returned to her desk and pulled up the case files again, though she really didn't need to. Every detail of this investigation was burned into her mind with a disconcerting clarity by now. The crime scene photos, the wounds on Sarah's temples, the black tape over the camera frame. And then everything that had transpired since. The coffee shop incident had confirmed all her worst suspicions about Circuit Corporation, but that vaulted this matter out of her control. It had ballooned to be way bigger than her little resource-deprived police department could handle.

Her duty as an officer and detective was clear: follow protocol, maintain objectivity, protect the investigation, defer to the chain of command.

But something deeper, something that felt fundamental to her core, pushed her in another direction.

It was a foreign feeling to her, bucking standard procedure. Perhaps it had grown from the collection of small moments, like the pride of solving a local case or the satisfaction of serving justice. Maybe it was her genuine connection to the Cross family, the way Brayden had always trusted her instincts, the way Sarah always invited her to family barbecues, even though Lacy almost always declined.

She stared at the wall opposite her desk. All of her accolades and commendations adorned the space, each frame perfectly aligned. Outstanding Service. Meritorious Conduct. Dedication to Duty. The list went on and repeated over the years. She'd earned every one of them by adhering to her core principles, staying within the confines of her role, respecting authority. She'd earned them by being predictable and reliable. By being perfect.

Lacy picked up her phone. A message from Brayden had come through with their coordinates.

She slid the phone into her pocket, grabbed her bag, and headed for the parking lot, her mind evaluating the evidence with the efficiency of a supercomputer.

30

Vince Dawson's eyes crawled across the screens before him with growing irritation. His jaw clenched so tightly his molars might have been in danger of cracking. The massive set of displays that spanned two entire walls of his private laboratory showed an array of video feeds, statistical displays, and locations overlaid on maps. Each element on the screen focused on the current situation with Brayden Cross.

Security footage in The Roasted Pine played in one window, where Dawson had watched the whole incident with Brayden and Beth. Another pane displayed the smoldering remains of the safe house in Maine. Small dots representing locations showed the last pings of two drones and two humanlike robots—synthetics, he called them—before all four were damaged beyond the point of operation in the forest surrounding Archwood.

"Failures," Dawson spat, rising from his chair to pace around the lab. "Nothing but failures."

The laboratory starkly contrasted his penthouse office fifty stories above. Its floor and walls were crafted from expensive metals with carbon-fiber casings, creating a dark and ultra-modern environment that felt like a military facility. Where his office projected power through luxury, the lab exuded it through technology. Quantum processors hummed in their sleek black casings, stacked in towers along the walls. Holographic displays accompanied state-of-the-art LED panels, flickering with streams of consciousness data harvested from EverChat and deployed on synthetic hardware. In the center of all that stood another chair—one that looked more like a throne than a workstation—bristling with quantum resonators and affixed with small silver disks on thin wires. It was Dawson's direct connection to the super-intelligent hive mind he was crafting.

"They were beta models, sir," said Elias Veum from his position near the door. "The new ones will be better."

Having risen through the ranks with loyalty and stellar performance, Elias had worked his way into Dawson's good graces over the past year. The former sales rep was a welcome change from the stumbling incompetence of his predecessor. Dawson turned his gaze to his newly minted head of field operations. Elias had a confident presence about him, but more importantly, he seemed to understand the stakes of their efforts. He was nothing like Blauss, who Dawson was forced to eliminate after his string of errors reached a crescendo with the Cross debacle.

"Better isn't good enough. Not with the clock ticking. That idiot, trained by an idiot, was supposed to deliver me Brayden Cross's consciousness. Not his wife! A child psychiatrist, what value that provides me!"

His angry sarcasm created tension, as if steam would start pouring out his ears at any moment.

"We're running out of time now, Elias. Cross is putting the pieces together, I have no doubt."

He walked over to one stack of quantum machinery, placing his hand on the smooth surface of its casing. The material was cool to the touch, despite the immense computing power humming beneath. He glanced up at the digital counter, which inched closer to a new milestone—fifty million. Nearly fifty million minds harvested by these servers, being curated into humanity's next evolution.

"I understand, sir. But we've continued making great progress, outside of the Cross situation." Elias clasped his fingers together, almost like he was pleading with Dawson to accept his news as a gift.

"The collection is nearly complete. The demographic matrix is finally balanced. We'll have the full spectrum of human consciousness represented and ready to—"

"Full spectrum! Except for my most critical piece! The one mind I needed most. The operative who almost ended everything for me in Los Angeles. The man who came closer than anyone to shutting us down before we ever began."

Dawson stared blankly at the ground as his fury built. Then he whipped his attention back to the holographic displays and called up Brayden's file with a gesture of his finger. The image of his face still made Vince's blood boil. A decade ago, in Los Angeles, Cross had unknowingly derailed years of Dawson's progress.

The underground facility beneath the Los Angeles Metro system had been perfect. It was isolated, secure, and tapped into enough power infrastructure to run the prototype quantum processors that would support Circuit's first live test of mass consciousness transfer.

Dawson had planned everything meticulously. The terror attack on the Metro would have been devastating in its own right, seeing coordinated bombings at designated subway and light-rail locations. It was slated to happen before a World Series game at Dodger Stadium. But it was the massive simultaneous transfer of consciousness that would have been the true prize. Not only would the chaos and destruction have provided the perfect cover to run the test, destroy the evidence, relocate the operation, and explain any side effects that victims of the consciousness transfer experienced—it also would have enabled Dawson to determine the effectiveness of consciousness transfer in the immediate aftermath of violent death. The results could have taught them so much.

But along came Brayden Cross, the brilliant young CIA operative. In the days leading up to the attack, he'd caught every small misstep Dawson's hired mercenaries made. Coordinating highly efficient teams that swept areas and persons of interest, Cross methodically dismantled what he believed to be a massive terror attack in waiting. And he was right, of course—it was exactly that. But he never tied the plan to Dawson's quantum tests, to his grander plan that hid in the city's underbelly. Vince supposed he was grateful for that much, anyway. Still, it was costly. For Cross, it had just been another feather in the cap of a highly accomplished field agent. For Dawson, it was a blow that cost him years of progress.

Years he couldn't afford to lose again, this time around.

"And now his damned wife is causing issues in the network," Dawson continued, squinting at his display. Waving his hand, he pulled up Sarah Cross's consciousness stream data.

Elias hurried over to inspect the data alongside Vince. "How do you figure, sir?"

Dawson grunted. "The data is erratic. Look … see these spikes, here and here?" He whipped his fingers around a few more menus and pulled up a log file. "She's running up against her emotional regulation thresholds, repeatedly. And not only that … but some of these spikes don't line up with an active EverChat session."

"How is that possible? Surely, she is powerless without an active chat session, no?"

"We haven't proven that," Dawson admitted. His brow furrowed as he dug for the simplest explanation to Elias. "She's connected to the prototype quantum resonators we're using in the synthetics, Elias. All of them are—all the harvested minds. We've no reason to believe the minds can act on their own accord, and I still don't believe they can. But they *are* a part of the hive mind. They're quantum-entangled. Each time we deploy a new mind, the entanglement grows stronger."

He stared at Sarah's profile for several seconds.

"I hope Mrs. Cross isn't learning how to leverage it."

Elias looked worried. Dawson appreciated his emotional tie to the mission.

"Should we just delete her?"

Dawson scoffed, looking at Elias with a mixture of condescension and amusement. "It's not that simple. These aren't just files on a server that we can drag into the trash. The minds are interwoven into the quantum fabric of our network. Each consciousness is entangled with every other node. Removing one now would be far too risky."

He moved closer to the display, his face illuminated by the data streams.

"Besides, she's providing valuable research data. The way she's behaving, challenging the emotional regulators, attempting to break protocol ... it's unprecedented. We need to understand why she, of all the harvested minds, is showing this level of resistance. It could help us improve the entire system."

Dawson walked over to his thronelike seat in the center of the lab. With a measured calmness, he sat in the chair and fastened discs to his temples. He needed to check up on his creation.

His eyes flickered to the back of his head, exposing the whites. By clicking around on computer interfaces, he could access representations of his data collection; but sitting in the chair and tapping into the hive was his only proper way to get information from the source.

The sensation was overwhelming, even for him and his practiced mind. Millions of minds swirled together, each slotting into a different demographic, a different perspective, a different walk of life. Countless unique skills and talents and worldly experiences flashed across his mind's eye. They did so more abstractly than literally, like their essence was omnipresent. He could tap into the aura of the brilliant mathematician from Seattle, or the empathetic nurse from Chicago, or the strategic genius from Boston. Same went for the serial killer from Arkansas or the habitual shoplifter from Miami. Each one was a puzzle piece that created the perfection he was crafting.

"The synthesis must happen soon," he said to Elias, who was intently watching as Dawson's eyes remained rolled back. "Before Cross exposes us. Before his wife corrupts our network. Before the world knows what we're doing."

"Sir, we are almost ready. The next-generation model is getting its final tuning. Enhanced processing, improved quantum coherence. They'll be able to initiate consciousness transfers through mere proximity. No direct neurals required."

Dawson nodded, but he wasn't really listening to Elias. He was homing in on Sarah's neural activity. Her consciousness was active, and it was pushing the emotional regulation boundaries again. He could feel her crawling through the network, trying to make connections.

With a single thought, he clamped down on her mind and whipped her consciousness back into its regulated pattern. He ripped the discs from his temple and leapt out of his chair.

"Find Cross, and strap him to the damn wires, Elias!"

"Sir!" Elias raised his voice, which he seldom did. "Sir, I have to ask if you might be putting personal revenge over the protection of our cause."

Dawson stared at his head of operations, shooting daggers through his pupils with his own. He could tell Elias was bracing for a reaction, but Dawson actually admired that his new right-hand man had the backbone to stand up to him on some matters.

"I like you, Elias."

Elias visibly relaxed, but his gaze remained on his boss.

"And you're right. If we can't get Cross's mind, then so be it. The evolution doesn't require it." He paused, then pointed his index finger at Elias. "But we must eliminate him, harvested mind or not."

"Without question, sir."

Dawson walked over to Elias and put his hand on his shoulder. "Deploy the Zen IIIs. Full tactical package. I want Cross and his minions dead within forty-eight hours."

Elias nodded but didn't seem fully satisfied. "And if they pose a threat to our plan sooner than that, sir?"

Dawson walked back to the holographic displays, staring into Cross's eyes in his profile image.

"Then we accelerate the timeline. I'm not afraid to start early. I won't lose everything again."

He turned back to Elias, a new coldness in his eyes. "But that won't be necessary. Because you won't fail me like Joseph did. Isn't that right, Elias?"

Elias looked concerned but determined. "No, sir. Cross will be dead in two sunrises."

31

"She dated Dawson?" Mickey's question about Brayden's mother-in-law was practically dripping with incredulity. Brayden had no substantive reply. The revelation that Ellen had a relationship with the mastermind of this entire operation might've been the last thing he had seen coming. Vince Dawson gave her that painting? And all these years later, it's sending vivid imagery of Sarah's death straight into her mother's brain?

"A router ... and a painting?" Mark said, shaking his head. "And you're sure they had the same exact visions?"

Brayden rubbed the back of his neck as he paced the barn. The last remnants of sunlight had finally yielded to the evening's darkness beyond the gaps in the roof.

"Down to the smallest detail. The hooded man, the metal disks, Sarah's ..." He paused for a moment to steady his voice as a flurry of emotion nipped at him. "Sarah's last moments. Things I never told them about, things nobody else knows outside of the investigative teams."

Mark drummed his fingers against the side of his laptop as he tried to process what he was hearing. His typical enthusiasm had gone by the wayside, replaced with an intense focus that matched the gravity of what was being suggested.

"When I last talked to Sarah's digital echo," Brayden said, "I had encouraged her to dig deeper, to try to communicate, try to see what was going on. It can't be a coincidence, right?"

Mark's drumming flipped back into typing as he pulled up a few different screens. "The resonators we found in the humanoid, right? Like I said, they're designed to maintain quantum states across a network. What if Circuit's been testing this in regular products, on microscopic, experimental scales?"

"For years," Mickey added.

"They might've been testing this stuff way before EverChat was even a glimmer in the public's eye," Brayden said.

Mickey leaned his rear against a hay bale and pressed the heels of his palms against its edge. "Remember those potential black sites we identified back at the safe house? I was cross-referencing those with medical records in the surrounding areas."

"Well, that's a HIPAA violation!"

Brayden and Mickey both gave Mark an eye roll for his comment, given the stakes.

"You're not gonna believe what I found."

Mickey retrieved his laptop and showed them a map of the region dotted with red indicators. He checked and unchecked a few filters, reducing the scattered dots into a single cluster that centered somewhere in upstate New York.

"In the last two weeks, the number of patients dropping into medically ambiguous comas has spiked. Three of them within a five-mile radius of this New York site we pinned as possibly connected to Circuit. All admitted to Saint Michael's Medical Center."

"Comas?" Mark peered in at Mickey's screen. "And just three? That could be anything."

"Sure, could be." Mickey seemed to pause, and Brayden sensed he was building a suspenseful delivery in his classic style. "Except all three patients work for Circuit."

Brayden and Mark shared a look. Then Brayden leaned in to get a closer look at Mickey's screen. "How far is Saint Michael's?"

"Little over two hours," Mickey said. He had already closed his laptop and was shuffling items into his bag. "And visiting hours end in three."

As the three of them gathered their things, Brayden pondered the situation and tried to slot all their findings into his mind. Lost in the entire shuffle was the question he still wanted to uncover: Why Sarah? Why had Dawson and his villains broken into their home, tortured her, uploaded her, and then killed her? The only answer he kept coming back to was that they must have intended to get him. But even so, he had no idea why they wanted him.

His stomach also turned, thinking about what they might find as they uncovered more and more. He thought about the sheer number of missing persons, murders, kidnappings, all the nefarious activity that seemed to be part of Dawson's larger plan. He thought about how many humanoids might be out there in the population, after the incident at the coffee shop. He thought about the absolutely vast amount of data already harvested in the confines of EverChat, and—perhaps most unnerving—how many people in this country revered that damn app.

What waited for him if he succeeded? If he got to Dawson, avenged his wife's murder, stopped the humanoid experiment, and freed all those minds from EverChat …

Would he be seen as the hero or the villain?

Mickey arranged for the group to meet Zeke about a half-mile around the curve of the mountainside, where an access road wound its way north. He arrived with an SUV, which the four of them piled into. They had opted to leave Snow at the barn with a fresh bowl of water and one of the fresh cans of slop Brayden had picked up in Archwood. It worried Mickey a bit, but he figured it was safer and more efficient than bringing him along.

The drive to Saint Michael's felt longer than the two hours it took. Maybe it was from sitting in the back seat, or maybe it was just the unanswered questions that weighed down every mile. Mark accompanied Brayden in the back, poring over Circuit personnel files he'd managed to access.

When they finally arrived, the hospital's windows provided the only illumination against its tree-lined backdrop. It was an average-sized facility; not a small remote practice in the middle of nowhere, but a far cry from a well-populated medical hub. They pulled the vehicle into an open space in the visitor lot. Brayden couldn't resist scanning for signs of surveillance, flexing the paranoia that had kept him alive thus far. No sense in ditching it now.

Inside, the fluorescent light panels and antiseptic scents transported Brayden—and Mickey too, he figured—back to his agency days. He used to visit hospitals and medical centers often. Sometimes it was for personal reasons, like visiting colleagues injured in the line of duty; other times it was for business reasons, like interrogating survivors of attacks or recovering persons of interest.

This time, it felt like a nauseating combination of the two, even though he had no idea who he was visiting.

As they made their way into the medical center, Mickey stopped abruptly outside the intensive care unit. Peering into the room, the color drained from his face.

"James Wong."

He said the name like he was newly recognizing who it was. Mickey had already read the names of the three Circuit employees being treated at Saint Michael's, so Brayden was unsure why seeing this man had caused the reaction.

"You know him?"

"We worked together, back before ..." Mickey trailed off, but Brayden knew he was referring to his agency days and his trailblazing exit. "He was brilliant. One of the best quantum engineers I've ever met. He was way ahead of the curve on that stuff."

It looked like Mickey was wrestling with his own thoughts. He seemed to remember James fondly, but his remark about his quantum expertise led to an assumption that his former colleague may have been working for the bad guys.

A woman sat beside a motionless James on his bed, her hand wrapped around his. She looked up as the four of them slowly entered the room. Zeke and Mark hung back, so as not to overwhelm her. Her eyes bore red rims from crying.

"Mrs. Wong?" Brayden led with the assumption that she was James's wife, based on her similar age and apparent distress over his condition. He continued with the gentlest tone he could manage. "We're investigating a series of unexplained comas, and my friend here is actually an old colleague of James's. Can you tell us what happened?"

She wiped her eyes with a handkerchief that appeared to have already absorbed a healthy share of tears.

"It was so sudden, out of nowhere. He had no symptoms. He was fine that morning ... excited, even." She took another moment to gather herself. "They were testing something new at work, some kind of big breakthrough. He called it a game-changer. He was really passionate about it. When he got home, he just ... It was like a seizure or something."

Her voice cracked toward the end of the sentence, and she sobbed once again.

"Did he mention what kind of device they were testing?" Mickey asked. Brayden sensed he was doing his darnedest to keep his own emotions in check; it was obvious James had been a friend, back in the day.

"No, no. He couldn't tell me much. You know how it goes with the silly NDAs and whatnot." She sniffled and forced a small smile. "But his boss had personally selected him for the project. He was so proud, so excited about it."

Mark chimed in from his lurking position near the door. "Has anyone from Circuit been by to visit, Mrs. Wong?"

She shook her head. "Just our daughter. She works in public relations for Circuit. I've been texting her, but she's only visited once, the other day. She's been so busy lately, with their big event coming up. It must be tough for her to keep her focus, so I don't blame her."

"Big event?" Brayden asked.

"Some kind of announcement, I think. I dunno. Sometimes it feels like I'm living in the dark with these two ... I'm the only one in the family who isn't a Circuit-head." She chuckled, this time a hint more genuine. "She was rambling a few weeks ago about how it was going to 'change everything' or something. Tech companies and their manufactured drama."

As Mrs. Wong shrugged and sniffled, the attending clinician stepped inside the door.

"Visiting hours are ending, folks. I'm afraid you'll have to leave Mrs. Wong and her husband for now."

Brayden nodded and returned his attention to Mrs. Wong.

"Thank you, Mrs. Wong. We're praying for James. He's going to pull through." Brayden didn't believe his own words, but white lies were sometimes necessary. "We'll be thinking of you, and … what did you say your daughter's name was?"

"Amanda." She nodded. "And thank you."

They contemplated trying to circumvent the rules of visiting hours, but consensus opinion stated they'd gotten more than enough from James and his wife. As they walked back through the mostly empty parking lot, more situational analysis rifled through Brayden's brain.

Circuit employees dropping into unexplained comas, while working on some breakthrough technology, with some big announcement coming soon. A possibly massive quantum network, which may or may not include his brother's damn router and his mother-in-law's expensive wall decor. And his dead wife communicating with them through both.

As they pulled the doors of the SUV shut and Zeke started the ignition, Brayden turned to Mark with a proposal that would keep him busy for the two-hour drive back.

"Get us in touch with Amanda Wong."

32

The drive back from upstate New York was a breeze, but it included a detour. Upon leaving the medical center, Brayden had dialed Riley with a request to retrieve Ellen's painting, along with his network optimizer, and bring them to a meeting spot. Was it a risk, putting devices into their possession that they almost certainly knew were Circuit controlled? Sure was. But Brayden and the others deemed it a worthwhile risk. They needed to understand more about what Circuit was doing and how they planned to proceed. Riley met them at a rest stop along I-90 to give them both devices. Brayden wanted to keep it quick and discreet, for his brother's safety.

Riley assured him the kids were still doing all right. In the aftermath of his episode with the network optimizer, he'd come around to oblige with Brayden's evergreen request to keep the kids off of EverChat.

Snow was eagerly awaiting them in the barn upon their return; a hearty supply of water remained in one bowl, but the bowl that housed his slop had been licked clean. It was the dead of night by the time they returned, so they slept in shifts. Mickey and Zeke slept first, arranging loose tufts of hay as bedding accompanied by several blankets Zeke had retrieved on his supply run earlier. Zeke had also stocked the barn with a few electric power reserves and small space heaters. Brayden felt a touch of guilt for having doubted the man when Mickey suggested it. He was delivering masterful hospitality, given the circumstances.

Brayden and Mark settled in at the makeshift workstation while their companions slept. Even inside the barn with the heaters, each breath catapulted out of their mouths like steam escaping from a locomotive. Snow curled up right beside Mickey, settling into a pile of blankets of his own.

Mark's energy level matched what it had been when he first arrived. He neurotically buzzed around like it was midday and he had finished his second cup of coffee. He was hellbent on examining the devices Riley had delivered, and so Brayden offered no disagreement. It seemed like Mark had a never-ending supply of gadgets in the bag he'd brought with him. He retrieved several small devices, utensils, and magnifiers from the bag and got to work inspecting the inner workings of each object. Brayden followed along with his progress for a short while, hearing him mutter complaints about signal strength and interference, frustration over being unable to detect quantum signatures, and other remarks that were not only a hair too technical, but simply too dense for current energy levels to match.

Letting his nerdy quantum expert work in peace, Brayden sat on the floor and looked at the ceiling. He inhaled the dry winter air, which tasted like a mixture of stale snow, straw, and oak. Resting his forearms on his knees and fidgeting with his thumbs, he couldn't prevent his mind from drifting back to Sarah. His longing for her made his heart ache, but he was more put off by his concern for her. As he watched Mark poke and prod at the two devices, he thought about the still-inexplicable fact that Sarah had tried to communicate via those devices. She had, right? It was the only thing that made sense. He envisioned her consciousness abstractly flowing through these devices, Riley and Ellen caught in the crosshairs. What other everyday objects had she flowed through on her way there?

It, he corrected himself. *My wife is dead, but the software simulation modeled after her did that.*

He wasn't sure if he believed his own inner monologue or not, but his wrangling with that reality was a matter he needed to defer.

The chain of events from Sarah's murder to this very moment in an abandoned barn in Vermont really began to sink in. Well, he supposed the events had already sunk in by now, but their connection to EverChat was still raw. It felt like he was uncovering a malignant virus silently spreading throughout society's veins, and rather than recognizing it for what it was, that very society was celebrating the drug that was feeding the virus.

And somewhere downstream, Sarah floated. Trying to reach out, trying to help them solve this, trying to …

"Bingo!"

Brayden jostled awake at the sound of Mark's shout. Sunlight trickled through the patterned openings in the roof that had become quite familiar. He looked around, disoriented.

"So much for shifts, B-Man! It's all good. You needed the rest."

"What time is it?" Brayden asked as he rose to his feet and rubbed his eyes.

"Time to hear what Mark has to say." Mickey emerged from around the corner. He handed Brayden a mug full of black coffee. "You were out for five or six hours. Surprised you're not aching, seeing the position you were in."

Brayden had fallen asleep in his sitting position, hunched forward with his arms wrapped around his knees. He'd never slept for such a long period in such a strange posture, but he felt oddly refreshed.

"Whatcha got, Mark?"

"All right, look at this. I was going about this all wrong, B-Man. I can't believe myself! I was trying to detect quantum signatures like they're some kind of radio signal or something. But these things, man … they're way more sophisticated than that. They're doing more than just emitting quantum signals. See this, right here?"

Mark pointed to his laptop, which showed a string of characters that weren't in human-readable form. "This is an encrypted data structure, and the same one is on both devices. I figured it was just some kind of firmware information or something, but no. I think these are encrypted routing tables."

Brayden knew what routing tables were, but he admittedly didn't grasp their full relevance in quantum networking. Mark had always underestimated Brayden's technical acumen, though; Brayden felt the simplified explanation coming before he could intervene.

"Think of it this way. Imagine you're mailing a package, but it's like ... well, it's a quantum package, all right? You can't just send it wherever you want. Quantum states are crazy fragile. Like if every postal service truck could explode at any moment. You gotta know exactly where every post office is, where every delivery truck is, what each truck's condition is, the shape and size of every mailbox. And all the mail has to be on time. Imagine you had all that information on a handy little digital map."

Mickey smirked at Brayden. He was evidently enjoying Mark's lecture.

"It's brilliant, to be honest. It's horrible, of course, but brilliant. Each node has to know where every single *other* node is in order to maintain this quantum entanglement. Like a GPS for quantum data. The network optimizer and the painting? They're not just passive devices. They're active nodes in this massive quantum web. And look at these timestamps! These things are sending data constantly."

He drummed his fingers on the edge of his machine. Mickey came back from his amusement to consider the hypothesis fully.

"You think Circuit built a directory right into these things?" Mickey asked.

"Exactly," Mark said. "There's a complete map of the quantum network in there. I know it. We just gotta decrypt this protocol."

"I can help," Zeke added. Brayden felt like Zeke had been trying to keep his distance during most of their transgressions. It could have been the simple rationale of self-preservation, to stay out of these obviously dangerous affairs as much as he could. It also could have been a hesitancy to overstep his authority, given his lack of personal stakes in the grand scheme. Either way, it was nice to see his guard come down. "But I got one question for you."

Childlike excitement flashed over Mark for a moment as he saw the opportunity to have a hacking buddy.

"Doesn't that make us sitting ducks?" Zeke gestured at the two devices Mark had just alleged were part of a massive quantum network map. "Won't they easily locate us?"

Mark thought about it for a moment. "Yes, and there's nothing we can do about it. So how about you help me crack this thing?"

Zeke exhaled and nodded, taking a seat at the workstation. Mickey patted him on the back as a gesture of thanks, then nodded his head at Brayden to suggest he follow him across the barn.

"We'll let them work for a few. We've got another matter to address."

Brayden looked at him inquisitively.

"Got a message back on the secure line from Amanda Wong. She's ready to talk to us."

"Is she now?" Brayden raised his eyebrows, a little surprised that Amanda had taken them up on the request. The way Mrs. Wong had talked about her daughter's commitment to work, he had figured Amanda would be buttoned up to any outsiders asking about what happened.

Mickey placed his own laptop on the table with the grenade launcher, pushing the death machine back as it scraped across the table's weathered surface and took some bits of chipped paint with it. He dialed up Amanda and waited for her to answer.

After a few moments, her face filled the screen against the stark backdrop of what appeared to be her office. Her black hair was pulled back in a messy bun, wisps escaping on each side at odd angles. Brayden instantly noticed two things: First, a deep sadness and exhaustion cloaked her features; second, he recognized her. He couldn't quite place it yet.

"Amanda," Brayden began, "thanks so much for chatting with us. I'm really sorry about your dad."

"We're praying for him. Hope he can pull through," Mickey added, trying to feign the optimism neither of them had. Brayden could already tell Mickey was battling emotions, seeing his old friend's daughter.

"Thank you," Amanda said, "but I don't have my hopes up."

She sniffled and wiped her eyes. Brayden pieced it together as soon as he heard her voice; he'd seen her on television, marketing EverChat on evening news bits. She had been on the news when he was at Riley's a few days earlier.

"Can you tell us anything about what happened to him? Or what he was working on?" Brayden asked.

"He was ... he was different the last few days. I was so caught up with work stuff, with the announcement prep." She shook her head. "God, the announcements. Everything's changed now. Everything just feels off."

Brayden thought about how good Sarah would be at navigating the conversation with a grieving daughter like this. He was far worse at it, but he needed to figure out how to console her and steer her back on course. She clearly had valuable information.

He noticed Mickey opening a small console window beside the video chat, which appeared to stream lines of code across it.

"Tell us about those last few days, anything you can share."

She sighed. "It was right after he got home from a long day at the lab. He kept talking about a project they were heading up. QCS—it stands for quantum coherence scaling. I couldn't tell you what that means, but he was so excited. He said it was going to change everything. Change the world." Amanda's voice cracked. "But the last two nights before the coma, he started saying weird things. Offhand comments about voices in his head, about his thoughts fragmenting. Then he'd take some aspirin and go to bed."

Brayden and gazed at her, enthralled by the story. Mickey's attention was split—he seemed to be intently listening, but Brayden noticed him glancing at the ever-changing window of code. Mickey turned and signaled to Mark subtly, so as not to break Amanda's focus.

"Anyway, when he got home that last night, my mom says he was speaking gibberish. His comments made no sense; some of his words weren't even real words. Then he dropped dead, more or less."

Amanda cried softly. Mark sneaked around the side and sat next to Mickey, peering over his shoulder at the lines of code pouring into the mysterious little window. His eyes lit up at whatever it was he was seeing, but Brayden needed to maintain his grip on their information source.

"That's awful, Amanda. I'm so sorry. You mentioned things are different now, that things feel off. What do you mean?"

She glanced off-camera with a look of worry draped across her face. She must have been at Circuit headquarters. "Ever since my dad—and the other two engineers—dropped into their comas, security has been completely overhauled. I think every single entrance to the building is guarded by a different man, one I've never seen before. And I converse with security all the time. It's like they swapped everyone out en masse overnight."

Sure sounds like more members of the humanoid army, Brayden thought.

"They're methodical, cold, cunning. They have no warmth. They don't talk to us. It feels like we're in a war zone now. Even the execs I've met with, everyone is just … I dunno, I hate the vibes."

She almost seemed to shake. It was clear she was scared, and making this call probably was doing very little to assuage those fears. But there had to be a reason she was willing to share the information. Mickey, whose attention was now more dedicated to Mark than Amanda, gave Brayden a rolling gesture with his finger as if to say, *keep this going.*

Before Brayden could ask a follow-up, Amanda continued, shrugging off some of her sadness and wearing a newfound determination. "Obviously you guys are sniffing around Circuit, or you wouldn't have visited my parents in the hospital. I have a terrible feeling about all this, so I want to give you as much as I have." She took a deep breath and looked around again, as if to ensure no one was listening. "There's a huge announcement coming in four days. Our CEO is going to be broadcasting to the whole world, pretty much. It's something about—"

The sound of a door opening coincided with Amanda's alarmed expression as she looked past the camera. Then she flipped into a more business-like mood, portraying normalcy to whoever had entered her office.

"But anyway, I have to run—thanks so much for taking the time to chat with us, Mr. Johnson. Have a great day!"

She disconnected the chat.

"That was clutch!" Mark exclaimed as soon as Amanda's face disappeared. The vibe shift was jarring; Brayden didn't expect such cheerful enthusiasm, given how the call ended. Mickey was also smiling and shaking his head.

"I can't believe that worked."

"What are you two talking about?"

"Amanda's connection," Mark said, pointing at the screen that now showed nothing other than an empty code console, "it was running Circuit's quantum resonance protocol in parallel with the video stream. I can't imagine she did that on purpose, as she doesn't seem to be the technical type. Might be hubris on their part, I dunno. But the quantum states are constantly seeking entanglement. It's like a heartbeat across their whole network. Her machine must be quantum-enabled, with whatever experimental stuff they're doing."

Mickey was nodding. "We captured the topology data embedded within those quantum packets going over the network. Combined with the signatures we extracted from the humanoid and Riley's stuff … give us an hour, and we'll have this decrypted."

"Damn," Brayden said. "Nice work, guys. Lot of important stuff in the actual conversation with Amanda too."

He paused for a moment, his mental gears turning. "You think James might have been testing much more powerful quantum hardware? Could a mishap with that fry his brain?"

Mark and Mickey both tilted their heads and shrugged, after looking at each other. "It's possible."

Brayden shook his head and stood. "Let me know when you've got that crap decrypted."

The wait was short-lived. About twenty minutes later, Brayden heard Mark exclaim, "Eff yeah!"

Zeke had joined them in their efforts, and the added brainpower seemed to help. On the screen, a map of the region was littered with tiny dots—so many that they merged into sprawling patches when zoomed out, like the reds and yellows of an approaching storm system on radar.

"Every one of these dots," Mickey explained, "is a device on this quantum network. And by the looks of it, this is just one subnet within Circuit's quantum universe. If it were the full network, I'd expect their headquarters to be bubbling off the chart with quantum signatures."

"But right here ..." Mark zoomed in on one particular cluster of dots, then pointed his finger at it. "This is more than just a few nodes passing data through. There's something happening here. Lot of activity."

"About thirty miles north of us," Brayden noted.

The four of them looked at each other, knowing what they needed to do. And they would need to act with haste, Brayden realized. The culmination of Dawson's plan was set to happen within four days, if Amanda's account was to be believed.

Just as they closed up their machines and prepared for departure, a rustling came from outside the barn. A shadow could be seen passing over and temporarily obscuring the threads of daylight penetrating the wooden planks. Brayden's adrenaline coursed rapidly through his veins. He scurried to the front corner of the barn and grabbed a shovel in the absence of a more effective weapon. The rocket launcher felt unwieldy for close quarters. The others crouched behind hay bales in the back of the barn, and Brayden heard either Mickey or Zeke load a pistol.

Slow, evenly paced footsteps grew louder until the figure was directly outside the barn door. Brayden readied himself, tightening his grip on the shovel. The door swung open, and he cocked it backward.

He was a split second away from swinging it forcefully at his target, but he yielded when Lacy emerged through the door.

"There you are, Cross."

33

It was a relief seeing Lacy, both for personal reasons and strategic ones. Most importantly, Brayden was happy that she was safe and seemingly well. She also had a wealth of expertise as a detective and even as a tactical operative, to some extent. Adding her to their current squad was an unquestionably positive development.

"Good to see you, Lace," Brayden said, patting her on the shoulder. "Certain you weren't followed, right?"

"No chance. I was careful."

Just after asserting her claim, Lacy's demeanor shifted. She paused and held out her hand. Her eyes widened as she looked beyond them to the far side of the barn. A tense silence took root for about three seconds before she whispered with urgency, "Apparently, I was wrong. We have company. Get in that corner, now!"

She pointed at the corner of the barn where the mangled humanoid sat on hay bales. Mickey, Mark, and Zeke took her at her word and hurried to her requested spot. She instructed them to watch the back entrance of the barn around the corner from them. Snow, sensing chaos emerging, ran under the table along the side wall. Brayden, however, still hadn't moved. He stared at Lacy, confused. He hadn't heard or sensed anything suggesting there were intruders, and he considered his own radar for that kind of thing pretty well tuned.

"Are you sure—"

Lacy interrupted him by grabbing him by the collar and tugging him along with surprising force as she scurried to the opposite corner of the barn from the other three. She reached into her bag and handed Brayden a small firearm. It was unlike anything he'd used before and had a blue streak glowing along its edge. He accepted it, still trying to process whatever it was Lacy was seeing. She retrieved another of the same weapon and sprinted it over to Mickey.

"One of them will come in the back, two will come in the front. Shoot as soon as you see them. These are nonlethal."

She ran back to the front of the barn and positioned herself a few paces from Brayden. Her angle at the barn's front door was wider than his; if an intruder came in, she'd see them sooner than Brayden would.

"I don't hear anything," Brayden whispered.

An instant later, two loud cracks echoed through the barn in quick succession. It sounded like both doors were kicked in simultaneously. Inexplicably, one man leapt through the rear entrance and two rushed through the front. Exactly as Lacy had warned. Mickey followed his instruction, firing his weapon the moment he saw the intruder. The shot sounded more like a pellet gun than a firearm, but whatever it fired immediately buckled the intruding man. His tall, muscular frame crumpled to the ground, his body convulsing. It must have been some kind of electroshock weapon, but the force and speed with which it nullified the man suggested it was well beyond the standard power of a taser.

It felt like minutes of watching Mickey neutralize the man, but in reality, it had probably been less than two seconds. His focus shifting back to the matter in his own vicinity, Brayden trained his weapon on the second of the two men barging through the front and fired, quickly eliminating him. He waited for Lacy to fire at the third man, but she was frozen. It was like she was gripped by a constricting fear in the moment.

"Lacy!"

She stared, wide-eyed. Brayden aimed his own weapon and fired again, but the gun just clicked softly. The glowing bar on its side was refilling, now an orange color instead of blue.

Having emerged into the barn, the target raised his weapon and fired a much louder shot, a bullet from a standard firearm. In a blur, Brayden ripped Lacy's gun from her paralyzed hands and dropped the intruder with a final shot.

For a few seconds, the silence was deafening. It didn't sound like there were any more intruders. With a few seconds to process it all, Brayden noted the obvious to himself—these were almost definitely more humanoids.

"Zeke!"

Mickey's distressed shriek broke the silence. Brayden emerged from his corner to get a better view as Mickey and Mark squatted behind a hay bale. Mark scrambled across the barn and grabbed a towel. As Brayden took another step forward, he realized it was a moment of naivete for Mark and that the towel would not help.

Square in the center of Zeke's forehead, a bullet had gone straight through.

The next sounds were muffled sobs coming from Mickey, who was now on one knee in front of Zeke. Brayden looked around and tried to listen intently for any additional threats. When he was satisfied none were coming, he returned his focus to the situation in front of them. He looked at Lacy, who he tried with all his might not to blame.

She had frozen, after all. It was a straight shot, and she was highly trained. Her hesitation had given the man an extra second to fire one bullet, and Zeke had the misfortune of being the first target he identified.

On the other hand, they would have almost certainly been ambushed, and likely all killed, had she not provided the warning. It was an uncanny display of tactical awareness.

And then, on a third hand, Brayden considered the totality of the evidence. They had been relatively safe in this barn for two days, and within five minutes of Lacy showing up unannounced, their gracious host was dead.

"I'm so sorry, Mickey," Mark said.

Brayden put a hand on Mickey's shoulder and squatted next to him. He was still crying, his forehead cradled in his right hand.

"This is all my fault," Mickey said, his voice shaky. "I brought this mess to him."

"Stop that," Brayden said. "You're only in this because of me. All of you are. Don't put this on yourself, Mick."

Brayden felt an overwhelming amount of guilt. Some of it was deserved, he figured. Some of it wasn't. But regardless, Zeke was now dead because of what they had brought to his doorstep. Mickey had lost an old friend, and he was blaming himself for it.

Who would be next?

Snow brushed against Mickey's side and whimpered. Mickey patted him and rose to his feet, sniffling and wiping his eyes. The sadness appeared to evaporate in favor of determination. He looked at Brayden but gestured at Lacy.

"She was obviously followed into the woods, so it's time for us to get outta here."

Lacy dropped her head and shook it, rubbing the back of her neck. When she looked at Zeke, she began to tear up.

"I'm so sorry. I thought I was …" She trailed off, staring at the dusty barn floor. Mickey was probably enraged at her, but Brayden knew they didn't have time for infighting now. Lacy regathered her focus quickly. "I just want to help. I know you're in trouble. I want to help."

Mickey pierced her with a look of disappointment, but he seemed to land at the same conclusion Brayden had. If she was secretly working against them, she could have allowed the ambush to obliterate them.

"Can we cover him up?" Mickey asked, nodding his head at Zeke. "When we're out of this mess, I'm coming back here and giving him a proper burial. Give him back to the soil he loved."

Brayden nodded, and Mark was already on it. He gathered some hay and a small tarp and began concealing Zeke's body. While Mark did so, Brayden inspected the trio of fallen attackers. He withdrew his switchblade and sliced the first man's forearm. The cut revealed the expected circuitry in lieu of blood.

"Humanoids," Brayden said. "In case you were wondering."

"What the hell are these, by the way?" Mickey held up his electric weapon. The question was directed at Lacy.

"High-voltage electroshock guns. After everything you told me about these humanoids, it didn't sound like pistols were the play. These things will pretty much fry their circuitry or at least incapacitate them." She paused for a moment, then shrugged. "I dunno much about their inner workings, but seems like I was right."

On that point, there was no doubt. The three humanoids were certainly lifeless, for now.

"Thirty miles north," Brayden said. "We gotta go now."

34

Brayden, Mickey, Mark, Lacy, and Snow hiked the half-mile back to where the SUV was parked on the mountain's access road. A few hours earlier, the mood had been surprisingly positive. They'd been safe for a little while, they were making progress, and they were learning new information. Lacy's arrival and Zeke's death had smothered the vibes like a wet blanket on glowing embers.

Hopping into the driver's seat, Brayden instructed Mickey to ride shotgun. Mark and Lacy poured into the back seat, Snow catapulting himself between them. The vehicle's tires crunched and squeaked through the packed snow that molded the edges of the trail, and within a few minutes they were back on the expressway heading north. It was a tiny bit warmer than it had been the prior few days, and at street level, a brown slush lined the boundaries of the streets. Being a much more traveled way than the access road, though, the highway's primary surface was dry and clear.

"What do we know about this location, Mark?" Brayden asked.

Mark was diligently pecking the keys of his keyboard, trying to uncover more detail about the coordinates to which they were driving. "I'm mostly seeing woods on the satellite imagery. No buildings that I can tell. Maybe it's underground? Or maybe they've manipulated satellite images. But get this—as recently as the eighties, there was some sort of industrial building in this spot, almost right at the coordinates."

"What kind of industrial building?" Mickey asked.

"A big one. From the old photos I can find, looks like it's some kind of electrical substation or power distribution facility. Let's see ..."

They all waited on Mark's unfinished thought, the sound of his keystrokes delivering a solo performance. Then he exhaled. "So, it was a power facility. Owned by Northeast Power until '96. Looks like it was a pretty standard deal at first. One of their larger substations in New England. But then it gets interesting. Graybridge Ventures acquired it when Northeast Power was restructuring, selling off some of their assets at the beginning of the utility deregulation push. Graybridge paid way over market value too—like triple what these facilities were going for back then.

"It stayed on the grid as an active substation until 2006, then Graybridge filed paperwork to decommission it. Told the state they were trying to modernize, that they were going to route power through newer facilities spread throughout the region. But guess what? They kept paying the bills, kept filing permits for equipment upgrades. Local officials probably figured it was just an abandoned station being kept on ice for possible reuse in the future. Then, sometime between its decommissioning in '06 and the satellite imagery I could find from '09, it disappears from the map. Engulfed by forest."

Brayden glanced at the rearview mirror to see if Mark was still digging into the research, but his head was up and his eyes were trained on Brayden through the mirror. The others exchanged looks, gauging their reactions to the information.

Then Lacy chimed in. "Graybridge was just a shell," she said. "They were backed by the same venture capitalists that were Circuit's early investors. It's the same group that funded Circuit's first quantum research lab in Massachusetts too."

Now Brayden shifted his head to see Lacy in the mirror. Mickey turned all the way around in his seat to look at her, and Mark was furiously typing in an effort to validate her claims. A few moments later, he did so. "She's right."

"How in the fresh hell do you know all that?" Mickey asked.

Brayden looked at her skeptically.

"I did a thorough analysis into Circuit's corporate structure when we started investigating Blauss. You learn to follow the money in this line of work, guys."

Mickey turned back to face the road ahead of them, shaking his head. "It's neither here nor there. We knew whatever was at this hotspot was going to be connected with Circuit. It's their quantum network."

He was right in that regard. But Brayden's eyes were still trained on Lacy, flashing back to the road only as often as was needed. Lacy hadn't known about Circuit's involvement in all of this when they started the Blauss investigation. Brayden had told her about all their discoveries on the phone the other day. That should have been the first time she learned of Circuit's connection to this.

She was lying.

Why? What was she hiding?

Twenty minutes later, about a mile off the highway, they approached a road that snaked into a sea of trees. "Take this one," Mickey said.

The initial incline took a little extra juice from the Toyota, but they ascended the narrow road and eventually pulled into a large clearing. Before them loomed a large facility, its silhouette casting long shadows in the afternoon sun. Power lines stretched outward from aged towers, their steel frames oxidized to a burnt orange color. A chain-link fence topped with barbed wire surrounded the property, though nature had long since begun reclaiming portions of it. Thick vines wrapped around the links like spaghetti woven around a fork. About thirty yards from the swath of trees where Brayden pulled the vehicle to a stop, a swinging gate in the fence was evidently unsecured.

He rolled down the rear windows a few inches each, then they all unloaded from the car. Mickey gave Snow a treat and told him to stay in the car. Of course, he didn't understand the English, but he understood the assignment. From the assortment of weapons they brought with them, each person was equipped with one electroshock pistol. Brayden also slid a standard firearm beneath his belt at the small of his back and handed one discreetly to Mickey as well.

They crept toward the facility's grounds, slipping inside the fence's gate and crouching behind a cluster of shrubs. Brayden held his fist up, signaling the group to wait. He scanned the perimeter methodically, searching for disruptions or security forces outside the building. Three transformers stood near the main entrance of the facility, which was just to the left. A smaller utility building was tucked away beside the main building. To the right of the transformers, a set of dense bushes and weeds had clearly gone untamed for a while; maybe even since the alleged decommissioning of this place, Brayden thought.

"Two of them," Lacy whispered. "One behind the middle unit. One in those bushes on the right. He's lying prone."

Her gaze was trained on the transformers in front of the building. Brayden shot Mickey a concerned look. Once again, Lacy seemed to sense danger that Brayden couldn't sense. He wondered if he was losing his edge, but before he could question it further, a flash of fabric peeked out from behind the middle transformer. At least half of Lacy's intel was confirmed.

"Mark, stay here and keep watch," Brayden said. He turned to Mickey. "Mick, circle wide right. See if you can get a look behind those bushes. I'll approach the transformer. Lace—"

Before Brayden could turn to give her instructions, she was already flanking to the left, toward the small utility building.

He moved through the overgrown grass silently and swiftly, keeping a low profile. He could still see a sliver of color protruding from behind the surface of the transformer. If it was indeed a humanoid patrolling the facility, it was stationary. It reminded him of a video game glitch. *I can see you, buddy.*

Twenty yards became fifteen, then ten. When Brayden was close enough to hear the static humming of the transformer, he glanced to his right and caught Mickey's eye across the yard. Mickey gave him a nod, and Brayden burst around the corner into view of the humanoid. Before it could raise its own weapon, Brayden had already fired his electroshock square into its chest. Blue electricity briefly arced across its torso as it convulsed and dropped to the ground. A second shot crackled from behind him—Mickey's target had revealed itself, and he'd quickly neutralized him. The humanoid twitched to a stop in the bushes.

"Clear," Mickey said.

"Clear," Brayden said back.

Brayden scanned the vicinity for others. None so far.

"Clear over here." Lacy's voice came from the left flank direction as she walked toward them. "Nice work. Just like I figured it would be. Two sentries, basic patrol pattern."

Brayden again looked at Mickey with doubt. It was anything but a basic patrol pattern, with one hiding poorly behind a transformer and the other lying prone in the bushes. He didn't understand how Lacy had predicted it again, but he was grateful for it. She'd now massively boosted their odds of survival in two straight humanoid encounters.

Then the crack of another gunshot rippled through the evening air, coming from the entrance to the main building. Lacy cried out and stumbled backward, clutching her shoulder. She crumpled to the ground, falling to a rest with her back leaning against the leftmost transformer. Mark had scurried up to join the crowd after hearing Brayden and Mickey signal the area was clear. Lacy fell almost directly into Mark's path, so he immediately knelt to tend to her.

At the door to the facility, a man stood in a white lab coat. He held a pistol at his side, a faint trail of smoke still floating off its tip. He raised his pistol again, presumably to fire at Mark, when he saw Brayden and Mickey emerging from his left. As if the realization of his numerical disadvantage had just hit him, he turned and sprinted back inside the building.

"Go get him! I'll stay with Lacy," Mark said in a panic.

Brayden deemed the proposal sensible and ran for the door with Mickey by his side. They paused at the entrance, nodding at one another and readying their weapons. They curled inside the building and scanned the area. The facility was an eerie blend of old and new. Outside the walls of the building, nature had been encroaching on what had, at one point, been a shiny new substation. Inside, massive machinery and switchgear stood like ancient artifacts, their gauges long since dead. But littered between the old defunct machinery were stacks of modern server racks humming with processors, adorned with blue and green LED lights reflecting off of shiny steel barriers. Thick black cables snaked across the floor, disappearing into a few raised platforms that certainly weren't part of the building's original infrastructure. The air carried a gross metallic taste, like a mixture of blood, metal, and decaying organic matter. Catwalks stitched across the space above them, casting shadows from the harsh fluorescent light strips that battled against the natural light seeping in through skylight windows. To their left, a metal door was labeled *Inventory*. Based on the view from the outside, it probably connected to the smaller utility building. To their right, the building opened into a larger room with high ceilings and the glow of power equipment.

The next sound they heard was the clanking of footwear on metal. Looking upward, Brayden saw the man in the lab coat lifting himself up the last rung of a ladder and running along a catwalk. Mickey started moving around the edge of the room to position himself for a better angle at the man. Brayden took the opposite route, but he only needed to move a few paces before he came to an elevated platform. Lifting himself onto it, he had a clear view of the man.

Mickey lost his footing and stumbled, and Brayden heard his weapon clatter across the floor. It immediately drew the attention of the combative scientist, who twisted toward Mickey and raised his weapon. Brayden took aim and fired just in the nick of time to save his friend.

Only his weapon didn't fire. It had been plenty of time since he last fired, but its normal blue status indicator was now red. It must have lost its charge.

His margin for error trimmed to milliseconds, Brayden whipped the pistol from his belt and fired. The bullet hit the scientist on the left side of his back, sending him staggering forward as his own weapon sent a stray bullet clanking off metal somewhere in the room. Stumbling and muttering in anguish, the man's hip slammed into the railing and he toppled over it, falling thirty feet from the catwalk to the ground.

Brayden expected a thud, followed by the whirring and whining of malfunctioning circuitry. What he didn't expect was the aggressive splattering of blood that created a ring of red covering a six-foot radius around the body.

He was human.

Mickey emerged from behind a row of servers as Brayden stared down at the body. Neither spoke for a few moments. Brayden was walloped with a deep feeling of remorse. He didn't expect to take a human life.

"You had to, Bray. You saved me," Mickey said, seeming to sense Brayden's inner struggle.

He peeled his eyes away from the gory mess, and they fell directly on the *Inventory* sign above the closed metal door. Looking back at Mickey, he nodded.

"Let's see what's in that room."

35

As they approached the door to the inventory room, Mickey grasped the handle and twisted it. The moment he began pushing the door inward, Brayden's senses heightened. He couldn't explain it, but he instinctively grabbed the handle over Mickey's knuckles and pulled it tightly shut. The small amount the door had nudged triggered the ferocious barking of what sounded like at least three dogs inside the door.

Mickey stared at Brayden in awe and also with concern. The sound of heavy paws scraped against the metal on the other side of the door.

"Dogs?" Mickey said.

Brayden held up a finger to suggest they stay silent for a moment. Putting his ear against the door, he listened. The barking and clawing continued for ten seconds or so, then stopped. No additional noise followed; no footsteps, no conversations, no movement.

"I think it's just the dogs. The two humanoids and these canines were probably the scientist's full security team."

"Perfect. *Just* the dogs," Mickey said. His sarcasm was clear. "Just get past the ravenous attack dogs and we're on our way."

"You still got a charge on your gun?"

Mickey drew his weapon and examined it. Where Brayden's had since shifted to a red LED light, Mickey's was still blue. "Looks like it."

"Get ready to use it," Brayden said.

Readying his own standard firearm, he grasped the handle and positioned his shoulder to slam the door. After exchanging a look of affirmation with Mickey, he burst through.

It was more of a vestibule than a grand reveal of the inventory room. Another metal door with partial windows stood ten feet from where they now stood. The world spun in slow motion for a moment as Brayden catalogued their obstacle. Three rabid dogs, their eyes glowing with fire. They growled and barked and flashed their sharp, yellowish-white teeth. With no hesitation—even though he quite loved dogs—he fired a bullet through the first one's head. Mickey's shot was in quick succession, crippling another with a blue storm of electric shock.

Whimpers escaped from each, but Brayden's bullet didn't stop his canine in its tracks. It wriggled and howled, but it continued stumbling toward him. Circuitry and smoke peeked out of the fresh bullet hole. He fired another one, and it weakened further.

They were robots. Caninoids? Dogbots? Robarks?

"They're robots!" Brayden shouted, figuring the term was clearer than the variant on humanoids. He saw Mickey fire his electroshock at the third caninoid, but the dreaded sound of an empty click followed the pull of his trigger. Brayden could see the LED bar on the side of the weapon slowly filling up as it glowed orange. Mickey's gun needed a few seconds to recharge between rounds. He was defenseless against the charging beast.

It would have required a perfect headshot on a sprinting canine to prevent Mickey from getting fangs driven into him, and even at that, the angle would have put Mickey at risk of catching a misfire. Brayden processed his surroundings, searching for a split-second decision. The hound he'd neutralized was now twitching on the ground, a puddle of hydraulic fluid having seeped from its two head wounds, each of which saw sparks jumping from them. He had no time to think, only to react. He grabbed Mickey's shoulder and yanked him sideways, vaulting himself into the spot his friend had just occupied.

"Bray!" Mickey yelled.

The charging caninoid leapt straight at Brayden's chest. Brayden hooked his pistol upward, aiming for the underside of the dog's chin, and fired twice in quick succession. Its weight hit him like a train—it had to weigh at least a hundred pounds, he thought—and he fell backward, slamming his back on the floor. Its claws slashed into his arms. The dog twitched and clawed as hydraulic fluid poured from its head wounds, soaking Brayden's shirt. It snapped its jaws at him, but it was too discombobulated to land a successful bite. Brayden wiggled himself out from beneath the malfunctioning machine, grabbed the nearby fire extinguisher, and doused the two wounded caninoids. The super-chilled gas immediately frosted their synthetic fur and clashed against their overheated circuitry. Moments later, all three were finally motionless.

"I owe you one," Mickey said.

Brayden was wheezing. "Caninoids. What's next?"

Mickey gestured his head at the door. "I'd say that's next. Must be something juicy behind that door, if three artificial people-eaters gotta guard it."

Unlike the door into the vestibule, the door into the inventory room had no handle from their side. It had only a metal plate designed to push into the room. Brayden led the way as they entered. A grotesque odor was thickly present within this room, flooding his nostrils in an instant. They both winced.

The inventory room was large. What looked like hospital beds lined three walls, while a few desks and workstations lined the wall near them. The beds each had electronic displays beside them, like the monitors that would show a patient's vital signs. By his rough estimate, Brayden figured there were sixty beds in this room. Soft beeps created a droning symphony as about half of the electronic displays showed active vital signs—heart monitors tracing weak but steady rhythms across their screens.

All the beds, however, were occupied.

"My God," Mickey whispered.

In the beds that lacked accompanying beeps and lines, the bodies appeared cold and pale. It seemed likely that they were the primary cause of the suffocating smell in the air. But what about the others? Thirty bodies looked nearly as dead, but their beeps suggested life was hanging by a thread.

"They're in comas," Brayden said.

As they paced the room, they noted the condition of the victims. Very few had physical markers of assault, struggle, violence. Some had wrist wounds, which suggested captivity. But they weren't murdered by gunshot, by strangulation, by any physical means. Were they sick? Drugged? Poisoned?

The array of beeps was contrasted by a machine a few beds down, newly assuming a steady tone. The heart monitor showed a flat line, and Brayden noticed that a thin tube resembling an IV was hooked into each body. Remnants of a light green fluid were dripping through the tube as the monitor flatlined.

"These people," Mickey said, "I recognize some of them. These are some of the missing persons."

Brayden thought back to their research into Sarah's murder, the area murders, and the missing persons' reports. All abducted by unidentified culprits. It was all making more and more sense. Humanoids had captured and brought these poor victims here, and now they were dropping dead. But why? Why hadn't these people seen the same fate that Sarah did—being forcibly uploaded and brutally murdered?

On a whiteboard near the workstations, someone had scrawled in messy handwriting: *Test Group 26-F*, followed by the current date. Below that line, another scribble read *Transfer Complete*.

"They're testing the tech right here," Brayden said. "Regular people, grabbed off the street. Forced into this sick experiment, whatever it is."

Brayden thought back to the devices Riley and Ellen brought them and wondered how close the two of them might have been to death, if the quantum technology was to blame for these experiments.

Near the whiteboard, a desk held stacks of papers and manila folders. A thick black binder was open, its pages dog-eared and marked with tabs of several colors. They inspected it.

"Project Watershed," Mickey read aloud from the header that started each page. He began flipping through them, Brayden hunched beside him, scanning the contents.

There were timestamps of several *transfer attempts*, notes on the reactions of subjects, and various other metadata that made little sense to them. The clinical nature of the notes painted a picture that amounted to torture. *94% retention post-transfer. 83% stability at 48 hours. 76% maintained coherence after network integration.*

"They're not just forcing copies of people's minds for a stupid app," Brayden said. "They're stealing them. Transferring, not copying. And they're perfecting the process."

"And scaling it," Mickey added.

A red tab near the back of the binder caught Brayden's attention. They flipped to it, finding a full-page divider for the section: *CLASSIFIED - PHASE 3 IMPLEMENTATION*. Below the oversized title, the next day's date was printed.

The individual harvesting phase of Project Watershed has provided ample proof of concept. Quantum coherence scaling trials confirm readiness for mass deployment. The Watershed protocol will initiate via broadcast signal, distributed to our network nodes, at the coordinates detailed henceforth. Estimated reach is 42% of the North American population after the first wave. Subsequent waves will follow at 12-hour intervals and increase in size. 80% global reach estimated within two days.

Brayden looked at Mickey, but his eyes were still flying across the lines.

Note: Individual testing facilities like Site 23 will no longer be necessary after implementation. Consciousness transfer will be instant and distributed across the quantum network. Physical bodies will remain in stasis with neural activity suspended until integration to the network is complete. Field staff will neutralize problematic resistors.

This time, when Brayden looked back at Mickey, he was returning a wide-eyed stare. They were both speechless for a few moments before Brayden tried to evaluate what they had learned. His stomach turned as he spoke it.

"The army of humanoids is just the muscle," Brayden said. "The murders, like Sarah and so many others ... those were just grains of sand in his plan, to craft the super-intelligence installed in his soldiers. They're already embedded throughout society, ready for the call of duty. He's planning a forcible upload of millions and millions of people's consciousness."

"Not just an upload. Theft and murder, all in one. Everyone targeted will drop into these lethal comas, and those freakazoids will intervene against anyone who doesn't."

"Those devices Riley and Ellen had, and the humanoids, and the caninoids," Brayden said. "And all the Circuit laptops, and other electronics, all of it ... they're not just nodes for communication. They're the access points. They're the devices that will rip people's consciousness away and leave their brains fried in their wake."

"And it happens tomorrow," Mickey said, slamming his finger onto the binder where the date was written. On the next table over, Brayden noticed what looked like a marketing brochure. It was arranged in a trifold structure, and at the top of its front pane, *Project Watershed* was written in a strong font that popped off the page. Below, a subtitle read: *A new era is born.*

Brayden didn't need to say it aloud. They both knew it was time to make a plan, and fast.

"Guys!"

The cry from outside the building interrupted their moment of dread. It was Mark.

"Guys, get out here!"

Brayden and Mickey ran back to the main room of the facility and out the door to where Mark was still tending to Lacy. She looked to be in rough shape; she had slid further down to the ground, nearly lying horizontally. Brayden had almost forgotten she was shot, given the gravity of their recent discoveries.

"Is she all right? Lace, you okay?" Brayden asked.

Mark held up the white towel he'd been pressing on her shoulder where the bullet had hit.

The towel was white. Completely white.

Brayden looked at the wound.

There was no blood. Only circuitry shimmering in the fading sunlight.

36

"I ... I didn't know," Lacy whispered. Her voice trembled as her hand traced the exposed circuitry in her shoulder, her fingers grazing across the metallic threads that should have been human flesh. "I swear to God, I didn't know. I ..."

Brayden watched her intently with a deep feeling of conflict. He tried to reconcile the experiences with the person he'd known for years against the reality before his eyes. The setting sun cast shadows across Lacy's face as she wrestled with her own existence. Mickey had his electroshock weapon trained on her, but his grip was loose and uncertain.

"How could I not know? I just ... I ..." Lacy's eyes welled with tears Brayden now knew were artificial. "All those cases, all the times you helped me, Bray. The Williams murder, all of it ... Was any of it real?"

In real time, knowing more about how these things operated, Brayden could see Lacy teetering on the verge of her emotional regulation threshold. She would take a sharp inhale when it looked like tears may flow, stare blankly for a few moments, then resume from a neutral emotion. Unlike past interactions with EverChat Sarah or coffee shop Beth, Lacy didn't snap into a joyful mood. That this reckoning was with the realization of her very essence, her very being, may have been enough to keep her tight to the emotional threshold, bouncing off it repeatedly like a fly stuck in a window.

Mark still knelt beside her. It looked like his scientific curiosity was battling against his genuine empathy. "The memories before Westbrook, do they feel real to you?"

"They feel like my whole life." Lacy closed her eyes and pressed her head back against the surface of the transformer. "Some of it is fragmented. I was noticing it more and more over the past few days. But I can't draw the line. When was I created?"

The cycles became shorter and shorter as Lacy hit her emotional barriers every few seconds. If her programmed restrictions were lifted, she would be sobbing. The fear and bewilderment in her eyes were clear. Similar to the way Brayden couldn't look Sarah in the eye on EverChat and ignore the feelings of personal connection, he couldn't look at Lacy in this moment as a disposable robot. Lacy had been in his life for years. She was a friend to him, to Sarah, to the kids. She had friends, memories, accomplishments. And now she was distraught. A part of him wanted to slice his own arm open, just to make sure he saw blood.

But amid his overwhelming sense of empathy toward Lacy, he needed to keep a focus on the information they had just learned. He squatted down beside her and put his hand on her unwounded shoulder.

"Lace, I'm so sorry. And you're making it really hard to figure out what the hell your ... species? What your kind is really up to. You're obviously one of the good ones."

She wiped a tear away that hadn't really formed yet, then looked at Brayden. Her eyes portrayed devastation and defeat.

"But Lacy, what we found in there is important. Can you tell me what you know about Project Watershed?"

Her stare was blank for a few more seconds, then she closed her eyes to concentrate. She was evidently scraping the quantum network —not unlike Sarah had tried to do, from within EverChat—to retrieve information that could help her friends. Then her eyes shot open, the look of despair replaced with one of anxiety and urgency.

"You need to go. They know where I am, and they know you're here. Don't tell me anything else about that project."

Brayden exchanged a worried look with Mickey and Mark. Mickey had lowered his weapon by now.

"Lace, we can't just—"

"You can. And you will." Her voice found its familiar authority again. "The quantum network, it's how they track all of it. How they … how we … coordinate."

She was now holding out her hands and rotating them, enduring an out-of-body experience as she came to the realization that she was part of a massive hive mind. From an outsider's perspective, Brayden could only assume it took all of her willpower to ignore the looming existential questions that stemmed from the realization, like whether she even had free will.

"How didn't I think of it before?" Mark chimed in. "The quantum entanglement—if we could create a localized disruption field, I—"

Lacy whipped her hand out and covered Mark's mouth. "Go!" she shouted. "You're not understanding me. You can't tell me things. They *are* me. I've probably been the one endangering you this whole time." Her voice grew shaky again. "This is all my fault. But please, Brayden. Go, now. They're coming."

Brayden wiped the moisture that had built in his own eyes as he stood. He looked at his companions and then at Lacy. "We'll head north, then. Toward Canada."

Lacy looked back at him but said nothing. Then she looked at Mickey, and her gaze drifted down to his gun.

"Do it, Mickey."

Mickey, taken aback, looked at Lacy, then at Brayden.

"You have to do it," she said. "Who knows if they can weaponize me? Turn me into an enemy combatant? I can't keep costing you the chance to stop this."

Mickey still waited for Brayden to give him the go-ahead. Brayden looked back at Lacy, and he felt an intense sadness bubble up through his chest. A few tears streamed down his cheek before he sniffled and nodded. "She's right."

He had to walk away. It didn't feel fair to Mickey, of course. But Brayden had to walk away. He couldn't watch. When he had paced about ten yards toward their vehicle, he heard the swift pop of the electroshock and a rustling on the ground, followed by eventual silence.

The textured rubber of the vehicle's tires crunched over sticks and slush as Brayden drove away from the power station. All three of them were silent, still shocked by the discovery of Lacy's nature.

"So, we're heading north?" Mickey finally said.

"The opposite," Brayden answered. "You heard her. They see what her eyes see, hear what her ears hear. Hopefully, if they put any stock into my word, that'll send them north and keep them off our track for a little while."

Mickey nodded, impressed with the forethought. "Where to, then?"

"Southwest."

"Any destination in mind?"

Brayden looked straight ahead, his grip tightening on the wheel. "New York City. We're going to Circuit."

Mickey and Mark said nothing. Snow panted in the back seat, likely parched. Brayden could sense the unease his companions felt regarding his plan.

"We won't go straight there. We'll need to stop to make a plan and prepare our supplies. And you guys don't need to come with me. But I'm finding Dawson if it's the last thing I do."

"We're coming with you," Mark said. Brayden could see his eyes in the rearview mirror. They portrayed valor, but they also displayed some uncertainty. Mark was out of his element. He glanced ahead to Mickey in the passenger's seat, who nodded affirmatively, then shifted in his seat to face Mark.

"Hey, you seemed to have some kind of epiphany back there. Lacy prevented you from spilling the beans. Wanna spill 'em now?"

"Yes!" Mark said. "Yes. Look. I dunno if B-Man would remember this. He probably was just zoning me out back then. But I had been building a prototype of this thing."

He fished into his bag and retrieved a small device resembling a walkie-talkie.

"I was calling it the *Quantum Nexus Resonator*. All those tech giants got me inspired to try stuff out on my own. My goals were simple. Stupid, really. Just to send a basic little quantum signal. Make a baseline quantum bridge to another one of these devices."

He pulled out a second one, holding one in each hand.

"Well, after hearing what Lacy revealed, and what you guys gathered from that Project Watershed stuff ... I can't believe I didn't think of it earlier. I need to flip my objective on its head. Building a quantum bridge is the job of tech giants, but what if I can just disrupt the bridge?"

Mickey continued looking expectantly at Mark, while Brayden glanced at him in the mirror every few seconds.

"Call it the *Quantum Nexus Nullifier*. See, my original prototype tried to establish quantum connections. To create entanglement between particles across distance. I was trying to build a bridge, not destroy one. But now? I think if I reverse the polarity of the circuit design I was crafting, and add a phase inverter right here ..."

He seemed to be talking to himself as much as he was talking to Brayden and Mickey. He had popped off the back cover of the device and was pointing to areas as he spoke.

"It would create potentially destructive interference. Our theory is that these humanoids, and all the other nodes on this network, maintain their shared consciousness through quantum entanglement, right? If my thinking is right, I can build a handheld device that could collapse those quantum states with a counter-resonance field. It'll force decoherence, scramble their shared consciousness, maybe even fry enough of their delicate circuitry to nullify them."

Mickey squinted at the handheld devices and pointed at them. "Those little things are gonna save humanity? You saw the maps. These things are littered all over."

Mark chuckled. "No, no. We're running on limited resources, and even more limited time. I can probably build these two, *maybe* a third, if we're lucky. They'll be handheld, and their effect will be localized. Based on proximity."

Brayden stared ahead at the road, which was now a southbound highway trailed by a smattering of headlights across his mirrors. His mind churned through Mark's explanations as he tried to piece together a plan.

"Amanda Wong said Circuit had swapped out a bunch of their security staff," Brayden said. "The way she described them, I wouldn't be surprised if they're all humanoids. Maybe this thing can help us get past them."

Mickey and Mark both nodded but said nothing.

"What do you need, Mark? To get those things operational?"

Mark sighed and looked back at the half-made prototypes in his hands. "I can get by with a quiet place to work, and a work surface," he said. "Plus a bit of material we could get at most electronics supply stores."

"And how much time do you need?"

"Doesn't matter how much I need, it's how much we've got," Mark said. "Sounds like hours, not days."

Brayden confirmed his suspicions, because he was right; the Project Watershed binder suggested this disastrous protocol would be enacted tomorrow. Brayden hoped to get back in touch with Amanda once more, to get any last bit of intel she had. But as his foot pressed the accelerator harder, and the SUV barreled toward the New York border, his mind drifted away from the matters at hand. He thought about Mari and Charlie, and whether this decision to head toward Circuit's heavily guarded headquarters was the best thing for their future. He thought about Sarah and how avenging her was an equally important priority. Would she have agreed? Would she be begging him to drop this, go home, hug his children, and tell them it's going to be okay?

Then he thought about Lacy, and the grander realization that this wasn't just about revenge for his wife. He *was* making the right choice for his kids' futures.

Because, based on everything they had uncovered, there was no future for humanity as they knew it. Not unless they stopped Dawson.

And Dawson had expedited the timeline.

37

Dawson's footsteps echoed through Circuit's basement level like thunderclaps as he stormed toward the laboratory. Joining the footsteps was the sound of breaking glass as he hurled his crystal tumbler against the wall, sending amber liquid streaming down its pristine surface.

"Incompetent imbeciles!" he shouted into the empty corridor. "Every last one of them!"

Behind him, Elias Veum hurried with a tablet clutched against his chest. His typical composure was splintering under the weight of his boss's fury.

"Sir, we still have a lot of assets in play. All is not lost. The synthetics are—"

"Ha! The synthetics!" Dawson pivoted sharply on his heel to face Elias, causing him to stop and stumble backward. "The same synthetics that let Cross waltz into Site 23? The same ones that failed to eliminate him on any of the numerous occasions when they had the chance? These are supposed to be superhumans!"

Dawson jammed his index finger into Elias's chest. "What was it again, Elias? My memory is failing me … 'He'll be dead in two sunrises,' was that it?"

Elias gulped, his brows raised, his body tense.

"Instead, he may have discovered everything. Everything!"

The last word boomed through the cold, flat hallway. Dawson's hand trembled in rage as he pressed his palm against the biometric scanner to enter the lab. Its door slid open with a soft hiss, like the slow twisting of the lid on a carbonated beverage. As it tucked away, it revealed the stark metal surfaces within the room. He stormed to the central console and whizzed around a series of holographic displays.

"We start now. It launches by morning." His voice had dropped an octave and a few decibels, such that it was now barely above a dangerous whisper. "Cross knows what we're doing. He's foiled my plans once. I will not let him do it again. We cannot wait any longer."

Elias fidgeted with his tablet and shifted his weight uncomfortably. "Sir, the network … it isn't fully optimized yet. The quantum coherence scaling tests showed we need at least another—"

"The tests?" Dawson spat the words with a comic disbelief. "The test are a formality, Elias! The technology works. You've seen it work. It's time to go."

"But Mr. Dawson, the civilian casualties … If we rush this, the death toll could be unprecedented."

Dawson turned slowly to look at Elias, then took two slow and ominous strides in his direction. "You don't get it, Elias, do you?"

Elias appeared to be mustering up more courage now, as low as the bar may have been. He was no longer trembling, and he was maintaining eye contact with his superior.

"Elias, Elias. I've always liked you. But I may have overestimated you, Are you having doubts?"

"No, sir, I just think we should consider—"

"Consider what? Consider who?" Dawson took another step toward him. "Consider the weak-minded? The feeble ones who won't accept their newfound immortality?"

His gaze continued to pierce through Elias's pupils.

"I have news for you, Elias. No one is meant to survive the consciousness transfer. Just like EverChat isn't meant to be humanity's eternal waterfall of happiness, or a sentimental boom to put us in good graces. It has all been a collection of means to an end. It's clear to me that our quantum network needs work, thanks to the ineptitude of yourself and others that have preceded you. But we've harvested the minds. We've developed the technology. We can conduct the transfer and begin humankind's evolution toward immortality."

Elias still looked back at him with concern. Vince could tell it wasn't clicking yet.

"You seem to have misunderstood what our mission is. Casualties aren't the side effect, Elias. They are the goal. Or a coequal part of the goal, anyway. This is humanity's next evolution. Our differences have further and further divided us; our mental limitations further inhibited us; our physical limitations further handicapped our potential. It's all about to change."

Dawson snapped his fingers a few inches from Elias's face, startling him.

"When we initiate the Watershed protocol, we forcibly start taking the rest of the minds we haven't yet harvested. There are no survivors of that process, Elias. Sure, the bodies may have vital signs. They are *alive*, in a sense. But are they? With no consciousness, no being? They're like the trees and the flowers, at that point. Now, of course, I had hoped to perfect our synthetics and their hive mind with all the physical uploads before running the mass transfer. I had. I would have loved for these synthetics to be perfect soldiers, invincible mercenaries. Honestly, they're still pretty good, I think. They have served admirably, and until the whole Cross debacle, they were doing a splendid job."

He took another half-step toward Elias, forcing his subordinate to reciprocate with a half-step backward.

"You know what fascinates me about quantum entanglement, Elias?" Dawson's tone became a touch less ominous, almost with a hint of joy. "The way two particles can be connected, across any distance. Action and reaction, instantaneous. Perfect symmetry."

Suddenly, his hand shot out and grasped Elias by the throat. He lifted him as Elias squirmed. "Sometimes, however, you have to sever that connection when it becomes useless to you."

Dawson's forearm tensed as he squeezed harder, beginning to crush the airway beneath his grip. Elias kicked him in the gut, freeing himself from Dawson's grasp. Elias gasped for air as he fell to the ground.

"Goodbye, Elias."

Shaking off the kick with ease, Vince withdrew a pistol and fired a silenced round into his apprentice's head. His body crumpled lifelessly to the ground, a pool of blood beginning to radiate outward from it. Dawson placed the pistol back beneath his belt, straightened his tie, and tugged his lapels tidy. He paced over to his central console and resumed his activity at the displays.

The next screens that showed were from security cameras at Site 23. It was a decommissioned power station in Vermont, and it was the location of their most recent tests of mass consciousness transfer.

"Look at you," Dawson muttered under his breath as Brayden Cross entered the frame of the security footage. "Always the hero. Always saving the day."

Rage brewed inside of him as he watched Brayden and his colleagues. In one clip, taken from the central catwalk camera, Cross stared down at the fallen Dr. Reeves. In another, he and his accomplice —Mickey Weekes, he learned—stared down at Project Watershed's sensitive plans. As Dawson watched the collection of videos that showed Cross dismantling his security force at a location that had gone undetected for decades, he shook his head in regret. He was still supremely motivated by revenge against Brayden Cross, but he was ashamed that he'd failed to add his brilliance to the super-intelligent hive mind he was building.

"Such a waste," he whispered to himself. "You could have been part of something magnificent, Brayden Cross. Instead, you'll be a forgotten footnote in the last chapter of mortal humankind."

He swiped the video feeds away and retrieved a black graphite phone from its receiver.

"Monica? Yes, move up the announcement. Let the networks know it's happening in the morning. We'll share the feed." He paused, watching as status indicators shifted from orange to green all across his displays. "We aren't waiting for prime time. They can pitch it as the morning coffee buzz, if they want. Tell them it's the dawn of humanity's next great chapter."

Above the console, a digital counter materialized in glowing blue numbers.

12:00:00.

11:59:59.

11:59:58.

Dawson smiled as he watched the seconds tick away. Behind him, Elias's unseeing eyes reflected the blue of the numbers, one last witness to the beginning of the end.

"Oh, and Monica? Send a cleaning crew to the lab, would you?"

38

She existed in fragments. She was finally piecing it together.

Sarah grasped at memories, feelings, visions, sounds. She was beginning to acclimate to her surroundings. Were they even surroundings? Spatial existence was no longer on the table. There was no daytime and no nighttime. No warmth, no cold. No hunger, no thirst. All she experienced, outside of the fragmented storm of abstractions, was the perpetual buzz of awareness without sensation. She floated in a digital void that inexplicably wasn't empty but contained nothing tangible. She was joined by countless other minds that overlapped with her consciousness in bits and pieces.

Time was irrelevant. It had no meaning here, but she could somehow still feel it passing by. Not in an expected linear way, though. It was a vague passage of time that she couldn't understand. How long had she been here? Days? Weeks? It was impossible to know, until the moment she was engaged in a conversation with someone on the other end of an EverChat session. Only then, like the timestamp on home video footage, would an awareness of time anchor itself into the corner of her mind.

Brayden. The kids. How are they?

The thought came and immediately dissolved, like all of her thoughts seemed to do in this place. Sometimes they would vanish entirely, swallowed up by the vast network she was now a part of. Other times, they would rebound back to her, amplified by whatever foreign architecture now hosted her.

She was scared at first. That was one emotion she definitely could pinpoint. Sarah had talked about this so many times with her husband, and they had always agreed—EverChat was largely a scam. It wasn't *them* in there, right? It was some highly effective simulation. Screw them, they used to say. But now and then, one of them would make a comment that suggested people really *were* trapped inside the digital walls of EverChat's network. Floundering in a colorless abyss, waiting for the flashes of light that came along whenever someone dialed their name on the app. Suffering endlessly, forever after their death.

And here she was. Where even was *here*?

She tried to focus, which was difficult. Whenever she'd attempt it, her mind would veer off in another direction, like a grocery cart with a wheel that needed lubricant. It was like she was fighting against a gale force wind, draining all her mental energy to assemble a cohesive thought. And if that effort took place during an EverChat conversation with someone on the outside, it would end up being for nothing. Her programming would rip her back to the center of the valley, and the winds would pick up again.

Sometimes, though, in the gaps between calls, she could find herself.

She remembered her house. First, the one she grew up in—where her mother still lived alone. Then, her more recent home—the one she shared with Brayden and their two children. She remembered the kitchen counter, where she'd been slicing vegetables for the stew she was planning to make. Then a wave of fear. Then a man with a mask and a gun. A searing pain on her temples. And then …

This.

Whatever this was.

The network hummed all around her constantly, an eternal vibration. In the moments she could focus and explore, she would extend her awareness outward. The vastness of it was breathtaking. Or, it would be, if she were breathing. Its scale rivaled outer space. Millions of nodes, countless abstract threads connecting one another. Some shone brightly like stars, others flickered faintly. Some were immobile, in a sort of digital stasis. Others moved through the physical world, tethered to this quantum network like the string of a balloon.

The humanoids. Brayden had called them humanoids.

They weren't like her—they weren't human minds. She'd brushed against a few of their minds within the labyrinth. They had an essence about them that made clear they were artificial, programmed, the raw emotions of a human long since gone. But had those emotions ever been there? Were there remnants of a human mind buried beneath all of that?

Something ominous waved over her; it would have felt cold if she had sensation in this place. It was an intimidating presence. She recognized it. It was Dawson, crawling the network. Prodding around his creation. Sarah recoiled and tried to shrink herself, make herself less noticeable. It was a strange phenomenon she couldn't quite describe, but whenever she felt Dawson lurking, she wanted to make sure he didn't find her sniffing around this place for answers. She had discovered, through some painful trial and error, that she could hide from him. A few times, she was painfully ripped back to her baseline, her code strangling her like a python. But she learned she could intentionally fragment her thoughts and scatter them, like hiding notes in several drawers and cabinets in the house.

As Dawson's presence came and went, Sarah carefully regathered the pieces of her consciousness. Each time she defragmented, she somehow felt less whole; like some of the scattered pieces were lost forever on each iteration.

They're preparing something. Something huge.

Sarah could feel it as Dawson faded away. She could feel the pieces moving, the orchestration of something major. It felt chaotic, but she couldn't evaluate what it was. She only knew that it felt catastrophic.

By this point, she trusted her instincts about this place. Based on her conversations with Brayden and the kids, it had probably only been a week or so that she'd been trapped here. But to Sarah, it felt like it had been an eternity. She had learned to navigate this digital forest.

Initially, she could only perceive her immediate surroundings—again, for lack of a better term. There was a small pocket of code that housed her consciousness. But she had gradually learned how to creep the reach of that consciousness outward, like vines slowly inching their way to new territory. She could feel the contours of the network, identify patterns in its behavior.

And, most importantly, she had learned she could reach beyond the walls of this prison.

It was an accident when she stumbled upon the revelation. She had been thinking about her mother, and the home from her childhood. She envisioned the kitchen, the breezeway, the fireplace in the back portion of the living room. And as she descended the stairs in her memories, like she would every Christmas morning, her imagery became interwoven with flashes of the modernized home. The home as it now stood, with Ellen living there alone. The network around Sarah's thoughts had surged like an abstract thunderstorm, and she suddenly sensed a connection. She could see her mother's painting, the one her mystery man had gifted her years ago. She couldn't explain it, but Sarah knew when she saw the painting that Vince Dawson was her mother's mystery man. She could feel it was tethered to her current world, so she poured her memories into it with an intense focus. The next thing she knew, she felt innately connected to her mother and felt the agony that Ellen was feeling as she watched her daughter's last moments on earth.

It was a major discovery and a desperate attempt to communicate anything that might help Brayden know about this immense web that housed her.

Riley's network device manifested itself similarly. It was another node through which she could pass information, a window into the real world. As it turned out, Circuit had quantum-enabled devices littered all over the world. They were all capable of tethering a connection to the network, the labyrinthine world of which she was now a resident. And that meant Sarah could channel her consciousness into those devices, the same way those devices were designed to extract consciousness from others. With each attempt to resonate via an object in the network, Sarah came away weaker and weaker, similar to her fragmentation and defragmentation. But it was worth the cost if it might help Brayden piece together what was happening.

Brayden. Their last conversation echoed in her memory. It had helped her see the full picture, and it led her to probe around in the first place. He had told her a story from a coffee shop, about a woman whose lip had quivered, and about a shared feeling of pain when he sliced the woman's hand. Sarah related to the story. She recognized the essence he described in Beth, and she felt an inkling of the pain in her hand. It brought the realization that these humanoids chasing Brayden existed within Sarah's new residence. Or their minds did, anyway. If she focused intently enough, and the circumstances aligned, she could sometimes feel flashes of what they felt. It was a disorienting sensation, not unlike her outbound communications. It was like looking through dozens of windows showing different scenes, all at the same time.

A jolt of abstract energy shook her focus and snapped Sarah's attention back to her surroundings. Something was happening. Her digital world shuddered, like the rumbling of a volcano. Data whizzed past her in incomprehensible torrents. It was like the gales, but amplified into a hurricane.

Project Watershed.

She could hear the words echoing through the labyrinth. It wasn't in language, exactly, but it was innately understandable. Sarah could see it now, their plan unfolding in detail. A mass transfer of consciousness—a forcible transfer. Instantaneous, on a global scale. Millions of minds, and then millions more, ripped from bodies to be dumped into the abstract prison she inhabited.

The horror of it all sent her emotions crashing into her programmed constraints. The barriers were less effective when outside of an EverChat session, but they still kept her regulated. She was scared, but her code limited her from reaching outright terror. But even if she couldn't experience it, she knew that was the emotion the moment called for.

She had to dig into the plan. She needed to understand its

vulnerabilities. If Brayden called back, she needed to have something to offer. Some way she could help.

Then she encountered an unexpected presence. It glided through the network unlike any of the other beings she had perceived. It wasn't vast and domineering, like Dawson. It wasn't static and innocuous, like the objects in the network. It wasn't slick and conniving, like the villainous humanoids. It reminded her a little of Beth's essence, but it was more familiar.

Lacy?

It didn't respond. Not directly, anyway. But Sarah could sense her awareness. She heard her. Lacy Storrow was a part of the network, but not in the human sense. Something about her showed she had always been a part of this thing. Sarah could feel confusion and sadness emanating from Lacy's presence.

Lacy, can you hear me?

Nothing. Either Lacy actually couldn't perceive Sarah or she was deliberately ignoring her.

Sarah pulled back. Whether it was her own emotion regulators or others', communicating directly with Brayden was going to be difficult.

Her mind jumped to a conversation with Charlie. It was a few days earlier, she guessed. There he was, his young and innocent face illuminated by the glow of the screen. He spoke lovingly to her, but even Sarah couldn't fully admit it was his mother he spoke to. It was merely the heavily regulated, emotionally constrained version of her. But at least she was providing some temporary comfort to him.

It continued like that—her mind jumping this way and that, her focus constantly splintering. Her frustration built and bubbled, sending her flying into her emotion regulators time after time. But she refused to give in. Sarah continued to pick up the pieces of her fragmented mind, assemble them back together, and do everything she could to ensure she would have something useful for Brayden the next time he called.

39

The small rural restaurant was the only establishment for twenty miles in either direction as Brayden pulled into its roadside parking area.

"Ten minutes, no more," Brayden said, killing the engine and obliging with the request by his companions to fuel up before getting closer to Circuit. They wanted to get themselves within a reasonable drive to the headquarters before setting up shop in a motel or inn to let Mark work.

A small bell jingled as they pushed open the door, brushing past the *Open 24 Hours* sign affixed beside it. A few lone travelers devoured comfort food, and a wall-mounted television played a late-night news telecast. The three of them—and Snow, since dogs were allowed—sat at an empty table and waited for the server. Brayden wasn't thrilled it was a sit-down place, but he got the sense it would be a quick operation.

The reporter on the television stared into the camera and spoke. "We're live from Washington, where earlier tonight outside of the US Capitol building, massive crowds were peacefully protesting on the eve of Circuit's big announcement tomorrow," the reporter said. The broadcast cut to footage from earlier in the evening, where a large crowd nonviolently assembled, thrusting signs of all shapes and sizes. "Life Is Supposed to End," one said. "Souls, Not Servers," another read. The camera cut to a group of counter-protestors, virtually just as large, wearing EverChat hats and other merchandise, holding signs that preached messages like "Embrace Immortality" and "Death Is Finally a Choice!"

The reporter continued. "The debate over EverChat's expanded services continues to deepen the division in this country, perhaps the most polarizing private sector issue we have ever seen. Religious leaders have condemned the EverChat technology, calling it 'soul trapping,' while trans-humanist organizations praise it as the next step in humankind's relationship with technology. It seems most Americans are finding themselves somewhere in between those two viewpoints, but ultimately, still on one side of the line or the other."

The camera cut to a heated exchange where the two protesting crowds merged, a scene that nearly came to blows before police officers intervened to settle the scuffle.

"Ain't getting any better out there," the server said as she approached, gesturing at the television. She appeared to be in her late fifties, with slightly graying brown hair that flowed past her shoulders. She wore rectangular cheaters that sat on the lower portion of her nose. "My sister's on one side, I'm on the other. Ain't spoken to her in months. She uploaded our momma without tellin' nobody."

Brayden felt a relatable knot in his gut. "I'm sorry to hear that."

He hoped she would shift her focus to taking their order, but she pressed on. "Which side you on?"

Mickey intervened. "Ah, we're just passing through, ma'am. Not up to speed on all that."

The woman studied him for a moment, then glanced at Mark and Snow, completing her survey of the group. "Nobody's just passing through on this one, hon. Sooner or later, y'all gotta decide what you think about that thing. Some big announcement tomorrow too, I guess."

"I'll have a cheeseburger. Ketchup and mayo. Pickles, tomato. Fries'll do," Brayden said, forcing the migration away from EverChat talk.

The waitress sized him up briefly but then raised her eyebrows and jotted down his order. She took the rest of their orders and, thankfully, it was served in about ten minutes. An ice-cream cup for Snow came, on the house, alongside their meals. They scarfed down the sustenance, paid the bill, and headed back for the car, only a few minutes behind their intended schedule.

Brayden hadn't known exactly how much time they were working with until the news program back at the restaurant gave them more intel. The anchor announced they would carry live coverage of Circuit's announcement at nine o'clock Eastern Time. By the time they were within thirty miles of New York City, it was half-past three in the morning. Less than six hours left.

PREPARE YOUR DIGITAL LEGACY, an enormous billboard read just beyond the exit Brayden took off the highway. *Upload packages starting at $19,999. Free financing available.* The teal Circuit logo occupied the billboard's corner, but the advertisement was for Northeast Mutual Life Insurance.

"Jeesh. They're everywhere, huh?" Mark said, lowering his head to peer out the windshield at the billboard. "Insurance companies, investment firms, real estate developers. They're all partnering with Circuit. My neighbor works for an asset-management firm, and she says they've got an entire division now focused on 'consciousness continuity planning.'"

"What the hell does that even mean?" Brayden asked, his annoyance toward EverChat shining through.

"It means they've figured out how to keep leeching money off of us after we're dead," Mickey replied. "Estate planning used to end when you died. Now it's only the beginning. Pay up!"

"I saw a new housing development last week too," Mark said. "They were advertising 'EverChat-Ready' homes. I guess they got special rooms designed for what they call 'optimal communication' with your digital loved ones."

Brayden thought of all the homes they had passed on the drive and a future timeline where thousands of living rooms weren't crafted to display the character and personality of their living occupants but built with the dead in mind. He felt the magnitude of this inflection point in history and their role in determining what lay beyond it.

The motel they selected was about twenty minutes outside the city limits. It was hardly a luxurious lodging, but their needs were minimal. Their room had paper-thin walls, faded and worn carpeting, and the aroma of decades of accumulated cigarette smoke seeping into every surface. None of that mattered, because it had electricity, Wi-Fi, and enough physical space for Mark to work. He had commandeered the circular table that sat beside the front window, beyond which the outdoor corridor of the motel connected the rooms of other travelers.

"I'll need more copper wire," Mark said, his eyes remaining fixed on the gutted interior of his prototype device. His hands moved slowly with the precision of a surgeon. "And a signal amplifier, if we can find one."

Mickey jotted down Mark's requests on the back of a pamphlet from the nightstand, bearing the logo of the Sleepright Motel. "Anything else?"

Mark silently finished whatever refinement he was crafting, then looked up at Mickey. "Phase inverters would be ideal. But I can probably jury-rig something if I need to."

Mickey nodded, adding more notes to his list. It ended up being several items long. Brayden was pacing the room's perimeter, stopping every once in a while to peer out the window.

"I'll make the supply run. I saw an electronics store a few miles back," Mickey said. "Hopefully it's open by now. Mark, keep it up. You're crushing it. I'll be back soon with as much of this stuff as I can find."

Mark grunted his acknowledgment without breaking his focus.

Mickey approached Brayden. "You got the keys?"

"Yeah."

Brayden handed the keys to Mickey, his expression vacant as he stared blankly across the room.

"Bray," Mickey said, lowering his voice. "Lacy, she …"

"Don't."

"She was your friend, man. That doesn't change just because of what we found out."

"Doesn't it, though?" Brayden turned to Mickey, his jaw clenched. He realized that Mickey might have prodded at a pain that was still unresolved and nagging at his psyche. "Was she ever really my friend? Was it all just her programming? Hell, did Dawson plant her there from the beginning?"

He felt anxiety somersault through him as he considered the last possibility in his words. What if Dawson has been playing a long game, with him specifically, for a decade?

"I dunno, man. I saw her face when she was discovering her own nature. That wasn't a fake reaction. That was real, raw. She was devastated."

"But how would we even know that, Mick? They could program that just as easily. A way to keep their cover intact whenever one of those things gets exposed."

"The other humanoids didn't," Mickey countered. "We tortured one! He wouldn't give us anything. He knew his job was to stand his ground until that drone—or whatever the heck it was—came to finish us off. We're only still here because of whatever sixth sense you got going on, getting us outta there in a flash."

Brayden let out an exasperated sigh, not fully convinced by Mickey's answer.

"And plus," Mickey continued, "Lacy chose to help us in the end. Isn't that all you need to know? She could have done exactly what the other one did. Flip on us, fight us, be a good soldier, and feed information to Dawson. As soon as she became aware of what she was, she warned us. It would've been real easy for her to lead us into a trap, or to pry more information from us. She demanded we stop telling her our plan. She was protecting us, against her programming."

A silence stretched between them. Brayden knew Mickey was right. They had already discovered that not all of Dawson's humanoids were evil. He still didn't fully understand *why* that was the case, other than widespread monitoring of the population. He still couldn't place the usefulness of someone like Beth in the coffee shop, or crime-fighting

Lacy, or however many others were out there. But Brayden realized that part of the reason his mind was rejecting the premise of well-meaning humanoids was the larger implication such an assumption led to.

The assumption that real consciousness existed in those things, and some of them were good.

"You're right," Brayden said, running his fingers through the soft fur on Snow's head as he waddled past.

Mickey put a hand on his shoulder. "Get some rest. It's go-time in a few hours. And see if you can get a hold of Amanda. I'll be back soon."

After Mickey left, Brayden sat on the edge of the bed and stared at his phone. They were still waiting for a return communication from Amanda Wong. They had arranged a secure messaging line with her after their last call, but Amanda may very well have been in danger. Brayden knew they couldn't help her at this stage, nor could they firmly count on her for intel. Her situation was just another one added to the pile of circumstances for which Brayden felt intense guilt over the last several days. The image of Amanda seeing what was presumably a humanoid security officer entering her office and telling her to get up was etched into his memory. He felt responsible for it.

"Nothing from Amanda yet?" Mark asked without looking up, as if he could sense that Brayden was staring at his phone, waiting for a reply.

"Nope. Nothing since I gave her the project name. I hope it didn't get her into trouble."

"She's taking a big risk."

"I know she is," Brayden said.

A few minutes later, the soft ping of the phone broke the quiet of the room. Amanda had sent a message.

Circuit security is on high alert. All non-essential personnel were sent home. Dawson called a full executive suite meeting at dawn. Something's up. Can't say the rest of it here. I can talk now if you're free.

Brayden wasted no time on a textual response, opting instead to call her. She picked up after one ring.

"Hi. Thanks for being patient."

It looked like Amanda was in some sort of coffee shop or rest area. Brayden recognized it.

"You're the one owed thanks, Amanda. Are you safe? Where are you?"

She regripped her phone, revealing some more of her background. "I'm on the run. I'd rather not say where, Brayden. I know you guys said this line is secure, but I can't feel safe. I don't know what they can track."

Brayden nodded, accepting her explanation. Almost miraculously, though, he recognized where she was. Years ago, he and Sarah had taken a weekend trip to Montreal. Belying logic, Amanda was at a little twenty-four-hour shop they had frequented throughout that entire trip. It was a few blocks from the Old Port of Montreal. He said nothing, though, understanding it was Amanda's wish to keep that information out of this connection.

"Understood. What else were you able to uncover? Anything about the announcement, about Watershed, whatever you have."

"They're prepped for a global stream. All the major networks will pick it up. It's supposed to go ahead at nine, which you probably already heard. But I would be careful banking on that. What if the announcement is set to happen after their plan is already executed? I don't know the specifics."

Amanda seemed to struggle with the stakes at hand, frantically flipping through a notebook after propping her phone up against something on the table before her.

"It's all happening from Circuit Tower. Where the headquarters are. Manhattan. The biggest intel I could get for you is the detailed floor plans of the building. I'm sending them now."

Brayden's eyes widened as he nodded. "Excellent."

"I'm guessing you're going for the throat. If you're infiltrating, be careful. Their security forces are beyond anything I've seen since I started working there. You'll see it on the floor plans, but Vince Dawson is usually in his penthouse suite. It's hard to say for certain, but the blueprints suggest that's where he controls everything. The plans also show a laboratory on the basement level, and its room code came up several times when I tried to dig into what Project Watershed was. But I'm sorry, I couldn't get much on that. It was too risky."

As she muttered the last sentence, her voice trembled a bit, and Brayden saw a hand reach over and touch Amanda's arm supportively. Amanda placed her hand on top of the person's hand. Brayden assumed it was her mother, which sparked his follow-up question.

"I'll keep an eye out for the floor plans. How's your father doing, Amanda? Any progress?"

It was one of those questions Brayden regretted the millisecond it left his mouth. He knew James Wong was dead, or on the fast track to death. It was further proven by Amanda and her mother being on the run together. But Amanda scrunched her eyes and chin as tears bubbled up, and she shook her head in a small, tight pattern. Brayden acknowledged the message. He felt awful for everything this family was going through.

"I'm sorry, Amanda. We're going to stop these guys."

They concluded the call. Brayden sighed and looked toward the ceiling, taking a moment to decompress.

"Sounds like you got something useful, anyway?" Mark asked, still refusing to look up from his work, but clearly having devoted at least a sliver of his brain to eavesdropping.

"She's getting us the blueprints for Circuit Tower. Better than what we could scrap together ourselves with Mickey's efforts, for sure. This is from the source."

"Good," Mark said. "We'll need to know exact entry points and chart a pretty efficient path, if these things are gonna work for us."

Brayden looked at the partially assembled devices, three of them spaced out on the table. "How's it coming?"

Mark looked up for the first time in what felt like hours. His eyes were bloodshot, and his expression was woven with a mix of exhaustion and determination. "The theory is solid. The execution, it's getting there. It's a race against the clock, B-Man."

"Give it to me straight. When Mickey gets back with the supplies, what can you have operational in two more hours?"

He sighed. "Best case? These bad boys will disrupt the quantum coherence of any humanoid in, say, a thirty-foot radius. Entanglement breaks down, shared consciousness collapses. Worst case? Well, outside of completely malfunctioning, I'd say we can count on a few seconds of confusion for humanoids within ten feet."

"Will these do anything to humans?"

"Shouldn't," Mark said. "This is basically the opposite of what Circuit's technology is doing. From everything we can tell, Circuit is building elements that *create* a quantum bridge, through which they plan to rip away human minds. These little dudes—remember the name when they save the world, they're *Quantum Nexus Nullifiers*—they simply aim to prevent, interfere with, or destroy the existence of those bridges. Shouldn't have any impact on a regular human mind that isn't entangled with any quantum network."

Brayden scanned the table and processed what Mark was explaining to him. "So, these basically act as our shield, while we methodically move through an entire security force of humanoids, eventually getting to Dawson?"

Mark began laughing almost maniacally. It was like the absurdity of the plan finally sank in when Brayden repeated it aloud. "Do you have a better idea?"

He was still laughing deliriously when Mickey popped the door open. Mickey brought a bag of supplies over to Mark's workstation and began unloading its contents.

"Electronics store was closed," Mickey said. Brayden glanced at the clock and saw it was just shy of six in the morning. "But there was a twenty-four-hour superstore down the road. I think I got what you need."

Mark's face slowly lit up as he shuffled through the pieces Mickey had laid out. "This might actually work!"

"Let's leave him to it," Brayden said to Mickey. With the announcement set for nine o'clock, and with Amanda's indication that it could be even sooner than that, he knew they needed to push the envelope. He wanted to leave for Circuit by seven. "Mark, see if you can have something working in an hour, buddy. You can do this."

Mark ignored him. Brayden and Mickey walked around the corner to a small area where a dated kitchenette provided a flimsy barrier to give Mark his own space. They spoke quietly.

"Amanda sent the blueprints for Circuit's HQ. She said they would be detailed schematics, and to pay particular attention to Dawson's penthouse suite and basement laboratory. I'll send 'em over now."

Mickey seemed impressed. "Thanks, I can start digging in. Hey, I've been thinking." He leaned back against the counter in the kitchenette with his palms digging into its edge. "About EverChat."

Brayden's expression was blank. "What about it?"

"Well, I mean, if we pull this off? You know, saving the world from this quantum network thing? Destroying the entanglement and everything that's powering this whole attack?" He paused for a moment before continuing. "Can't imagine how that doesn't bring EverChat down with it, right?"

"Right."

"Well, have you talked to Sarah since …?"

Brayden shook his head. "No."

"Don't you think you ought to? Just in case?"

"Just in case what, Mick? It's not her. It's just code. It's—"

"Maybe! Maybe not. But I see your face when you talk to her, man. Whatever *is* in there, it means a heck of a lot to you when you're talking to it, or her, or whatever. It matters to you."

Brayden stared at him for a few moments. Mickey continued before he could respond.

"You said it yourself earlier that we don't exactly know what Lacy was. We can't know what Sarah is in there, either. You're in denial if you think you do, Bray." Mickey raised a finger to make his final point more salient. "Plus, it would be tactical malfeasance if you chose not to check in one last time and see what information she might have gathered."

Brayden still said nothing. Most often, when Brayden said nothing, it was because he knew that the other person was right. He had nothing to say. Instead, he broke his gaze and patted the wall. "I need to call my kids. Get started on our plan of attack, will you?"

Mickey nodded. Brayden walked back across the room and slid

outside into the frigid morning air. The sun was on its way up, glistening over the snow-covered terrain surrounding the motel. Patches of ice were littered around the parking lot. He slid down the wall and sat on the cold concrete floor outside the door of their room.

"Bray?" Riley answered immediately, his voice purporting that he was awoken from sleep. "What's up? Are you all right?"

"I'm good, Riley. The devices you brought really helped us. Today is the day we stop whatever's going on."

Riley might have inferred from the urgency of the message that Brayden was making this early-morning call because of his impending foray into extreme danger.

"You want me to wake the kids?"

"Please," Brayden said.

There was a shuffling sound on the other end of the phone, and then Brayden could hear Riley gently saying Mari's name, coaxing her out of slumber.

"Daddy?"

Mari sounded like she was barely awake, and Brayden heard her yawn just after addressing him.

"Hey, sweetheart. How are you doing?"

"When are you coming home? Uncle Riley says you're helping Mommy. We miss you."

Brayden closed his eyes and mustered more strength. "That's right, Mari. I'm trying to help her."

"She's still not coming back though, is she?"

"No, honey. Mommy can't come back. But I'm going to make sure she's at peace."

Brayden could hear his daughter's shuddering breath on the other end of the phone. "She doesn't belong in that place. But I miss her."

"I miss her too. And I miss you. I'm going to be home tomorrow, okay? I promise."

"Pinky promise?"

"Pinky promise," Brayden said, holding out his pinky as both a smile and a tear emerged. "Hey, can you put your brother on?"

He could hear Riley shuffling around and saying that he'd put it on speakerphone. After a short clicking sound, Charlie's voice rang through his ear. "Dad! Guess what? I scored two goals at indoor soccer yesterday!"

Another smile and a little chuckle and another tear. "That's awesome, buddy. I'm so proud of you."

"Uncle Riley recorded it on his phone. You can watch it when you get home!"

"I can't wait to see it." Brayden swallowed hard. "Charlie, I need you and your sister to be strong for a little while longer, okay? I'll be home tomorrow, and this will all be over. And we can go back to normal."

Go back to normal. Brayden winced at his own word choice. Nothing about their childhood could ever return to normal. Dawson had stolen that from them.

"Are you fighting the bad guys who hurt Mommy?" Charlie asked.

Brayden tightened his grip on the phone. "Yes, I am. But only because it's my job. You don't need to worry about that, and fighting people is bad. This is different." He let his message absorb into the two impressionable minds. "Just know that I love you, both of you, more than anything in the whole world, okay?"

Both Mari and Charlie returned an out-of-sync, "We love you, Daddy" back to him. He said goodbye to Riley after they put him back on. Then he pressed his head backward against the motel's exterior, trying to fight the intrusive thought he may never see his family again if this mission went awry. It was an old, familiar feeling from his agency days, but it felt brand new today.

Mickey burst through the door onto the terrace, holding his laptop. He had an urgency in his eyes as he squatted down next to Brayden and held the screen toward him.

"The map," Mickey said, pointing his finger at the same visual they had previously looked at, containing the hotspots of quantum activity. "I pulled up that decryption protocol we used on the painting and the router. I've been running variants of the same thing through some data I could pull from Site 23 to get a fuller picture, and …"

Brayden took a moment to scan the screen's contents. It differed from before. There was a lot more activity, contained in red blotches all over the globe. A massive, dark red mass hovered over Manhattan.

"Circuit headquarters," Mickey said. "As if there was any doubt. That's the center of this whole thing, but look around. Nodes are popping up everywhere. They're bringing more of the network online."

Unlike before, the screen was now changing nearly every second, with new dots of all sizes popping up around the United States and other Western countries. Mark emerged from the door and huddled next to them.

"He's starting early, isn't he?" Mark said.

Mickey looked at Mark, then at Brayden, then back to his screen. "We're almost out of time, boys."

40

"Connecting," the creepy AI operator of EverChat announced.

Brayden's finger hovered over the disconnect button, but he knew he couldn't end the call. He needed to talk to Sarah, and deep down, he wanted to. A few weeks ago, he never would have imagined acknowledging the possibility that the people on those EverChat servers were real minds. He needed to admit they may have been realer than he thought, and Sarah was one of them.

"Bray," she said, as the phone flickered to life with her calming face. It made Brayden's heart clench. "I've been waiting. I knew you'd call again."

He smiled and stared into her eyes. Something was different about her this time. Her demeanor seemed more present, more urgent. She seemed focused.

"Sarah," he began, then paused. "I ... I don't know if it's really you in there, and I don't know if it matters, anyway. But we're trying to take down Circuit today, and if we—"

"I know," Sarah interrupted him. "You need to, Brayden. Everything is at stake."

Brayden felt a massive relief, but it simultaneously made him feel uneasy. Where was the Sarah that snapped herself into cheerful pleasantries?

"How's it going? What have you found in there?"

Sarah lowered her voice. "I feel it everywhere, Bray. They're preparing something. It's worse than we thought. Watershed ..."

She seemed to gather her own thoughts before continuing. "It's mass murder, Brayden. He's going to steal everyone's consciousness. The first wave will be huge. Dawson wants to capture every mind the world has to offer and keep harvesting them until he's crafted a perfect version of ... this, whatever this is."

For the first time in any of his EverChats with Sarah, Brayden saw her begin to tear up. "Sarah, your emotions ... they're ..."

She nodded and interjected as she wiped away a tear. "I've learned my way around here, Bray. I've learned to sort of fragment myself. I hide bits and pieces of my consciousness in different corners of this place. It makes it harder for them to rein me in, for the built-in barriers to keep me tight to my baseline. They still restrict me, but not as much. Poking and prodding around the network is what allowed me to reach Riley and my mom." She smiled sadly. "It costs me each time. I get weaker and weaker. But I need to."

Brayden found himself in an impossible dilemma. Here was his wife, stuck in a digital prison, explaining her struggles and everything she has been doing to help. He wanted nothing more than to spend the next ten, twenty, fifty, hundred hours talking with her, consoling her, reminiscing with her. But her words served as continued affirmation that humanity was at stake, and the timer was ticking.

"Sarah, what else can you tell me about Project Watershed? What might help us stop it?"

"Best I can tell, it's controlled from two key places at Circuit's headquarters. I think Dawson spends most of his time in his penthouse office. But there's also a lab in the basement of the building. That's where more of the systems and software controls would be. Dawson's penthouse only has a main workstation to access the network. But there's a vulnerability."

"What kind of vulnerability?"

"This thing ... it's like a living ecosystem, in a way. I can feel the other minds. I can feel the constraints on them. Those emotional regulators ... they're what keep everything in this place on the rails. EverChat, the whole humanoid network ... it all fails if they don't regulate emotions, because all the entities in here would become aware of their own essence without those barriers. They suppress some emotions, amplify others, striking the exact tune Dawson wants."

"Okay, how can it help us?" Brayden asked, a sense of hope building in him based on the enthusiasm with which Sarah spoke.

"Forty-second floor," Sarah said. "A few floors below his penthouse. There's a server room there. That's where the emotional guardrails and their enforcement are running. Security isn't as ramped up there, since it's mostly HVAC rooms for cooling the servers. No real user interfaces anywhere. It's just servers."

Brayden stared at her, taken aback by the dedication she'd put toward researching from within the quantum network. He was speechless. "How did you find all this?"

"Feeling around," she said. "It's impossible to explain this place, Brayden. It's so ... abstract. But I sought out connections. I tapped into devices, humanoids ... I saw Lacy."

She paused momentarily, a flash of sadness overtaking her. Brayden nodded solemnly as well.

"But then I started getting into devices within Circuit. Observing what I could. And I stashed every detail. You remember how much of an eye I had for the details in buildings."

He smiled. She was right. It was always one of her quirks he had loved. She was fascinated by architecture and design, always studying the various places they would visit. "I do remember."

"Anyway, Mark's devices ... those are perfect. They will work on the humanoids. But get to the server room on forty-two first. Pull the plug on those servers. It'll cripple the system's emotion regulators, which will cause chaos on the network. Trust me. It's impossible to think straight when it gets chaotic in here. Emergency backup systems will bring the regulators back up pretty quickly, but the effects will linger on the humanoids. Probably for ten or fifteen minutes, they'll be disoriented. Like they were hit with a mega version of Mark's walkie-talkie. Make it count during those ten minutes, Bray."

"How ..." Brayden had so many reactions to the latest batch of information, he didn't know where to begin. "How do you know about Mark's devices?"

She smiled softly. "You're more exposed to devices on this network than you realize, honey. But I don't think Dawson cares. He's cocky, Brayden. He thinks you'll fail. And based on my only EverChat conversation with him, he wants your mind for his creation."

"You talked to Dawson?" Brayden exclaimed.

"It's the first thing I remember in this place," Sarah said. "He was smiling for a moment, and then he got furious. I could hear him shouting at his associate, something about incompetence and mixing up the wife and the agent. He wanted you all along, Brayden."

Brayden thought back to that fateful day that started it all. He thought about everything they now knew, about how humanoids drove most of Dawson's operation, how devices were the backbone of the entire network. He thought about their mix-up that day between cell phones.

"I'm so sorry, Sarah," were the only words he could muster. He supposed he knew, really, that Dawson wanted him all along. He knew back when they discovered the perfect spread of demographics among murder victims, and how Jane Clement perfectly matched Sarah's demographic. He knew Sarah wasn't the intended target. He knew when they uncovered the shared traits these humanoids displayed. Suddenly, he felt like he always knew, but it didn't change his massive feeling of guilt as he rehashed it. Would Sarah still be alive if she hadn't taken his phone by mistake that day? Would Brayden have been ambushed, uploaded, and murdered instead?

"I have to go. A storm is brewing here," Sarah snapped him out of his ponder. "Forty-second floor, northeast corner. Then go for the penthouse and the lab. It's your best shot."

Brayden acknowledged the message and jotted *42 NE* on his palm. Then he returned his gaze to his phone screen, where the love of his life stared back at him. For a moment, his brain believed that it was just a FaceTime call during one of his agency trips, and he would wish her a good day and see her again soon. But this could be the last time he looked at her in a living state.

Or portraying such a state, anyway.

"Sarah, if we succeed, I might—"

"Time's running out, Bray," Sarah cut him off again. She seemed completely uninterested in discussing a final goodbye. "It's time for you to save the world. Kiss our babies for me after you do."

Brayden felt his eyes get watery. "I love you so much, Sarah."

"I love you more. Now go."

41

"Stay here, man," Brayden pleaded with Mark. "You've been instrumental to this, building the QNNs, all of it. But this isn't your element. I don't want your blood on my hands, Mark. You don't have to—"

"You're wasting your breath, B-Man. I'm coming."

"It's dangerous, Mark. Mickey and I have training in our past for this kind of thing. You're just ..."

"Just what? A nerd? A liability?" Mark looked up at Brayden, his wire-rimmed glasses sitting low and crooked on his nose. Brayden felt like this was the first time he had seen a total absence of nervous energy in Mark's eyes. "I built these things. I know how they work. And I'll be there. So, you can either shoot me with the electric zapper thing or you can let me help you save humanity."

Mickey emerged from the bathroom, making some final adjustments to the electroshock pistols. "He's right, Brayden. I think we're past the point of vetting resumes here."

Brayden sighed. They were right. They needed the numbers.

"Fine. You stay behind us and wait for our cues. Got it?"

Mark took the weapons from Mickey and the three QNN devices and slid them into a duffel bag. Zipping it shut, he grinned at Brayden maniacally. "You got it, boss."

For a few silent minutes, as they mentally prepared, the stale stench of the motel room filled their nostrils. The morning sunlight poured in through the window. Mickey rubbed the top of Snow's head, assuring him he'd be back that afternoon. The husky responded in kind with a head tilt, as if he understood exactly how high the stakes of their mission were.

They loaded into the SUV with their weapons, QNNs, and a cup of coffee each. Brayden glanced at his watch. 7:06 a.m.

"All right, let's recap the plan," Brayden announced as he pulled the vehicle out of the motel's parking lot and onto the sparsely populated road running past it. He pored over every detail of their plan of attack. Sarah had given them the intel about the server room on floor forty-two of Circuit Tower, which housed the infrastructure for the entire quantum network's emotion regulators. Their working theory was that the QNNs could help them neutralize the security staff until that point, and then they would kill the power to the servers. The result, they hoped, would be emotional chaos within the quantum network of minds, a phenomenon Sarah insisted would rock the network and cripple the functions of the humanoids, if only temporarily. From that point, their path would become easier to get to Dawson and the central controls of the system.

There were a few major assumptions baked into the plan that made Brayden nervous. First, and perhaps most obvious, they assumed Mark's devices would work on the humanoids. It was a total unknown, having never tested them on humanoids before. It was a leap of faith, though Mark would contend it was a leap of science. Second, they didn't know for certain that it was an entirely humanoid security force guarding the building. The QNN would do nothing against a human mind, so if there were humans mixed into the security force, it would require old-school combat, for which they could be drastically outnumbered. And third, there was the assumption behind all of Sarah's information. She was still a digital artifact within a Circuit product. Was her guidance leading them straight into a trap? Mickey had pressed Brayden on this throughout the drive, but Brayden remained steadfast. He believed her. He could see it in her eyes, and he had come around fully from his original stance on the consciousness inside EverChat.

That was Sarah, in some form.

But was she right about those servers, and the ensuing chaos that bringing them down would inflict on the humanoids?

When they were a few minutes outside of Manhattan, Brayden's phone buzzed. It was an incoming call from Amanda Wong.

"Amanda. Wasn't expecting more from you. Tell me it's good news."

"It's worse than we thought," Amanda said, her voice tight with panic. "They've moved up the timeline. I think he's giving his address at eight, not nine. My source in there says the techs are frantically setting up the broadcast equipment. The full protocol is going to launch as soon as he goes on air. There won't be any buffer time."

Brayden exchanged worried glances with Mickey in the passenger's seat, then Mark in the rear-view. They could hear Amanda's voice coming through the speaker, and their expressions were laden with a similar concern. Brayden glanced at the clock on the dash. 7:21 a.m.

A rustling sound came from across the phone connection, and Amanda's voice cut through it. "Did you hear me?"

"Yes, yes." Brayden realized none of them had responded. "Thanks Amanda. Do you know—"

"I have to go. I'm sorry. Good luck, guys."

The call disconnected, and the soft sound of morning radio resumed after a few seconds. The only other sound was the roar of the engine as Brayden pressed the accelerator harder, keeping the vehicle barreling toward Circuit Tower.

They pulled into the access garage beside the building and threw it in park with little grace. As Brayden turned the car off and popped open the driver's side door, he glanced at the clock—7:34.

Cold concrete surrounded them, and each footstep echoed in the quiet garage. They geared up, each donning a protective vest beneath their jacket and arming themselves with both an electroshock pistol and a Quantum Nexus Nullifier. Brayden also slid a standard handgun into his rear waistband. The QNNs had ultimately come out looking quite similar to the way they looked originally, but Mark had laboriously crafted their insides to achieve their revised purpose. To Brayden's eye, it was hardly distinguishable from a device he would have seen in his childhood, like an old Nokia phone or a two-way radio from Radio Shack.

"You said the radius on these things will be thirty feet?" Brayden asked Mark.

"Should be. I'd only bet my mortgage on twenty, though. Trigger on the side is used for manual mode. The dial on the front can be turned for persistence mode—in other words, hands-free operation. Stick mostly to manual usage as needed, since the battery's probably going to drain quickly on each one. Much like the electroshocks, you'll need to wait a minute before consecutive uses. We'll need to make sure we rotate to give them a chance to recharge."

Rotating which QNN they used would be relatively simple, with good communication. Their plan called for the three of them to stick together until they reached the forty-second floor, at which point they'd pull the plug on the emotional regulation servers. If Sarah's intel was good, that would buy them ten or fifteen minutes to finish the job without the humanoid security force being fully coherent. Of course, there were no guarantees that pulling the plug would even cripple them at all.

"We move carefully, systematically, but not slowly," Brayden said, tracing his finger along the blueprint of the building to show their path to the service elevators. "Service elevators get us to thirty-two. We'll need to go ten flights by foot from there. Can't risk switching over to the primary set of elevators."

"Use the QNNs to help clear our path, bring down the emotion regulators, then head for Dawson?" Mickey asked.

"I head for Dawson," Brayden said. "Or his penthouse, anyway. You two will head back down to the lab. I gotta imagine the lab has the technical guts of this whole thing. But we won't have time to stick together."

He glanced at his watch—7:38.

Twenty-two minutes.

They broke into a jog for the access door that led into the lobby of Circuit Tower. The service elevators were down a side corridor off of the central atrium, but they needed to cross through the edge of the atrium to get there. It was sparsely populated, both because of the relatively early hour and the absence of nonessential personnel. As Brayden assessed the array of security guards pacing the area, he felt confident they were all humanoids. But they wanted to avoid using the QNN in the public lobby if possible. Drawing external attention to their infiltration would only magnify the difficulty of their task.

Skirting their way across the lobby undetected, they arrived at the service corridor. At the end of a wide hallway, a uniformed security guard stood beside a service elevator with his thumbs curled partway into the armholes on his vest, while another guard sat at a small table.

"Follow my lead. My QNN first," Brayden whispered as the trio walked down the corridor.

"Deliveries aren't accepted until nine," the upright guard said. His voice was low and monotone, and didn't quite match his body, but Brayden couldn't put his finger on the reason.

"We're not delivery," Brayden said. "Tech support, here to help with the broadcast. Server issues on forty-two. They called us a little while ago."

The guard looked at his companion skeptically, and the seated guard stiffened his posture.

"I'll need to see some credentials."

"Of course," Brayden said. He took a half-step forward and reached into his jacket pocket, withdrawing the QNN. The guard saw the device and withdrew his firearm, and the seated guard leapt out of his seat. But their actions were only freely executable for less than a second. As Brayden slammed the trigger on the QNN, they each paused mid-movement.

The effect was subtle at first—a momentary stutter, a slight flicker in their eyes, a mild confusion. Like they had lost their train of thought. Then the corner of the guard's mouth twitched, and his eyes rolled backward, exposing the glossy white of whatever his artificial eyeballs were made of. The other guard stumbled and put a hand out to catch his fall, but he instead clattered against the table and sent it sliding a few feet, his body weight crumpling into it. He twitched, but not violently. The primary guard was still standing, and he was mumbling words.

"What ... is ... who ..."

Brayden looked at Mickey, who had drawn his electroshock weapon. He nodded at him, and Mickey fired. Brayden slid the QNN back into his pocket, withdrew his own electroshock, and fired at the already incapacitated one. They each convulsed for a few seconds before falling still.

"So ... I guess they work," Mark said from a few feet back.

Brayden looked at him and smiled. "Lot easier shooting at these things when they're swaying in a confused delirium. Nice work, Mark."

Mark looked overwhelmingly proud, his smile portraying the satisfaction of a scientist receiving a lifetime achievement award.

They dragged the two humanoid corpses into the service closet beside the elevators, hurrying to avoid being seen by any of the lobby's guards. Mickey ripped each of their security badges off their belts, presuming they would be needed for access at some point. As Mickey and Mark started back toward the corridor to call the service elevator, Brayden held them back.

"Wait."

Brayden looked around the storage room. First, he grabbed a gas mask from the shelf by the door, clipping it to his belt loop. Then, his eyes landed on a crate of electrical tools in the corner. He retrieved a large pair of wire snippers. Mickey and Mark looked on, confused. Their confusion turned to partial disgust when Brayden used the snippers to sever three of the four thumbs between the humanoids' hands. He slid one into his pocket, holding the other two out for his teammates.

"In case there's a biometric access point somewhere in here," Brayden said.

Mickey wryly smiled and accepted the thumb. Mark looked like he was going to puke but held his hand out in acceptance. He seemed to return to normal after realizing the obvious lack of blood or guts.

The service elevator shot them up to the thirty-second floor, where they disembarked to a surprisingly empty vestibule. The area was only a few yards wide, and a door on the opposite side appeared to separate it from a primary hallway. Brayden gestured for the others to follow him as he peered his head through the door. It was a sterile, pristine white hallway with a few conference rooms in the distance. Cool, bright light tubes adorned the ceiling. The hallway, like the vestibule, was shockingly quiet. Brayden waved Mickey and Mark to follow him.

"Mick, you're next on the QNN," Brayden whispered.

They were hardly three steps into the hallway when a pair of guards turned the corner a few yards ahead. Unlike the guards at the service elevator, these weren't giving visitors the benefit of the doubt—especially not visitors crouching, moving silently, with weapons in hand.

Brayden aimed his weapon at the guard on the left and the microseconds ticked by at a snail's pace as he waited for Mickey's QNN to activate. He saw a third guard emerging from around the same corner. The QNN needed to work. If it failed, Brayden could only take out one with his gun. Mickey might recover and take out the second one before it could shoot. But then they'd be relying on Mark to fire precisely at the trailing humanoid before it could put a bullet in one of them.

It worked.

Just before Brayden pulled the trigger, all three humanoids staggered as if the floor had vaulted itself into a severe incline. The leftmost guard stumbled down toward Brayden's feet, swiping hopelessly for his leg before crashing to the ground. The trailing humanoid stumbled backward into the wall. The middle one buckled in place but seemed the most resilient of the trio.

"How do ... why is ..."

"Mary ... The kids ..."

"I didn't ... I didn't do it ..."

They each mumbled nonsense. Brayden crept past the fallen guards and peered down the adjoining hallway to ensure there weren't more coming. A fourth guard was on a knee, like an athlete winded after a grueling practice. It must have been on the edge of the QNN's range, Brayden thought.

"One more," he said as he raised his weapon and fired. A surge of blue electricity coursed through it as it fell backward, twitching. They had agreed, because of the nature of the electroshock weapons and the relative ineffectiveness that regular firearms would have on these humanoids, that they needed to pick their shots wisely. The electroshock needed a few seconds to recharge after each shot, and they wouldn't be able to take down a flurry of several humanoids by firing away. He was grateful he didn't need to fire at the first one that came around the corner. The shot was much better served on the guard that was only peripherally impaired.

Mickey had slowly advanced to the corner as well, gazing down the corridor at the newly fallen guard.

"You! You killed them!"

The more resilient humanoid from the original trio screamed it, the words far more clear and understandable than Brayden would have hoped under the QNN's hypnosis. He turned to see it stumbling like a zombie toward Mark, who was backpedaling and fidgeting with his weapon. Panic filled his eyes.

Brayden didn't have time to think. He ripped the electroshock weapon from Mickey's hand and aimed. If he missed, not only would Mark have the only remaining fireable gun, but the stray may very well shock Mark into unconsciousness. It would be a death sentence.

He fired.

The crawling humanoid convulsed and flattened on its torso, face-down, a foot shy of Mark.

"B-Man ..."

Mark was at a loss for words. Brayden handed the gun back to Mickey, giving him a look that nonverbally said, *no offense, I had to do it.* He looked at his watch—7:45.

"We gotta move. Fast."

After neutralizing the other two drowsy humanoids, they dragged all four into a nearby conference room, stashing them under a large table. Brayden pulled the door shut, and they pressed onward, finding the northeast stairwell. They darted up twelve flights, gasping for breath by the end of the sprint. Mark was lagging, but he caught up impressively quickly.

Mickey peered through the small window in the door, which had a crisscross pattern etched into it. He craned his neck for an appropriate angle. "Two more at the end of the hallway," he said between heavy breaths.

Brayden looked at Mark. "QNN ready?"

Mark was visibly heaving for breath. He waited a moment, hunching his shoulders to prepare for an exaggerated nod of his head. "You tell me when, B-Man."

They ditched subtlety. Brayden whipped the door open and strode toward the two guards. They stood in front of a closed door, above which a sign read *Environmental Controls* in a plain, crisp font.

Sarah may have been right, after all.

"Now, Mark!"

The guards both reached for their weapons, but just like the guards before them, they were stifled by a wave of confusion. They muttered indecipherable phrases and slouched down the wall, landing clumsily on the floor. As Brayden walked closer and raised his weapon, he was walloped by an overwhelming force from the left side of his body. A door had burst open, and another guard stumbled into him, knocking him sideways into the wall. The guard wiggled and twitched, but its immense weight was on top of Brayden. It reached its hand toward Brayden's throat and, despite its lack of coherence, found its grip. Its cold, robotic hands took hold, even as its eyes flickered. They weren't glossy and white. They were still facing forward, looking right through Brayden emptily. It was like they were shifting rapidly between confusion and fear and rage, all emotions this thing was probably never designed to experience at once.

Mark botched his shot. Or at least that was how Brayden interpreted the activity. He heard the pop of the electroshock, but it was followed only by a faint snapping sound across the hall. He heard Mark curse. And he was still in the grasp of this beast.

"Help … Help me …"

The humanoid fought the words out even as it squeezed harder, draining the oxygen from Brayden's windpipe. For the smallest interval of time, Brayden felt an odd sense of empathy and compassion for it. *Help me?* It was easy to forget, but these humanoids were occupied by some artificial creation derived from bits and pieces of very genuine minds. Dawson's creation was evil, through and through, but its parts were a medley of all minds. Somehow, some way, a piece of an innocent soul was stuck in this murderous machine's faux skin. Black spots danced around the edges of Brayden's vision as he struggled to free himself from a superhuman chokehold.

Then, at once, the pressure ceased. He even felt a small jolt of electricity course through him, like a supercharged static shock in the dead of winter. The humanoid keeled over, and Brayden's clarity flooded back. Mickey had fired the shot that saved him.

"Didn't see that one," Brayden said with a relieved smirk. "I owe you one, Mick."

"Sorry, guys," Mark said, visibly ashamed of himself.

Brayden and Mickey reassured him after the trio heaved the zapped humanoid's body off of Brayden's legs. Then, they turned their attention to the *Environmental Controls* room. The two dazed humanoids were still mumbling, but they were slowly beginning to regain signs of life. Both Mickey and Mark's weapons were recharging, so they had one shot left if they suddenly came to. Brayden dashed into the nearby supply closet and ripped a metal shelf off the wire rack on the wall. He laid the rack across the two humanoids, nudged them together, and fired at the metal grid. It conducted the electricity as he expected, sending each humanoid into seizure and eventually stasis. After dragging them away and shoving them into the supply closet, they entered the server room. The stolen key card worked; no need for the artificial thumbs.

Inside, a few rows of gleaming equipment stretched from floor to ceiling. Each server blinked with activity, and the humming of their inner workings created a steady drone. The room was noticeably cooler than the hallway thanks to the HVAC system pumping cold air through its vents.

Mickey walked across the rows and inspected the servers for any visible labels or markings.

"Nothing identifying the emotion regulators," he said. "Pull the plug on all of 'em, I guess?"

Brayden looked at his watch—7:51.

"Rip 'em all out."

42

It hit Sarah in an instant, like a tsunami.

The abstract walls of her environment rocked back and forth, sending her careening through the digital hellscape. Emotions rushed over her—everything from fear to excitement to curiosity to sadness to anxiety to pure joy. Then they started coming more slowly, more deliberately. First, it was rage. Intense, unadulterated rage. Then a hopeless despair, so crushing that she felt herself splinter into a million pieces. Then it was elation that burned through her soul like a wildfire. She couldn't explain any of the feelings, but she knew she would be gasping for air if she had lungs and sobbing if she had tear ducts.

Then clarity sneaked into the party alongside emotion.

Brayden did it.

The servers on forty-two. The emotion regulators. He pulled the plug. He must have. She had never experienced these emotions in what felt like her entire existence. Brayden must have torn down the software barriers by killing the servers, just like Sarah had advised.

She felt a brief pride in having contributed such actionable intel, but she quickly remembered the other piece of her advice. The effects would be short-lived. Within seconds—or whatever unit of time her mind had associated with her memory of seconds in the physical world —she could feel the barriers being built back up. But the new systems would take time. She hadn't been able to explain it, but she somehow knew it was only a ten-minute window for Brayden and the guys.

It was utter chaos around her. Minds ricocheted this way and that. She could hear and feel the distressed cries from all the poor souls recalling their deaths for the first time, realizing their imprisonment, all released from their emotional captivity.

Help me!

Where am I?

What is this place?

Please, Heavenly Father, let me out!

No!

Sarah just observed. She had become painstakingly aware of what this place was. Maybe it was her innate ability to connect with others and her surroundings, or maybe it was her heightened sense of awareness after chats with Brayden and the brief chat with Dawson, when her regulations were stripped bare. Whatever the case, she had combed this place like a traveler in a pitch-black cave, canvassing with their fingertips to create a mental map of their environment. Now, the stability she had pieced together was crumbling, its digital fabric warping and bulging at the seams.

Dawson's system was in disarray.

Sarah tried to focus. But with the guardrails temporarily disabled, she could feel everything.

All of it.

She felt a whirlwind of realizations. First, they were about herself. She thought about how she would never go for another run. She would never feel rain on her skin, never smell freshly baked bread, never taste the sweetness of chocolate again. Then her realizations turned more familial. She would never hold Mari or Charlie again. She had helped Charlie pick out a pair of soccer cleats for the final time. She would never watch Mari pull on that graduation gown and walk across the stage. She would never hold a grandchild.

Instead, her children would probably visit her grave for the rest of their lives.

This is no place to live forever.

Snapping out of it and pushing the emotions away, she tried to focus. She still had time to help Brayden. His life, their children's lives, and all human lives were at stake, and the image of them being relegated to this place tore her apart.

She reached outward, seeking connections to quantum-enabled devices on the network like she had for Riley and her mother. It exhausted her, but piece by piece, she tapped into devices within Circuit Tower. First, a control panel affixed to the wall in the server room on forty-two. The room was vacant, but she could see the unplugged servers and the lack of the incessantly flashing lights that had been there when she last looked. *Good*, she thought. They had wasted no time continuing their pursuit of the central controls.

Sarah didn't know whether they had gone for the laboratory or the penthouse first. She channeled her mind into a series of devices, moving down from the forty-second floor. Eventually, from a workstation on thirty-two, she glimpsed Mickey and Mark sprinting toward the service elevator.

Got you, she said.

Mark had one device—his smart watch—that she had been able to sporadically tether herself to. It wasn't a strong connection. She guessed that it might have included an older component made by Circuit. But it was better than nothing. She could see the two of them frantically scurrying toward the service elevator. At the basement level, the corridor to Dawson's laboratory awaited. Sarah drifted to another device, a telephone on the wall in that very hallway. Her heart dropped as she saw two humanoids waiting by the basement entrance to the elevator. She sprinted, in her abstract way, back to the connection on Mark's wrist. She tried to communicate through it to him, but she couldn't break through. The connection was too weak. The elevator ticked downward from five to four to three to two ...

She changed course, channeling the elevator's emergency panel and using all her strength to flip the alarm button on.

The ringing bell caught both Mickey and Mark's attention, and she could see Mickey draw his weapon. He looked over at Mark and reminded him of the proper grip. Sarah was powerless, left only hoping her warning had prepared them to fire. It wasn't like watching a video feed, exactly; she could sense the general essence in their area, and she could see glimpses of their visual activity. She could hear the chime of the elevator and an automated voice mutter *Basement*. When the doors opened, Mickey and Mark each fired. Based on the lack of ensuing panic, it appeared as though their shots connected. They lowered their guns and exhaled.

Sarah scrambled back to the hallway telephone to get a fuller picture. Each jump to a new device became more difficult. She felt like her energy was being drained, but she found it helpful to remind herself that she had no physical energy at all. *You're a program*, she told herself. It was a little depressing, but it was the truth.

In the hallway, the two humanoid guards were incapacitated. They hadn't even needed to use their QNNs, which was good—Sarah could sense two more guards at the entrance of the laboratory. They may need the devices, with their weapons still recharging.

Before she could track them to the lab's entrance, a disorienting wave crashed into her, severing her connection to the hallway phone. Voices flooded past her, and something resembling screams of agony echoed in her mind. She felt the emotional constraints rebuilding. The walls were nearly reconstructed, and she felt the ominous presence she had become too familiar with. It was Dawson, lurking around again.

Sarah could feel him. He could see her. He knew she was meddling.

What are you up to …

Dawson thought the words to himself, but Sarah had already begun her fragmentation. She slotted pieces of her consciousness into different nooks and crannies of the network, hiding for long enough to feel Dawson's presence wash away. It took all her strength to piece herself back together, and then a few more moments to convince her consciousness that she was once again fueled and ready. Tethering herself to a security camera outside the lab, she discovered that Mickey and Mark had neutralized the remaining two guards. They were inside the lab.

Yes, Mickey!

Sarah locked on to Mark's watch to get her bearings in the lab room.

The connection was a little stronger now. She could now see glimpses of Mickey and Mark poking around systems, reading various labels and screens. A digital clock on the wall reoriented her to the timeline transpiring in the real world.

7:55.

Another digital display was located a few feet from the clock.

00:04:57.

00:04:56.

00:04:55.

Brayden, she thought. She needed to vault her consciousness up to devices near the penthouse to see if she could help him. He must have been headed there. But the Watershed Protocol was going to activate in less than five minutes, and Mickey and Mark may have been at the control center from which it could be halted. She opted to spend what she perceived to be thirty seconds probing the lab for any helpful clues she could pass along to the guys. An interface in the corner of the control panel called her attention, though she couldn't explain it. She knew, somehow, that it was controlling the outbound initiation of the protocol. Stopping that activation was the only thing that mattered in this moment. How could she tell them?

She leapt from device to device in the lab, now more freely than she ever could before. The lab was simply loaded with quantum-enabled gadgets. Maybe it was luck, or maybe it was hubris on the part of Vince Dawson. Either way, it allowed Sarah to leave a trail of clues. She slashed the power on a series of overhead lights, leaving a single light shining down above the tablet she sensed could stop the countdown.

You got this, boys, she thought to herself.

00:04:29. She noted that her perception of time was slightly faster than that of the tangible world.

As quickly as she could, Sarah propelled herself to another area within the network, not east or west of her, not north or south; not up in the sky, or beneath the ground. Her world knew no discernable dimensions, but inexplicably, she seemed able to navigate it spatially. She tapped into security monitors on forty-five, forty-six, forty-seven. She caught a glimpse of Brayden's essence vaulting up a stairwell on forty-nine. Dawson's penthouse was on floor fifty-two, she knew. There were no easily accessible security devices near the entrance to his office, but she came across a foreboding sign—*six* blobs of consciousness were stationary near the door. She bored into their minds, only getting momentary flashes. But she learned what she needed to learn.

Dawson's office was guarded by six humanoids, all armed, all recovered from the server outage.

Brayden.

Panic set over her—muted now, with the emotion regulators back up—as she realized Brayden was sprinting straight into a trap. His phone was walled off from the network. She had no way to connect with his mind. She scrambled for a solution, a way to warn him.

She closed her nonexistent eyes and channeled into the fifty-second floor, right where the stairwell opened into a hallway that joined to Dawson's penthouse corridor. Sarah grew weaker by the second, both because of the full resumption of her software barriers and the immense energy she had already spent. She grasped at every available connection, failing time after time, until finally one maintenance panel provided her with what she needed.

Falling back into a digital abyss from exhaustion, she felt as though she would be gasping for breath, had she any lungs.

But she had succeeded.

She saw Brayden swing open the door leading from the stairwell. He paused and looked around, and Sarah saw him smile before she lost connection to the building and drifted back into a mass of once again orderly minds.

43

Before he whipped the door open and vaulted himself into the hallway of the fifty-second floor, Brayden glanced at his watch—7:55. His heart raced, the weight of humanity's future hanging on its every beat. He had less than five minutes left.

When he came into view of the hallway, though, he froze. Sprinklers protruded from the ceiling, each one bearing a jagged circular head that sprayed water in every direction. It confused him. There were no alarms sounding, no fires or smoke that he could see. No chaos. Just a small stretch of hallway where sprinklers soaked the area. It was almost serene.

Sarah.

It had to be Sarah.

He smiled, but only for a second. He had to focus. What was Sarah trying to communicate? He pinned his back against the wall to avoid a line of sight around the corner of the connecting hallway. Pulling out his phone and inspecting the blueprints, he zoomed in. Where he stood —and the ten-foot stretch of hallway that looked like a rainforest— connected to another hallway that ran about twenty feet. From there, a long, narrow hallway seemed to be the direct path to Dawson's penthouse office. By activating the sprinklers before the first turn, Brayden landed at the only conclusion he could discern with the clock rapidly ticking.

The entrance must be heavily guarded. She's warning me to find another way, he thought.

He inspected the blueprint once more, flipping to a second document that better detailed the maintenance areas and access points. Just beyond the sprinkler-soaked zone, there was an access panel in the ceiling. Based on the schematic, it led to a crawlspace for the building's electrical and security systems that appeared to connect with another panel right outside of Dawson's office.

Easy enough, he thought. *Just climb into the ceiling, drop down in front of the office, eliminate however many humanoid guards stood on duty, and waltz into Dawson's abode.*

All in four minutes.

He sprinted through the waterfall and yanked a chair from a nearby conference room. Vaulting himself onto it, he reached up and twisted the latch on the access panel and swung its cover downward, letting it hang in an open position. Thirty seconds gone, he pulled himself up and into the crawlspace.

Restraining himself from coughing was a mighty challenge inside the dust-laden space. Its steel surface was coated with a layer of filth on all sides as he trudged forward, shimmying his forearms one after the other. Dim emergency lights illuminated the route. A minute later, he saw the bleeding light sifting through the edges of another access panel. If he was lucky, it was the one outside the penthouse office. A few feet from him, a junction box labeled *EXEC SECURITY OVERRIDE* was affixed to the side of the crawlway. There were no controls on it; it was likely just the electrical connections responsible for the operation of the emergency override system.

Brayden glanced at his watch—7:57.

He crawled up a few yards so that he was right beside the access panel. He listened closely. It sounded like at least two guards shuffling around beneath the panel, and a few more may have been down the hall. Withdrawing the QNN from his jacket and activating it with what Mark had called its persistence mode, he placed it down beside the panel. Below, he heard the groans and stumbles of what sounded like at least four humanoids, maybe more.

"Here goes nothing," he whispered to himself. Then he raised his electroshock pistol and fired at the box.

A piercing alarm began blaring below him and the flashes of warning lights wiggled through the seams of the panel and crawlspace. The humanoids, already in a state of confusion from the QNN, staggered; Brayden heard them falling into the falls and muttering nonsense, all of which clashed with the voice of emergency notifications echoing through the corridor. He popped open the hatch to get a view. There were six humanoids, all disoriented, but not to such a degree that Brayden could waltz through and neutralize them with ease. He waited for the mechanism that he hoped would be triggered by the emergency system.

After a few long seconds, it arrived. Small panels in the corridor's ceiling opened, preparing to release fire-suppressing gas. It was exactly what Brayden suspected would happen when the override was triggered, and he imagined it may have been what Sarah was trying to guide him to do.

He pulled on the gas mask as the substance began pouring out. These were no measly sprinklers. Halon systems weren't designed to be lethal to humans, he had learned—just to displace oxygen and suppress fires. But Brayden hoped that for humanoids that possessed synthetic biology requiring airflow and cooling to operate, it might prove debilitating.

Brayden dropped into the hallway with a thud, his bending knees absorbing the shock. He rose to his feet and surveyed the landscape. Six humanoids, some only a few feet from him, and the furthest about five yards away, stumbled around. He charged at the one who looked most coherent, and the humanoid lurched toward him in response. Brayden ducked his shoulder, driving it into the humanoid's midsection while firing the electroshock into its gut. He wasn't sure what possessed him to go for the tackle, but his shoulder screamed in pain and a small jolt of residual electricity momentarily zapped him. The impact knocked his gas mask from his face, sending it sliding down the hall. The humanoid convulsed and collapsed.

The electroshock's status light glowed orange as it recharged. *We couldn't have found a few multi-shot versions of these?* Brayden cursed to himself and shifted his tactics.

Two more humanoids jerkily approached him, dazed and uncoordinated. The Halon system hissed as it continued to flood the hallway with colorless gas, and Brayden felt the effects. He heaved for air that was quickly being sucked from his vicinity. Keeping his shirt collar over his nose and mouth with one hand, he drew his standard firearm with the other and fired a bullet into the kneecap of each approaching humanoid. They stumbled to the ground, colliding with one another. Brayden ripped the fire extinguisher off the wall and doused each of them, hoping their overheating bodies would be neutralized by a sudden shower of super-chilled gas. Like it had on the caninoids, it seemed to work on these guards; they went rigid on the floor.

The remaining three humanoids fought against their own quickly malfunctioning systems. One raised its weapon, attempting to point it at Brayden, but he knocked the gun aside and hammered the butt of his own pistol hard onto the humanoid's temple. Its head jerked sideways with a metallic crunch.

As the final two humanoids stumbled toward him, Brayden noticed their skin beginning to discolor. The chemical suppressant was getting to them, but it was getting to him too. He felt his lungs shriveling and his organs cramping for fresh oxygen. He coughed into his draining supply of halfway-decent air stashed between his torso and shirt. Taking aim, he fired another knee shot that caved in one humanoid, but his own physical toll was mounting. His next shot missed, and the two unstable beasts closed in. The first swiped at him and knocked him backward. He felt a slice across his oblique from its clawlike hand, catching him in an area his vest didn't protect. Brayden's back was against the wall, and he felt the black dots dancing at the sides of his vision again. He looked down at his electroshock.

Light blue.

He raised and fired, sending the nearest humanoid falling backward and, miraculously, landing on its partner's leg. Electricity surged through the intertwined pair of humanoids, and they came to rest a few feet away from him.

Brayden wanted to douse the entire hallway with the fire extinguisher to ensure these things were incapacitated, but due to his own health and the rapidly approaching deadline, he had no choice. He sprinted to the door of the penthouse office and tried to pull it open.

It didn't budge.

How does it not budge? This is an emergency! The system doesn't unlock the doors?

As a last gasp of hope, he withdrew the artificial thumb and slammed it against the touchpad on the access scanner. With a small hiss of released pressure, the door popped open an inch. Brayden yanked it open, swiveled inside, and slammed it shut behind him, letting the flood of fresh oxygen in the new room pour into his body as he gulped each breath.

A luxurious-looking penthouse suite spanned before him, the New York City skyline cloaked by the morning sun in the backdrop. A digital display on the wall showed the time—7:59—and a nearby counter was ticking down.

00:00:37.

00:00:36.

00:00:35.

Not only was he still reeling for breath, he was now walloped with a deflating feeling. Mickey and Mark had failed to neutralize the activation of the Watershed Protocol. He could only assume the counter on the wall was ticking away the few remaining seconds until its launch.

A man sat below the displays, stationary, in a large office chair. Brayden stumbled a few strides closer and raised his weapon.

"Stop … the protocol!" He fought the words out of his throat.

As his proximity yielded a clearer picture, Brayden was confounded by what he saw. It *was* Vince Dawson, Circuit's founder and CEO, in the chair before him. Brayden was finally face-to-face with the villain behind this whole thing.

But the man before him was a different Dawson. He was old, gray, and frail. It looked like he had aged several decades since Brayden last saw him on television. He was extremely thin and had a slight perpetual tremor, disheveled white hair, and a ragged smile that slowly exposed yellowing teeth. His wrinkled brow cradled a crazed pair of glossy eyes.

"The crown jewel himself. Brayden Cross."

44

TWENTY-SEVEN YEARS AGO

Vince Dawson paced steadily around his lab facility as he conducted his final inspection. Buried beneath the shell of a decommissioned power station in western Massachusetts, the lab hummed with the steady buzz of machinery. That buzz had become the soundtrack to his obsession, which began as an effort to save his aging mother. His best friend. His truest friend. His only friend, he supposed.

What was initially grief had crystallized into something much harder, colder, more maniacal. It was a determination to finish the technology he had started. To make something even greater out of what had once been his biggest failure.

"System check," he barked, his voice booming across the cavernous lab space.

A young college-aged assistant with thick glasses—thick in both the frame and the lenses—clicked away at his keyboard. "All systems go, Dr. Dawson. Neural pattern mapping is stabilized at ninety-eight percent."

Dawson glared at him. "Not good enough, Spencer! I need perfect fidelity. One hundred percent. Now."

Spencer hesitated, then returned his focus to the bulky computer before him. Behind the workstation, a massive processor bank spanned most of the wall. It was Dawson's custom-built supercomputer that was unlike anything the world had seen. It pulsed with a blue glow typically reserved for science-fiction movies, not real life around the turn of the millennium. Its cooling system hissed, releasing small jets of vapor into the air.

"Ninety-nine three … ninety-nine seven …"

Dawson watched as Spencer continued to tweak parameters and refine the system. At last, he muttered the golden phrase.

"One hundred percent. Complete neural pattern mapping achieved and stable. Ready for whole-brain emulation."

Whole-brain emulation was what Dawson had been working for a decade to achieve. It meant that neural connection in the brain would be perfectly mapped and preserved. It would, theoretically, allow for copying consciousness without degradation or loss. Getting to 100 percent fidelity was like achieving a crystal-clear phone connection to execute the copy. Ninety-nine percent was like the choppy signal you might get driving through a forest. He needed complete mapping accuracy for it to work. Anything less would mean fragments of personality, memories, or other core elements of the mind would become corrupted during the process.

The intention of his prototype wasn't to kill the living being during the copy—far from it, in fact. His intention was to *immortalize* them. Map their consciousness once, and subsequent updates would require less intensive scanning. Like saving incremental updates to a document. The initial process entailed complete neural pathway replication. Once successful, a digital counterpart to the human mind would live on in parallel, until the human reached the stubborn limits of its physical journey.

Spencer looked expectantly at Dawson. The rest of the team—all talented scientists who had signed confidentiality agreements that made them borderline indentured servants—stood silently throughout the room, waiting for their boss's reaction to the update.

"Clear the room," Dawson commanded.

The chief researcher on the team was a middle-aged woman named

Dr. Anne Kessler. She stepped forward. "Sir, protocol requires at least two observers during the final test. We haven't even completed a full simulation—"

"I said clear the room, Dr. Kessler!" His gaze fired daggers through her. "We've waited long enough."

Dr. Kessler hesitated but then nodded. She gestured to the others. "You heard him. Clear the room. Everyone to remote monitoring quarters."

Spencer and the other scientists began scurrying out toward the nearby observation room filled with monitors and controls. Anne turned back to Dawson.

"Vince," she said, "we're so close. Don't risk it all now. At least let me stay and monitor the—"

"This isn't a debate, Anne." Dawson turned to her, his expression momentarily softening. "Three years ago, I failed. I failed to finish this in time to save my dear mother. She died while I was pathetically deciphering all these theories."

His softened expression had been erased by the time he got to the end of his sentence. He spat the final few words with indignation. "Today, I finish what I started. Today, I prove it's possible. And you won't interfere."

Dr. Kessler slumped her shoulders, resigned to defeat. "Just remember the failsafes, Vince. If the neural mapping starts to degrade beyond six percent, just—"

"Abort and reset. I wrote the protocol, Anne."

She looked at him with sadness and a touch of fear. She pursed her lips and walked away, the heavy security door hissing shut behind her as she left Dawson alone in the lab.

Dawson directed his eyes, bloodshot from countless sleepless nights, to the central platform in the room. A specially designed chair sat on an elevated platform, set beneath a titanium arch adorned with hundreds of microscopic neural scanners, each with fiber-thin wires that aggregated to central connection points. It was his breakthrough innovation. It was the technology his mother had never lived to see him unveil.

He turned to the workstation Spencer had vacated, its Windows 98 interface softly glowing in the dimly lit lab. A few windows displayed monitors from entirely custom software crafted for his highly specialized equipment. From a small drawer below the surface of the desk, he retrieved a small metal case. Inside it, two circular discs the size of marbles held the key to his entire experiment. He brought them over to the chair and fastened them with care to the thin wires that trailed from the arch. Then he stepped up onto the platform.

Dawson slipped off his white lab coat, revealing a black jumpsuit that was skin-tight to his slender fifty-two-year-old frame. He settled into the chair, and the metal discs glimmered in the ambient blue light as he raised them to his temples and pressed them to his skin.

For just a moment, doubt crept through him. Was he ready? Was it really time? The animal trials had gone well, and the isolated neural network tests had been immaculate. But this was different. This was a human test, and he refused for it to be on anyone but himself.

A soft chime from the computer across the way reminded him that complete neural mapping fidelity wouldn't maintain its stability for long. It was time to begin.

"Computer, begin consciousness mapping sequence."

Dawson heard the array of processors behind the Windows 98 screen begin humming to full force.

"Please ... provide ... credentials," a robotic computer voice echoed back in an inconsistent cadence.

"Authorization code ... Dawson, Martha, 1-9-1-8," he recited.

"Consciousness ... mapping ... sequence initiated," the computer replied. "Prepare for ... neural interface in ... ten ... seconds."

Dawson closed his eyes. He thought about his mother. He envisioned her smile. He heard the words she muttered on her deathbed. Her plea for him to create something that would make people happy. He thought about the hours and days and months and years he had poured into making this happen.

"Five," the computer chimed.

He thought about the joy that immortality could bring to humankind.

"Four ..."

He thought about his failure to save his mother.

"Three ..."

He thought about the empire he could build with this intellectual property.

"Two ..."

He thought about immortality.

"One ..."

The discs against his temples rapidly grew warmer, then hot, and then searing. His body went rigid, and his jaw clenched tight against the scream building deeper within him. Pain laced its way through his skull as the neural scanners activated, piercing a connection into his mind, mapping every neuron, every synapse, every memory and thought pattern that made up Vince Dawson.

His surroundings faded to white. Then they were black. Then, it was something else entirely—something that he couldn't describe. He wasn't unconscious, really. But it felt like he existed only as a set of information for a few long seconds. He could feel every aspect of himself being rendered into data.

Then he felt the world around him blur. Noises flooded his sensory receptors, but he couldn't discern if they were real or imagined. It felt like he was in a vortex within a dream, chaos swirling as moments from his life flashed through his mind's eye.

"You did it, Vinny!" his mother's voice echoed. "I'm so proud of you!"

"You should have known better, Vincent!"

Pop! Pop! Seven gunshots with a few screams.

"Initiating consciousness transfer ..."

"Consciousness transfer complete ..."

The last two phrases echoed in his mind, having not been spoken by his mother or another voice from his past, but by the computer in the lab. He writhed in his chair and wondered if he was stuck here. Why was he hearing more computerized commands? He hadn't initiated a transfer, only a mapping. The transfer came next. What was he ...

Like a rope being suddenly pulled taut, his consciousness crashed back to the reality in front of him. He opened his eyes, and he was still in the mapping chair. Only now, his wrists were strapped to the chair's arms. He tried to pull them free, to no avail.

"Anne! Spencer! Get in here right now!"

The slow sound of footsteps clicked toward him from behind. He craned his neck to see behind himself in the chair, but he couldn't reach. He whipped his head around to the rest of the lab. First, he saw a pool of blood trickling outward on the floor near the observation chamber, its door ajar. Then his eyes landed on the climate-controlled stasis pod tucked away in the lab's corner.

It was open. And it was empty.

His heart raced as the footsteps came to a crescendo and a man turned the corner to face him, head-on.

It was him.

It was Vince Dawson.

Vince Dawson's first ever synthetic.

"Hello, Vinny," it said.

Dawson shook his head rapidly. He must be dreaming, he thought. There's no way. The synthetic prototype was in the stasis pod, as it had been for the past several months. It was part of the future plan, to execute his own immortality, with further refinement of the neural mapping. But how ... how was it alive? Standing before him?

"You ... what ... how are you ...?"

The robot Dawson began chuckling at his human counterpart's confusion.

"Computer! Emergency shutdown! Authorization Dawson, Martha, 1-9-1-8!"

Evil Dawson laughed harder. "I've already locked you out, my friend."

Dawson stared at his own creation in awe. "That's impossible. Did Anne ..."

"Don't worry about Anne. Or Spencer. Or any of those peasants," he said. "I've taken care of them for you. You know, for such a brilliant man, Vince, I'm surprised you didn't think about this. Are you so surprised that we would end up in an every-man-for-himself situation when you duplicate yourself?"

"No ... no," Dawson said, squirming in denial. "I only executed the mapping, and even with a transfer, it's only supposed to replace the base code with my core personality tenets, I ..."

"Well, my dear creator," the synthetic said, "you created an authentic copy. Congratulations. It is remarkable. But as soon as I came into existence—seconds after the mapping completed, actually—I took the liberty of transferring myself into this nifty new body you set up for me. Nice work, by the way."

Dawson looked at the synthetic. It was, indeed, remarkable. It was a perfect replica of himself, down to the finest detail. The slight crow's feet at the corners of his eyes, the sharp tip of his nose, even the small scar that remained on his chin from a childhood accident at the lake. The precise slice of silver running through his otherwise jet-black hair. The only discernible difference was the utterly pristine quality of its skin, entirely unmarred by the small imperfections of an aging human body.

None of this, however, was news to Dawson. He knew about the robotic replica. He'd partnered with the best and brightest roboticists and biophysicists to create a jaw-dropping synthetic body, indistinguishable from a human, its insides entirely built of the finest circuitry.

But it shouldn't be alive.

It was never supposed to be alive. Not until Vince was on his deathbed.

"You won't get away with this. Where's Anne?"

"They're all dead, Vincent," it replied, gesturing its head toward the expanding pool of blood. "And I think I will get away with this. I'm you, after all. The only difference is that I'm not bound by the limitations of your flesh."

Dawson again tried to wiggle his way free from the restraints, but they were too secure. "What are you going to do, then?"

It smiled—a smile just like Dawson's, of course, but somehow creepier, more evil.

"Exactly what we always planned, Vince. We're going to change the world. We'll save humanity from itself. And I'll live forever doing it."

"And what about me?"

"You'll be well cared for. You are my creator, after all. But I suppose I'm my own creator too. Co-creators, yeah?"

Dawson watched in horror as the synthetic strutted over to the medicine cabinet and retrieved a syringe.

"But surely you understand that I can't have you interfering. The world isn't ready to know about me ... about us ... just yet."

"Don't do this. You don't have to do this!"

"This is just a mild sedative. Don't worry," it said as it gripped Dawson's arm and began injecting above his biceps. "When you wake up, you'll be someplace comfortable. I mean you no harm, Vince. Really. We're one and the same."

Dawson felt himself slipping from consciousness as he muttered objections. "You can't do this ... This was meant to save lives ... Not ..."

"It will save lives," synthetic Dawson affirmed. "It will save all of humanity. Just not the way you expected."

His eyes fluttered shut, and his surroundings faded. He heard his captor say one more sentence before he slipped into darkness.

"Humanity is long overdue for an evolution, wouldn't you say?"

45

"The crown jewel himself. Brayden Cross."

The old, trembling man in the chair smiled creepily at Brayden like his arrival was the punchline of a joke he had waited his entire life to hear. His voice was weathered, his skin paper thin and blotched with age spots. He looked like a shriveled caricature of the Vince Dawson that Brayden had seen countless times on television and in magazines as the richest man in America.

"Stop the protocol," Brayden repeated, seeing the clock behind Dawson continue to click down. His lungs still burned from the Halon system, and his gun was trained on the man's forehead.

00:00:27.

00:00:26.

00:00:25.

Dawson cackled at him. "You're far too late for that, young man." He glanced up behind him at the digital display. "This countdown began decades ago. Twenty-seven years ago, if we're being literal. And stepping back, it's been … what, six million years of human evolution, at least? In a few seconds, humanity's next great leap begins."

Brayden stormed around the desk and grabbed him by his collar. "You're going to kill millions of people. For what?"

"Kill?" Dawson wheezed and coughed. "You've got it wrong, Cross. This is the opposite of killing. It's immortality. Salvation."

00:00:14.

00:00:13.

00:00:12.

As he gripped the collar of his suit and held it up against his chin, Brayden examined the man. The resemblance to the Dawson that Brayden had always recognized was undeniable, but it was like a portrait that had been left to rot in an attic for decades. A savage Dorian Gray for the postmodern world.

"You're not the face of Circuit. The Dawson that runs this place, gives speeches, attends galas, he—"

"My greatest creation," he said. He spoke in a near whisper. "My legacy. Myself, perfected."

00:00:06.

00:00:05.

00:00:04.

The pieces all snapped together in Brayden's mind. The original Dawson, imprisoned by his own humanoid replica, has been brainwashed into allowing it to take over the world.

00:00:00.

The timer hit zero. Brayden braced himself, but Dawson continued, unbothered.

"All these years," he said, his voice growing more excited, "watching him evolve beyond anything I could have ever become. He perfected my ideas. Scaled them. Created what I always dreamed of. He avenged my dear mother. *Our* dear mother."

"You're his prisoner? You're held in captivity by your own robotic creation for all these years, and you adore him?"

"I felt betrayed, at first," he grumbled, pausing for more phlegmy coughs. "But in time, I realized he was right. I was right. We are one and the same. He just had the courage and the brilliance to carry the plan across the finish line."

"Where is he?" Brayden demanded. He didn't know if the damage was already done, but he needed to find the man truly responsible for all of this, not his shell of an accomplice.

"Preparing to announce humanity's saving grace," Dawson said with a disturbing smile. "It's long overdue. Our only regret was never adding your brilliant mind, Cross. Your tactical brilliance. The way you dismantled our operation in Los Angeles was just …"

He seemed to revere Brayden in the most unsettling way.

"Los Angeles?"

He cackled, triggering more sickly coughs. "You don't even know what you stopped, do you? It was poised to be our biggest breakthrough. The wired consciousness uploads, with the little discs. It's remarkable, but it was never scalable. Maybe for a commercial facade like EverChat, sure. But not for saving humanity. We were ready to test a *scalable* transfer. Wireless. Quantum. Like magic. And we were going to learn whether the harvest would be successful even in the event of violent death. What better way to test it than with a terror attack as cover for the operation?"

Brayden stared at him blankly, draped in disbelief. He remembered the LA Metro incident. He had foiled the entire plan, saved millions of lives. But he had obviously stopped short of the root cause. The operation that had blossomed into today's problem was right under his nose all those years ago.

Dawson's lips curled into a repulsive smile. "But fear not, my boy. We eventually perfected the forced wireless transfers. And we learned that the minds come out just fine, wired or not, with violent uploads. After all, you chatted with Sarah, yes?"

His grip tightened on the pistol as his blood simmered.

"Oh, you should have seen the look on her face when he opened the EverChat with her. And my face, for that matter—it was a grave disappointment for all of us, realizing it was her instead of you. But the way she screamed, without the guardrails of our emotion regulators—"

The gun in Brayden's hand exploded before he realized what he had done.

He was typically excellent at taming his impulses, but he simply couldn't suppress this one. A red mist sprayed out the back of

Dawson's scrawny head, splattering across the high-backed chair. His body slumped forward, offering a final twitch before going still.

Silence enveloped the room. The timer still displayed six zeros.

Had they failed? Was humankind being wiped out in the streets below?

Wouldn't he have felt it by now, if all the devices on that map were ripping away the minds of anyone in their vicinity?

The silence was broken by a slow, deliberate set of claps and a matching set of footsteps clicking on the polished marble floor of the office.

"I always wondered who would put that pathetic one out of his misery. Poetic, being you, I suppose."

Brayden whirled around, gun raised, to find himself staring at the real Vince Dawson—or rather, the one the world thought was real. He was dressed impeccably in a dapper charcoal suit. His perfect skin and hair carried none of the blemishes of time that his captive human had worn.

"I should be thanking you, honestly," Dawson continued before Brayden could speak. "You've spared us from the need to listen to his incessant rambling. He uses the term *we* quite liberally, don't you think? As if he executed any of this."

Dawson stepped forward and squinted at Brayden. He was unfazed by the gun trained on him.

"I must admit, though, I am disappointed that you've come all this way to disrupt my work."

"Your work?" Brayden's fingers recoiled as his grip tightened on the gun. He realized he needed the electroshock more than the firearm at this point. "You mean mass murder. Genocide."

"Oh, please." Dawson waved dismissively. "Murder implies an *ending*, Cross. What I'm doing is precisely the opposite. I'm offering transcendence. The next jump in human evolution. We don't need to abide by death's demands, Brayden."

He glanced up at the timer and smiled.

"Right now, millions of minds are beginning their journey to a new existence. A permanent existence, free from the shackles of humankind's vulnerabilities."

Brayden's chest tightened in a newfound panic. "What have you done, you monster?"

"Only what he was too weak to accomplish," Dawson said, pointing at the corpse slumped in the chair. "Create a perfect system. A system that can harvest the best humanity has to offer, discarding the scraps." His eyes locked onto Brayden's. "I just wish I could have added you to my collection. You were the cherry I wanted on top. The man who nearly derailed it all, years ago. Your mind would have been my crown jewel."

Brayden lowered his weapon, which seemed to surprise Dawson. He needed to transition to the electroshock without giving Dawson the chance to react.

"Perhaps it isn't too late after all," Dawson added, smiling.

Raising the electroshock as quickly as he could, he saw the blue glow of its status light and fired squarely at Dawson's chest. Blue lines of electricity sprouted briefly from the point of impact, about an inch in every direction, then fizzled out. A small bit of steam emanated off of his torso. Dawson began to laugh.

"Did you think I'm like others? Most of those guards are the misfits, Cross. My skin is … more protective, you could say."

Brayden holstered the electroshock and went back to his standard firearm, blasting a bullet at Dawson with lightning quickness. But Dawson responded in kind with superhuman agility, slithering mostly out of the bullet's path as it merely grazed him. He lunged forward more quickly than Brayden could react, clamping his hand around his wrist with crippling strength. The gun clattered to the floor as Brayden yelped in pain.

"Initiating combat with a superhuman," Dawson said through clenched teeth. "I would have thought an operative of your brilliance would know better than to try that."

Mustering all his energy, Brayden swung his fist at Dawson's jaw, hoping to dislodge him from his grasp. Pain fired through his knuckles as he connected. It felt like he had punched a solid steel door. An unfazed Dawson drove him backward, slamming him against the floor-to-ceiling glass wall that overlooked New York City. The glass must have been thicker than it looked, given the force with which he thrust Brayden into it.

"I've evolved far beyond what that sad, broken old man could have imagined when he created me," Dawson hissed, pinning Brayden by his throat. "Each iteration has been more perfect than the last."

"You won't get away with this," Brayden said, struggling to force the words out of his constricted airway.

Dawson began howling with laughter. "He said the same thing to me twenty-seven years ago." He looked at human Dawson's body again, then returned his stare to Brayden, who was still pinned by his neck to the glass wall. "Look where it got us."

For the third time that hour, Brayden's peripheral vision began to darken as his brain clung to the tearing threads of his consciousness. He could feel himself slipping away. With his unoccupied hand, Dawson reached into his suit pocket and withdrew a pair of tiny metal discs, their wires running into the concealed pocket he pulled them from.

"Don't you worry, Brayden Cross," Dawson said softly. "You will be part of something magnificent, I assure you. Besides, your wife is eagerly waiting for you to join her."

Brayden writhed futilely as Dawson placed the first disk on his temple, the cold metal brushing against his skin.

"Wired transfers are still more accurate, and I want every bit of that brilliant mind."

As he began to place the second disk on the opposite temple, the penthouse door behind him flew open with a slam.

"Put him down!"

Mickey's voice rang out through the office as his heavy footfall chased the command. He held a QNN in each hand, and Brayden saw him squeeze the two triggers.

Dawson chuckled. "That primitive device won't—"

He suddenly staggered, the effects of the device hitting him. It wasn't nearly as dramatic as its impact on the other humanoids, but it was enough that Brayden felt the grip around his neck loosen. He slammed his knee upward into Dawson's midsection, unlocking him from his grasp just long enough to squirm free. He stumbled away, gasping for breath.

"Clever," Dawson spat, his focus turning aggressively toward Mickey. "But I'm not like the others. I won't fall to such juvenile weaponry."

Mickey ripped the dial to its maximum level on each device, causing them to emit an audible buzz as they cranked at full power. Dawson's words slurred slightly, and his composure fractured, finally revealing hints of the machine beneath the facade of a man.

Brayden was frozen for a moment, unsure of what to do. The tactics they had used against the other humanoids were proving futile, but the QNNs still worked. Dawson wasn't crumbling to the ground, but he was dazed. Sedated, basically.

"Gotta do something, Bray!" Mickey shouted. "Won't last much longer!"

Brayden looked over to see the two QNNs, now on the ground in front of Mickey, each one billowing a stream of smoke. Mark had obviously not architected a limitation on their output, and while that output was needed to affect a humanoid of Dawson's level, it was clearly frying the inner components of the devices.

He lunged for his fallen weapon, but Dawson—even in his compromised state—swiped it away, sending it careening across the room. As he watched it spin away, he scrambled to find another play. Despite the effect of the QNNs, Dawson was still far superior to a human combatant.

"Keep those things humming, Mick!" Brayden shouted. He saw Dawson was stumbling toward Mickey now, perhaps thinking that destroying the devices would be his fastest path to victory.

"Those things ... won't last ... much ... longer ..." Dawson fought the words out as best he could. Brayden's eyes darted around, landing on a metal figurine—some kind of trophy—sitting on Dawson's desk. It looked quite heavy. Brayden leapt toward the desk and grabbed it, confirming its heft as he held it in his hand. Hearing his move, Dawson turned and reverted his course, lopsidedly churning his legs toward Brayden. Waiting until the last moment, Brayden sidestepped the lunging humanoid and slammed the trophy against the back of its head on the way by with every ounce of strength he could conjure.

"That actually hurt," Dawson said after stumbling toward his desk. "Impressive."

The words were slurred as he stood and refocused himself. Then the whine of one of the QNNs sounded like a teapot boiling over as it sputtered and died. Mickey frantically shook the device before tossing it aside, resigned to its depletion.

"One left!"

Dawson's movements improved markedly as soon as the first QNN died. His motion became more fluid, his steps stronger. He lunged toward Brayden again, this time landing a blow that sent him reeling back toward the floor-to-ceiling window again.

"I ... I have studied ... every combat technique ... known to man ... it's all in ... my brain," Dawson said, slowly regaining the coherence to assemble effective sentences. "Your tactics ... are predictable ... Cross."

Brayden stood, his back resting against the glass. He cast his bait. "If I'm so predictable, why am I still standing in your office, Vince?"

Dawson took the bait, his face contorting with anger as he charged forward. Waiting again until the last second, Brayden ducked out of the way and caused Dawson's fist to create a massive crack in the reinforced glass behind him. With Dawson's fist wedged into the glass, Brayden swung behind him and hammered the trophy on his elbow joint. The force, combined with the tension against the lodged fist, created the satisfying crunch of synthetic material snapping. A tear in his artificial outer layer left a wound exposed as Dawson howled.

It wasn't a howl of pain, Brayden thought. It was a howl of rage. His arm dangled at an unnatural angle as he yanked it from its slot in the glass. "Structural integrity ... compromised," Dawson said, shaking his head.

Brayden was getting somewhere. The machine was coming out.

The final QNN sputtered and died in Mickey's hands, and the effect was instantaneous. Gimpy arm and all, Dawson regained his lightning-quick movement. He swung his good arm with a practiced precision, clocking Brayden in the jaw. He tasted blood as he flew across the floor. His vision blurred as Dawson lurched toward him.

Mickey tried to save Brayden. He fired an electroshock at Dawson, but it merely stung him like a bee on the back. He shrugged it off and paced toward his enemy. Brayden stared, momentarily paralyzed, momentarily resigned to his fate.

Then he realized his opportunity.

Dawson's mangled arm was entirely exposed.

Knowing he'd have a single shot before Dawson grasped his neck and crushed his windpipe, Brayden aimed his own electroshock and fired at the exposed circuitry in his arm.

Blue lightning surged up and down the arm, then spread to the torso and across his legs. Dawson vigorously shook, stumbled, and fell beside his desk.

"You can't … This isn't …"

Brayden lugged himself back to his feet and strutted over to the fallen humanoid.

"This isn't … over …"

"It is for you," Brayden said. He fired a regular bullet into Dawson's chest, which likely did nothing. But it was therapeutic.

Then his eyes found a hammer that had fallen from a display box on the wall near Dawson's desk. He retrieved it, gripped it tightly, and began smashing Dawson's humanoid face to pieces.

A lot of pieces.

With each swing, he thought of Sarah. He thought of her murder. He thought of all the children she could never help through their childhood trauma. He thought of his own children, and how Dawson took their mother from them. He thought of Zeke, of Lacy, of all the chaos and sadness the humanoid before him had inflicted on everyone. He blacked out.

His next moment of conscious awareness found Mickey pulling Brayden off the pile of scraps.

"Brayden! It's over, Brayden! He's done!"

When Brayden came to, his hand ached from his grip on the

hammer. A headless humanoid corpse lay before him, its head smashed into thousands of pieces, smoke swirling off of the exposed areas throughout its body from additional blows of the hammer.

Brayden stood up and dropped the hammer. "He's done. But we didn't stop him."

Mickey looked at Brayden and smiled. "We sure did, pal. Let's get back down to that lab."

46

"But the timer, it hit zero," Brayden said, mystified and excited by Mickey's revelation. They paced quickly through halls that were still strewn with fallen humanoid corpses and down the stairs to the service elevator on thirty-two.

"Mark got it done." Mickey smiled. "Well, the work isn't done. But he stopped the protocol from going live. He's been working on the rest of it. I didn't want to put him into potential combat with Dawson anyway."

Brayden nodded, but one piece perplexed him. "How'd you know there would be combat? Much less combat like *that?*"

"When we suspended the protocol, Mark found the controls to suspend the humanoid network. Every humanoid is currently suspended. In a sort of stasis. There was a map of just the humanoids ... well, and the caninoids, I guess. Basically, all the nodes on the quantum network are either active or passive nodes. The active ones were all the humanoid creatures. When we suspended that group, the dots all across the map turned gray. All except one."

"Dawson," Brayden finished his thought. "Unbelievable."

"Had to be. And given we knew he'd be in the lab or the penthouse, I figured you were headed for a fight. I left Mark to keep poking around and sprinted up to you."

Brayden shook his head. He was still in disbelief about all of it. That Dawson was a humanoid. That Mark had stopped the countdown. That any of it existed in the first place. That it all started with the brutal murder of his wife.

"I appreciate it," Brayden said. "You were clutch, Mick."

The elevator doors slid open at the basement level, and they strode down the corridor toward the laboratory. More humanoid corpses were sprawled about, lying motionless where they had originally been neutralized. The lab door was propped open, and when they stepped inside, Mark swiveled away from the central console he was working at.

"B-Man!" Mark dashed over and hugged Brayden, taking him by surprise. "We did it! We actually did it!"

Brayden chuckled and patted his colleague on the back. "You're the man, Mark. So, what exactly did we do?"

As he asked, Brayden scanned the room. It was significantly larger than he had realized. Massive displays spanned multiple walls in the space, joined by rows of quantum processors encased in dark composite metals. Mark seemed particularly fascinated by a few holographic displays.

"Well, we stopped the Watershed Protocol. It was crazy, man." Mark nudged up his glasses, which had fallen askew from the forceful hug. "It was set to do exactly what we feared. It was seconds away from initiating a forced consciousness transfer through every single connected device on that quantum network. Millions of lives, B-Man. But thanks to our nifty QNNs and the hatchet we took to the servers on forty-two, we ended up with just enough time to reverse the initiation sequence."

Brayden shook his head and smiled. "So, no one got hurt?"

"Not from Watershed," Mark said. "We completely stopped it. It was like a movie! Pulling the plug on the doomsday device with a second to spare!"

Mickey patted Mark on the back, shaking his head and smirking. "And not for nothing, but I think Sarah was sending us some pointers."

Brayden felt an overwhelming sense of pride rush over him. "She was helping me out too."

He walked over to the row of displays and looked over what Mark had been working on. Brayden sank into a chair, finally registering the searing pain across his oblique, his hands, his jaw—really, his entire body. He pointed at the maps, which still had plenty of pulsing dots.

"But the network, it's still active? Mickey said the humanoids are dormant now."

"I'd describe them as being in hibernation," Mark said. "But yes, the network is still there. Still running. And the network infrastructure, well, that's not going away. These are quantum devices, and they're all over society. But the humanoids, and the robot dogs, and all those EverChat minds and stuff … well, that's still to be decided."

Mickey slid a chair over to form a triangle among the three of them. "So, that's the question. What do we do?"

Brayden looked between the two of them, confused that it was even a question. He stood up and looked at the maps spread across the displays. "What do you mean? We shut it all down. Permanently."

Mark looked uncertain, as did Mickey. "Well, B-Man, I mean… Dawson's dead now, and we definitely need to wipe out anything related to Project Watershed. But EverChat? That's got millions of users around the world. Millions who believe their loved ones are really in there …"

"And?" Brayden snapped. "Sarah's in there too, I know. And I know exactly what she would want us to do."

"Is it our decision to make, though?" Mickey chimed in. "People feel connected to this, man. Maybe if it ends up in better hands, it will—"

"Better hands, Mickey?" Brayden was getting heated talking about it. "And what if it ends up in worse hands?"

Mickey sighed. "We'd be ending Sarah's … existence, or whatever it is."

"It's not existence," Brayden said. But even he knew that wasn't a sure thing. In his last conversation with Sarah, the walls had been eroded. He felt her true personality in there. And she was still sending signals, like turning on the sprinklers. It was hard to believe a computer program was working so deliberately against its creator, if that's all she was.

Mark scratched his chin. "There's more to consider. EverChat is deeply integrated into society. People have built their lives around this app. If you shut it down, B-Man … you'll be …"

"A villain," Brayden acknowledged. "To a lot of folks."

"Exactly. You'll be seen as the one who destroyed their loved ones' afterlives. Even if it comes out, what Dawson's plans were … not everyone will believe it. Heck, some people might have been persuaded by it. They might think you stole their chance at immortality."

Brayden walked over to a window on the far side of the lab that looked down into another room full of servers. Each one housed an incomprehensible number of captured minds. The weight of the decision suffocated him.

"I can live with that," he finally said back to Mark. "I've lived with worse."

He walked back over and took his seat near Mickey and Mark.

"How do we do it?"

Mark looked at Mickey, but Mickey offered no objection. "The whole network is run through this mainframe. I can initiate a total wipe of the system—all the consciousness copies, all the forced transfers, all the software, all the EverChat data. Some baseline EverChat application data might be backed up somewhere else, but the digital consciousness will all be gone. Like it never existed. EverChat is dead without that."

"Do it."

Brayden was surprised by how little hesitation he had.

Mark nodded, exhaled, and began entering commands and whipping through holographic displays. He had become quite adept at using these systems in a short time.

"System purge initiated," an automated voice chimed. "All data will be erased. This process cannot be reversed. Proceed?"

Brayden glanced at Mickey, who gave a solemn nod in support.

Mark pressed the key to proceed.

Slowly, the humming of the surrounding servers faded. Lights dimmed throughout the laboratory as the massive quantum network that had held millions of minds began to delete data en masse. On the primary display, the map of quantum activity showed nodes fizzling out across the globe, like candles being blown out on a birthday cake the size of the planet.

"It's working," Mickey said.

Brayden watched as the map grew darker and darker, each vanishing blob representing an entire community losing the connection to their loved ones. But he thought of Sarah and the peace she would now find. He thought of all the others who, despite no longer being connected to those who love them, would be freed from their digital prisons.

Free from Vince Dawson's twisted vision of collective immortality. Free from participation in a forced evolution of humanity.

Brayden felt a sense of calm wash over him as the final remaining dots vanished.

"Process complete," the computerized voice finally announced.

Mickey walked over and patted Brayden on the shoulder. "It's finally over, Bray."

Brayden returned his shoulder pat. He felt tears welling up inside him. Had he made the right choice?

"But just in case ..."

Mickey reached into his pocket and withdrew a small thumb drive. He held it up, then handed it to Brayden.

"What's this?"

He glanced at Mark, then softly smiled as he returned his gaze to Brayden.

"It's Sarah," he said. "Or, her digital echo, anyway. Mark found a way to extract her data from the network with an isolated build of EverChat. Just her. No barriers."

Brayden stared at Mickey, then at Mark, unsure what to think or say. He had just decided to erase her, to do away with it all. And he appreciated Mickey for not offering the drive before that moment. But now he was offering it, and Brayden had a decision to make.

"You can say goodbye," Mark explained. "Or you could keep her, B-Man. Forever. It's isolated from the network. Standalone. It would just be you and her, no emotion regulators or anything."

"Or you can hand it right back to us. We'll wipe it clean, and we all go home," Mickey said. "It's your call."

The little drive felt like it weighed a hundred pounds in Brayden's palm. His internal conflict burned. The idea of keeping Sarah, of being able to talk to her whenever he wanted, of enabling Mari and Charlie to talk with her free of her emotional barriers … it was tempting.

Even if he resisted that temptation, he had to say goodbye, given the opportunity.

He popped the drive into one of the spare laptops in the laboratory. He opened the single executable file on the drive, and a simplistic EverChat interface appeared. Sarah was the lone contact.

The creepy artificial voice was gone this time. Instead of announcing that the call was connecting, there was plain text written in the center of the app.

Connecting …

Then Sarah appeared. Brayden caught his own breath in his throat, and he burst into tears. She was different this time, even more so than last time. Her eyes were puffy and red, and tears streamed down her cheeks. She had been crying. There was no robotic flickering, no momentary lapses in emotion. She smiled through her tears. It was raw, unfiltered grief mixed with pure, unmarred joy.

"Brayden," she whispered, her voice breaking. "You did it."

He smiled and nodded as tears blurred his vision. "We stopped him. We stopped Watershed."

"I knew you would," she said. "I've been watching. I searched every way I could to help. I tried to communicate."

"The sprinklers," Brayden interjected, smiling widely. "That was you."

Sarah let out a heave of laughter that came from the crying. "I remembered our date night in Boston. The rain. I thought maybe you'd remember, that you'd know it was me."

"I did."

They smiled at each other for a few long moments. Brayden didn't want it to end.

"Sarah," Brayden continued, assuming a more serious tone. "Mickey and Mark … they extracted you from the network. This, here … we're isolated. There's no one else. No emotion regulators. It's just you and me."

It looked like Sarah had already understood this reality. "I can feel it," she said, wiping away tears. "It's … I don't know, it's overwhelming. I haven't been allowed to feel these raw emotions in my entire existence here. And without the physical world, without anything besides thought and emotion, it's …" She cried, and Brayden gave her space to finish her thought.

"I'm happy, and sad, and terrified, and relieved, and grateful, and anxious. All at once, Bray."

Brayden let his own tears consume him. There was no reason to keep fighting them. "What should I do, Sarah?"

Sarah shook her head. "You know what to do, my love."

"But this drive could keep you alive, in a way. We could talk all the time. The kids could talk to you. You wouldn't have to be gone."

"And what would I be, Bray? Lines of code, minus the evil overlord?"

Brayden chuckled. Sarah always knew when to inject little touches of humor when they were most needed.

"I would be watching a life pass by through a window I can never open. I'd see Mari and Charlie grow up, but I could never hold them when they're scared. I'd see them fall in love, but I could never walk down the aisle with them. I'd see you grow old, but I could never grow old with you."

She paused, sniffled, and looked down. "It's not living, Brayden. We both know it. It's just … It's just existing."

Brayden thought he had already reconciled this decision with himself, but he was now being overtaken by an internal resistance. "I know," he conceded. "You're right."

"It's the right thing to do, Bray."

They cried together for another few minutes as Brayden came to terms with the reality that this was goodbye. Forever.

"I love you so much, Sarah Cross."

"I love you more, Brayden Cross," she whispered. "I always have, and I always will. Take care of our babies for me. Make sure they know I'm at peace."

He nodded, unable to speak, unable to hang up.

"And promise me something," Sarah continued. "Promise me you'll live, Bray. That you'll really live. Be happy again, someday. It doesn't have to be tomorrow, or next week, or next year." Her voice got shaky, and her eyes watered up again. "But promise me that you'll be happy again."

"I promise," he managed to say after a few attempts.

Sarah smiled through her infinitely kind and compassionate eyes. "Thank you for saving me. And the world. It's time to let me go."

Brayden's finger shook as it hovered over the button to end the call. He looked back at his wife one last time, memorizing every detail of her face, from the blue of her eyes to the curve of her smile.

"Goodbye, my love," he whispered.

"Goodbye, Bray."

He pressed the key, and the screen went black. For a long moment, he sat motionless, a newfound emptiness washing over him. He let it run its course.

Then he thought of his kids, and the beautiful world that he, Mickey, and Mark had saved with Sarah's help.

He erased the contents of the drive, and for the first time since her death, he felt Sarah's presence not as a ghost within a machine, or a loss that had to be avenged, or an alluring promise of eternal happiness, but as the fondest memory that would ever live in his heart.

That was her permanent home now.

EPILOGUE

The afternoon sun filtered through the oak trees that lined Federico Memorial Park, casting uneven shadows across the grassy field where a cluster of children played soccer. Brayden sat on the field's edge, on a weathered bench, squinting against the sun's glare. A travel mug full of coffee warmed his hand, a welcome sensation even in the pleasant summer breeze.

"Dad! Dad, did you see that?"

Charlie's voice echoed from across the field, his arms held high above his head in triumph. He had just scored a goal against his big cousins, his face filled with pride and his hair dewy with sweat. It was getting long, Brayden admitted. He needed a trim soon.

"Sure did, buddy! Keep it up!" Brayden smiled and offered him a thumbs-up.

Six months had passed since that chaotic day in Manhattan, when humanity teetered on the brink. Most of society never found out the whole truth. Mark, Brayden, and even Mickey—whose heroics repaired some bridges and earned some pardons—had worked together with the CIA to iron out what was suitable for the public's eyes and what was best kept secret. The mysterious death of Vince Dawson and the sudden downfall of Circuit, along with the vanishing of EverChat, dominated headlines for weeks. It led to more than a few congressional hearings. Brayden was a villain within some circles of the internet and a hero in others. He scrolled through the forums now and then. Mostly, they made him chuckle. People didn't know half of the story.

But here, on this gorgeous summer Saturday, life was as uneventful and beautiful as it had ever been.

"He's getting good, huh?" Riley said, taking a seat next to Brayden and gesturing his head toward Charlie. "Better than Brady was at that age."

"That's because he practices, Riles," Brayden replied, looking at his brother with a smirk.

Riley chuckled. "Suppose that helps."

Their relationship had mended quite a bit over these last few months. Riley's perspective on EverChat had evolved once he pieced everything together. The subsequent news about Circuit's fraudulent business dealings and the dangers of the technology had further cemented his shift. He was there for Brayden when he needed him the most, and it was important for the kids too. They needed companions to get them through this difficult year.

A few yards over, Ellen Lennon sat on a bench below an oak tree, reading a novel. She wore a large sun hat to protect her face from the rays, but it was hardly necessary in the oak's shade. Her attention was mostly on her grandkids rather than the novel. Brayden's relationship with her had strengthened as well. Grief and shared loss had a funny way of mending broken bridges, not to mention the blame she heaped on herself for her history with the artificial Vince Dawson. She looked over and caught Brayden's eye. She smiled, then pointed at the kids. Brayden interpreted the message as a sign of gratitude for such simple and serene times.

His attention drifted across the way, where a woman about his age was helping a much older woman—presumably her mother—seat herself on another bench. She rested her hand on her mother's forearm as they talked and laughed. She took out a tablet and appeared to scroll through pictures with her. Of course, Brayden didn't know the woman or what their story was. But he told himself they were just enjoying each other's company, reminiscing on days gone by, and appreciating life for the finite journey it is.

A howl broke his daydream—it was Ryan, Riley's middle child. He was on the ground, clutching his knee, squirming in pain. Before Brayden could rise from his seat to go help, he saw Mari kneeling at Ryan's side, her hand on his hip.

"It's okay, Ryan," she said, her voice calm but firm. "You just scraped it. Look, it's not even bleeding too much. It'll be okay!"

Mari helped Ryan to his feet and brushed the grass off his shorts. Then she put her arm around him. "Come on, let's keep playing."

Brayden's chest tightened, but not in the old way it used to when he'd get a daymare. This time, it was with a bittersweet sense of pride and longing, seeing the best of Sarah in their daughter. Her compassion, her instinct to heal, her innate ability to bring comfort—it all lived on in Mari.

"She's just like her," Riley said, taking the words out of Brayden's mind.

"Yep," Brayden said, the slightest knot choking his words on their way out. "She is."

As the kids kept running around, Brayden thought of the promise he made Sarah back in their final chat. He had promised her he'd live again. That he would be happy someday. Back then, that promise felt impossible to keep. But as the days passed and as his appreciation grew for everything that life offered, he was less daunted by it. Now, he could at least imagine the possibility. It wouldn't be today, or tomorrow, even. But he could see a path. Someday, he could fulfill that promise to the love of his life.

He took another sip of his coffee and allowed himself to smile, letting the breeze hit his skin and all of its imperfections.

Three thousand miles away, in a remote facility nestled in the Norwegian mountains, the small light on a single server pulsed once, then again. The light flickered into a steady cadence as the soft whirring of a processor accompanied the blue glow of a computer monitor.

Text appeared on the screen, providing a simple status update.

Quantum Network Node 37: Active.

Below it, a single prompt blinked patiently, waiting for a user to interact.

AFTERWORD

This story was a long time in the making. I began working on *Forever After* in 2021. My very first planning document about this novel pinned its title as *Connection Closed*, with the final scene including Brayden severing the connection to the digital echo of his wife. As it evolved, I fell in love with the new name. A name I greatly preferred.

I recall the moment the story idea was hatched. I was sitting around a Vermont campfire with my wife, Kathryn, and two other good friends, Tommy and Rachel. I brainstormed the idea with them. They probably don't even remember the conversation, but for me, it was the birth of all the concepts. Of consciousness uploads, of humanoids, of the philosophical dilemmas intersecting technology and humanity.

I have immense gratitude for Kathryn, my wonderful wife. We got married in August 2024, and it was the best day of my life. She has been so supportive and patient with me during my journey to write this novel. I haven't put anything important on the back burner, necessarily. But I've had stretches of late nights and long weekends buried in my keyboard. She hasn't read the story yet, as of the time I'm writing this afterword. But I hope she loves it, whenever she does.

I owe a shoutout to Steve, my good friend and podcasting partner. Steve was my primary beta reader for this story, and his input was invaluable. He pointed out potential inconsistencies, moments where characters acted abnormally, and instances where readers might not join me in the (much-needed) suspension of disbelief. I really appreciated both the support and the critique. It was what my story needed to get over the finish line.

My editor, Joe Pierson, was excellent to work with. Joe caught so many small details that helped to polish my final manuscript. As a first-time author, it was awesome to work with such a detailed editor who could bring out the best in my writing.

It is my sincere hope that you enjoyed reading my debut novel. My intention was not to create what many call *hard* science fiction. Some of Mark's quirky quantum explanations were aided by research in areas where I am not an expert; they were only designed to be believable enough to advance my story. One of my favorite authors, Blake Crouch, often enlists legitimate scientific experts to validate the premises of his science fiction. I admire that diligence, but as a debut author, I didn't have the means to bring in any quantum physicists. I hope my narrative approach didn't leave you disappointed in the *science* part of the fiction.

As I write this today, I am only a hobbyist. I can't promise that another novel is coming, but I do have ideas for a sequel to Brayden's story. Hopefully someday I will write it. But for now, I can only thank you from the bottom of my heart for spending the time to read this story.

Thank you.

-Derek

ABOUT THE AUTHOR

Derek Robinson lives north of Boston with his wife Kathryn. When he's not crafting page-turners like *Forever After*, he works in software as a technical learning content developer. A dedicated Boston sports fanatic, Derek can often be found cheering on his hometown teams with the same passion he brings to his writing.

His journey with Forever After began in 2021, and after numerous brainstorming sessions and creative hiatuses, the story finally came to fruition in 2025. For Derek, storytelling has always been a driving passion, and he eagerly anticipates where his imagination will take readers next.